M000210154

AN ENCHANTED MOMENT ON EVER AFTER STREET

JAIMIE ADMANS

Boldwood

First published in Great Britain in 2024 by Boldwood Books Ltd.

Copyright © Jaimie Admans, 2024

Cover Design by Alexandra Allden

Cover Photography: Shutterstock

The moral right of Jaimie Admans to be identified as the author of this work has been asserted in accordance with the Copyright, Designs and Patents Act 1988.

All rights reserved. No part of this book may be reproduced in any form or by any electronic or mechanical means, including information storage and retrieval systems, without written permission from the author, except for the use of brief quotations in a book review.

This book is a work of fiction and, except in the case of historical fact, any resemblance to actual persons, living or dead, is purely coincidental.

Every effort has been made to obtain the necessary permissions with reference to copyright material, both illustrative and quoted. We apologise for any omissions in this respect and will be pleased to make the appropriate acknowledgements in any future edition.

A CIP catalogue record for this book is available from the British Library.

Paperback ISBN 978-1-80483-871-6

Large Print ISBN 978-1-80483-870-9

Hardback ISBN 978-1-80483-872-3

Ebook ISBN 978-1-80483-868-6

Kindle ISBN 978-1-80483-869-3

Audio CD ISBN 978-1-80483-877-8

MP3 CD ISBN 978-1-80483-876-1

Digital audio download ISBN 978-1-80483-874-7

Boldwood Books Ltd
23 Bowerdean Street
London SW6 3TN
www.boldwoodbooks.com

This one is for all the members and admins of the following Facebook groups:
Riveting Reads and Vintage Vibes
The Friendly Book Community
The Spirituality Café
Chick Lit and Prosecco
Book Swap Central
Fiction Addicts at Socially Distanced Book Club

Thank you all for making our book-loving corners of the internet a gorgeous place to be, and proving that bookish people are the best people!

1

"'I'm so glad I live in a world where there are Octobers.'" I quote *Anne of Green Gables* to Mrs Potts as I throw open the bookshop curtains, ready for another day on Ever After Street.

She looks up at me uninterestedly from the floor, waits for me to straighten out her bed in the window, and then jumps into the display and settles down with her back to me. Sometimes it feels like I'll never win over my grumpy old lady of a cat.

It's not personal, I tell myself. Mrs Potts doesn't like anything except Dreamies and leaving mouse intestines by the front door.

As I open up the shop, Mickey, who runs The Mermaid's Treasure Trove, is walking past and she pokes her head round the door. 'You okay, Marnie?'

'Fine, thanks.' I pretend to be rearranging the other window display and concentrate intently on it so I don't have to make eye contact. I know she means well, the other shopkeepers who work on this street always do when they pop in to check on me, but every time they do, it's a sharp reminder of how alone I am now.

'Well, you know where we all are if you need anything. Have a good day.'

I give her a wave as she disappears down the street towards her own shop, but it's too late for her to see it. It's not that I don't appreciate them checking on me, but I just keep hoping they'll stop coming, and maybe things will start to feel normal again.

Things haven't been normal in A Tale As Old As Time for a while now, not since Mum died, taking with her my enthusiasm for running the bookshop we owned together.

In the window, there's a vase holding bare tree branches hung with laminated miniature book covers, a liberal scattering of fabric autumn leaves around my book picks for this week, and brown and yellow leaf bunting that's draped from one side of the display to the other. I adjust that and rearrange my favourite book that has a permanent spot in one of the two bookshop windows – *Once Upon Another Time* by U.N.Known – an anonymous author who happens to have written the best book ever. It's my go-to recommendation for *anyone* looking for a book. It appeals to all ages, from disinterested teenagers to cynical adults who need to see the good in the world again. It's the ultimate comfort book. Escapism that reminds you of what's important in life and inspires you to follow your dreams. I stroke my fingers over the embossed cover and tilt it on the stand so the shiny lettering catches the morning sunlight and draws in passersby. Hopefully, anyway.

A Tale As Old As Time is a little bookshop on Ever After Street, a fairy-tale-themed shopping street in the foothills of a castle in the Wye Valley. I stock mainly fairy tales and their retellings and other books that have a hint of magic, myth, legend, or enchantment about them. And romance, because falling in love is like experiencing a fairy tale in real life. So I'm told, anyway. My experience of love so far is the exact opposite of a happy ending.

It's not nine o'clock yet so I run upstairs to make a cup of tea. The elderly gent who used to rent this shop before we took it on lived here, but my mum left her bungalow to me when she died, so

I live in a little row of cottages on the other side of the forest, and the upstairs here is just storage with a dingy kitchen and a kitty litter tray for Mrs Potts, who only deigns herself to go outside when the bloodthirsty need to murder a mouse arises. Most of the time – perfectly normal contented cat. Couple of nights a month – bloodthirsty harbinger of death to every rodent within the Herefordshire land borders.

I pop a lemon shortbread biscuit into my mouth for good measure and go back downstairs and head to the counter with my cuppa. The counter is probably the best thing in the shop. It's hexagonal and made from dark wood, with shelves for displaying books on each of its sides. The sixth side at the back is a door that lets me into the middle of it, where the till and computer is, and there's loads of under-counter shelving to stash my current read and any errant cups of tea.

I tidy the displays of bookmarks, postcards and notebooks, a few of the other bookish gifts on sale here, and wait for the first customers to come in.

And wait…

And wait…

All right, customers are few and far between at the moment, but it'll pick up. It's autumn now – the perfect time of year for snuggling under blankets with a good book and a hot chocolate, preferably in front of a crackling fire.

And it's Monday. It's always quieter early in the week. It'll be better at the weekend. And there's the after-school club this afternoon. Maybe one of them will buy a book for a change, and not just find a book they like and watch as one of their parents gets their phone out and orders it from Amazon.

It's times like this that I miss Mum more than anything. She was my co-owner and running this shop was our dream, together. Once upon a time, the place was filled with customers and full of the constant chatter of book recommendations and the ding of the till as people couldn't queue up fast enough. We had a shop assistant back then, we were so busy that it was more than two people could handle, and it was nice that there was always someone to talk to, although given what happened with Shannon, my *ex*-shop assistant and Rick, my *ex*-boyfriend, maybe there's something to be said for working alone.

Thankfully, it's picked up a bit by the afternoon. There are a few people browsing, and a mum reading a Heidi Swain book while her toddler runs riot in the kids' section play area, scribbling with crayons on the table itself as opposed to on the blank paper set nicely in front of him. I want to say something because that'll take me a lot of scrubbing later to clean up, but I'm not very good at saying things to people, and I'm hoping the mum will actually buy that Heidi Swain, given how much she's creasing the spine.

'Anything new by U.N.Known yet?' one of my regular customers asks as she comes up to the counter with a pile of fantasy books.

'Nothing, disappointingly.'

She comes in every week and we have the same conversation. I talked her into buying *Once Upon Another Time* months ago. She loved it, and now she's as desperate to read something else by its unknown author as I am, but unfortunately he hasn't written anything else, and in the seven years since it was published, he seems to have disappeared from the face of the earth. No website, no social media, no other mentions anywhere online. It was initially advertised as the first book in a trilogy, but over the years, all mention of that has been removed from existence, so much so that I'm half-convinced I imagined it. Even a movie that was being made of the book has now been canned with no explanation.

'One day,' she says hopefully as I put her books into a brown paper bag with a print of the Beast's enchanted rose on it. 'What I wouldn't give to meet that man. The things he can do with words. I'd ask him to marry me on the spot.'

No one knows for sure that U.N.Known is a man, but that's the general consensus. It's hard to believe that someone who can write a story like that can suddenly stop and never write anything again, and I – along with a *lot* of other fans – live in continual hope that he will. There's a forum on the internet dedicated to *Once Upon Another Time* and its mysterious author, with people determined to find out something about the unknown man.

I wave goodbye to my regular customer and turn back to serve the next one.

'Think we'd better take this.' The mum has put the Heidi Swain back on the shelf, put her toddler in reins, and reluctantly come to buy the book he's scribbled all over while I wasn't looking. 'A sneaky idea to put crayons in the children's section, bet you get a lot of sales this way.'

I'm not sure if she's joking or not, but I do an awkward laugh like it's the funniest thing I've heard all day, which to be fair, as she's only the second person who's spoken to me today, it actually *is* the funniest thing I've heard all day. Most people scurry out without purchasing anything and don't want to make conversation with the person they haven't purchased anything *from*. I want to tell her that the only reason she has to buy it has nothing to do with my placement of crayons and everything to do with her not bothering to watch what her precious moppet was up to, but I'm not brave enough to say it. I don't have enough customers to risk offending the ones I do have.

At least she had the decency to buy it because most people who damage books just slip them back on the shelves and hope I won't notice.

I put it in the bag and the toddler scrunches his hands for it, so

I hand it over, and his mum gives me a glare when he immediately tries to eat it.

'Thanks for your purchase,' I call after them. 'Have an enchanted day!' Our go-to farewell sounded quirky at first, but with customers like that, I fear it's taken on a patronising tone.

There's a display of pumpkins in a stack by the door, and the toddler smacks it as his mum drags him outside, sending it clattering to the ground and mini plastic pumpkins rolling across the shop. Charming.

I apologise to Mrs Potts, who has woken up with a start, and go over to set the display right.

I'm still gathering up pumpkins when a group of three women come out of The Beast's Enchanted Rose Garden, the flower shop next door, and come straight in through my door, one of them carrying a miniature rose bush in a pot under her arm. Each pristine white flower has a delicate lemon centre and the shop is instantly filled with a subtle floral scent.

'That place is so weird,' she says as I scramble out of the way with my armful of pumpkins. 'The guy who owns it isn't really a beast, is he?'

As a bookseller, you'd think the questions I get asked the most are in some way related to books, but in reality, the one and only thing most people want to know about is my Scary Neighbour. 'I don't know, I haven't seen him.'

'Aren't you two, you know...' She lowers her voice and waggles her eyebrows. '...together?'

'Just a coincidence, I promise.' I give her my brightest smile. It's a misconception that I have to correct several times a week. The Beast's Enchanted Rose Garden being right next door to the Tale As Old As Time bookshop really is just a coincidence. When I was a little girl, I told my mum that I wanted a bookshop named A Tale As Old As Time one day, after watching *Beauty and the Beast* for the thousandth time in my young life. The Beast's Enchanted Rose Garden was already here when we arrived on Ever After Street, but that just made it even more of a perfect fit for this fairy-tale-themed street.

The only thing I know about my neighbour is that he exists. The Beast's Enchanted Rose Garden is run by a man who is hardly ever seen, and on the rare occasions that he *is* seen, he's always wearing some kind of disguise that keeps him hidden. He's also the gardener up at the castle in the hills at the end of Ever After Street, the one who kept it neat and tidy while it was abandoned, before Witt and Sadie from The Cinderella Shop across the street moved back in earlier this year.

Maybe I should be grateful. Given the kinds of problems that people can have with their neighbours, I never hear a peep out of mine. I may as well be living next door to a ghost. People say he lives in the flat above his shop, but the only time I know he's there at all is if I'm upstairs and he happens to be upstairs at the same time – the walls are thin enough to give away the sound of movement on the other side: footsteps or the creak of opening and closing doors.

When we first opened our shop a few years ago, I went next door to say hello and although I could see him moving around in the back of his shop, he didn't respond or acknowledge me in any way, and he's never tried to introduce himself since, so it's probably safe to assume he's not one for neighbourly goodwill. He's obviously some kind of rose specialist though, because everything in his shop revolves around them. He's got bouquets of cut roses in a rainbow of colours; growing roses in decorative pots, from huge established bushes to tiny windowsill plants; bare-rooted stems for people to take home and plant themselves, and an array of seasonal wreaths and garlands that all feature roses in some way. His window displays make you stop and stare at them, open-mouthed, as you wonder how anyone can do *so* much with a simple flower. His shop is beautiful, but *he* is terrifying. In fact, he seems determined to drive customers away. Every time I've looked in, there's no one manning the till, just a cash box where he expects people to put the correct money for anything they want to buy, and anyone who has made the mistake of seeking him out for flower-related advice has found themselves growled at or shouted at, and apparently chased away with a broom once. Which seems like an odd way to run a business to me, and surely the broom is overkill.

There are security cameras everywhere in there, so I can only assume he monitors everything via video and relies on his scary reputation to deter customers from attempting anything dodgy.

The postman is next to arrive at the bookshop, depositing a pile of letters on my counter with a cheery smile as I ask the women about the last books they read. I can't resist chatting about books at any given opportunity, and I'm always happy to hear book recommendations despite the fact my to-read pile is so big that it's liable to topple over and crush me one day.

I leaf through the letters distractedly, dreading the thought of *more* bills or problems to deal with. There's an official-looking letter with my landlord's return address on the back and a stone settles in the pit of my stomach. My lease renewal is coming up... Maybe it will be something nice about that, like saying my rent has gone *down* perhaps? Unlikely, but a girl can dream.

The three women are chattering between themselves so I open the letter and scan it quickly, not expecting anything too bad, but my eyes pick out words like 'complaint', 'prosecuted', and 'evict'. *What*?

Panic rises, but I don't have time to read it properly as a man comes up to the counter with a stack of romance books and tells me he's buying them to cheer his wife up. It warms my cold heart to think there are still some good men out there, but all I can think about is the letter I've just shoved onto the shelf beneath the counter with such force that it's still billowing around, like one of those fortune-telling fish you get in Christmas crackers, warning me it's something far from good.

It takes forever for the women to leave, without buying anything, of course. My stomach is rolling and my hands are shaking as I get the letter out and try to make sense of it.

Dear Miss Platt,

I'm writing to inform you that I've received a complaint about the state of the garden area at the back of my property. I've received documentation suggesting a vast amount of neglect on your behalf. The garden behind the bookshop is as much a part of the property as the bookshop itself, and you signed a lease agreeing to look after the property.

You have failed to do this. The garden has been left to dereliction, and as such, it is now devaluing my building. This is unacceptable behaviour from any tenant. I have been more than lenient, given your personal circumstances, but this cannot be ignored for a moment longer.

A patch of Japanese knotweed has been brought to my attention. While it is not illegal to have it on the property, it is illegal not to declare it, and you, Miss Platt, have not declared it. As it is close to the property boundary, we are at risk of it spreading onto public land, for which we could both be prosecuted.

I take the letter and go to look out the window. I don't even know what Japanese knotweed *is*, never mind that I was supposed to declare it. And 'illegal' sounds all sorts of terrifying. I picture myself in court, a scary judge bearing down on me as I wibble about not being able to declare something I can't even recognise. The garden is a mass of greenery. There could be *anything* lurking out there.

Therefore, if work is not undertaken to rectify this immediately, you will be liable for the charges to put things back as they were when you signed the tenancy agreement, and I will not be renewing your lease for another term.

I work in accordance with the local council and the complaint has prompted them to look again at the popularity of A Tale As Old As Time, and quite frankly, the council and I agree that your bookshop is simply not attracting the attention that it once did, and therefore, if things do not improve within six weeks, I will be evicting you when your lease expires. I will be in the area at that time and I will be coming to inspect the property, and I politely suggest you have a very good case to put forward as to why Ever After Street needs a bookshop at all. The novelty of a Beauty and the Beast-themed bookshop has clearly worn off and the council are keen to fill the street with shops that attract customers, bring in revenue, and get people talking about the area. Your shop, Miss Platt, is doing none of those things.

Regards,
Mr Rowbotham

The garden? The *garden* has caused all this? Pure dread is flooding my veins and I can't get enough air into my lungs. I lean a hip against the counter to steady myself because my legs are shaking. Mum loved gardening. The garden was always her department. She kept it looking lovely and spent many sunny afternoons sitting out there when she needed to take the weight off her feet. Since she died, I haven't been able to face the garden at all. I've tried not to think about it, tried to ignore how overgrown it was getting in the hopes that... I don't know. Maybe fairies would come along and sort it out for me?

I can't cry, there are customers in. Someone's telling me about a book she bought for her son last week and how much he enjoyed it. I can see her lips moving but I can't hear her words coming out.

What am I going to do? A Tale As Old As Time has been my sanctuary for the past eighteen months. It's given me something to focus on. It's the only thing that's kept me going, and now it's going to be taken away?

I know I've been avoiding the garden, but I didn't think anyone *else* had noticed. I'm not much of an outdoorsy person, and the garden at the back of the bookshop is... well, all right, it's a bit on the unkempt side, but there's a little path because Mrs Potts and I cut through the back way to get into work every day. Who the hell has complained about it? And why? What has my garden got to do with anyone else? Who can even see it? The window to the back is in the children's section, but I painted it with blue sky, sun, and green hills, so no one can see out. No one walks down the back lane apart from the other shopkeepers who work on this side of the street. Was it one of them? Or some miserable customer intent on sticking their nose in where it doesn't belong? The garden doesn't harm anyone. It's just a tad overgrown. I glance towards the back window, where the branches of an overhanging bush are scraping along the glass outside, clamouring to get in. All right, maybe more than a *tad* overgrown.

And okay, trade has been quiet lately but since Mum died, so has my enthusiasm for doing anything other than losing myself in books. I read so I don't have to think about real life. The bookshop *isn't* pulling its weight with reaching new people. Earlier this year, The Cinderella Shop staged their own real-life Cinderella story that went viral and pulled in tonnes of visitors for all the shops on

Ever After Street, but now a few months have passed and things are quiet again. Schools have gone back after the summer holidays, parents are spent-out on uniform and every other expense that comes with a new school year, but things always pick up as we move towards Christmas. They *have* to. Because I can't lose this place.

The thought makes my nose burn and a lump forms in my throat. I glance up at the clock: 3.30 p.m. The after-school club will arrive in half an hour – I can't let myself cry. Children notice and are quick to point out things like red blotchy faces. I'm reading Beatrix Potter tonight; I can't be a sniffling mess when they come in.

I won't think about it, not now, not in the middle of a working day. Professionalism and all that. I distract myself by scrubbing the crayon off the table and tidying up again. I talk a constant litany of nonsense to Mrs Potts because if I stop for even a second, my mind goes to the letter under the counter. It feels like it's watching me as I work, biding its time until it can leap out and clamp my leg between its metaphorical teeth.

The after-school club was inspired by Meg Ryan reading to children in her bookshop in *You've Got Mail*, but tonight's session is like torture, not because of the kids or *The Tale of Jemima Puddle-Duck*, but because of me. I mess up words and I can't hide the distress in my voice, even on the cheeriest parts, where I overcompensate and become high-pitched and squeaky. A small child bursts into tears. An accompanying grandma takes her hearing aid out and replaces the battery in case it's on the blink.

I'm a wreck by the time they leave, not a sale between them, and even though it's only half past four, I shut the door and flip the sign over to 'closed'. Being open for another half an hour is not the magic wand I need to save this shop. Unless it's the difference between a billionaire stopping by and buying 13,692 books, anyway.

Mrs Potts has had some cat biscuits and is sleeping on a chair upstairs now, where she swiftly takes herself at the appearance of any significant number of small children who tend to scream 'kitty!' and usually want to do one of two things – smoosh her to their little chests or pull her tail, and in her grouchy old age, Mrs Potts no longer has the patience for smooshing or tail pulling.

I get the letter out again with shaking hands. Maybe it will make more sense with a re-read, like really clever paragraphs of really clever books, except clever paragraphs excite me, there's a joy in learning new words or seeing what someone has done with text, but there is nothing good about this letter.

This letter is the end of the only good thing in my life.

2

I don't know what to do. I read the letter over and over again, but no magical solution springs out at me. No fairy godmother appears to wave a magic wand and make it all go away. I'm just... alone. There's no one I can turn to. No one I can ask for advice. Mum would've known what to do. But if she was still here, the garden wouldn't be in the state it's in, and the shop probably wouldn't be either.

It's at moments like this when you realise how few friends you *really* have. I want life to be like a made-for-TV movie where the heroine would lose a big job promotion and immediately be surrounded by friends to commiserate and pour wine and give a much-needed hug. I have never needed a hug more than I need one right now. But there's no one to hug. It never feels like I'm friendless, but characters in books can't give you hugs when you need one, even if they feel like friends while you're reading. But in real life... I really am friendless.

My mum was my best friend, but now she's gone, and the hole she's left in my life seems to get bigger every day. I'm friends with a lovely group of readers on a few Facebook booklover groups, but I couldn't share something like this with people I only know online. I've lost touch with everyone I was friends with in school or in previous jobs. And now I'm alone, apart from Mrs Potts, who, although lovely, is not really very good at giving legal advice. Or pouring wine, for that matter. And the tendency to claw my arms to shreds if the mood catches her doesn't make her the *best* choice for a cuddle buddy. The other girls who work on Ever After Street are friendly, they offer help all the time, but I wouldn't know how to turn to them with this. What would I say? I've let my garden slip into disrepair because all I can think about when I go out there is how much Mum loved it and I've lost all my customers because some mornings it's been too hard to get out of bed, let alone follow through on promotions and other things we had planned now I'm by myself?

Even if it was just one thing, like needing to sort out the garden *or* get more customers then maybe it would be manageable, but both together seems insurmountable. I keep the letter in my hands as I open the back door and peek out, and immediately wish I could go back inside and block it out like I have for the past few months, but I force myself to step out and shut the door behind me.

The evening breeze is fresh and cool and there's an autumnal smell in the air. The nearest tree on the opposite side of the path is a tall sycamore, and its leaves are a blaze of yellow while its brown helicopter seeds already litter the ground.

The garden is overwhelming. There's green plant life everywhere, and I don't know what any of it is. Brambles are just about the only thing I can identify. And stinging nettles. And tonnes of other weeds and nasty-looking things. Even though I walk through this garden every day, I keep my head down and hurry Mrs Potts along the path from the gate to the door. I imagine the garden is still as it used to be – wonky paving slabs, borders filled with flowers, and somewhere in the midst of it, there was a rusting metal-work table and two chairs once, but it's been swallowed completely by nature. I force myself to look at the wooden bench where Mum used to sit, over by the far wall. I haven't looked over there in months because it hurts that she *isn't* still sitting there. I can only see one end of it through the greenery now, and that's on an angle where at least one leg has rotted away. Mum would be devastated to see the garden like this. How have I let things get this bad?

No wonder someone's complained. It's a jungle. Most of the weeds are taller than I am, and the stinging nettles are so beefed-up that they look like they've been eating spinach on a daily basis. Even with one step, weeds have reached out and clung onto my jeans and a bramble has snagged a thread from the sleeve of my knitted jumper. I try to tread down the brambles. Maybe if I can make a bit of a path to the other side of the garden and at least *get* over there, could I think about... weedkiller, maybe? I could buy a bottle of weedkiller and spray it, couldn't I? And if it all died, then I could clear it away...

'People kill weeds all the time,' I say to myself. 'Shops have shelves full of products for this exact purpose. It can't be that hard, can it?'

It's the first time I've felt the slightest spark of hope since that letter arrived.

I have to do something about this. I've let things slide, buried my head in the proverbial sand, but this shop is the only thing left in my life that I love. I can't let it slip away because I'm not brave enough to face my grief. This letter is a wake-up call, giving me a chance to turn things around before it's too late.

I take another step through the undergrowth, but I've trodden on a bramble and pulled it taut, and my other foot catches in it, and I flail around to keep my balance, but it's no good.

I shriek as I go flying face-first into the weeds, throwing my arms out to catch myself as I crash down, my fall cushioned by the thicket covering the hard ground underneath.

I lie there for a moment, adrenaline coursing through me as I assess myself for injuries. I'm scratched from the brambles, but my jumper is thick enough to have protected me from the worst of the damage. My face is scratched and a stinging sensation has started to burn through my left hand. I landed in a patch of nettles. Of course I did. I push myself back up onto my knees and there are bramble thorns embedded in both my palms, and my limbs are shaking from the shock of the fall. I feel too unsteady to get up, so I turn myself over into a sitting position, and I sit there in a bramble bush, feeling small and stupid for not being more careful, for getting ahead of myself and thinking a bit of weedkiller could win against this jungle, and the patheticness overwhelms me.

The emotions I've been fighting all day finally build up until they explode in a noise of anguish and a flood of tears.

It's all so much. Too much. I can't even take two steps into the garden without falling over and then crying like a child who's grazed their knee in primary school and needs a parent to kiss it better.

Heaving, shuddering sobs wrack my body. Everything feels jarred from how hard I hit the ground. Each thorn in my hand is throbbing, the scratches on my face are stinging as salty tears drip over them, and my hand is burning and tingling as though pins are being pushed in and out of it and the sensation is spreading up my arm too, and I sit there and let all the feelings come bursting out. I swipe blood from a scratch on my nose, feeling so stupid. How the heck am I supposed to do something about this when I can't even take a step without making a mess of myself?

'Bloody hell, will you stop making that godawful noise?'

I freeze in shock. A voice. A voice from the other side of the hedge.

Scary Neighbour. It *must* be my Scary Neighbour. He's *there*? He must be out in his garden too, and I had no idea. How long has he been there? I've been talking to myself, has he heard all that?

Usually I'd be quite excited at the prospect of contact with this unknown entity of a person, but tonight... tonight, I've absolutely *had* it. I cannot take another thing today, and now I can't even cry in my own garden in peace? Not today, Scary Neighbour, *not* today.

'I'm sorry if my misery impinges on your day!' I shout back.

'I'm trying to work over here. I want peace and quiet, and all I can hear is the wailing cry of an elephant seal giving birth! This is a peaceful garden, go and yowl somewhere else!'

The nerve of him! No flipping wonder he keeps to himself if that's how he speaks to people.

'I'm not an elephant seal,' I yell back. Quite possibly the most unexpected sentence I've ever uttered. 'I'm going to be evicted for letting the garden get out of hand, and I just fell over and landed half in a patch of stinging nettles and half in a bramble bush, and it's really painful!'

'Go and tell someone who cares!'

'There *is* no one who cares!' My tears had stopped with the surprise of hearing him speak, but the truth of that sentence hits me like a bramble bush to the face. There is *no one* who cares. When did my life become this empty? When did I become this lonely? I try to stifle the sob that rises in my throat. I shouldn't – whoever he is, he has no say over what I do in my own garden, but I've got enough trouble without riling up Scary Neighbour too.

He doesn't speak for a while, and I think that last outburst must've been enough to shut him up, but then his voice filters through the hedge again.

'I know that feeling.' It's a quiet mutter this time, so low that I might've imagined it. 'Open your gate, and on the right side, there's a clump of dock leaves growing. Crush one up and rub it over the stings.'

Is there? I never knew there were dock leaves so close by. I push myself onto my feet and go along the path on still-shaky legs to look out the gate, and sure enough, he's right. I lean down to pluck one, crush it a bit, and rub it over my hand. 'Thanks.'

No response. I wait, and a few minutes pass in silence. It seems that the extent of my contact with Scary Neighbour is going to be a couple of insults and a helpful observation about dock leaves. I lean against the gatepost and carry on rubbing the leaf, appreciating the cooling sensation that turns the red and lumpy part of my hand from prickling to only tingling.

'Heads up!' The voice from the other side of the hedge speaks again, and something small comes flying over the greenery and hits the ground with a metal clink.

'What's that?' I pick it up and gingerly turn over a pair of small, sharp tweezers.

'You're incapable of identifying a pair of tweezers?'

'Obviously I know what they are, what I don't know is why you're lobbing them over the hedge at me.'

'They're thorn tweezers, good for getting blackberry thorns out of your hands.'

'Oh! Right.' That was surprisingly thoughtful of him. I was just going to try picking them out when my other hand had stopped feeling like it's on fire. 'Thank you.'

'Take your time. If you try to rush it, you'll only push them in deeper.'

'And you'd know, would you?' I mutter under my breath, not intending it to be a question, and looking up in surprise when he answers.

'I grow roses. I'm used to working with pricks.'

It takes a few seconds to comprehend what he's said, and then the unintentional innuendo makes me laugh out loud.

'I'm sure we've all felt like that at some point or another,' I say, thinking of some ex-colleagues who are better left forgotten.

'Prick*les*,' he corrects, but it's too late for me. I can't stop laughing. My eyes are watering again for an altogether different reason now, even though I'm sure he's going to yell at me for laughing like a walrus or something equally insulting.

Instead, I'm surprised when there's a reluctant but deep rumble of laughter from the other side of the hedge too.

I've laughed so hard that I've given myself hiccups and I hold my breath for a couple of minutes to make them stop, and then release it, panting. The laugh was a much-needed distraction, and everything feels momentarily less overwhelming.

The stinging nettle sensation is fading now, but the bramble thorns in my right hand are still throbbing. I find a spot on the path beside the hedge that separates our gardens, and sit down so I can brace my elbows against my legs and use the tweezers left-handed.

I can sense Scary Neighbour is still there. I hear him take a breath like he's about to speak a few times, but he doesn't.

'Tell me what's wrong,' he barks eventually.

It's said with the same tone as the Beast demanding Belle join him for dinner, and I feel equally obstinate in the face of such a harsh demand. 'No, thank you.'

I'm sitting with my back to the hedge between us, but I can hear movement behind me, footsteps that make me think he's pacing, and then a quiet groan and the unmistakeable sound of him lowering himself to the ground. I glance over my shoulder as if I can somehow see through the thick hedge. He's sat down with me? *Really*?

It takes a while for him to speak again. 'Look, I'm not very good at saying what people want to hear, or knowing what to say in any given situation, but I don't see how they have any right to evict you. You're in trouble because of the garden?'

I focus on picking bramble thorns out of my skin. I wasn't intending to share any of this, but this time, his voice sounds soft and encouraging, and something about it makes me feel calmer than I have all day. He doesn't push any further, just lets the question hang in the air, and as I concentrate on pulling out each thorn with his little tweezers, the whole story comes spilling out.

'You can't blame Mr Rowbotham for being angry about the garden,' he says when I've finished. 'Anyone can see it's a disaster zone. Apart from the total chaos of brambles, stinging nettles and giant hogweed, which is invasive *and* dangerous if you cut it, you've got that ever-increasing patch of Japanese knotweed. If that spreads outside of your property boundary, you'll be prosecuted and fined, and you'll need a professional removal expert to get rid of it. Trying to do it yourself will spread it further.'

Why does it seem like I'm the only person in the universe who doesn't know what Japanese-sodding-knotweed is?

'Aside from that, you've got willowherb spreading in such a quantity that it could be termed a biohazard, and ivy climbing up the walls.'

'Ivy is pretty. Who wouldn't want to live in a little cottage covered by ivy?'

'Ivy sends out roots that drill into cracks in the mortar and cause structural damage to the building.'

'Oh. Right.'

'Not to be a killjoy or anything.' He laughs at how desolate I must sound.

This day just gets better. Although, since he appeared, it inexplicably *has* got better. There's something about the way he's pragmatic and sensible, and clearly knowledgeable about plants.

Without realising it, he's exactly the kind of person I needed to talk to today.

'I'm sorry about the rest of it though. It's unfair that they've dragged the shop into things. It should've just been about the garden.'

'They're not wrong,' I admit eventually. 'Trade has been quiet lately. I barely earn enough to cover the rent most months. The amount of disposable income customers have got is going down and the price of books is going up, apart from on the big retail websites who can afford to sell them for much cheaper than I can. If I cut prices any more, I'm going to be paying the customer to take books away.'

He laughs. 'A memorable but rather ineffective marketing strategy.'

I laugh too, but it quickly turns to a groan of hopelessness. 'I need to make a change. My mum and I used to run the shop together. We had all these plans for marketing and advertising but now it's just me and it's all been a bit much. I tweet pictures of my cat into a social media void and hope customers will stumble upon my shop. I do a rotating selection of heavily discounted books every week and most of my sales come from those. My customers are people who are visiting Ever After Street anyway – no one comes *to* visit the bookshop, I think that's what the letter is getting at – I don't pull my weight when it comes to dragging in visitors. I've been buried by the grief and I've let everything slide, and this letter shows that other people have noticed too. I have to do something about it.'

He's quiet before he speaks again. 'May I see the letter?'

The letter is now a scrunched-up ball where I fell on it, and I fish it out of the bramble bush and clamber to my feet and... the hedge separating us is about nine-feet high and so thick that you can't see through it. Handing a piece of paper over it isn't going to be easy. 'Paper aeroplane?'

'Put it on the gatepost and then walk away.'

The gates at the bottom of our gardens are attached to a shared gatepost, except my gate is at waist height and his is six-feet high, ensuring no one can see into his garden from anywhere. I put the crumpled letter on the flat-topped square post, and then take a couple of steps back, hovering close by, hoping to catch a glimpse of him.

'That's not walking away.'

How does he even know? The hedge towers above my head, and although I'm sure it's neatly trimmed on his side, on my side... well, you could park a couple of double-decker buses in there and no one would be any the wiser. The unruly green branches spring out in every direction, and the whole thing has bowed outwards so it takes up a good chunk of the garden. The gaps between branches are small enough for only the tiniest birds to take refuge in. There's no way he can actually see through, but I dutifully traipse up the path, and when I look back at the gatepost, the letter is gone.

'Wow. You really were *angry* at this letter.'

I stay quiet, listening to the rustle of paper while he flattens it and reads it.

'I'm sorry, this is hideously unfair.' There's silence for a moment, and the letter reappears on the gatepost without me seeing even so much as a flash of him. 'Mr Rowbotham always was a dingbat.'

'Is he your landlord too?'

'No, I own outright. I bought the building – that was more than enough contact with him for one lifetime.'

'Must be nice,' I mutter as I walk down to collect the letter. The thought of being my own boss, of not living a life where letters like this can turn up at any given moment and knock you totally off course... I wish I could afford that. 'People say you're also a gardener at the castle?'

He doesn't answer. Too personal a question, maybe? I go for something simpler. 'I'm Marnie, by the way.'

I expect him to introduce himself in return, but he doesn't. 'Do you have a name?'

'Yes.'

Again, I wait for him to do the traditional thing of actually telling me what it is, but he doesn't.

'Would you like to share it with the rest of the class?'

He lets out a sharp bark of laughter and then quickly cuts it off as though it wasn't intended. 'I see no reason to. We are not friends. I should have gone inside long ago and left you making the elephant seal in labour nois—'

'Don't, please.' I interrupt him because the panic of earlier has dampened down since we've been talking, but the thought of being alone out here stokes the flames again.

'Why not? You surely know my reputation. You *want* to talk to me?' The words are laced with contempt, and it makes me wonder if I'm more surprised that Scary Neighbour is talking to me... or if he's more surprised that *I'm* talking to *him*.

'Would you like to come round? I can make a cuppa and there's some biscui—'

'No, thank you.'

I don't think anyone's ever sounded quite so horrified at the offer of tea and biscuits before. 'Do you mind me asking why you're so...' I realise this is a sentence that could go badly wrong. What do I end it with? Standoffish? Rude? Shouty? So uninvolved with the rest of Ever After Street?

'Reclusive?' I eventually settle on. It seems the least offensive possibility.

'Yes.'

'Yes, you mind me asking?'

'Yes.'

Okay then. I almost laugh at the awkwardness.

'Does my shop name not give it away? I'm a beast. That's why you never see me – and never will.'

I can't help being taken aback by his sharp answer. He can't mean that literally, can he? 'But surely that's just a rumour, made up because no one knows you. Everyone knows everyone else on this street, apart from you.'

'People are entitled to be different.'

I stutter for an answer because while he's not wrong, it's just not how things are on Ever After Street. 'There's no requirement to make friends with the other shopkeepers, obviously.'

'Good. Friends are a waste of time. They'll do nothing but disappoint you in the end. Everyone is better off alone – anyone who thinks otherwise just hasn't realised that simple truth yet.'

'Wow.' I'm surprised by how much his words pull at something deep in my chest. 'That's so sad.'

'Not sad, just common sense. If you never form attachments to anyone, you never get hurt.' He's quiet for a moment. 'And you never hurt them.'

There's that hint of self-loathing again. Who *is* this guy? He seems angry and bitter, and yet he was kind enough to tell me about the dock leaves, throw me his thorn tweezers, and read the letter, and yet...

'Why are you talking to me about all this anyway? Why not share it with your boyfriend?'

My head tilts in confusion. 'I don't have a boyfriend.'

'Yeah, you do.'

'I assure you, I do not. I think I'd know.'

'That guy who always buys flowers for you.'

'Oh! Rick!' I do the bleat of annoyance that thinking of Rick always generates. 'He's not my boyfriend. He was, once. He *was* my fiancé, until I caught him shagging my shop assistant in the romance section last year.'

Scary Neighbour laughs out loud, but it's not an unkind laugh. 'That seems like a very unromantic use of the romance section.'

'The books thought so too! They were traumatised for life! I wasn't too happy about it either. I sacked her and broke up with him, but he's the kind of guy who doesn't take no for an answer. He's decided we were happy together and has vowed to win me back, which is *never* going to happen.'

'Good. He's a smarmy twit who calls me Scary Neighbour and proudly taunts my CCTV cameras by not paying full price for his flowers.'

I cringe. Scary Neighbour is *my* nickname for him. Rick was never meant to say it to his face. Well, not literally. I don't think anyone's ever actually seen his face. 'I'm so sorry. I don't even want the flowers. I refuse them, and if he leaves them on my doorstep while I'm at work, I give them to my neighbour at home. Better she enjoys them than me be reminded of him every time I see them.'

'You give away my flowers?' He sounds mortally offended, and I can imagine his eyebrows have just shot up.

'Not because of the flowers, because of the giver. No offence to your flowers, they're always beautiful, *he's* the problem. And he always buys bouquets with lilies in them, and lilies are poisonous to cats. I told him multiple times while we were still dating but he never listens.'

'Want me to refuse him service?'

'No, of course not.' That seems like a surprisingly nice thing to offer. 'That would affect your profits. He'd only find somewhere else and give his money to a rival florist; that's not fair on you.'

'I'll refuse him service.' I can hear the decisive nod of his head.

'Er, thanks, I think.' Given the stories we've heard about Scary Neighbour's apparent contempt for his customers, it sounds vaguely threatening and a bit foreboding. 'Want me to give you his full name and address so you can report him to the police for shoplifting?'

'Nah. Don't worry about it.'

'Don't you worry about people stealing from you? The temptation must be higher than in other shops because you're hardly ever there.'

He makes a noise of indifference. 'I'm of the opinion that anyone desperate enough to steal flowers probably needs them more than I do.'

I blink in surprise at his mellow answer. 'That's a surprisingly laid-back attitude for someone who calls himself a beast.'

'Losing a few flowers to less-than-honest customers is a small price to pay in exchange for not having to be there in person.' He sighs like he knows he's about to say something he'll regret. 'I *am* the gardener at the castle. It was my father's job and I took over when he died three years ago. The shop is just a sideline, a way to sell excess stock. I don't like people, but without the shop, my roses would die unseen in the castle grounds. Having to deal with the occasional customer is a marginally better alternative.'

'Your displays are spectacular. Your windows are always incredible, and the scent... Sometimes I open my door just to let the scent of your flowers in.'

'Thank you. I didn't know anyone noticed. I prefer it when people don't.'

Don't what, notice him? He is noticeable on Ever After Street by his absence. He's never come to a shopkeeper meeting, and never does anything that the street gets involved in, never puts up posters or anything else we all do to support the other shops. He never seems to do anything other than scare his own customers away.

'Okay, I have a question for you – how does someone let their garden get into this state in the first place?'

'My mum died.' Even now, it feels so final to say it. I usually say things like 'gone' or 'passed', but something about him makes me want to be direct. 'Eighteen months ago. Cancer. We ran the shop together. I hefted boxes of books around and she did the garden. And since then, I haven't been able to face it. She was always green-fingered, and I'm the opposite. My fingers are like death to plants.'

'Which would arguably be a good thing in this situation. The one thing those weeds need is a swift death.'

It makes me laugh out loud again. He's the strangest conundrum of a man. Sharp and snappy, so closed off that he won't even tell me his name, and yet he says things that are unexpectedly hilarious. It's well after 5 p.m. now, and the chill from the stone underneath me has long since seeped through the fabric of my jeans. He must be in the same position, and yet... he's still here, and seems in no rush to go anywhere. 'I know it's going to seem strange to someone who gardens for a living, but I'm not an outdoorsy person. I don't even know why a bookshop needs a garden.'

'A lot of people enjoy sitting in the garden to read, so I'm told. As a bookshop owner, you strike me as someone who might enjoy reading.'

The deadpan tone in his voice makes me laugh again. 'Yes, I do *quite* enjoy reading, but I'd rather curl up in an armchair with a hot chocolate and a fluffy blanket.'

'Even in summer?'

'Well, maybe with an iced coffee and a fan instead then. Indoors, there's nothing that wants to sting you or bite you. I prefer to read inside where I can relax, rather than be on alert for rogue horseflies, wasps divebombing your cup of tea, and sunburn. My skin has two settings – ghost and post box. I switch from so pale I'm almost translucent to so red that it would make a lobster cringe in less than three minutes in the sun.'

Now it's his turn to laugh. 'You've never heard of suncream?'

'Then you've got grease everywhere and leave handprints on your book, or your Kindle slides out of your slippery grip. It's easier to read inside, especially at this time of year. Reading is *made* for getting cosy in front of a fire, a scented candle burning, hot chocolate full of whipped cream, a snuggly blanket and soft and fluffy socks. Cat on lap is optional, depending on cat's mood and tolerance levels.'

He laughs again. 'I can't argue with excuses like that. And I suspect me and your cat might have similar levels of tolerance.'

I wonder how much tolerance he's got left for me tonight. I bite my lip as I bite the bullet. 'I have no right to ask, but as a gardener, do you have any advice on what to do about my garden?'

I expect him to shout at me, because it's not his problem and I shouldn't be asking him, but he's a *gardener* and the one thing I'm in desperate need of is garden advice.

Instead, his answer is instantaneous. 'Oh, that? That's no big deal.'

'No big deal? I'm going to be evicted if I don't do something about it and I've started by throwing myself headfirst into stinging nettles and a bramble bush. You might be an expert but I'm not.'

He's laughing at my indignation, but it's a kind laugh, one that's laughing *with* me, whereas anytime Rick laughed, it was always *at* me, which is something I only started noticing after we broke up. 'Start by chopping it all down.'

'With... scissors?' I try to be helpful.

'No, with a spoon.' I can *hear* the eye roll. 'You know how to use a chainsaw?'

I laugh, but he doesn't. 'Oh, you're serious? No, funnily enough, I don't know how to use a chainsaw. I don't even own a chainsaw.'

'You can borrow mine. And yes, I'll teach you how to use it.'

'Thanks,' I say, unable to hide the surprise in my voice. Scary Neighbour is quickly turning into Surprising Neighbour. 'I was *not* expecting that.'

'Neither was I.' He sounds as surprised as I am, but I like his honesty.

Everything about him intrigues me, from why he calls himself a beast and stays so hidden to his blasé attitude towards shoplifters and why he's been so unexpectedly kind tonight.

And there's a little unwarranted flutter of excitement because it means I'll see him again. Well, maybe not *see* him, but talk to him again. It's a promise that this isn't a one-off thing.

There's something so easy about talking to him. Maybe it's because I can't see him. It takes the pressure off. I'm not great at talking to people. I'm awkward, and rubbish at making conversation, and terrible at eye contact. People know me as the quiet bookworm who does nothing but read books and walk her cat to work every day. It doesn't help with making friends. But there seems to be no expectation with him. This is the easiest conversation I've had lately, and it's with a stranger without a name, an age, or a face. He could be *anyone*, but he's nothing like what I thought he'd be.

After the despair of earlier, the panic of the letter and the shock of hurting myself, everything feels manageable again. The nettle stings have reduced to just a bit of numbness because of his tip about the dock leaves. The thorns are gone from my other hand because of his tweezers, and the garden that seemed so overwhelming an hour ago... now seems like it isn't entirely unfixable. All because of him.

Someone who must be so lonely has made me feel less alone than I have for a very long time. And even though it's cold and the sky is rapidly darkening, and Mrs Potts will be after me for her dinner before long, I'm lingering out here, hoping he'll stay longer too.

'Thank you,' I say. 'Earlier on, I didn't know what to do. I desperately needed someone like you to talk to, and there you were.'

'There I was.' He sighs. 'You don't need to thank me. I don't speak to many people, and it was... unexpectedly enjoyable.' He makes a noise of... what... pain? Like a groan, a few grunts as he moves, and the direction that his voice is coming from shifts upwards.

Now it's my turn to laugh again. Unexpectedly enjoyable. I heave myself to my feet and turn to look at the hedge, standing on tiptoes and then bending down, hoping there might be a gap to catch even the smallest glimpse of him through the branches, but the hedge is disappointingly tight. 'I'll take that as a compliment.'

'As it was intended.'

It makes me feel warm in the chilly evening air as I stamp my feet up and down to get feeling back in my legs, and I can hear stomping from the other side of the hedge that suggests he's doing the same. 'So I guess I'll say goodnight then...'

'Yes. Um... goodnight...' There's a slight reluctance in his voice, I'm sure of it.

'Okay. Goodnight.'

'Goodnight.'

Surely we're going to need an independent adjudicator to verify this world record attempt at how many times people can say goodnight in a single two-minute period? I've made my way back up the path and my hand is on the door handle before he speaks again.

'Darcy.'

'What?' I look at the hedge in confusion.

'My name. It's Darcy.'

Darcy! 'As in, Mr Darcy?'

'Just Darcy, but I believe that's who my mother was thinking of. Jane Austen was her favourite author.'

'I *love* Jane Austen too. *Pride and Prejudice* is one of my favourite books ever, and still one of my biggest sellers, and you're telling me that for the past few years, I've worked next door to someone named after Mr Darcy and this is the first I'm hearing of it?'

'It would seem that way, yes.'

It's a name that seems to suit him very well. Mr Darcy was cold and standoffish on the surface, but he was deep, multi-layered, and good-hearted underneath his pride. And there's definitely more to my Scary Neighbour than meets the eye.

I hear his door click shut, but I stand on my doorstep for a while longer, looking at the hedge that separates us. This has been one of the most surprising nights of my life, and *that* was one of the most enchanting encounters I've ever experienced... without actually encountering anyone at all.

3

Darcy. I get a thrill every time I think of his name. And it's not just that – it's the fact he *told* me. He revealed something about himself, something that he clearly wasn't intending to reveal earlier in our conversation last night.

As Mrs Potts and I walk to work, I delete a text from Rick, suggesting a weekend trip to Paris to 'reacquaint ourselves with our lost love' which is so sickening, it nearly makes me lose my breakfast. Because Rick uses sentences like that and can afford things like skipping off to Paris at the drop of a hat, because he has no adult responsibilities whatsoever. I nearly type a reply asking how many times he's taken Shannon to Paris, but I don't, because the best thing I can do with Rick is ignore him. A reply, even one that tells him exactly where he can shove his Eiffel Tower, suggests that I care, and if he thinks I care, it will be a weakness for him to chip away at, and there are already enough of them. My mum loved Rick, she thought he'd be my happily ever after, and he reminds me of that regularly.

The trees are an artist's palette of autumn colours, and the paths are covered in yellow and brown leaves, and I love every crunchy step I take at this time of year. Mrs Potts is on her leash and harness, leading the way along the paths through the woods from the little row of bungalows where I live. On the other side of Ever After Street, there's the Full Moon Forest, a pretty winding trail full of fairy doors and solar lights, and there was talk of doing the same with this part of the woods too, but we're closer to the river here, and there are crevices and sharp drops where the water cuts through the trees at the bottom of an embankment. It's unsafe if you don't know where you're going, whereas an overenthusiastic earthworm is the most trouble anyone is likely to run into in the more civilised part of the forest.

As the lane behind our row of shops comes into view, there's a flash of colour on the gatepost. Rick must've left his invitation in person too, although he never usually comes round the back – he prefers his romantic gestures to be performed in full view, so everyone on Ever After Street who once witnessed him being thrown from the bookshop, naked from the waist down, with his boxers hitting him in the face shortly afterwards, swiftly followed by my engagement ring, will know how sorry he is and what a wonderful boyfriend he'll be if I'd only give him another chance.

I tighten my grip on Mrs Potts' lead in case it's lilies again, but as we get closer, I realise it's definitely not from Rick.

On the gatepost is a red mini rose in a ceramic pot, a pair of thick gardening gloves, a pair of shears, and a tube of after-sting cream. There's a card attached to a stick that's poking out of the soil in the plant pot.

A little thornless rose to help you acclimatise to nature by bringing the outside in. Put it in the shop, water it when it looks dry, try not to kill it.

He's written on the other side too.

The shears are sharp but probably less daunting than a chainsaw to start with. Wear gloves. Don't cuddle any more stinging nettles.

Darcy has got gorgeous handwriting. Is that a weird thing to notice?

And even in writing, he makes me laugh. I run my fingers over the petals of one of the nearly open red rose buds. It's so pretty – small, but perfectly formed – and I'm so touched that my eyes have welled up.

After last night, I thought he would've gone inside and not given me a second thought, but to have gone to all this trouble... It's so thoughtful. Even the tube of sting relief cream. Or he expects me to fall into stinging nettles many more times, which is also possible. The gloves are a thick fabric with rubber-covered palms, and the shears are lightweight, and when I take the sheath off them, their razor-sharp blades glint in the morning sunlight.

'Thank you!' I call out. I've got no idea if he's even there, but I'm kind of glad it gives me an excuse to seek him out again later to thank him.

I can't get Darcy out of my head all day. The shop is dishearteningly quiet, which gives me even more time to imagine what he might look like. He sounded young-ish, maybe in his thirties, around my age, but how much can you really tell from a voice alone? He could be twenty and he could equally be sixty, and I wouldn't know.

There are a few customers here and there. A lady who comes in and does the classic, 'My friend told me about a book. I can't remember the title, but it was something to do with hedgehogs.'

When I suggest the *Hedgehog Hollow* series by Jessica Redland, she thanks me and leaves without even asking if I have any copies in stock. A family who take over the children's section and admire the *Beauty and the Beast* mural on the back wall. There's book-page wallpaper, and a life-size painting of the Beast carrying a wobbling stack of books while Belle walks in front of him, reading. The family take selfies with the mural, do a bit of browsing, but don't buy anything.

I change the window display around Mrs Potts – like U.N.-Known's *Once Upon Another Time*, she's the one thing that stays a constant in my window, no matter the season. I stare out at the empty street while I'm doing it. The garden might feel conquerable now, but it doesn't seem like anything will help with getting more customers into the shop, or getting them to buy something once they're here.

It's just after lunch that Witt comes in. He's the owner of the castle in the hills at the end of Ever After Street. After it was abandoned for decades, he moved back a few months ago, fell in love with Sadie who owns The Cinderella Shop across the street, and now they've had structural safety work done on the castle and are planning to use it as an event space. He approaches the counter with a stack of flyers in his hand. 'As you know, Sadie and I are starting to think about hiring the castle out for events. The correct insurances have come through, and we wanted to offer everybody on Ever After Street the chance to hire it free of charge. We're aiming to put together a portfolio of events we've held, along with photos and testimonials for the website, so we thought we'd start by waiving the fee for anyone local, and it would be beneficial for all of us.'

He hands me one of the flyers, which shows a picture of the castle from the outside, and a few smaller photos of the glamorous rooms inside, and there's a short blurb underneath, along with a website to visit and a number to ring with booking enquiries.

Live your own fairy tale at the Ever After Street castle. Weddings, receptions, ballrooms, conference rooms, and intricate castle gardens, suitable for all kinds of event hosting, in gorgeous Wye Valley surroundings. Welcome to a real-life Disney castle for your world of imagination.

It's a nice gesture, but he's obviously handing the flyers out to every shop on the street and didn't want me to feel left out. 'What would a bookshop want with event hosting?'

Witt's got a stammer and it often takes him a while to find the right words to say, which is fine with me because it usually takes me a while too. 'I don't know. That's where you'd come in. We're just trying to hit the ground running when we open for bookings officially.'

At first I want to laugh it off. Why would I ever need to hire a castle? But it reminds me of something Mum and I talked about... two, maybe three, years ago now. Before the diagnosis. Back when things were normal and we were planning for the future of the bookshop. We'd talked about hosting a book festival. An event where booklovers would come together to share their love of books, and there'd be author guests, talks and Q&A sessions, creative writing... We never made any actual plans, but it was easy to bat ideas back and forth when there were two of us. We'd chatted about how much fun it would be, wondered about what kind of money it would cost to hire an event space, and what kind of place we'd need, but the discussion had petered out because, back then, there was nowhere around here that would've been a viable option.

A book festival.

I went to a ball in the castle once, and it was a spectacular evening. The rooms are gigantic and full of opulent glamour. The ballroom was so perfect that you could easily imagine Belle and the Beast waltzing around it while a sentient teapot sings the song my shop is named after.

A book festival. The idea repeats itself in my head. It's a silly idea. Not the book festival itself, but the thought of me running it on my own. It's way beyond my level of expertise, and... I must've been staring into space because Witt has said goodbye and is opening the door to leave. It's now or never.

I call after him so loudly that I make both him and Mrs Potts jump. I didn't intend to be so loud, I just had to work myself up to it and apparently working myself up to something increases my volume as well. 'What's your availability like?'

'We've got a pretty much open schedule.' He comes back to the counter and gets his phone out. 'There's a Halloween party on October thirty-first, and then nothing until a wedding in December and then the Ever After Street Christmas party.'

'You're free mid-November?'

He turns his phone around to show me a calendar. 'Totally free. It's all yours if you want it.'

'I... er... I don't know. I was just asking. Being brave.' Because if I'd let him walk away, I'd never have plucked up the courage to ask again.

'No pressure.' He pats the counter. 'Give Sadie a shout if you decide on anything, she'll sort out the booking. Some of the others have expressed interest, so I'd get in quick. Ali from the 1001 Nights restaurant wants to do a themed dining night, and the shopkeepers from Christmas Ever After are thinking of a holiday market...'

These are people who know what they're doing. Ali is the owner of a restaurant that's got a brilliant marketing campaign.

He's always doing promotions and stuff. Christmas Ever After is like a little festive world of its own at the end of the opposite side of the road, where Ever After Street parts like two ends of a wishbone. I couldn't do something like that. I don't know the first thing about events. I curl up in an armchair and read books, not plan social gatherings for booklovers...

Witt must notice I've tuned out because he goes to walk away again. 'Better go and leave a leaflet for your Scary Neighbour. I doubt he'll want one, but he's not going to be excluded on my watch.'

I regret ever naming Darcy that. He must know it was me – he's *my* neighbour. Our two shops stand side by side in a block of their own. Who *else* would've given him that nickname?

I'm incapable of starting a conversation at a normal moment and must always wait until someone's halfway out the door before thinking of what to say. 'Witt, you know Darcy, right?'

He looks at me in surprise. 'Got to admit, that's the first time anyone's ever used his name. I didn't think anyone knew it.'

'They didn't.' That warmth flushes through me again. He definitely didn't intend to tell me that last night. 'Have you ever seen him?'

Witt's eyes flick to the red rose on my counter as though he knows who it came from. 'I've *seen* him. Never without a hat, scarf, gloves, and sunglasses on if that's what you're asking. I don't think anyone's *ever* seen him without those on. His father used to work for my father. He took over the job when his old man passed on, long before I came back. He's a bit prickly if anyone tries to talk to him. He likes privacy while he works. I don't disturb him and he doesn't disturb me, an arrangement that suits us both.'

'Same here,' I mutter. Darcy really is like a ghost, even to his employer. It's like he exists on the sidelines. There, but never noticed, never bothering anyone, never disturbing anyone and never being disturbed. Forgotten, like the Beast shut away in his enchanted castle. 'Has he ever told you why? Because I assume he's covering scarring, maybe burns or something...' I say it casually, like it *hasn't* been at the forefront of my mind since last night.

'No. No more than calling himself a beast, anyway. But even if he had, I don't...' He stutters, searching for the rest of the sentence. 'I don't think he'd appreciate being the subject of Ever After Street gossip.'

I see what he's saying. Even if he did know something about Darcy, it wouldn't be his place to tell me. 'And yet, he makes himself the subject of gossip.'

'He keeps to himself. He might not be particularly friendly, but he doesn't do any harm or cause trouble to anyone. You only need to glance at the castle gardens to see how talented he is. He might not run his shop in a traditional way, but that's up to him.'

'Fair point.' I wave goodbye as he ducks back out the door. Mrs Potts stretches and gets up to turn around and find a more comfortable position in her bed.

I can't get the idea of a book festival out of my head for the rest of the afternoon, which at least makes a change from Darcy, who has occupied every inch of my mind since last night.

In previous jobs, I've spent every afternoon clock-watching, counting down the minutes until going-home time, but I've never done that here. I *love* owning this shop. I love being surrounded by books. I love the nods to *Beauty and the Beast* everywhere. The rose on the counter fits right into the theme in the shop, where as well as the mural on the back wall, I've got framed watercolour paintings of Belle with her nose in a book, and ones of the Beast feeding birds, and them dancing together hung around the walls too, but tonight I'm clock-watching for a different reason.

Typically, at five, there's a customer in who seems to be browsing *every* book, and I struggle to get excited when she buys two Sophie Kinsellas, because I can't wait to close the shop and go outside.

When she leaves, I run upstairs and throw open the window to peer out, and I can hear the *plink* of secateurs snapping together as he prunes something on his side of the hedge. While I want to race down there so fast that I fall over myself, I also want to do something nice for him, and the only thing I can think of is what he refused last night. If he won't come to the tea and biscuits, the tea and biscuits can come to him instead.

I make the fastest cups of tea possible without compromising on optimum brewing time, grab a packet of Custard Creams, and rush down the stairs while trying not to spill them.

'Ahoy there, neighbour.' My volume control has gone again and I'm out of breath by the time I stumble through the back door. Composure, Marnie. Twenty-four hours ago, this guy was mildly terrifying, you cannot be in *that* much of a rush to see him. Well, not *see* him exactly.

'I wondered if you'd be brave enough to run the stinging nettle gauntlet today.'

I'm grinning because of the way he said that... like he was *hoping* I might be out here again today. 'I'm going to put something down on the gatepost.'

He doesn't answer, so to avoid a spillage, I take both mugs to the gatepost and put them down, tear open the Custard Creams and take a couple out for myself, and then carry my own mug back up the garden.

'Tea?' There's confusion in his voice. 'You made me tea?'

'Yes.'

'How do you know I like tea?'

'You're British. At least, you sound British. What self-respecting Brit dislikes tea?'

'Yeah. I am. I do, I just... didn't expect that.'

'I'm nowhere near the gatepost; you can come and get it before a leaf lands in it.' Even though he can't see me, I nod towards the beech trees in the forest past our gardens, which are losing yellowed leaves like a snowstorm with each gust of autumn wind.

'Biscuits too,' he says, while I'm trying not to watch as the mug disappears from the gatepost and the rustle of the packet as he takes some Custard Creams, and his footsteps come back up his garden until he's standing near me on the opposite side of the hedge. 'In a *Beauty and the Beast* mug. Very on-brand.'

'I love that story. Belle is a mascot for bookworms everywhere, and I think everyone can relate to her wanting adventure in an otherwise boring life, and the whole moral of the story that beauty is found within and love can grow in the most unexpected places. It's my favourite. Favourite book as a child. Favourite Disney movie. You must like it – you named your shop after it too,' I say, curious about this completely coincidental thing we have in common.

'I fit the character, nothing more.'

'He was really a prin—'

'Not that part. Just the monster part. A hideous, growling beast who'd throw an old man in a cell just for picking a rose, that's me.'

Says the man whose attitude towards being stolen from is 'they need it more than I do'. Something doesn't add up in the difference between his words and his actions.

'Thank you for this.' It sounds like he's got an entire Custard Cream in his mouth. 'I can't remember the last time someone made me a cuppa.'

Really? Is he really *so* alone that he doesn't have anyone to make him a hot drink? I mean, I can't remember the last time anyone made me one either, other than Lilith. Does it count if you pay for it and the person owns a tearoom? Probably not.

'Thank you for the stuff on my gatepost this morning.' The words don't get across how touched I am.

'Ah, it was nothing. I kept thinking about you last night and thought of a few bits that might help.'

'The rose is beautiful.'

'Still alive?'

'Your faith in my ability to keep plants alive is inspiring. I've only had it for a day; it would have been pretty difficult to kill it in that time.'

'Difficult, but *not* impossible.' He's laughing as he says it and I end up laughing too, even though I'm sure there's an insult in there somewhere. He's got a nice laugh, a deep rumble that wraps around you and makes you want to laugh in response.

'You seemed daunted by my chainsaw suggestion, so I thought the shears might be less intimidating for a beginner, and we can graduate onto big scary power tools later.'

We. That word warms me to the core, despite the fact there's a nip in the October air that makes me wish I'd stopped to shrug my coat on in the hurry to get out here. He obviously only means it in a general sense, but it's the first time in years that I haven't felt as alone as I do usually.

'I thought about coming in to make a start last night, but your gate was locked, presumably in case the garden gets *out* and terrorises the local population.'

He's good at unexpected laughs. He seems like quite a serious person, and yet his sense of humour is sarcastic and deadpan, and I never expected him to be as funny as he is. And *this* is exactly why I spent most of the afternoon clock-watching. This weird little connection I feel to this unseen man on the other side of the hedge. 'It does feel like the garden could eat me alive if it wanted to. It's a bit like a vampire. I satisfied it with a taste of blood last night, but it won't be long until it needs more.'

'Ah yes, vampiric gardens are all the rage these days. It started with Audrey II in *Little Shop of Horrors* and just got worse from there.'

Every conversation with him leaves me wondering how we ended up here, and yet it feels good-natured and teasing. 'I always thought it fed on the pulled threads of jumpers and the snagged ladders of new tights.'

There's something so satisfying about getting him to laugh. There's an essence of surprise in it, like he isn't used to laughing and it surprises him every time one pops out.

In the quiet, I hear his footsteps approaching the gatepost again and the clink as he puts his empty mug down, and then the rustle of the biscuit packet as he takes another. 'You make a good cup of tea.'

'Now that's a top-tier compliment right there. Most girls would appreciate a comment on their hair, make-up, or style, but not me. I think tea-making skills are sorely underappreciated in this world.'

'If it helps, I also think your hair looks pretty.'

I finger my short brown hair self-consciously, twisting a few strands around my index finger. Short at the back, longer and straight-ish at the front so it falls over my forehead like a fringe, the kind of dull-brown that doesn't stand out in any way and has been in the same style for decades, and every time I've tried to do something different with it, the promised 'warm blonde' high-lights have come out neon orange, and the in-between stage of growing it out once made a scarecrow look at me with envy. 'I didn't think you'd ever even seen my hair, much less taken any notice of it.'

'I see you around. Not in a creepy way. Just that you *do* see your neighbours, don't you? You can't really avoid seeing them from time to time, even if you're not looking, they're just there.' He huffs out a long breath. 'Sorry, I'm useless at talking to people. I hadn't realised how out of practice I was until today.'

'Me too. Conversations are *hard*, right?'

'Right,' he agrees. He's got a local Herefordshire accent in his gruff voice that can be equal parts growly or cheerful, and it makes me want to carry on talking to him.

We're both lingering. I need to make a start with the shears, and it sounded like he was pruning his flowers before I came out, and yet even though the tea is long gone, we're both just standing here, next to each other, with a giant overgrown hedge between us.

'Can I ask you something that's been bothering me all day?' I blurt out.

He grunts. 'Oh, here we go. Let me guess. What's wrong with you? Why are you such a loner? A weirdo? Why do you wear a scarf even in the summer?'

His voice is harsh, but there's a sadness in the words that makes me wonder how many times he's been asked similar inconsiderate questions. 'How old are you?'

'Of all the things people want to know about me, that's never been one of them.' The sharpness of his laughter is edged with a sigh of resignation, like he knows he's about to say something he might regret. 'How old do you think I am?'

'Flattering or insulting?'

That laugh again. 'You tell me and I'll tell you.'

'Thirty?' I suggest.

'Flattering.'

'Forty?'

'Insulting!' He's laughing, and I want to continue saying random numbers just to keep hearing his laugh.

'Ah-ha! I knew you were around my age. Thirty-five?'

'Still flattering, mildly.'

'Thirty-si—'

'We'll still be having this conversation in January at this rate,' he interrupts. 'I'm thirty-eight, all right?'

'Victory!' I punch my hand in the air. 'I know your name and your age! Baby steps and all that.'

'Give it 'til November and you might know my shoe size.'

'I'm not overly interested in your shoe size.'

'Why *are* you interested? People are always better off if they don't know anything about me.'

'They are or *you* are?'

He doesn't reply. Not that I expected him to.

'Because it's weird not to know anything about a new friend.' I reply to his original question when the silence has grown heavy.

'We're not friends.'

I probably shouldn't be as stung as I am by his harsh response. Of course we're not friends. This is our second conversation, no one becomes friends that fast, but maybe in time? 'A new acquaintance, then. You're someone I know now who I didn't know two days ago.'

'Beginning to think it should've stayed that way,' he mutters, and I'm pretty sure I hear a growl under his breath.

I look up at the cloudy and rapidly darkening sky. I'm reluctant to put an end to this conversation, but it's going to get dark soon, if it doesn't rain first, and I *did* come out here to do some gardening. 'Well, I'd better get on.'

'Yeah, I'll be out here for a while yet pruning my roses. Shout if you want any pointers.'

I might not be allowed to call him a friend yet, but the fact he hasn't completely closed down the conversation makes me really happy, and I force myself to walk away. I go back inside, check on Mrs Potts, and pull on my coat and the gardening gloves he gave me. They're fleece-lined and thick and cosy around my fingers that are already cold from being outside and then go back out.

I unsheathe the shears and snip them together a few times to get a feel for them and approach a patch of brambles nearest the gate. I crouch down, pull the handles apart and then snip them back together, slicing off stalks and sending the cut stems spilling to the ground.

I must make a noise of amazement because his good-natured laugh lifts over the hedge again, and I carry on, chopping through weeds with reckless abandon.

The shears aren't the fastest thing to use. After a few minutes, my arms are aching and my lower back is protesting the repetitive movement, and when I've done a patch, I gather up armfuls of chopped weeds and leave them in a pile to one side.

I get into a rhythm with it. The gloves are miracle workers and I can pull away stinging nettles without fear, and I can still hear the *plink* of Darcy's secateurs as he works on his roses, and it feels comradely, neighbours side by side, tending our gardens, except his is neat and tidy, and you could land a plane in mine and it would never be seen again.

'Have you ever been to a book festival?' The idea I had earlier won't leave my head, and I don't know who else to blurt it out to.

He sounds confused by the randomness of the question. 'Do I seem like the kind of person who goes to book festivals?'

'No, I guess not. Sorry, forget I said anything.'

He doesn't reply and I'm kind of glad he really is going to forget I said anything. This is a silly idea that needs to be forgotten all about. Daydreams that Mum and I shared years ago are not a magic wand for saving the shop now.

'You asked that for a reason...' he says after a while, his tone leading, and I try to ignore the little fizzle that runs through me because he cares enough to ask when he could've just left it.

'It's silly. It was just that Witt came in today with flyers about hiring out the castle, and it put the thought of a book festival in my head. You know, if I could get a few local authors together to do book signings, readings from their books, maybe a couple of talks about writing or publishing or something... If I could bring a load of booklovers to Ever After Street, they'd naturally visit the bookshop, and that would bring in customers, and...' My voice is speeding up and I stop myself. 'Sorry, it sounded better when I said it to my cat.'

'It sounds pretty good when you say it to me too.' His secateurs have stopped *plinking* and his voice is closer to the hedge again. 'Why are you stopping yourself?'

'Because I don't know the first thing about hosting a book festival. I've never even *been* to a book festival. I know a great group of readers online who could give me some tips on what would be expected, and there are a couple of brilliant romance authors from the Herefordshire and Gloucestershire areas who do talks in local libraries occasionally, if I could get them to come...' I'm getting carried away again and force myself to stop.

'Have you always been a bookseller?' he asks, and it's my turn to be surprised by the randomness of his question.

'No. Before A Tale As Old As Time, I worked in retail. I managed a stationery shop until it closed down, then worked as an assistant in a clothing shop, then supermarket checkouts.'

'And yet, you took on your own bookshop without any hands-on bookshop experience. I know you weren't alone then, but that still must've been a risk, a big step outside your comfort zone, but you went for it. And you're talking to me – so you're clearly not afraid of a challenge.'

I bite my lip because that self-deprecation is just a little bit too close to the surface. Without realising it, I've migrated across the garden to the hedge too. I'm standing right opposite him but we're invisible to each other. 'It's not a challenge to talk to you.'

He does a grunt of disbelief but clearly isn't going to continue this thread of the conversation. 'So what's changed in the past couple of years? That dynamic young woman who can take on anything is still in there somewhere. Grief, I know. I've lost people too. But your mother wouldn't want you to lose a place you obviously both loved because of her absence.'

'You don't know what my mum would've wanted,' I snap and then sigh at myself because this is what I do. I take well-meaning comments too seriously and push away people who are trying to help. 'Sorry. You're right, I know you are. She'd be devastated if she knew how much I've let things slide. I've done the basics to keep the shop afloat. I rearrange books, I order as much stock as I can afford with the dwindling budget, and mainly I lose myself in books to avoid the real world. I've pushed the other shopkeepers away. I have no right to expect their support now, and I don't know how to do it on my own.' I chew on my lip. Where the heck did all *that* come from? I hadn't even realised I felt that way until it spilled out. This poor guy. He did *not* bank on getting all that in answer to his simple question.

I expect him to backtrack in horror at his oversharing neighbour, but instead there's a rustle from the other side of the hedge and the grunts and groans of him sitting down.

If he's really thirty-eight, he makes the noises of an eighty-year-old when moving around.

'Sit down with me a minute. Maybe I can help. I know a little bit about pushing people away, and if there's one thing I know about this place, it's that they don't leave you alone, even if you wish they would. Even if you growl at them.'

I appreciate the laugh, even though I doubt he's joking about the growling. Despite the cold concrete of my garden path, I sit down cross-legged again like last night and lean my head back against the hedge. I'm directly opposite him, back to back, with just the vast expanse of green branches between us. Maybe my next job should be thinning it out on my side just to be a bit nearer to him.

'When are you thinking?'

'Mid-November.' I say it quickly without giving myself time to overthink. 'It has to be before my lease is up. I have to have something to show Mr Rowbotham, and prove to the council that A Tale As Old As Time deserves its place on Ever After Street. I was thinking we could use a few rooms in the castle. Author talks in one. Book signings in another. Maybe an author question and answer session. Nibbles and drinks. If I held it over a weekend, we could have a bookish fancy-dress party for a finale on the Sunday night – a "come as your favourite literary character" type thing and there's a prize for best costume.'

I love the sound of it – it's something *I'd* go to, but I've never done anything like this before and I don't know where to start. 'But it depends on so much. How many people are going to have free time at such short notice? And if any authors agree, I can't expect them to come for free, I'll need to pay them out of my already dwindling budget, and that's without everything else that costs money. Caterers. Decorators. Prizes.'

'I'll provide floral decorations. And one prize could be a delivery of flowers to their door every month for a year or something.'

'Seriously?' My head spins towards the hedge in surprise. 'You'd do that?'

'Yeah, why not?'

'Because you're...' I don't know how to end that sentence without offending him.

'Yeah, I am.'

'I just meant... You're not usually one for getting involved in anything to do with Ever After Street.'

'No, I'm not.'

'So why...' Another sentence I can't finish.

'Because I hate seeing people excited about something and letting self-doubt stop them. Let the excitement consume you and see where it leads. What would *you* want to see in a book festival?'

'Romance,' I say instantly. 'We could make it a romance festival. I love romantic fiction and it always gets a bad rep as being cute and fluffy, but it tackles real issues in a relatable way, and authors of it deserve celebrating. I can think of three local authors I adore who write romance. And I'm a member of a booklovers group on Facebook where loads of authors are members too... I could put a post up and see if anyone would be interested in travelling from further afield, and...' I trail off again.

'*Everything that is real was imagined first.*'

'Is that...' It takes me a minute to remember where that line comes from. 'Is that a *Velveteen Rabbit* quote?'

'It's very fitting. Everything that exists only exists because someone had the courage to do it.'

It makes me smile to myself and repeat the words in my head. There's something about book quotes that makes things feel achievable, and somehow, Darcy chose the exact one I needed to hear.

This strange and mysterious man has got a better understanding of me than most people I've known for years. I only wish I had a better understanding of him.

4

———————

When I got home last night, I put out feelers online to see if any authors or readers would be interested in attending a book festival in November, and so far, I've got three local authors who have offered to come for just the price of travel costs, and twenty readers who have said they'd buy a ticket if it didn't cost a fortune, and then I couldn't sleep for a strong mixture of fear and excitement, so I opened my laptop and started playing around with my graphics program, and I've made a couple of mock-up flyers for the event, and researched the practical things like how to sell tickets, and it's made me feel a lot more on top of things, despite only snatching a couple of hours of sleep.

There's a definite spring in my step the next morning as I crunch my way through masses of autumn leaves on the way to work and reach down to pick some up and toss them to Mrs Potts, who looks suitably uninterested.

As we approach the back lane from the woods, another splash of colour on the gatepost catches my eye. Like yesterday, there's a mini rose plant waiting for me, yellow buds this time, sitting in a blue china pot. There's another card on a stick poking out of it, written in Darcy's gorgeous handwriting.

Yellow, the colour of Belle's dress, because she was a woman who could do anything she set her mind to…

I turn it over.

And so are you.

I take a deep breath and hold it to stop myself crying. 'Thank you!'

I linger for a few minutes, hoping he'll come outside if he's heard me, if he's even there, but he doesn't.

I've got the printed mock-ups of the flyers in my bag, so I take out one that's sunshine yellow with a red rose border, and an open book in the centre that's got 'Bookishly Ever After' written across it. I've put three spaces for author photos and added some potential events, like the author talks, a literary-themed afternoon tea, and the book character costume party we talked about yesterday. I leave it on the gatepost and pick up a stone to weigh it down before the autumn breeze blows it away.

I'll catch him later to thank him properly, and the thought of seeing him again sends a lovely little thrill through me, but first, I have to do something else before I lose my nerve.

I feel a bit stalkery as I watch The Cinderella Shop, which is directly across the street from A Tale As Old As Time, waiting for opening time to roll around. I'm trying to be casual as I walk-*not*-run over to catch Sadie when she arrives, hoping she won't turn me away after how nice everyone's been to me and I've barely given them eye contact in return.

All thoughts of being casual are gone as I blurt out my idea about the book festival so fast that it sounds like one sentence. I'm abuzz with nerves and excitement, and Sadie's laughing by the time I finish, and it would be generous to assume she's understood approximately a third of what I said.

'Marnie, relax,' she says like we're old friends. 'Come inside, let me get it booked in.'

I look back across the road to check Mrs Potts is okay in her window seat, and then follow Sadie into The Cinderella Shop. It's the most beautiful dress shop, full of Disney-style princess gowns and, since Sadie took over earlier this year, they've increased their range to include more accessible and affordable everyday dresses that appeal to everyone, as evidenced by how many customers they have now.

My awkwardness with talking to people comes to the forefront again as I try to slow down and tell Sadie about my idea. She's a booklover too, and she listens to everything, scribbling down notes, oohing and ahhing over the mock-up flyers, and gasping in surprise when I tell her about the authors who have tentatively said they'd be interested in coming.

'I can't think of anything nicer than having an influx of booklovers visiting Ever After Street. The castle is yours for that weekend.' She scribbles my name into a big diary. 'Get these authors confirmed and get the flyers printed up for real. Everyone on the street will display them and hand them out to customers, and we can put some on the noticeboard by the carousel. How are you selling tickets?'

'I don't know. I did some research online last night, but...'

'Digital tickets are always hassle-free, so guests can just show them on their phones on the day, but a bookshop needs something more traditional too, so get some paper tickets that customers can buy directly from you, or over the phone, and you either post them out or they can collect them on arrival. Everyone on Ever After Street can advertise them too and direct buyers to you, so make sure you put the shop's phone number on the flyers.'

'You'd really do that?' I say, wishing I'd brought a notebook to jot down all her advice.

'Of course.' She must realise that I don't have much of a budget. 'You won't have to do everything yourself, we'll all help. Witt's brilliant at decorating so he and I will deck out the castle. For catering, we could ask Ali from 1001 Nights; he'd love the extra publicity.'

'I can't afford much.'

'Oh, nonsense, no one's going to charge you for anything beyond basic ingredients. It's all for the good of Ever After Street; we help each other out around here, and we'll all benefit in the long run, you know that. And this costume party idea... Witt and I were talking about hosting another ball, so why don't we combine that and make it a big literary ball where the dress code is to come as their favourite characters?'

I can barely contain my excitement. Sadie has got the type of can-do attitude that makes me feel like I can-do too, and by the time we've finished talking, I'm buzzing with anticipation. I'd half-expected that everyone would laugh at the idea of me running a book festival, but her enthusiasm spills over into me too and leaves me feeling like anything is possible.

When I get back to A Tale As Old As Time, I email the three authors who showed interest last night to get concrete confirmation, and spend the rest of the day hunched over my laptop at the shop counter, perfecting the flyers and making a batch of postcards too, enjoying the scent of the roses perfuming the shop, making me think of Darcy every time I inhale.

My U.N.Known loving customer comes in, and she sees the mock-up flyer on the counter and picks it up.

'Oh my gosh, a book festival! Here? But nothing ever happens here! Are tickets available yet?'

I find myself laughing at her eagerness, majorly buoyed by her enthusiasm, and having to explain that we haven't got quite so far as tickets yet.

'I'll be there with bells on. The only thing that could make it any better is if you got U.N.Known to come. Can you imagine the excitement?' She lets out a squeak. 'I'll pop in again later in the week when you've got the tickets ready.'

I *can* imagine the excitement. Getting U.N.Known as a guest author would be the scoop of the book world. Talk about creating a buzz around Ever After Street...

I always have a copy of *Once Upon Another Time* behind the counter so I can flick through it and re-read paragraphs when I'm staring at an empty shop and need to remind myself that owning a bookshop is my lifelong dream. I turn to the inside cover of the hardback book, but where there would usually be a photo of the author and a short biography, the image is a stock photo of a silhouette, and the biography reads 'U.N.Known wishes to remain unknown.'

The book came out seven years ago and no one has ever found out who he is. But if I could... if I could somehow persuade him to be one of the authors at the Bookishly Ever After event...

'*Everything that is real was imagined first.*' I repeat the quote to myself as my fingers rub across the blank photo.

* * *

I close up at five and run upstairs to set about making two cups of tea and getting the Custard Creams out again.

This time, I grab a tray to transport it and put it down long enough to shrug my coat on over my brown and cream striped autumn jumper and then hurry out the door.

'Tea up, neighbour!'

'Are you serious?' Darcy says from the other side of the hedge.

'Who doesn't need a cup of tea at the end of a long day?' I take the mugs down to the gatepost, take a few biscuits for myself and then come back, and I hear his footsteps on a concrete path as he goes to collect his mug and then returns.

'Thanks for this, Marnie.' There's so much satisfaction in hearing him take a sip and then let out a sigh of pleasure.

He must be able to tell I've sat down because there's the sound of his under-breath grunts as he sits too. There's something odd in the subconscious noises he makes with almost every movement.

'Your flyer is fantastic. Thanks for showing me.' He takes in a breath, like he's questioning his next sentence before he's even said it. 'It's... surprisingly nice to be involved in something like this.'

The warmth that fills my chest is enough to shut out the chill filtering through my jeans from the cold ground. I want to jump on the sentence and say he could be a part of everything on Ever After Street if he came along to a shopkeepers' meeting or engaged with anyone else at all. 'Three authors confirmed today,' I say instead.

'That's incredible.'

'Everyone has been so supportive. Independent bookshops are dropping like gravely ill flies that have been on the wrong end of a squirt of fly spray and the general response has been that no one wants to lose another one. I've never really posted about A Tale As Old As Time in my Facebook booklover groups before, but I did last night, and so many readers said they'd visit if they lived nearer, which is promising, even if they live miles away.'

It's a reminder of how things used to be, how excited I used to feel about A Tale As Old As Time and all the possibilities here. This week has felt like the before times, when I wanted to put all my energy into making our shop the best it could be, whereas recently, I've channelled every bit of energy I could scrounge up into ignoring the world.

'People are drawn to a genuine passion for something.' His words are gentle, calm, and deep, and I close my eyes, let my head drop back, and wayward hedge branches spear me in the neck as I look up at the sky.

I never complain when the winter starts coming on – I love the darker evenings and the prospect of going home to have home-made soup for tea and snuggle on the sofa under blankets with a good book, but it's getting dark, and I wish we had longer, because I need to make a decent start on cutting back the garden and I also *really* want to talk to Darcy.

'I don't suppose there's any chance you'd come, is there?'

'Hell, no!' he barks, followed by a scoff of derisive laughter.

Oh, well, that's telling me. So much for it being 'surprisingly nice' to be involved. I stomp down the disappointment. The man has *never* before attended an event on Ever After Street – what did I think his answer was going to be? I want so badly to push and prod, to get him to explain why he's so reclusive, but it would do nothing but push him away. 'Do you like to read?' I ask instead.

He does that disbelieving scoff again. 'No.'

'No?' I say in surprise. 'You don't read?'

'No.'

'What kind of person doesn't read?'

'The kind who doesn't enjoy reading, perhaps?'

'But what kind of person *doesn't* enjoy reading? Books are the best way to escape from the misery of the world. You can immerse yourself in these brilliant worlds for hours on end using nothing but your imagination. It's not like staring mindlessly at a TV or endlessly doomscrolling on social media.'

'We're in luck then because I don't like TV or social media either.'

Well, that answers the question I hadn't got around to asking about why his shop doesn't have its own Instagram account. 'You say you're a beast, but nothing has ever made you more of a beast than not reading.'

'People are allowed to like different things.'

'Apart from gardening, it doesn't seem like you *like* anything at all.'

'I don't.'

Is he for real? Everyone likes *something*. Don't they? 'I like to think I can spot bookish people from a mile away. You seem like someone who'd be well read.'

No response. I don't think I've ever been more disappointed in my life. Not liking books is a deal-breaker for me in any friendship or relationship... not that this is either, but still. Most women probably dream of getting into bed with a gorgeous man and having hot sex – I dream of getting into bed with a gorgeous man and reading our respective novels, and then putting them on our bedside tables, turning out the light, and snuggling down for the night.

It's like when the Beast shows Belle his library. Talk about every girl's dream. When they sang 'Something There', the thing that hadn't been there before was clearly the revelation that the Beast loves to read. I could never understand why Belle wanted to leave the Beast's castle after that. A bookish friend who was nowhere near as beastly as he first seemed, a huge library, and sentient homeware to tend your every whim – sounds like heaven to me.

And Darcy, who is literally named after a book, and who seems kind, empathic, and intelligent, when it's well-known that these are qualities found in readers... it doesn't add up that he doesn't like books.

'I used to.' His voice has an air of surprise to it, like he's as surprised as I am by what he's saying. 'But not any more. I fell out of love with reading.'

I let out an actual sigh of relief. Now *that* makes so much more sense. 'Everyone hits a reading slump once in a while.'

'That implies someone's got a bit disillusioned after reading a couple of mediocre books. It's more than that with me. I lost any joy I once found within the pages of books. It's not something I'll ever get back again.'

'That's impossibly sad.' I chew on my lip. 'Do you know why?'

'Yes.'

I wait for him to elaborate even though I already know that was a one-word answer and I won't be getting anything else out of him.

'Okay, hold that thought, I have a solution to that problem.' I down the rest of my tea and jump to my feet.

'It isn't a *problem*,' he calls after me as I rush back inside.

I run to the fantasy section and grab a copy of *Once Upon Another Time* – a book I recommend to *everyone* who's struggling in any way. This book is the solution to *every* problem.

'This is my favourite book in the world,' I say as I put the book down on the gatepost and walk back up the garden and sit down, once again listening to the suppressed grumbles as he hauls himself to his feet. 'It's life-affirming. It's literary-fiction-meets-fantasy about this woman who's feeling lost in life. She's stuck in a dead-end job, her family are disappointed that she hasn't settled down and had children, her friendship group is growing apart as her old friends are busy with their partners and families. Everything's dull and lacking excitement, and she doesn't know where to go in life. And then, one evening, she's browsing in a bookshop and she falls down the ladder into the children's section, like falling down the rabbit hole into Wonderland. The ladder breaks so she can't get out, and the owner closes up and leaves without hearing her shout, so she's stuck in the children's section of the bookshop overnight. With nothing else to do, she pulls out some of her childhood favourites and rereads them, and she reconnects with characters she loved as a child. You know when you're little and you get so consumed by a book that it seems like the characters are right there in the room with you? It's like she meets old friends who she'd forgotten, and who all meant something to her when she was young, and over the course of the night, she goes on all these magical adventures with Alice, and Darrell Rivers, and Peter Pan, and Anne Shirley, and Jo, Bessie, and Fanny, and the Pevensie children, and it reminds her of who she used to be and what she wanted, and how she's let life drag her along rather than taking control of her own destiny and doing what she wants rather than what other people think she should do. She learns that it's okay to do things that bring you joy, and to ignore other people's expectations and put yourself first in your own life.'

He's quiet. Maybe he's reading the blurb and appreciating the gesture, and I make myself stop talking because I could talk about *Once Upon Another Time* until the cows come home, have their supper, and pop off back out again.

'Are you kidding me?' There's the slam of a book shutting and a whoosh, and the book comes sailing over the hedge above me and lands limply in a bramble bush.

'Oi! That's my stock!' I scramble to my feet and retrieve the precious book, smooth it down, and hold it to my chest protectively. 'Don't throw my books around! What is *wrong* with you?'

'What is wrong with *you*? Why the hell would you give me that pile of... crap?' He settles on a word eventually, sounding like he's being reluctantly polite.

'It's the best book ever written!'

He tuts. 'I thought you had better taste than that.'

'Are *you* kidding *me*?' I repeat his own question. 'What's wrong with *Once Upon Another Time*? It's a really special book.'

'Yeah, if you're a duck!'

'A duck?' I pull a confused face at the hedge. 'What have ducks got to do with anything?'

'It was a figure of speech. I meant you'd have to be illiterate to enjoy it. It belongs on a bonfire... Actually, give it back, I'll start a bonfire especially for it.'

'Don't you dare say that about my favourite book!' I didn't realise I was so protective of it, but I'm moments away from stalking round there and beating him over the head with this hefty hardback. 'It's life-affirming and positive. Have you read it?'

'No.' He sounds like he's sulking.

'You can't possibly judge it if you haven't read it.' I don't know how long I've been staring at the hedge with my mouth hanging open in shock, but I snap it closed when my jaw starts to ache. 'For someone who has said multiple times that people are allowed to like different things, you're being very judgemental.'

'Anyone daft enough to like that stupid book deserves to be judged on their horrific tastes. You have that displayed in your window – no wonder your shop isn't pulling in enough customers.'

I... well, I intend to pace up and down the path, but I end up clomping around angrily. 'This is an incredibly important book to me. I wouldn't have found it without Ever After Street, and I wouldn't have found A Tale As Old As Time without *it*.'

He's pacing too, and he stops and turns towards me and takes a few calming breaths, and when his voice comes out, it's a lot more composed than I expected it to be. 'How'd you work that one out?'

I do the same because I'm getting too worked up at him. 'I was like the main character. Totally lost in life. Stuck in a dead-end job, feeling like the world was passing by without me being a part of it. I knew of Ever After Street, but I thought it was somewhere for children and adults had no place here. My mum's bungalow is on the other side of the woods, and I was out walking one day and got turned around. It was winter, cold, wet, and misty, and I stumbled through the trees and came out on Ever After Street. I didn't have any money on me, but I went into the tearoom for warmth and, obviously I didn't know Lilith at the time, but she took pity on me and made me a cuppa and gave me a cake even though I couldn't pay for it, and I felt this sense of being somewhere I was meant to be. When I left, I stood and watched the carousel turning by the evening light and the vintage music took me right back to my childhood, and when I turned around, this old guy was outside his bookshop, and I've never been able to ignore a bookshop. He was a book restorer and antique book dealer, but in the window was a copy of *Once Upon Another Time*, even though it wasn't an antique or in need of restoration. I asked him about it, and he said his daughter loved it and insisted he have a copy in the shop. I must've looked so intrigued that he gave it to me and told me to come back the next day to pay for it. I read it that night. I went on these adventures with the main character. I emerged feeling like *I'd* been stuck in a bookshop overnight, like *I'd* revisited my fictional child-hood friends and they reminded me of my younger self and what I thought life would be like by now, and most importantly, how much I loved books, and how much of a childhood dream it had been to own a bookshop. When I came back the next day with the money, the old guy was outside his shop again, putting up a "for rent" sign.' I'm hugging the book to my chest as I speak. 'I asked him to write down the details for me, and by the time I went home and told Mum, she was reading it as well. She'd always dreamed of owning a bookshop too, and she'd recently retired and was wondering how she'd fill her days, and it all just clicked into place. This was something we'd both always wanted to do, the timing was perfect, the place was perfect, and... here we are.' I stop myself abruptly when I realise I've been talking for ages. I didn't intend to share my life story with him, just as much as I'm sure he didn't want to hear it.

There's silence from the other side of the hedge, and I'm half-convinced that he's gone inside and left me to it. 'Have you fallen asleep?'

'No,' he grunts, but his voice sounds thick and, with the absence of any other sound, I can hear the shaky breath he takes. 'I'm sorry, I didn't realise it meant that much to you.'

'I feel like we all need to be reminded of who we were once, what we wanted when we were younger and how much we dreamed impossible things could be real, before life got in the way and turned us into cynical old adults. *Once Upon Another Time* is the antidote to adult life.'

He lets out an unexpected laugh. 'You have a unique way of seeing the world, Marnie. I wish I could be more like that.'

'Why can't you?'

'I'm too old.'

'I thought you were thirty-eight,' I say in confusion. Thirty-eight isn't old by anyone's standards, unless he was lying about it.

'Not in an age way. I'm too... cynical. Jaded. Worn down. Life has chewed me up and spat me back out. I will never be able to see the world through hopeful eyes again, end of story.'

'No story ever has to end. I've got a great book here you could start by reading...'

'No, thank you.'

I like how he never loses his politeness. He can be rude and sharp and blunt, but he's always polite about it. 'It's never too late to start believing in fairy tales again.'

'Hah.'

It is not the good kind of 'hah'.

I hadn't realised we'd both sat back down until there are the familiar noises of discomfort as he moves. 'You know what it *is* going to be too late for at this rate? Gardening.'

I let out a groan of my own. It's gone half past five and the light is fading fast. I get to my feet and pick up the shears again, listening to the snip of his pruners as he cuts off rosehips and tells me it's to stop the plants wasting energy on producing seeds.

I kneel on the kneeling pad he's lent me and start snipping through weeds and brambles, and self-sown hazelnut trees that have grown from squirrel-dropped nuts in the cracks between concrete. 'You're probably the wrong person to say this to, but I thought about trying to get in touch with U.N.Known and asking him to come to the book festival as a guest author and give a talk or something...'

I can sense the horror from across the hedge without even looking up from my weed cutting.

'Oh, I'm probably the right person to say it to because I won't hesitate to say – what the *hell* are you thinking? The unknown author, whose name literally revolves around being unknown, who has remained unknown for years... Why do you think that unknown person will suddenly reveal themselves because you ask nicely?'

'His book changed my life.' I'm surprised by how much I've had to defend *Once Upon Another Time* tonight. Does he hate *all* books this much or is there just something about this one? 'A lot of other people love his book because of me, because I talk it up at every chance I get and foist it into the hands of unsuspecting customers at any given opportunity. Maybe if he knew how much people around here love him, he'd want to share that...'

'And while I'm sure the anonymous prat appreciates your efforts, spend your time on something more rewarding, because with six weeks until the festival, you don't have time to waste chasing down a wild goose. And if you do, might I suggest that an actual wild goose would be a better festival guest?'

'What have you got about birdlife today?'

He laughs. 'I'm just saying, an actual goose, honking, pooing everywhere, and attacking the guests, would give a more appealing author talk.'

Oh, what a mental image that brings to mind. He might dislike reading, and most other things, but even I'm perplexed by how much he seems to dislike *this* book. 'If I could get U.N.Known to agree, it would attract so much attention to Bookishly Ever After. People are curious, even now after seven years, people still want to know who he is and why he didn't write anything else.'

I can't get the thought out of my head. U.N.Known's book has been with me since the start of this journey. It's never been out of the window display. Barely a week passes without me talking someone into buying a copy. Mum and I would never have had our shop without *Once Upon Another Time*, and maybe its author is also the key to saving it.

'How do you know it's a guy?' Darcy asks.

'Oh, that's easy. There's a line about period pain where it's described as a minor inconvenience, and that could only have been written by someone who *hasn't* experienced their ovaries turning themselves inside out while their uterus goes on a one-organ quest for revenge in seething anger because you didn't get pregnant that month.'

He guffaws. Really truly laughs, like it's the funniest thing he's ever heard. 'Who am I to argue with that?'

I go back to chomping through stinging nettles, enjoying the satisfaction of watching the sharp blades of the shears slice through thick stalks and the plants that seemed so overwhelming becoming nothing more than a limp pile on the ground.

'Don't you ever miss getting lost in a good book?' I ask because curiosity will always get the better of me. 'The world is hellish and books are nice. Everyone deserves that escape.'

'Not monsters like me.'

I can't work him out. Is he serious? Is he *really* some kind of beast? Something that shouldn't exist in this world but somehow does? Or is it more metaphorical? I go back to what he said about life spitting him out. Does he feel like a monster because of something that's happened to him? 'Books are magical. They have power. A book can show you how the world *could* be. Everyone deserves to know the joy of getting lost inside one. Especially someone who sounds like the one thing they desperately need is to get out of their own head for a while.'

I could be pushing it. I'm only guessing at what's going on with Darcy and our friendship still feels fragile and like if I push him too far, he'll walk away and never come outside again.

He grunts in response, and while I think it was meant to be evasive, it sounds a little bit like he wants to believe me, and I can't help grinning to myself as I go back to chopping down weeds.

Maybe, just maybe, no one is really a lost cause when it comes to books.

5

'Two tickets to the book festival, please!' a husband and wife say as she puts a ten-pound note on the counter. I went with selling tickets for a fiver each, because although extra income would be nice, it's more important to show that A Tale As Old As Time can bring people to Ever After Street than it is to earn money. There will be time for earning money later, but if I don't convince Mr Rowbotham and the council to give my shop another chance, then it's all over anyway.

A few tickets have sold online since I put them up a few days ago, but this is my first in-person ticket sale, and I'm not sure who's more excited – me or the woman bouncing on her feet as she waits for me to get two book-shaped tickets out and scribble their names on them. 'I've always wanted to go to a book festival but they're so far away.'

'That's exactly why we're doing it.' I try to project confidence rather than letting out a sob and thanking her like Grateful McGratefulson.

Excitement is fizzing through me as they leave. This could actually work out. I've struggled to muster up excitement for anything lately, but this festival makes it feel like Mum is still with me, supporting this idea that we never got around to doing together.

The thrill lasts until Rick saunters in, a bunch of flowers grasped in his fist.

'Not today, thanks, go away.' I try to be polite, but every day without Rick is a good day, and today has rapidly turned into a bad one.

He stayed away for months after we split up, but then he came back, saying life wasn't the same without me. I was touched at first. I'd felt so lonely since Mum died and Rick had loved her too. Someone to reminisce with was nice. But that encouraged him, made him think there was a chance for reconciliation, and he hasn't given up on that idea yet.

'For you.' He crosses one hand across his wide chest and bows while holding the flowers out to me with his other hand.

They are *not* Darcy's flowers. They look like a mix of weeds and grass, and they really... smell. And not in the traditional way. 'Where on earth did you get those? It looks like you picked them from the roadside.'

'I did pick them from the roadside. And some from the window box outside that old biddy's tearoom.'

'You can't do that! Lilith works hard on those flower boxes. God knows how she's managed to keep them flowering into October.'

'Don't worry, she'd never be fast enough to catch me, she's really old.'

Was he always this disrespectful? He was wonderful to my mum, a prince among men, but I still haven't worked out if he's changed since our break up or if he was always like this and I was too caught up in Mum's illness to notice. 'They smell of dog's pee and exhaust fumes.' I ignore the childish urge to add, 'And so do you.' Because he doesn't. He smells of his usual £400-a-bottle aftershave, of course.

'I had to improvise. Can you believe that weirdo next door refused to let me in?'

'I'm not surprised when you're stealing flowers from him. You're lucky he hasn't called the police.'

I shouldn't have said that in case he wonders how I know, but he's too wound-up to listen. 'As I went to walk in, he appeared from nowhere, full scarf and glasses nonsense on, blocked the door, and told me I wasn't welcome. I'll give that pathetic recluse a reason to make me unwelcome!' Rick's nasally voice rises as he shakes his fist at the wall between us and The Beast's Enchanted Rose Garden.

He lays the raggedy bundle of flowers on the counter, and then leans on his elbows and reaches a hand out towards me like he's going to stroke my face. I step back sharply. 'We're not together any more.'

'No, but we could be...' he says hopefully, and then sighs when I don't immediately fall into his arms. 'Why are you doing this? Don't push me away too. We were supposed to get married. We still could. Give your mum the day she always dreamed of seeing...'

And *that*, right there, is exactly why I'm 'doing this'. Yes, my mum loved him, and the fact he thinks he can win me back by reminding me of that constantly is one of the many, many reasons I don't want anything more to do with him, even though there are many women who would *kill* to have him bringing them flowers, even roadside ones.

Rick is *gorgeous*. The kind of gorgeous that makes you wonder what he's doing walking around amongst us mere mortals when he should be in his boxer shorts on a Calvin Klein billboard, or at the very least, a Hollywood leading actor. Tall, dark-haired, and handsome, with green eyes usually only seen in Disney cartoon heroes, huge muscles, a perfectly sculpted body... and an ego that outsizes the solar system.

He was so exciting, once. He's a Michelin-starred chef with his own catering business, important clients, and invitations to fancy, celebrity-filled events. He's outgoing, loud, and confident – the opposite of me. Every day was a new adventure in our year-long relationship.

We met through a charity event. Mum and I had donated a shopping spree at the bookshop, and Rick had donated a series of cooking lessons, and I won them. He invited me to his restaurant kitchen. I didn't learn much about cooking, but there was chemistry sizzling between us. He was sweet and attentive, funny and exciting. At the last lesson, he poured us a glass of wine each and shyly asked me to go on a date with him.

It didn't seem to matter that we didn't have anything in common, not even reading or an interest in books. Opposites attract, I told myself. My mum was overjoyed when he proposed. He was the son she'd never had and she was the mum he'd always wanted. He was everything she'd ever wished for in a son-in-law. He treated her like a queen. Nothing was too much trouble.

And then the diagnosis came. He was wonderful throughout it. He was by my side, from driving us to hospital appointments to choosing a coffin. My mum's last ambition in life was to make it to our wedding, which never happened – neither her making it nor it ever occurring. Because other things happened instead.

One of the things Rick did that I thought was so lovely and supportive of him was to look after the shop for me. When I was with Mum throughout the treatment, when I didn't want to leave her side, and then after she'd gone and the grief pressed down so heavy that I'd rather have chewed my own arm off than stand behind the counter and face conversational enquiries about where my co-owner was from well-meaning customers who were used to seeing two of us, Rick was there instead of me, always. My rock. The man I thought I'd marry one day, despite our differences.

And then I caught him with his bookmark in Shannon's pages and discovered that the main reason he'd been so eager to cover the shop for me was because he'd been getting closer to my shop assistant, which he then blamed on me for being too preoccupied to give him the attention he needed, and revealed true colours that had been well hidden until then.

'Roses.' He points to the yellow and red flowered plants, one on either side of my hexagonal counter. 'Who's been buying you them then?'

'No one,' I say, because he's already made enough disparaging comments about Darcy, I certainly don't want him to know we've been talking.

'You're never going to find another man who'd treat you like a princess, you know that, don't you?' He raises an eyebrow in what's probably meant to be a seductive way, but it makes my stomach churn, which is not a reaction Rick will have ever experienced before.

'Good thing I've never wanted to be a princess then, isn't it?'

'Sure you have. That woman with her head in the books all the time.' He waves a dismissive hand towards the watercolour paintings on the walls. 'I could buy you a castle with a library. Just say the word and it's yours.'

'No, thank you.' I give him a polite smile. 'There's the door.'

Instead of listening, he starts walking between my display tables and bookcases, moving books that I've just put out and painstakingly placed at the best angles to catch people's eye. I hate this feeling of powerlessness. I cannot get this man out of my shop. Asking politely doesn't do it, and I'm not big enough to physically push him out. I'm alone, and I desperately want to *not* be alone with him.

That loneliness settles over me again. I am *always* alone. I don't know why it's reared its ugly head lately, but instead of enjoying my own company, I'm wishing I had someone to talk to, someone to laugh with, someone to share problems with. The only times lately when I haven't felt alone are when I've been outside talking to Darcy.

'Please stop doing that.' I look longingly towards the door, willing someone, anyone, to come in.

'Trying to help, Marn. Not like you're any good at this stuff by yourself, is it?'

'Yes!' I snap. 'This is my shop. We're organising a book festival and everything. It's going really well.'

'You?' He glances at me with a raised eyebrow. 'That's a bit far out of your comfort zone, isn't it? And we all know Marnie Platt doesn't leave her comfort zone, ever. Who'd come to something as dull as a book festival anyway?' He does that familiar laughing-*at*-me sound. 'Although I'll cater it for you, if you like. Give it at least a chance of succeeding.'

'No, thank you,' I say through gritted teeth as my nails dig into my palms and my hands clench into fists. Do not rise to it. That's what he wants. He's trying to make me feel like I need him – exactly what he did when we were together.

'Your silly board is looking dusty.' He goes over to the board that's mounted on the wall directly opposite the counter and waves a hand in front of it, disturbing dust motes and the odd cobweb. 'No one's using it, I see. *Quelle surprise* – people just aren't that nice.'

'You'd know,' I mutter. 'And it's not a silly board, it's a pay-it-forward board. It's there for people who can afford to leave a little extra towards the cost of a book for a stranger who can't afford one.'

'Yeah, but no one's that generous, are they?' He gestures to the two paltry tags on the board that have, admittedly, been there for a few months, undisturbed.

The idea is that someone pays an extra amount of their choice, and then they put a book-shaped tag of that value on the board. Anyone who can't afford a book can take a tag and use it to pay for their purchase with no questions asked. It was heart-warming at first, but now the only tags are two I put up, and no one's bothered to take one or add one in ages.

'The greedy beggars who used them won't have needed them anyway, they're just trying to swindle you out of a free book. And if anyone's *that* poor, they're not going to bother about boring old books, are they?'

'Oh, sod off,' I snap, at a loss for anything more fitting to say. I defended my pay-it-forward board many times when we were together – Rick thought it should be taken down and replaced with another display shelf to show off more stock – and I disagreed. Such a simple act of kindness can make all the difference to someone who's struggling and I refused to give up hope that customers who have money to spare would pay for an extra book on behalf of a stranger who doesn't.

'Happily. All these dull books are sucking the life right out of me.' He returns to the counter with a cheerful grin. 'So, Paris?'

'No, thank you,' I repeat, hoping how disinterested I sound will make him take the hint. 'We're over, Rick. I wouldn't go to the end of the street with you, never mind a different country.'

'Oh, you are in a mood today. Time of the month, is it?' He taps his nose like it'll be our little secret. 'Say no more. I'll come back at a less premenstrual moment.'

'Don't come back ever, you sexist pig,' I shout after him as he finally heads for the door. 'I don't need to be PMSing to despise you!'

I brush his flowers carefully into the bin. I didn't want to be rude to him. He was good to me when he *was* good, and there's still the lingering feeling that my mum would be disappointed to know I'd broken up with him. He was all she ever wanted for me in a partner – excitement, chivalry, financial stability and a head for business, the looks of a Disney prince... but that doesn't make him what *I* want, especially now. There will never be anything between us again, and no matter how obvious I make it, he never takes the hint. I make a noise of frustration at the ceiling and a customer chooses that exact moment to come in.

Perfect timing. It's a bloke looking for a book for his son as a reward for having a good week in school, and he picks out a Roald Dahl and comes to pay at the counter.

I've put a poster about the book festival on the front edge of my hexagonal counter, and a stack of postcards beside me. He takes one and reads it while I put his book through the till, and then says his wife loves one of our attending authors and buys two tickets.

He's the first customer of what turns out to be a busy day. Sadie posted about the book festival on the Ever After Street website this morning, and it's reminded people that A Tale As Old As Time exists, because there's a constant stream of customers in and out, and it's busy for a Wednesday. The postcard stack is shrinking rapidly and I'm seeing flyers being passed between families and slid into bags as people walk out the door with their purchases.

Between customers, I'm on my laptop, scouring the internet for any trace of U.N.Known and getting more despondent by the minute. Whoever he is, he *really* does not want to be found. It takes most of the day, but I eventually find an old announcement about the sale of film rights for *Once Upon Another Time* in the archives of a now-defunct publishing industry magazine, which mentions the literary agent he was once represented by. I find the agency and dash off a quick email, explaining where I work and why I want to get in touch with U.N.Known, not expecting to get anything back.

At least it stopped me looking at the clock for a few minutes. I *miss* Darcy. My mind keeps flicking to him. He could be just on the other side of the wall behind me, but he seems a million light-years away and I'm trying to ignore the fluttery feeling I've got about seeing him at five o'clock.

At five to five, as the last customer is browsing the classics shelves, I absent-mindedly check my emails again and see a reply in my inbox.

Dear Miss Platt,

I must admit that U.N.Known is a name I never expected to hear again. You are right, he was once represented by this agency. He was an ex-colleague's client, and after her retirement, his contract was passed to another agent to look after, and then another, and she's currently on maternity leave, so in a roundabout way, I'm now responsible.

However, for want of a better way of putting it, U.N.Known disappeared many years ago. After delivering only one book of a three-book contract, he simply vanished. All responses to emails ceased. Phone calls went unanswered. Letters sent to his address were not acknowledged, and when the publisher themselves tried using a tracked service, the letters were all returned as undeliverable. Over the years, and many changes in staff both here and at the publisher, I'm afraid we've all but given up.

The only reason he is still connected to this agency at all is due to financial reasons – we still accept royalties on his behalf, although payments to his bank account started being returned at the same time as contact was dropped.

He was never a client of mine, and as you are acting in a professional capacity, I see no harm in passing along his email address, although please be warned that if you can get a reply out of him, you are a better woman than myself and many who have tried before me. His email is the-unknown-author@gmail.-com. Do let me know if you have any luck!

I let out a squeal that makes the customer drop his book in surprise, and then apologise profusely when it lands squarely on his toe and he yelps in pain. Instead of buying anything, he limps out empty-handed, apart from a flyer about the book festival, and even though I'm trying to tell myself not to get overexcited, I keep staring at that email address.

I have a way of contacting U.N.Known. All right, it doesn't bode well that even his agent hasn't been able to get in touch with him for years and it sounds unlikely that he'd reply to a random book-seller, but it puts me one step closer to the dream of getting him to appear at the book festival.

One teeny, tiny step, but still.

6

I send the agent a quick thank you in response, and now it's ten past five, and I rush upstairs to make the usual two cups of tea. I can't help the wild grin and the flutter in my chest at the thought of seeing Darcy again.

'Tea up, neighbour,' I say when I get my coat on and push my feet into my boots.

His warm laugh is the first thing that greets me. 'You don't have to keep doing that.'

'I want to.' I don't add that his befuddled reaction at someone making tea for him is a huge part of why. When I walk down the path towards the gates at the end, I see a dash of colour waiting for me.

'Oh, Darcy, what are these for?' I lift the tray onto the post and take the ribbon-tied bouquet. They're yellow roses, but each petal is splashed with splotches of pink, red, and white.

'I don't know. It's getting late in the season for summer roses and I was cutting them last night and thought you'd like them.'

I thank him and run back upstairs to dig out an old vase left behind by the previous bookshop tenant, fill it with water, and take it back downstairs to display them behind the counter. My clattering around has disturbed Mrs Potts, who's meowing and rubbing her slinky body around my feet, clearly angling for extra kitty biscuits.

'You've already eaten.' I give her head a rub, and because she's up and about rather than sleeping, I leave the back door open in case she wants to follow me when I go back outside.

'Thank you. They're beautiful. Do you grow them yourself?'

'Well, I *am* a gardener who specialises in roses... It would be quite odd if I'd nipped out and bought them from Tesco.' He sounds amused by my lack of knowledge of the correct gardening terminology.

'No, I mean... I've never seen roses like that before. They don't exist anywhere else, do they? You... invented them?'

His amusement turns into outright laughter. 'I *bred* them, yes. Every year, I select different roses and cross-pollinate them, and then the rosehips they produce at the end of the season contain seeds that are a cross between the parent plants. Grow those seeds and voila. The possibilities are endless, and the hybrids that result are one of a kind.'

'Wow. That's exceptional, Darcy.'

'It's just a hobby. I like roses. They're easy to grow – they can look spectacular with very little care, and they come back every year. Each spring, there will be rosebuds waiting to open with these perfect flowers. They always bloom, no matter how harsh a winter has been.'

Flower buds in spring speak of new beginnings and the promise of better days to come. A rose in the spring is hopeful. There's more to this than he's saying. His roses are special, and the fact he does this is special, even if he insists on downplaying it. People go into his shop to buy roses and no one has any idea that these are roses they can't get anywhere else in the world. Each petal is totally unique because of *him*. He deserves recognition for how meaningful that is.

'Rick came in today and said you'd shut him out of your shop. I'm not used to men doing what they say they will, so thank you for that too.'

'Ahh, what a charmer that guy is. I didn't think there were many swearwords I hadn't heard, but he's invented his own batch of them. The threats were a nice touch too.' I can almost *hear* him rolling his eyes. 'What on earth did you ever see in him? Well, other than money, prestige, and insanely good looks.'

'Something I ask myself every day,' I mutter.

We're standing directly opposite each other again, and I lower myself down to the concrete path and sit cross-legged, and listen to the familiar pained noises as he does the same. I want to ask him about them. We all grunt and groan a little bit as we move, but his seems... excessive, and I don't think he's even aware of it.

'I know you like *Beauty and the Beast*, but you seem to have taken a wrong turn and accidentally dated Gaston... He doesn't enjoy hunting, decorating with antlers, and singing songs about how wonderful he is, does he?'

The fact he knows the story so well makes my heart swell, and I laugh, because Rick does have some Gaston-like qualities. If you could call them qualities. And he'd definitely like his friends to gather in a bar and sing his praises. I tell Darcy the whole story, from his endless support while Mum was ill to his stamping of Shannon's library card.

'Ahh, I get that. Relationships with people who are only happy if you're unhappy. Been there, done that.'

Ah-ha! So he can't always have been as withdrawn as he is these days. 'Are you single now?'

'What do you think?' His tone is so sarcastically incredulous that it makes me smile.

'Are you looking?' I'm trying to sound casual, but I'm suddenly desperately invested in his answer.

'Hah.' He lets out such a shrill laugh that it makes me jump, and when he speaks, there's an irate tone to his voice. 'I hate people and avoid them at all costs. Funnily enough, no, I'm not looking for a relationship and never will be again. I'm alone, forever.'

I wince because it sounds so sharp and so final, and so very sad. 'You're okay with that?'

'Y-yes.' He swallows before he answers, and there's just enough of a hesitation to convince me he isn't *quite* as assured as he sounds. 'I would never subject another human to getting close to me. I curse everything I come into contact with.'

I chew the inside of my lip. He sounds so raw and broken, and for the first time, I desperately want to give him a hug. 'Who's told you that?'

'No one needs to tell me. There are mirrors that show me every day. There's a trail of destruction behind me – the destroyed lives of people I once loved.'

I want to say something like I'm sure that's not true, but I don't want to trivialise it. He's obviously been through *something*, I just don't know what and don't think he'll ever tell me. 'Rick is living proof that beasts can be princes in disguise, and equally, princes can be disguised as beasts. No one is all good or all bad.'

'I can think of a few ex-prime ministers who are the exception to that rule.'

I laugh again because no one can argue with that astute observation.

The half-open back door to the shop moves and Mrs Potts puts a tentative paw out onto the step and then slinks the rest of her body outside with a *brrrrip* noise.

'Oh, hello, Madam.' I make a squeaking noise and pat my lap, even though she rarely sits on my lap at the best of times. 'Mrs Potts just came out to see if she can wrangle any more kitty biscuits.'

'You called your cat Mrs Potts?' Darcy asks from the other side of the hedge.

'Technically she was my mum's cat, but I inherited her. She's grey and white and as soon as we saw her at the rescue centre, we both said she reminded us of Mrs Potts from the animated film, so that became her name.'

He's laughing to himself and I imagine him shaking his head fondly. 'Your dedication to *Beauty and the Beast* is unrivalled.'

'It's the love story every lonely bookworm dreams of, isn't it? I thought I *was* Belle when I was younger. I loved to read and I never fitted in at school, and I wanted life to be more exciting and fairy tale-esque than it actually is. I fell in love with the "tale as old as time" scene and dreamed of waltzing around a ballroom with a handsome Beast.'

'I think you mean prince.'

'No. Even as a child, the scene where the Beast became a prince again was the most disappointing moment of the entire film to me. I loved him as he was. He didn't need to be a prince again to show he was kind-hearted and good.'

There's just a hint of a quiver in his good-natured scoff. 'So *Beauty and the Beast* really is a lifelong obsession then?'

'I was certain that a big magical adventure was coming my way, like it does in all Disney movies. My father died when I was young and I always thought he wasn't really dead and one day I'd stumble across a castle in the forest where a Beast was keeping him a prisoner and I'd save him by taking his place and then fall in love with said Beast.' Mrs Potts comes to sit beside me, flipping her tail from side to side. She bats my hand away when I go to stroke her – no claws this time, but a severe warning that it won't be clawless next time. 'Obviously with adult hindsight, I see those were the thoughts of a grieving child, but even now, the movie reminds me of everything that's good about the world. I *want* there to be an enchanted castle filled with magical things.'

'*The world is full of magic things, patiently waiting for our senses to grow sharper.*'

'W.B. Yeats,' I say, impressed. Darcy never stops surprising me. 'You're very well read for someone who hates books.'

'I don't hate books, I just... reading isn't for me these days.'

Mrs Potts gives an inquisitive meow, her head tilted to the side as she listens to the voice from behind the hedge and then walks down the garden path, like she's trying to work out where it's coming from. She jumps onto the gatepost, surveys what she can see of Darcy's garden and then jumps down on his side.

'Oh,' I say in surprise because she rarely ventures to the door, never mind into someone else's garden. 'Mrs Potts is coming to see you. Is that all right or do you want me to get her back? Not everyone likes cats.'

'No, it's fine. Even I am not so much of a monster that I would dislike our furry friends.' Mrs Potts obviously reaches him, because he greets her and makes coaxing noises and I can hear him rubbing two fingers together to encourage her over. 'She really does look like Mrs Potts. That's uncanny. Hello, lovely pussy-cat. You are gorgeous, aren't you?'

Mrs Potts makes a series of delighted noises and Darcy laughs as, I'm guessing, she headbutts his hands and lets him tickle the back of her head, and I shift around until I'm sitting sideways against the hedge. I try to part the branches for a peep through, but it's no use, the hedge has the entire summer's worth of green leaves and growth spurts behind it; it's as dense as a wall.

Mrs Potts *meow-ows* at Darcy and he makes similar noises back at her, like they're having a full-blown conversation in cat-speak. I lean my head against the hedge and listen to the sound of them getting acquainted.

There's a sense of peace that's settled across our gardens. Even his voice changed when she went over there. It switched into a gentle baby-talk-ish voice, and I hadn't noticed how much tension I could sense from him, but I notice the shift in atmosphere when it dissipates.

'She's lovely. A credit to her owner. She's standing on my lap, making pies in my knees.' His laugh sounds happy rather than sarcastic for once.

'Do you want some Dreamies?'

'By going to *sleepies*?'

I laugh out loud. 'They're cat treats. She's so addicted to them that I might have to stage an intervention soon.'

'Nah. Because she's getting comfortable on me and I don't want to disturb her by getting up. Next time.'

She's getting comfortable on him? Mrs Potts is a very self-contained cat. She sleeps in her own bed and only comes to me when she's hungry, and occasionally deigns herself to sit beside me on the sofa if it's cold on a winter's night and I've got the fluffy fleece blankets out. I'm surprised that within minutes of meeting him, she's kneading his lap and curling up on him, but they say animals are good judges of character, don't they?

There's contented purring coming from beside me. Mrs Potts is rumbling loudly, and Darcy is murmuring sweet nothings to her, and he's so *nice*, and I can't get my head around why *he* thinks otherwise. We've been talking for a few days now and he's made no suggestion of coming round or seeing each other *without* the hedge between us, and the questions I want to ask keep multiplying and I'm going to burst if he doesn't explain *something* soon.

Eventually, I can't tamp it down any longer and blurt out a question. 'Why?'

He sighs.

'Come on, Darcy, give me something. I'm not trying to push you or change you or persuade you to come over. I just want to know *why* you stay so hidden and hate people so much?'

He's quiet for so long that I start suspecting if he didn't have Mrs Potts on his lap, he'd have got up and walked away.

'Because I don't look like other people.'

'No one looks like anyone else. We're all different. The world would be boring if we all looked the same.' I hate things about the way I look too. My lips are too big; they look like I've had fillers even though I haven't. My hair is too short, but it looks weird if I try to grow it out. 'Very few people wouldn't change something about themselves.'

'It's more than that. I'm... damaged.'

I'm trying to piece together a theory about him. The general avoidance of people, the way he keeps to himself, the disguise he's never seen without on the rare occasions he's seen at all. He's mentioned things he used to enjoy but now doesn't. 'Something happened to you?'

'More like *I* happened to *something*.' He snaps it so bitterly that it must wake Mrs Potts because he whispers a profuse apology to her and promises he won't do it again.

I can't work out what his words mean. 'No one is so damaged that they don't deserve love. Friendship. Support. You don't have to be alone, Darcy.'

'Oh, don't you start. You're *never* alone on Ever After Street, even if you want to be. As evidenced by Witt inviting himself into my shop to tell me, many, many times. Ali from 1001 Nights, that magician who wears eyeliner from the carousel, Sadie and her cousin who I think I've terrified enough that they always come together... safety in numbers when visiting the street's resident beast.'

He tries to make a joke of it, but there's a shuddery sound in his breathing and I get the feeling that he's just a little bit more touched than he wants to admit that our neighbours are constantly trying to bring him out of his shell, a bit like they do with me by checking in every morning, and how they still come, even when I push them away.

The night air is growing chillier. I'm wishing I'd bought a blanket or something to sit on because the cold concrete path is turning my backside numb, but there's nowhere else I'd rather be. I should get up and tackle some more weeds, but I sit there for a while longer, enjoying the feeling of having a companion here, someone who is kind, generous, clearly an animal lover, funny, and always does what he says he will. The world needs more people like Darcy, even if *he* doesn't think so. 'I got an email address for U.N.Known today.'

He snorts and then apologises to Mrs Potts for another disturbance before he realises I'm not joking. 'Oh, you're serious? Who the hell is giving out his email address?'

'Someone at the agency he was once represented by.'

'Well, let's hope they enjoy getting sued for invasion of privacy. Pretty sure it's not okay for them to hand out authors' private contact details to anyone who asks for them.'

'It's nice of you to be so concerned for the "anonymous prat" author of this book you hate.' I quote his own words back to him. 'And I'm not anyone, I'm a professional bookseller. And I think it was a last-ditch attempt at getting through to him.' I tell him about the aggravated agent, wishing I hadn't said anything given how riled up he gets by any mention of my favourite book.

He must be leaning back against the hedge because the branches move when he shakes his head. 'Have you sent anything yet?'

'No. I wanted to take my time and think about what to say. *Once*

Upon Another Time means *so* much to me. It changed my life and I want U.N.Known to know that.'

You wouldn't think it was easy to communicate in non-verbal noises, but Darcy's replying grunt clearly says 'you're an idiot'.

I leave Mrs Potts in his care, pick up the shears and carry on tackling the weeds. My forearms are aching from the repetitive force of the movement over the last few days, but it's also starting to feel like I'm making progress. Bit by bit, the weeds are being hacked down and the garden underneath them is reappearing. Cracked concrete and overgrown borders. The roots that are left will need to be dug up, and Darcy has suggested a good dose of weedkiller to prevent them from regrowing in the spring. Tonight, the soundtrack of Mrs Potts' purring accompanies the snick of the blades slicing together and the whoosh of tall weeds flopping down around me.

'Did you ever have a favourite book?' I ask Darcy, unable to give up on the opportunity to learn *something* more about him.

'Yes.'

Here we go again. I ready myself for another round of Twenty Questions as I try to wheedle a title from him, but he surprises me.

'You're going to laugh.'

'I'm not.'

'It's *Beauty and the Beast*.'

I laugh. 'No, it's not.'

'It honestly is. The original 1740 unabridged version. It didn't used to be, but since...' He pauses, which again suggests *something* happened that changed his life, and then the words come out in a rush, making me wonder if he didn't intend to say them. 'I identify with the Beast and his feeling of loneliness and self-hatred and desire to shut himself away from the world. The language is so old-fashioned that you get lost in trying to decipher it – and I used to love studying the way words and their meanings have changed over the centuries and things like that, but now it's just a reminder of what my life has become. All books are.'

Earlier, it took all my willpower to stop myself marching round there and hugging him, but now, I feel like I could vault over this nine-foot hedge with sheer determination alone, so I could look into his eyes and quote that original version of *Beauty and the Beast* to him, particularly one line that Beauty says to the Beast. *Among mankind, there are many who deserve that name more than you.*

* * *

At home that night, once Mrs Potts is fed and I've scarfed down a sandwich, I open my laptop and start composing an email to U.N.-Known. Even though it's unlikely he'll read it, I can't shake the good feeling I have, and I don't want to mess up my first and probably only contact with my favourite author.

I introduce myself and try to do a non-fangirly, non-gushy appreciation of his book, but I want him to know how much of an impact *Once Upon Another Time* had on me. I tell him a short version of how I found the book, and then get onto the kicker.

Ever After Street is hosting a book festival, and I'd like to personally invite you to attend as a guest of honour. I know this is not what you're known for, but there is so much love for *Once Upon Another Time* in my little shop, so many people who admire and respect you, and would love nothing more than a chance to thank their favourite author in person.

Any concessions to retain your anonymity can be put in place. Please know this email is sent with love and respect, from someone who feels a little less alone in the world because of your gorgeous book.

Best wishes,

Marnie Platt, A Tale As Old As Time

I cross the fingers on both hands and hit send. I don't expect to hear anything back, but it was worth a shot. I close the lid of the laptop to avoid the temptation to sit here staring at my screen all night. Within a few minutes, the willpower has gone and I've opened it again.

And there, right at the top of my inbox with a 'new' flag, is a reply from The Unknown Author.

'Oh my God,' I say out loud even though there's no one to hear, apart from Mrs Potts, who's curled up under a blanket on the sofa. My fingers are shaking as I click onto the email.

U.N.Known is dead.

I gasp in shock. No. No, no, no, no, no. It can't be. He can't be. This wonderful, inventive, mould-breaking man cannot be gone from this world.

It certainly explains his disappearance from the publishing industry. But how can no one know? I stare at the screen open-mouthed, trying to process the heartbreak I feel. A light in the universe has gone out, and the world feels smaller and darker knowing he's no longer there. Despite the fact I never knew him, it feels like someone's told me a family member has died. I know his words so well that it's almost like I've come to know him too, and absolute devastation sweeps through my little house.

My fingers can't stop shaking as I write back.

Oh my goodness, I'm so sorry. I'm devastated, as I know many of his fans will be. He leaves behind an unfillable hole in the book world. *Once Upon Another Time* is a shining beacon for everyone who has ever felt lonely or like they don't fit in.

Providing a light in the darkness will always be his legacy. I'm so sorry for the loss of your friend... or relative. Do you mind me asking who I'm speaking to? I'd like to properly express my sympathy.

I send the email off with tears in my eyes, and lean my elbows on the table and stare at the inbox onscreen, hoping whoever it is will get back to me quickly.

Sure enough, within a few minutes, there's another email.

This is his evil twin, LeaveMeAlown.

The hair on the back of my neck stands on end and I push myself upright and narrow my eyes at the screen. Whoever this is... they're making jokes at their dead friend's expense? And that wordplay... *Once Upon Another Time* is full of wordplay like that – words spelled differently to match the look or sound of other words so it gives an almost poetic rhythm to the prose.

And twin... Unless he really does have a twin, why would anyone describe themselves that way? Unless... this *really* is U.N.-Known and he wants to be left alone?

And if he's dead, why does no one know? Wouldn't someone, somewhere, have informed his publisher and agent? Surely someone couldn't die without *anyone* knowing? And this person is obviously monitoring his email account. Whoever it is would have seen all the attempts to get in touch with him... He's taken the time to respond to me, so why wouldn't he send a quick response to other emails from other people, letting them know that U.N.-Known is dead? Unless U.N.Known is *not* really dead, and... he just wants people to think he is.

A gut feeling tells me there's more to this than meets the eye and I can't stop myself pushing back on it.

Are you playing the clown? (Pronounced own not ow-n!)

Two seconds later, he replies again.

Ha ha.

You're not really dead, are you?

Yes. You're talking to a well-developed ghost.

I laugh out loud at the mental image that brings to mind, but there's something so familiar in the tone of these messages. I'm almost positive this is U.N.Known himself. I reply again.

Well-developed as in large-chested?

A ghost of ample bosom, yes. I meant technologically advanced, obviously.

The reply makes me laugh again, and before I've formulated a response, my email pings again.

It's been a while since I laughed so much. Cheers for that. Goodnight.

While I realise he's shutting down the conversation, it isn't quite as closed off as I expected. Maybe if I email him again some other time, we'll progress beyond single-sentence exchanges, and I'll get a bit closer to working out what's going on and, if he isn't dead, why the heck he's telling people he is.

7

I'm already outside at 5 p.m. a couple of nights later. The garden is looking so much better. I can see paving slabs again between the overgrown greenery, and there's been so much interest in the book festival. The phone's been ringing off the hook, even a reporter from the local newspaper wanted to interview me so they can feature it, and I've sold about twenty tickets today between in-person and online sales.

The wind blows and the sycamore tree at the edge of the forest sends out a scattering of helicopter seeds that twizzle to the ground. Mrs Potts pounces on one and wraps her paws around it, attacking it with teeth and claws as though it's caused her the greatest imposition.

After satisfactorily killing the helicopter seed, she sits by the gatepost, looking up at it, like she's remembering where Darcy was before and hoping she'll see him again.

There's something that appeals about Darcy, whether you're human *or* feline. I look at the hedge. How can I be so eager to see someone I've never *seen*?

It doesn't feel like I've never seen him. I've got a picture forming in my mind, even though I haven't the foggiest idea what he looks like. I picture someone tall; his voice sounds like it comes from somewhere above me when we're standing opposite each other. And he must be fit and muscular from the outdoor work he does. His deep voice makes him sound rugged, and then I try to imagine what colour his eyes might be, what his hair might be like. It's strange to lie awake at night thinking about someone, but not to know the most basic details about them.

'Can I ask you something?' I'm hacking down weeds and gradually forging a path towards the opposite side of the garden, and Darcy has come outside and is tending his roses on the other side of the hedge.

'If you must.' He doesn't outright refuse, but his sigh quite clearly states his reluctance. 'What?'

It's a bark of a word that makes me flinch and reconsider. 'I don't know. Something. Anything. I want to know more about you than I currently do.'

I thought he might be more forthcoming if I left the question open-ended and let him offer something he feels comfortable talking about, but he remains stubbornly silent, and his only response is the scrape of his garden fork as he digs autumn fertiliser into his potted roses. 'What do you look like?'

'Unremarkable.'

'Everyone looks unremarkable until they're seen through the eyes of someone who thinks they're remarkable...' It's my turn to sigh when he doesn't respond. 'Hair colour?'

'Brown.'

Yet another gruff, one-word answer that makes me feel like I'm interrogating him. Maybe I'm on dangerous ground asking about his looks. I know he's self-conscious of *something* but I thought by asking *around* that thing, he might open up a bit. 'Is it long? I hear you running your hand through it sometimes when we're talking; it sounds like it's long.'

'Long-ish, I guess? I've never tried to define it before. I just hack bits off when it starts getting in the way.'

I laugh because we have a similar approach to haircare. 'Same. When I realise I can't see, I snip at my fringe and then regret it when it ends up looking like a drunken Edward Scissorhands has gone to town on me.'

He laughs but still doesn't offer anything more.

'Eye colour?' I prompt, stomping down a patch of stinging nettles and moving onto a green thing with thick bristly stems that's towering above me.

'Bl— DON'T CUT THAT!'

I freeze in shock at his sudden bellow, wondering how he can even see what I'm doing and what plant would cause that volume in his reaction.

'Don't go near it! Just back away slowly and I'll...' He makes a noise of frustration and I'm convinced I hear him throwing his hands up in the air. 'I'll be right over. Just give me a few minutes, okay?'

'Okay...' I say to the sound of his footsteps going up his garden and inside his shop. I look at the plant in front of me. I have no idea what it is. It looks innocuous enough but it must be something serious to cause that response, and... he's coming round. Really? After all these days of talking with the hedge between us, in a matter of minutes, he's going to be in my garden. Face to face after so long wondering what his face might look like...

I'd started to think I was never going to see him and I can't help the little flutter that starts in my belly and moves up to my chest at the thought. Maybe he'll let me give him that hug I wanted so badly the other day.

'That's giant hogweed.'

I've been so caught up in my thoughts that I hadn't heard his gate opening and the voice behind me makes me squeak in surprise as Darcy reaches over to unlatch my gate and lets himself in.

'It's got phototoxic sap. If you get it on your skin, it causes severe burns. Even brushing against it is dangerous. You can't just cut it willy-nilly. Did you get it on you?' He sounds worried as he strides across the garden and holds his hand open, palm up, demanding I show him my hands. I'm wearing gardening gloves but hold my hands out in front of me and look up at him.

I don't know why I expected him to be disguise-less, but he isn't. He's wearing jeans and a black coat, a baseball cap pulled down to his eyebrows, a scarf pulled up over his nose, and a pair of dark glasses that block out any remaining strip of his face that might be visible. A pair of thick black gloves cover his hands. This must be why he went back inside – to don all of this.

And I know it shouldn't, but the sight of this grouchy figure dressed all in black, using the term 'willy-nilly' has brought out my inner child and such an unserious word coming from someone so serious makes me giggle.

'Burns are not funny,' he snarls.

'No, of course not.' I swallow and try to straighten my face, wondering if that answers something about him. The consensus of the other shopkeepers on Ever After Street has always been that he's hiding burn scars, so maybe the rumours aren't too far off base.

He twists a finger around, gesturing for me to turn my hands over, which I dutifully do, and he peers at my gloves through his dark glasses, and then makes a noise that I interpret to mean that they pass inspection so I drop my hands, and he goes to stride away.

'I'm sorry,' I say quickly because the last thing I want him to do is leave. 'It wasn't the potential sap burns that were funny, it was the "willy-nilly". It's such a good word and you do *not* seem like the type of person who'd use a word like that, and...' I trail off because his hidden face gives me no clue as to whether he's about to yell at me or stalk off like this never happened.

Until he starts laughing. I didn't realise how tense his shoulders were until they drop as the laugh overtakes him. 'You're absolutely right. Willy-nilly is one of the best words and I endeavour to use it as often as possible.'

I can't help grinning at the utterly unforeseen way tonight has gone, and he takes an awkward step back towards me. 'Sorry, Marnie. I'm not very good at seeing people face to face.'

I can't tear my eyes away from this figure standing so close to me. He's tall, an inch or two over six feet at a guess, and strong built. The garb he's wearing doesn't hide the expanse of his chest and well-defined arms that undoubtedly come from outdoor work. 'I didn't think I'd ever see you.'

'If only it had stayed that way,' he mutters. 'I shouldn't be here.'

'Well, you're here now. Why don't I make you a cuppa?'

'No, tha—'

'Please, Darcy,' I say instantly. 'Don't go yet.'

He turns towards the hedge, looking as if he desperately wants to be on the other side of it and then he looks back towards me. 'Go on then.' He sounds reluctant and confused, like he isn't sure why he's saying it, and then he goes over to the gatepost where Mrs Potts is watching on. He strokes her and picks her up, and she meows and rubs at him as he brings her back up the garden and deposits her into my arms. 'I'll get rid of the giant hogweed. Just go inside and *don't* let Mrs Potts out; you do not want her getting this stuff on herself.'

I go to argue that I can help, but even without a millimetre of his face visible, I know he's glaring at me, so I hurry back inside before he changes his mind, and run upstairs to keep an eye on him from the window, although I'm not watching to see what he does with the hogweed – I'm watching to make sure he doesn't have a chance to run away.

He goes out the gate and returns with another pair of gloves that he pulls on over his other gloves, and a shovel, and I watch as he shoves it into the earth and rams it down with his foot, digging around the giant plant without cutting it, like he knows exactly what to do.

I wait until he uses the shovel to lever the huge rootball and towering plant out of the ground as one, and then quickly set about making the teas and go back outside, leaving the door ajar in case Mrs Potts wants to join us again.

He comes back in the gate, the extra pair of gloves have gone as well as the plant, and he's breathing hard, like the rootball put up more of a fight than I could tell from upstairs.

'Thanks, Darcy. Tea's ready.' I give the tray in my hands a jiggle. 'Do you want to sit down?'

His covered face looks around, as though he's trying to work out where to sit, and I jerk my foot towards the doorstep, offering him the best and only seat in the garden, apart from Mum's old bench that looks like it would collapse if so much as a butterfly sat on it.

'I'll take the hogweed up to the incinerator in the castle gardens tonight.' He says it as he sits down, probably to hide the pained grunts that escape without him even realising it.

I put the tray on the ground in front of him and then because the doorstep is barely big enough for two, I sit beside him, perching on the edge, and his head turns sharply towards me. I don't think he expected me to sit so close, and he inches as far across as he can, although whether he's trying to give me more space or get away from me is up for interpretation.

He leans over to take his mug from the tray and out of the corner of my eye, I'm watching as his gloved hand comes up and wriggles the scarf down just far enough for him to take a sip. I desperately want to turn towards him, to catch even a glimpse, but he's obviously self-conscious and I get the sense that he didn't think things through before agreeing to sit down with me and now he's regretting it.

'I looked up knotweed contractors online.' I'm keeping my eyes averted and trying to sound conversational and pretend not to have even noticed the way his scarf is pulled down as he dunks a Malted Milk biscuit into his mug. 'Their suggested pricing is well into the thousands. You don't have any insider connections that would do it a bit cheaper, do you? Because I cannot afford hundreds, never mind thousands.'

'You're making me want an ice cream.'

I laugh but it does nothing to ease the knots in my stomach about how much I'm going to have to shell out for this knotweed removal.

'I'll see what I can find out.'

'Thank you.' I nudge my elbow against his and he pulls back and looks at me, and if I could see his face, I think there'd be an aghast look on it at my nerve for not only daring to sit so close but actually having the gall to touch him too, no matter how innocent a touch it is.

'So, how was your day today?' I ask conversationally, really because I'm not sure if he's about to leap up and stomp away at the injustice of an elbow bump and asking him a question might give him something else to focus on. 'Do you have—'

'Are you lonely or something?' he interrupts before I can finish. 'Why are you always trying to talk to me?'

'Why shouldn't I talk to you? We're neighbours, aren't we?' I'd best not suggest that we might be friends again. It didn't go well the last time.

At least that's a question that he can't deny. We unequivocally *are* neighbours. He's saved from having to think of an answer when the back door creaks and Mrs Potts slinks her way through the gap.

He makes an indisputable noise of joy, and pushes his scarf back up so he can give her his full attention, and she immediately climbs onto his lap, making a series of delighted *prrrups*.

'I am lonely.' I nibble around the edges of the Malted Milk biscuit and then dunk the remaining bit with the cows on it in my tea. 'Talking to you has made me realise how I don't have anyone to talk to. I always convinced myself that my life was full of friends, but not the kind who are there for you when you need them.'

'But the kind who expect you to be there when *they* want *you* though, right?'

'You too?'

'Kind of. My life was riddled with people who pretend to be friends until you've outlasted your usefulness to them and then drop you like a stone.'

'Pulverising your self-worth in the process?' I finish for him.

'Something like that.'

'I don't know how to make new friends,' I admit quietly. 'I'm shy and awkward. I don't like talking to people. Or, well, I do like talking to people but I get self-conscious and always think I'll say the wrong thing, and then I spout something stupid and people laugh at me, and it makes me not want to talk to people. When we started A Tale As Old As Time, I thought it would be a great way of meeting more book-loving people. People really connect over books. It's easy to chat to someone about books they love, and there's always a joy in finding someone who's loved the same book as you. Everyone takes something different away from each book they read. I thought A Tale As Old As Time would be full of people wanting to chat about books and make new friends who enjoy the same things I do, but people don't want that. And I'm the professional; I can't bounce up to a customer and say, "Hey, I like you, will you be my friend?"' I think of my U.N.Known-loving customer, who I'm sure I'd get on with. 'It would be weird and creepy and a little desperate. I don't know how people make friends as adults. It's easy when we're kids. Making friends is as simple as "that's a cool Barbie, let's be friends", but as adults, it's a minefield. Even if you get on with someone, at our age, people already have their friends, and jobs, families, children, responsibilities. They have no room in their lives for new friends.'

'Or you could just accept being alone forever and never having to change yourself to fit other people's opinions of how you should act, and never having to worry that people only want you for what they can get from you.'

That bitterness tinges his voice again, and I know without a shadow of a doubt that he's been hurt by people who were once close to him. 'Well, you've made a new friend over the past couple of nights.' I nod towards Mrs Potts who is sitting on his lap and keeping a paw on one of his gloved fingers in case he dares to stop stroking her.

'The kind of friend everyone needs.' He says it in the baby-talk voice he uses for Mrs Potts and then switches back to his normal voice. 'It's a shame friendships aren't like romantic relationships. You meet someone, go on dates with the intention of getting to know them and moving onto the next level of a romantic relation-ship, but there's nothing like that with friendship. Which is a shame because I'd totally go on a date with a cat. We could hold paws across the table and share longing looks over pouches of Whiskas and exchange our best mouse-catching tips.'

'Oh my God!' It's like a lightbulb pings on in my head. I put my hand on his knee in excitement and then quickly remove it when he flinches. 'Darcy, you're a genius!'

'I am?' He sounds confused. 'I'm not sure pouches of Whiskas are much to get excited about or that I have any mouse-catching tips that a cat would be interested in.'

I laugh, but his words have set an idea in motion. 'Everything you just said is right. It's *so* hard to make friends as an adult. I can't be the only one who doesn't know how. Why *aren't* there such a thing as friendship dates? Why *don't* we go on dates with potential friends to see if there's a spark of friendship there? If people want to make friends, why don't they spend time together to see if they're a good match – if they have similar interests, laugh at the same things, or enjoy doing the same activities? Why isn't it normal to say, "I'd like more friends in my life and I don't know how to find them?"'

'Er, I don't know...' He sounds caught between laughing and being concerned for my sanity.

'And what do people connect over like nothing else? Books!'

He shifts around, murmuring an apology to Mrs Potts for disturbing her, and turns towards me, pulling back until he can see my face and making me extra aware that I can't see his. 'So, what, you want to match up potential friends based on what books they like, and... send them on friendship dates?'

'Yes! Why not? We can't be the only people who feel lonely and aren't sure what to do about it.'

'I'm not lonely.'

'No, of course not.' I glance over at him. He sounds like he's *trying* to be growly and harsh, but he's sitting on a freezing cold doorstep in October and he hasn't left yet. As far as I know, I'm the only person on Ever After Street who's ever had this much of a conversation with him. I think he's lonelier than he wants to admit. 'There's something that draws booklovers together. It's always lovely to chat to someone who loves a book that you love. There's this regular customer and I always look forward to talking to her because we both love *Once Upon Another Time*. It's like a little bookish connection between two people. There must be others who'd like to talk about books with people who like the same books, and there must be other adults who'd like to make new friends but aren't sure where to start.'

'So you're going to match people up based on what books they enjoy, like a platonic Cupid shooting bookmarks instead of arrows, and then send them on blind friendship dates like Cilla Black on nineties' TV? Do we need to hire "Our Graham" for a quick reminder?' He does a perfect impression of Cilla's Liverpool accent.

'Yes!' Everything he says makes me crack up. 'Well, maybe not the "Our Graham" bit, that would just be weird.'

'And where will these dates be? Have you got a budget for sending multiple pairs of people out to fancy restaurants?'

'Well, no, but maybe they could sit out here. When the garden's finished, that is,' I say hurriedly. Although it's improving daily, it still looks like a wild boar could emerge from the undergrowth at any moment. After the excitement of thinking up something that could really make a difference to mine and my customers' lives, the garden makes me feel overwhelmingly deflated. The only living creature that would be happy out here is a rat. No matter how much progress I'm making, it will take a *long* time to get it to the stage where it's suitable for hosting visitors. This is something that could make a huge difference to Mr Rowbotham and the importance of A Tale As Old As Time to Ever After Street, but it would need to be implemented before mid-November, four weeks away.

Darcy is quiet for a while. 'They could go to mine.'

My head spins towards him so fast that a bone in my neck clicks. 'Seriously?'

'Yeah, why not? My garden is a neat and tidy rose haven. There are tables and chairs at the castle that I could borrow, and you could get some finger food from Lilith in the tearooms, and set up your booklovers on their platonic dates and send them through your back gate and into mine. They could have a chat over tea and cake, and then come back to you with their... I don't know, marks out of ten and verdict on whether they're going to see each other again?'

'But... but...' I struggle to find the words for how astounding this offer is. 'But you avoid people. That's a lot of privacy invasion for someone so private.'

'I wouldn't *be* there, Marnie. You'd have to deal with the people. If you snip a rose for each table, rest assured I won't lock you up in my tower for all eternity. Obviously the aim will be to use your own garden, but considering that last I knew, you had one rusty table and wonky-legged chair, currently MIA and last seen being swallowed by greenery some months ago, it would be a compromise for now. If you want to, that is.'

'Yes! Yes, yes, yes.' His support is something I've never known before. Someone who just *gets* what I'm trying to do and doesn't make me feel like an idiot every time I open my mouth. 'Thank you. Darcy, you're...' A lump forms in my throat that won't let words out. I've never met anyone like him before. Kind, calm, logical, and supportive. *He* is the kind of person everyone needs in their life.

'It's a good idea.' He deliberately doesn't let me finish the sentence, and I'm once again certain he knows what I'm thinking. 'How are you going to do it?'

'I don't know. Ask people to fill in forms listing their favourite books, maybe a bit of other info about hobbies or interests, and then go through them to see if there are any matches? It doesn't have to be exact. Even reading within the same genre would give them something to talk about... Maybe I could give them both the same book and they could come outside to sit at a table, have a cuppa and a cake, chat, have a little read...'

'And in bad weather?' he asks. 'It's mid-October, we're heading into winter, it won't always be clear and dry with the last hints of the autumnal sun dropping behind the mountains. Some days, there's going to be thunderstorms and hailstones and temperatures cold enough to freeze your nan's balls off.'

Trust him to think of the practical things, including anyone's nan's balls. 'I don't know. It's more of a summertime thing, but I need to start it now to prove that I deserve my place here. I could move shelves around to create space for a few tables inside...' It's far from ideal, but he's right. The weather is still reasonable for October, but it isn't going to stay this way for much longer.

'In nicer weather, we could send people on walks around the castle gardens or tours of the castle library,' he suggests. 'Or on a trail through the Full Moon Forest, and for now, we could offer a date to the book festival if the matched friendship couples hit it off.'

We.

I hadn't realised how alone I've felt in the last couple of years, but I do realise how alone I suddenly *don't* feel, ever since the moment Darcy burst into my life.

'I've got to admit, it sounds nice, even to someone who doesn't want another human in their life ever again. I'd go for that.' He pauses. 'I mean, I would have. In years gone by. Not now, obviously.'

I'm not imagining the dejection in his voice when he says that. I've got a niggling feeling that Darcy is much, much lonelier than he lets on, and that pause was a bit too long. Just long enough for an idea to form...

'Would you?' I say casually.

His face shifts towards me. 'Why does that leading tone in your voice give me a really, really bad feeling?'

'Because you're the perfect person for this! The unfriendliest man on Ever After Street! What a start that would be! If I could match *you* up with the perfect friend, no one would ever doubt how good an idea this is. It would be the best start I could ever have hoped for. If I had *your* backing, this couldn't fail.'

'I give you my backing unreservedly. No human contact needed.' He looks down at Mrs Potts like he's trying to think of the least disruptive way to move her off his lap so he can run away.

'Oh come on, Darcy, aren't you lonely?'

'N—'

'Honestly?' I interrupt before he can finish the denial. 'If you're in your shop at all, you're hiding out the back. You slink between here and the castle like a ghost. If anyone ever sees you, it's as you disappear into the distance like you were never there.'

'There's a reason for that.'

'There is *no* reason for never speaking to anyone on Ever After Street. You're so far away from the beast you claim to be.' I bump my shoulder into his gently, no matter how much he disliked it before, surprised he hasn't moved out of reach yet. 'You've just come in to remove some dangerous plant for me because you're much nicer than you'd have people believe. Wouldn't it be nice to have someone to chat to? Someone to share frustrations with? Someone to talk with, joke with, compare horrible customer stories with...'

He looks away obstinately. 'How could *I* ever make a friend, Marnie? Look at me!'

I look at him.

'Don't look at me! That was metaphorical! I don't want anyone to look at me, ever.' He sighs when I look away.

Maybe I'm barking up the wrong tree. He seems so much more mellow than he'd have anyone believe, and I feel like I've known him for much longer than I have.

'What about the other poor soul who'd have to agree to talk to me? Who would? I've... I'm not... I mean...' He's obviously stumped for words after a few minutes of silence. 'Not many people around here would be up for that challenge.'

'I am.'

'You are.' He glances at me again. 'But you're different. You're you. I've got to know you over the past couple of weeks.'

'You could get to know other people, it just takes one tiny first step.'

He doesn't say anything, but more importantly, he doesn't say no.

'How about Witt?' I suggest. 'He doesn't have the easiest time talking to people, and he's a lovely guy, empathetic and understanding.'

'Witt's my employer at the castle. And for someone who doesn't find talking easy, he *never* stops trying to engage with me – I don't want to encourage him.'

'Ali from 1001 Nights then. He often says that he'd like to get to know you...'

'Ali is always inviting me to eat in his restaurant. But I... I don't eat in public.' He waves a hand in front of his face, meaning the garb he's wearing to disguise whatever he's trying to hide. 'So I ignore him. I know he's only trying to be nice, but I don't deser—'

He cuts off the sentence, but surely that was going to be 'deserve'? Is this what's really going on with Darcy? For some reason, he feels like he doesn't *deserve* love and kindness?

'You'd be the perfect person. You're a representation of people who are lonely, people who find it difficult to make friends. Do this for me, please. It's a brilliant way to bring people to Ever After Street. If I can show Mr Rowbotham and the council that I have something that will attract interest and set A Tale As Old As Time apart...'

'That's what Bookishly Ever After is for.'

'But that's just a one-time thing. It may bring an extra hit of visitors in that weekend, it may get a few people mentioning our name, but it's not long-term. This is something that could continue indefinitely. Something that will make my shop stand out. And it's important to me. Books make people feel less alone and loneliness has been a big part of my life lately. If I can do something to help other people who feel the same then that would be an even better use of a bookshop than just being a bookshop.'

He ignores my impassioned plea as he gently excuses himself from Mrs Potts and urges her off his lap until he can stand up, stomping his boots on the ground to get feeling back into his legs.

I stand up too and look up at him, trying to make eye contact through those dark glasses, and he stills, looking back at me.

I hear his barely audible intake of breath. 'Stop looking at me. You're doing something to me with your eyes. I can feel my resolve weakening and my resolve never weakens. I'm not going to say yes to this. Ever.'

I give him a wink, because, for as determined as he is to refuse, I'm determined that he'd be the perfect candidate for a friendship date, a test run to make sure it works, and I'm not giving up. 'You know what they say about things like that – everything that is real was imagined first.'

8

'It'll be fine. You might even have fun.'

Darcy is pacing up and down the neat path of his garden, alternating between folding his arms and shoving his gloved hands into his pockets angrily.

'I just need a couple of phot—'

'Photos?' he bellows. He's still in his full disguise. A cap pulled down low, a scarf pulled up high, gloves and dark glasses.

'For the plan I want to show Mr Rowbotham. You can sit here...' There's a table and two chairs set up on the grass beside me. 'So you're facing the shop and your back is to the camera, and Ali will sit there, facing this way, and I'll take a couple of snaps through your open gate. You won't even know I'm there. And then you and Ali can both give me glowing testimonials for the website, and you will have made a connection with another human being. It's win-win and win again because you get something out of it, I get something out of it, and Ali gets something out of it too. He gets to meet you and then he can tell everyone else on Ever After Street how nice you are, and they all get to meet you too.'

'No! No more meetings. I don't know how you talked me into this one!'

'Because you're a great big softie who can't refuse a bookworm in distress and you want to help your friend and neighbour?' I say hopefully.

'Slipped something in my tea, more like,' he mutters. 'Hypnotism. Mind control. A magic spell. Poison. The possibilities are endless.'

'Darcy! You might like the guy. Ali is lovely. He's really clever, he's a brilliant cook, his granddaughters love *Beauty and the Beast*, and he likes *The Velveteen Rabbit*, which I had to assume that you do too because you've been totally unforthcoming with any other info that may help. His wife died a few years ago and left him with a huge rose plant that's taking over the garden and he doesn't know how to take care of it. He'd love your advice. Please give this a chance.'

He paces back towards me and huffs in annoyance, and I'm pretty sure that behind the scarf and glasses, he's glaring at me.

'Hello, anyone home?' Ali calls cheerfully, opening the back door of Darcy's shop and coming out into the garden. 'I did knock but no one answered, I thought you might already be out here, and here you are.'

Darcy makes a noise of indignation, like Ali has done something akin to entering the forbidden West Wing by inviting himself into The Beast's Enchanted Rose Garden and coming to look for us.

'Here we are!' I overcompensate by throwing my arms out and nearly dropping my phone. 'Thank you for coming! Ali, Darcy. Darcy, Ali. I know you already know each other but...'

It seems weird to introduce them. Both of them have worked on this street for longer than I have, but this is probably the first time they've progressed beyond a few grunts.

'It's a pleasure to meet you, friend.' Ali has got a bottle of wine in one hand and he holds the other out for Darcy to shake, which he reluctantly does, and then Ali hands him the wine. 'Just a little something to say thanks for having me over.'

Darcy takes it and puts it down on the table, right in the centre so it will block their view of each other.

'Sit down,' I say chirpily. 'I'm just going to take a couple of snaps and I'll make you cups of tea.'

'This is a beautiful garden,' Ali says as they both sit down, and I back away slowly, lurking behind the open gate with my phone, trying to get an artsy shot of the scene, two strangers at a table in a pretty garden. If I can show Mr Rowbotham that this is something A Tale As Old As Time could do on a regular basis, use books to bring people together, surely he would see that I have long-term plans for the future *and* a reason to keep my garden as neatly maintained as Darcy's is.

I take a few pictures. Darcy's back is to me and from this angle, you wouldn't know he was anything other than a man wearing a baseball cap on an autumn evening, and Ali has gone from looking around the garden in awe to listening intently to something Darcy is saying, and as much as I *really* want to stay and eavesdrop, they deserve their privacy, and I reluctantly go back into the bookshop to make them a cup of tea each.

Unfortunately, the kettle hasn't finished boiling before there's the sound of yelling, and I race back down the stairs and skid round to Darcy's garden in time to see Ali fleeing through the shop door as the bottle of wine hits the wall nanoseconds behind him, shattering into pieces and flooding the steps up to Darcy's back door with red wine.

'What are you doing? You can't throw bottles of wine at people!'

'I threw it beside him! I have a good aim, believe me, if I'd wanted to throw it *at* him, I would have!' Darcy whirls round to me, breathing hard under his disguise. 'What the hell was I thinking in agreeing to this? What the hell were *you* thinking setting me up with that smug know-it-all?'

'Ali's nothing like that!'

'Look at that bloody insult!' He throws a hand out towards the spilled red wine, dripping forlornly down from the top step to the one below. 'He was trying to gawp at me! Trying to get me drunk in the hopes I might loosen up and give him a good look!'

'Oh, come on. He was being polite. It's nice to bring a gift when someone invites you into their home! There's no way he had any intention of you sharing it there and then! He's working tonight. It's the busiest time at the restaurant, but he left someone else in charge so he could come when our shops are closed for *your* convenience!'

Darcy mutters a string of expletives, still pacing angrily. I stay quiet for a few moments and then approach him, trying to be gentle. I wasn't here – who knows what was said or done. I'm assuming Darcy is overreacting, but he deserves the benefit of the doubt.

I reach out, trying to put my hand on his arm comfortingly, to show I'm on his side. 'What did he say?'

He yanks his arm out of my reach and then turns to stare in my direction. 'He assumed I was a burn victim and started mansplaining how to treat burn scars. I don't know if you can be mansplained to while actually being a man, but he managed it. Patronising pillock.'

'Are you *not* a burn victim?' I snap, because Darcy was deter-mined to be insulted by *something* tonight, no matter what it was.

He stares at me again, and I fold my arms and pull myself up straighter, challenging him with my eyes. We dance around and around the reason he wears that disguise, but I've never had the courage to ask him outright before.

He swallows hard. 'No, I'm not.'

'Well, that's what everyone thinks. If you don't want people to make assumpt—'

'Everyone has no business thinking anything. What I wear is no concern of anyone else's.'

I go to snap a response, but it's undeniably true. I take a few breaths because I'm getting as het-up as he is. '*I* know that, but *you* know what small places like this are like. Everyone knows everyone else, and believe it or not, people worry about you.'

'I don't deserve anyone to worry about me.' He snarls the words instantly, and then takes a step backwards and lets out a breath when he seems to realise what he's said.

That 'deserve' thing again. Something happened to Darcy, of that I have no doubt, but it was something that left him feeling like he doesn't deserve to be part of the world, so he exists on the outskirts, staying away from people, and covering up whatever scars it left him with... to avoid attention? Or to avoid anyone caring about him?

'*This* is exactly why I avoid people,' he barks before I can come up with a response. 'Thank you for showing me that is *not* a mistake.'

'Ali didn't mean any harm. You could have just corrected him.'

'And you could've just left me alone with no one else to think of or care about!'

We stare at each other for a second, at least I assume he's looking at me as I try to process what he didn't intend to say there. Is that his unintentional way of suggesting that he cares about me? 'Darcy...'

'Leave me alone, as you should have from the start!' He stomps up the path, the broken glass of the wine bottle crunching under his boots as he storms in the door.

'You need to control your temper!' I shout after him, feeling more like Belle than ever before. 'No one cares about what you're hiding under that scarf as much as you do, Darcy.'

The back door slamming is my reply.

I make a noise of frustration and go back round to A Tale As Old As Time.

There will be a free book swap table at Bookishly Ever After and I'm sorting out unsellable or damaged stock for that when Ali knocks on my door a couple of hours later, looking sheepish in the rain that's started up, reflecting my mood after the disaster of what was supposed to be a great start for the friendship dates.

'Sorry, Marnie.' He's still got his chef's hat on and he takes it off and clasps it in his hand when I invite him in. 'I was trying to help. I'd looked up burn scarring on the internet, I thought he might feel comfortable opening up to me if I knew what I was talking about. Which I obviously didn't. I didn't mean to ruin things.'

'No, not at all. Maybe it was a terrible idea. I just thought, with his reputation, if I could show that books can bring even the unlikeliest of people together... Maybe I lost the plot. Got caught up in it and thought I could...' I look at the wall between me and The Beast's Enchanted Rose Garden sadly. '...change the unchangeable.'

Maybe that's where I'm going wrong – by acting like Darcy needs to change rather than just accepting him. He's pretty great exactly as he is... even with the tendency to throw objects at people.

9

_____

Not to be discouraged by the disastrous start, over the weekend, I've started work on the idea of friendship dates and how to get it functioning. I've created a spreadsheet to cross-reference answers, and printed out a blank form to be filled in, hopefully by people who actually want to find friends, unlike one half of my first couple, who definitely did not.

So far I've got options for – favourite book, other favourite books because every booklover knows it's unfair to ask for just one, favourite author, favourite childhood book, last book read and enjoyed, last book read and hated, other interests and hobbies, and a box for any additional comments the filler-in might want to share.

I'm leaning on the counter working on it when my U.N.-Known-loving customer comes in.

'Anything new this week?' she asks cheerily.

'Nothing.' I try to hide the disappointment in my voice, but the budget hasn't stretched to new stock for a few months now, and with Christmas not far off, I've concentrated on children's books and gift books.

'And nothing from our favourite mysterious author, I guess?' Her tone suggests that she's wondering why she bothers to ask.

I shake my head, keeping my lips clamped closed because I'm *dying* to tell her I emailed him, but I can't. It's not my secret to share.

She's the only customer, so she wanders around the shop, telling me about her latest read from the other side of the shelves. Even Mrs Potts welcomes the scritch she offers her, which is unusual because Mrs Potts isn't generally a fan of customers, but she seems happier since Darcy came into her life.

My favourite customer picks up a couple of bookmarks painted by local artists and a new witchy rom com by Holly Martin and comes over to the counter to pay. 'You're certainly doing all the things lately. What's a friendship questionnaire?' Her eyes are on the form I've just pushed aside and then her cheeks flare red. 'Sorry, that's hideously nosy, isn't it? Ignore me, I only open my mouth to change feet most days.'

There's something about her that puts me at ease and it buoys my confidence that someone is interested enough to ask, so I give her a brief explanation of the idea of friendship dates and connecting platonically over a love of the same books.

'Oh, that sounds brilliant, sign me up!'

'Really?' I try to hide the grin that bursts across my face, but I can't quite manage it. I was half-convinced that most people would think I'd finally lost the last one of my remaining marbles.

'Yeah, definitely! I don't have many friends and it always feels odd to admit that. It's so difficult in real life. I either feel uncomfortable around strangers and barely talk or I feel too comfortable around them and don't stop talking, and both options are off-putting. It would be nice to meet someone else who understood that awkwardness, and to have the bookish chat to break the ice, because things are always stilted at first, and I usually come out with something random and weird like, "Do you think conkers would taste nice?" thereby ensuring they back away slowly before running for the hills. I never feel like I fit in anywhere, no matter how hard I try, you know?'

'Oh, more than you can imagine,' I mutter, wondering how on earth someone who's so pretty, chatty, and seemingly outgoing could feel like they don't fit in, and it builds my confidence once again. People are going to get behind this idea. None of us know what other people struggle with, and I'm more convinced than ever that I'm not the only person who struggles to make friends and would like more nice people in my life.

She's turned the form around to face her and is reading the options. 'Know anyone who likes *Once Upon Another Time*?'

'Well, other than me, we haven't really got start—'

'You're who I was hoping for.'

'Me?'

'Yeah. We obviously have similar tastes in books. I'm eternally grateful to you for bringing that book into my life. I look forward to chatting to you every time I come in... Couldn't *we* go on a friendship date and see what else we have in common?'

I don't intend to start giggling, but it's such a coincidence that it feels like a nudge from the universe. Actually, it feels more like the universe is giving me a drop-kick up the backside. 'You're not going to believe this, but when I came up with this idea, I thought of you. You've always seemed like someone I'd get along with, but it would be so unprofessional, not to mention quite sad and desperate, to accost you and say, "I like you, will you be friends with me?" so I've never said anything.'

'You should have! I would've said yes in a heartbeat! I'm Cleo, by the way.'

'Marnie.'

'See? We've been chatting for ages – *how* is this the first time we've known each other's names?'

'I don't know. It's weird trying to befriend customers. I want to jump all over them and squeal about books we like, but I feel like I should remain professional and keep an aloof distance.'

'Making friends in a bookshop is a great idea. I don't think anyone feels alone in a bookshop. It must be incredible to work here. I'd never want to leave.'

I'm staring at her with hearts in my eyes. That's exactly how I feel about A Tale As Old As Time and someone who understands that is exactly the kind of person I want to be friends with. I can already picture us going to visit libraries together, sharing our favourite books, swapping bookish memes online, and excitedly recommending books to each other. 'What's your favourite book, other than *Once Upon Another Time*?'

'*Alice in Wonderland*,' she says without a nanosecond of hesitation.

'Oh, I love Alice. It's timeless. Even so many years later, it's still relevant to kids everywhere learning to push boundaries, stand up for what's right and question authority figures, and believe in the impossible.'

Now Cleo's looking at me with hearts in her eyes. 'I feel like you're my new best friend already. No one appreciates the genius of *Alice in Wonderland* like I do, and you've been right in front of me all along and I've always been too nervous to push you for much of a chat in case you're busy. Shall we really go on a friendship date?'

'I'd love to! I was thinking of doing an initial set-up evening to start with. People could mix in the bookshop, then go on their dates, then fill in a reaction form. If it's a success then I'll give them free tickets to Bookishly Ever After for their next date, and if there's enough interest, then we do it again with a new set of people. We could make it a semi-regular occurrence, and take it online to open it up to a wider range. People might want to make virtual friends even if they don't live close by...' I'm getting overexcited and force myself to stop yammering before I scare her off completely.

'Are all the dates going to be in here?' She looks around my little shop in awe.

'If the weather's nice, I'm going to send everyone to next door's garden for tea and cake.'

'The weird angry guy's place?'

'He's not that weird. And not... always... that angry.' I try not to think about the doomed meeting with poor Ali the other night. 'He's...' I don't know quite how to describe Darcy, and I stall long enough for the right word that Cleo's eyebrow starts rising in a suggestive way. 'I'm sure he's got his reasons, and his kindness outshines his weirdness.' I didn't know I was going to say that until the words are out, but I realise how true it is as I say it. I've always thought of Darcy as the Scary Neighbour next door too, but now I've got to know him, he's a real prince under the beastly reputation.

She looks at me curiously. 'That's good to know. Usually I avoid his shop because he's lurking out the back and he ignores you if you try to speak to him, but if you say he's sound, I'll pop in and get myself something on the way home.' She takes one of the friendship questionnaires, promises to pop it back in soon, and waves as she goes out the door, leaving me feeling like I've finally found the thing I was meant to be doing. Something good can come of my loneliness with these friendship dates. Maybe my awkwardness can help make other outsiders feel less alone too.

10

Just after 3.30 p.m. a couple of nights later, I'm awaiting the arrival of the after-school group for story time, when there's a knock on the front door, which is weird because the shop is open and customers would be very, very welcome. I push myself up on my hands on the counter and lean over, but I can only make out a shadow standing outside.

I walk over to the door, ready to greet eager book shoppers and reassure them that knocking isn't necessary. The bell tinkles as I pull the door open, and the person who was facing away, looking out at Ever After Street, turns back my way.

It is not a customer.

It's a man dressed head to toe in a white Hazmat suit. Not a centimetre of him is visible, from the hooded visor covering his face, to the rubbery suit covering every part of his body, long gloves that reach his elbows, and plastic boot covers covering knee-height black boots.

The man clears his throat. 'Heard you've got a knotweed problem.'

Every hair on the back of my neck stands on end and goose-bumps race across my arms. 'Darcy?'

'And there was me thinking you might not recognise my voice.'

'I'd know your voice *anywhere*.' Usually, when you're feeling tingly about someone, you picture them every time you close your eyes, but I can't picture Darcy, so his voice is all I've got. I've come to know every nuance, from every breath to every grunt and groan. I've heard every smile and imagined every laugh lighting up a face that I can't imagine at all. And now I'm standing in the doorway, staring at him like a mute lemon because he's never come to the front door before, and this is the first time we've spoken since he stormed off after the friendship date last week. I've continued chopping down weeds and digging out their roots every evening, listening for the sound of him in his garden, but it's been wretch-edly quiet. 'I thought I needed a specialist contractor to get rid of the knotweed?'

'It just so happens that I *am* an experienced removal expert.'

I don't know why, but it makes me laugh. He's a gardener – of *course* he is.

'And I owe you an apology for the other night.'

'You owe Ali an apology for the other night.' I fold my arms and raise an eyebrow.

'Yeah.' He sounds contrite. 'I know. But I was supposed to be doing *you* a favour and instead I got too worked up and let my nerves get the better of me. Do you know how long it's been since I sat down with another human face to face and tried to make a conversation that I couldn't growl and walk away from? I worked myself up into a ball of angry frazzled nerves. I expected the worst and I didn't give him a chance. And I'm sorry.'

'A prickly, spiky ball.'

'A selfish and inconsiderate prickly spiky ball who's trying to make it up to you via the medium of invasive plant removal?' His voice sounds hopeful, and I'm trying not to smile but it isn't working. 'Thought it might give you a fright if I appeared in your garden looking like someone from a forensic investigation team and started digging. Can I come through?'

He's nervous. He must be self-conscious, standing there on Ever After Street, maybe not so oblivious to the curious looks passersby are throwing our way.

I step back to let him in. 'Can I help?'

'No, it's a one-man job. Besides, aren't you working?'

Oh hell's bells, I'd forgotten all about that. 'Yes. The after-school club will be here in less than half an hour and I haven't even decided what I'm reading yet.'

He glances towards the front like they might turn up at any moment, and I follow him as he heads past my 'books of the week' display shelves and through the children's section, hesitating like he wants to look around, but time is limited. He lets himself out the back door and I fight the overwhelming sense of not wanting him to go yet. This is the first time he's ever been *in* my shop. I don't want it to be the only time.

'You know where I am if you need a hand, right?'

He salutes me with a gloved hand as he goes to collect tools from where he's left them outside the back gate.

I stand in the doorway watching for a few moments, and Mrs Potts meows and wraps herself around my legs, like she's sensed Darcy's presence too. I herd her back inside and reluctantly close the door. I don't know what knotweed removal entails, but it's probably not something a cat should be getting involved in.

Usually I love after-school night. It reminds me of why I wanted to open a bookshop in the first place, and how much a love of books can affect a child's life and turn them into a lifelong bookworm, but today I can barely concentrate because of Darcy in the garden.

I can't stop myself glancing out the window, trying to see between the painted blue sky and green hills and watch what he's doing, and my mind is not on the children waiting for my next sentence. I went for *The Princess and the Pea* in the end. I've got a dried pea and everyone takes it in turns to place another layer of fabric over it to see if the plasticine princess I hastily rolled together can still feel the pea, and when the story is over, the group of kids all clamour for another one. Parents are still wandering around the shop, hopefully doing some early Christmas shopping, so I read *The Ugly Duckling* too, and absolutely no one pays the slightest bit of attention to the sounds of chopping and digging from the garden.

When I next glance up, the back door is slightly ajar and a figure dressed in white fills the gap. Darcy has come to story time too.

I'm fluttery because he *wants* to listen in, and sad because he's outside looking in, hiding behind a door, never brave enough to step into the light, even in his Hazmat suit disguise. It feels like a metaphor for his life – a part of the world but so alone that it can't feel like it sometimes.

It seems to take forever to get the stories finished, ring up the parents' purchases, and wave goodbye to the little group as they flood out onto Ever After Street with cries for cake from Lilith's tearooms. I lock up and go straight to the back door, where Darcy is outside finishing up.

The towering knotweed has gone and is currently burning in an incinerator drum he's brought with him, and Darcy pulls off his plastic boot covers and stuffs them into a bin bag, followed by stripping off his elbow-length gloves, and I think I'm finally going to get to see the hands that produce such beautiful handwriting, but underneath the long gloves is another pair of gloves that tuck under the sleeves of his suit. Not a millimetre of him is exposed, and I can't help the twinge of disappointment.

A little thrill shivers through me when he starts walking towards me. His visor must be made of two-way mirrored plastic because he can definitely see out, but I can't see in. If I could see his face, I think he'd look quite perplexed by the width of my smile.

The garden looks so much different than it did. There's something about a patch of knotweed that's imposing and, even without knowing what it is, you know it's something sinister. Darcy's also stripped down the ivy and it's all starting to come together now and look like it might've been a garden once. 'I don't know how I can ever thank you.'

'Getting to witness story time was thanks enough. I saw all this light and laughter from inside and wanted to see what it was all about. It's been a *long* time since I read a fairy tale. It was nice, actually. We don't hear those kinds of stories as adults and it made me want to raid the children's section and reminiscence about the olden days.'

'If I remember rightly, I tried to give you a book that's perfect for that.' I give him a pointed frown, and he looks back at me for a long moment. At least, I think he does. I can *see* where his face must be, but I still can't see his face.

'I'm done for now, anyway. The area will need another dose of herbicide within a few weeks to make sure it won't come back, so I'll go...' He gestures vaguely in the direction of the gate.

'No, don't. Come in! Please!' I say it so quickly that the words come out as a shout, and I'm moments away from leaping forth and hauling him into the shop. Seeing him inside seems like a new realm of our relationship. It's like there's an escape route outside and shutting himself in a building with me is the largest amount of trust he's shown so far. 'Everyone's gone and it's past closing time. No one else will be in.'

'I don't... um...' He wrings his gloved hands together.

'Mrs Potts would really like to see you.' I'm not above using feline-related blackmail.

He looks up at the door and I get the sense he's about to do something he'll regret. 'Oh, go on then, your cat has got me wrapped around her little finger.'

I narrowly avoid victory-punching the air as I step back and let him in, and he wipes his boots on the doormat and pulls the door closed to shut the October air out.

'I never knew you read to children.' The children's area is right by the back door, and the book of Hans Christian Andersen fairy tales is still open on the table. He flicks through it. 'I used to do that.'

'Really?' My mouth falls open in shock. 'Where?'

'A library, before it closed down. A long time ago. I used to host a creative writing class for kids there.'

I don't know why I bothered closing my mouth because it falls open in shock again. '*You* taught creative writing? Mr "Won't Even Read A Damn Book"?'

I can't see his face, but if I could, I think there'd be a pinched grimace on it because he's definitely said more than he intended to. 'A *very* long time ago.'

His body language has gone so tense that he'd snap like a taut rubber band if a feather touched him, and I think a subject change is in order before he bolts from the shop for good. 'Reading to kids was inspired by *You've Got Mail*.'

'What's that? The film with Tom Ryan and Meg Hanks?'

I burst out laughing so hard that I might never stop. 'I think you mean *Tom* Hanks and *Meg* Ryan,' I say between gasps for breath. 'Have you seen it?'

He shakes his head. 'I'm not a romantic movie kind of person. People don't get happy endings in real life; I don't see the point in pretending fictional characters somehow do. It's not worth the disappointment that inevitably comes with reality.'

I ignore his cynicism. 'Meg Ryan's character reads to kids in her bookshop, and it just seemed so magical. I said I'd do that if I ever had my own bookshop.'

'And now you do.'

'And now I do.'

'You forget how amazing that is sometimes, don't you?'

I bite my lip. No one has ever been able to make me go from crying to laughing to crying again as rapidly as Darcy can. Every time he speaks, his words seem able to say things that other people can't or won't say. 'It's not that I forget. It's that I never expected to do it on my own and since losing Mum, it's become more of a dread than anything else. I needed a reminder of how much joy books can bring.'

'Maybe I did too.' His voice is barely above a whisper.

'Do you ever miss...' I falter, searching for a way to put it. 'I don't know. Seeing people. Taking a class. Talking to kids.'

He goes to answer with what I'm fairly sure was going to be a swift 'no', but then he stops himself and thinks it over. 'I never thought I did, but seeing that tonight, seeing how their faces were enraptured as you read, how much fun they had with the plasticine princess... If I'm honest, maybe. More than I thought I did.'

'I've got a group of kids every week who'd love to have a change from me. You could do it again if you wanted to.'

The noise he lets out was probably intended to be a laugh, but it's nothing like a laugh. 'No, I couldn't.'

In that moment, I would do anything to take the pain out of his voice. 'You could dress up. Kids love costumes. You could be a tiger reading *The Tiger Who Came to Tea*, or a bear reading *Winnie the Pooh*, or I bet they sell Gruffalo costumes, or...'

'No, thank you. I'm not a part of this world and I don't want to be. I'm fine with my life the way it is. And I'm too old for fairy tales of any kind.'

Try that without a wobble in your voice, matey. 'It's a sign of true adulthood when people are old enough to start believing in fairy tales again. When we're young, we're so keen to appear grown-up and reject anything that's deemed childish, and I think everyone goes through a full circle in life and comes back to a love of fairy tales when they're ready. As I've grown up, I find myself more and more drawn to those books of early childhood, those Disney-esque fairy tales that teach us valuable lessons and always have a happy ending.'

'Like where *The Little Mermaid* turns into seafoam and dies at the end? Or *The Little Match Girl* runs out of matches and freezes to death?'

'No. It's like *Peter Pan*. When we're children, all we want to do is grow up. When we're adults, we desperately search for that child-hood innocence again and wish we could go back to simpler times. One way of doing that is re-reading old favourite books. What was your favourite when you were little?'

'I have fond memories of *The Faraway Tree* series. My mum sitting on my bed and reading it to me. Begging her for one more chapter even though I was already half asleep and inevitably wouldn't hear much of it.' His voice has taken on a soft and nostalgic tone, and I'm convinced there'd be a wistful look on his face too, if I could only see it.

'I loved it too. I *still* can't walk past a big tree without knocking on the trunk to see if there's a Slippery-Slip inside or to look for Silky and Moon-Face, and if there's anything wrong with a tree, I always wonder if there are trolls mining in its roots.'

'The number one cause of all garden problems – trolls in the roots.'

I love that he makes me laugh just as much in person as he does from behind a hedge. It's a relief somehow, especially after the other night when I wondered if I'd pushed him too far and blown it for good. He's the same person, whether he's a voice only or whether he's actually here. I want to reach out and squeeze his hand. And mainly, I want him to stay longer. 'Do you want a cuppa?'

He shakes his head and points to his visor. Unlike the scarf, it's not something he can pull down a little bit. He's either got to leave it down or show his whole face to me.

'You could take it off.'

'No, I couldn't.'

'Yes, you could, Darcy. I don't now and never will care what you look like. Who you are is what's important.'

At first, I think my words might've struck a chord and he's thinking about it, but then he takes a step away and starts looking around the shop.

His eyes, I think, fall on the mini rose plants on either side of the counter. 'You know, a blonde woman came in today and bought two mini roses, and said she'd just seen the roses in your shop and had to get some for herself. Why do I think you're responsible for that?'

'They weren't red and white, were they?'

'Yes. How'd you know?'

'Alice in... never mind. That was Cleo, I think she might be my new friend.'

'You got someone to sign up already?' His voice is excited and I love how supportive he is about this. 'You didn't have to send her to me.'

'I didn't. She saw the roses and thought they were beautiful. All

I did was reassure her you're not as scary as you'd have people believe.'

For just one second, my words catch him off guard. I think he smiles or at least wants to smile, but then he shakes himself and walks away instead. He circles the children's section again, tidying the shelves up as he goes, putting wonky books back the right way and pushing them into rows as neat as the variety of heights, thicknesses, and sizes will allow.

I'm at the counter, supposedly trying to balance the end-of-day bookkeeping, but it's impossible to concentrate on anything with Darcy so near. A soft scent of aftershave follows him around, a giddy mix of wood and spice and fresh air. Not overpowering, but a gentle reminder that he's there. I hear his every soft footstep on my grey carpet, so hyperaware of his presence that it's like I'm in tune with his every breath.

'It's been so long since I was in a bookshop,' he says from somewhere between the shelves. 'I'd forgotten how special they are.'

That long-ago thing again. He talks often about things he used to enjoy, but it always sounds like he doesn't do them any more. I'm desperate to find out why – what changed him from being someone who taught creative writing and loved bookshops to being who he is today?

There's the unmistakeable sound of books being removed from shelves, flipped through, and then returned to their rightful positions, before he reappears from between the bookcases. 'Your shop is beautiful.'

It sounds so genuine that it makes my eyes sting again. He isn't the kind of person who says things just because someone else wants to hear it. He must mean it.

There are display tables filling the space in front of the counter and he wanders around them, straightening up piles of flyers for the book festival and neatening stacks of postcards that have been rifled through by customers and I haven't had a chance to tidy yet. Now he's in front of me, it's even more impossible to drag my eyes away.

'How's the interest in the festival been?'

'Good.' I sigh. 'Better than expected...'

He looks up from the modern-day retelling of *The Nutcracker* he was leafing through. 'Why does that sound like a bad thing?'

'Because more interest equals more people to disappoint.' I sigh again. 'Three authors have confirmed and I keep wanting to email them and make *sure*-sure that it's not a practical joke. Something is bound to go wrong. Things like this cost money I don't have and need expertise I don't have. In fact, the only thing I will have is many disappointed people when it fails.'

'Or...' He holds a finger up. 'An alternative point of view – it all works out, you show Mr Rowbotham who's boss and tell the council to shove it where the sun wouldn't dream of shining, and along the way, you gain many new customers, new friends, and even match up some friendship couples of your own.'

I go to protest but I look up at him, and somewhere behind that visor, he's looking at me, and the words die in my throat. '*You* still support the friendship dates after the other night?'

'That had nothing to do with the concept itself. That was me. It was a mistake to let anyone pretend I could be normal. And it's you. You make it easy to support anything you do because you love it so much.'

'Thank you,' I say, because I'm not sure how to fight the first part of that sentence. His continual support and unwavering faith in me is something that I haven't had in my life for a long time, and for once, I don't want to contradict him, I just want to believe him.

He's still wandering the shop and he does a double take when he looks into the window display and sees Mrs Potts there. 'So that's where you've been hiding. Hello, darling lady.'

Never mind Mrs Potts, *my* ovaries explode at that term of endearment.

She meows and gets up, *brrrrrip*ing and rubbing around the hand he's holding out to her. He crouches in front of her, inviting her to step into the cradle of his arms, and she rubs against him so hard that he nearly overbalances and then throws herself against his chest, rubbing at his chin as he stands up with her in his arms.

'Have you liberally coated yourself in Dreamies? Started using tins of cat food as deodorant?'

'No, but I'll bear that in mind for next time.' He carries on wandering the shop with Mrs Potts in his arms, talking softly to her like he's taking her on a tour of the bookshop, stopping to look at the watercolour prints of Belle and the Beast on the walls.

'This place reminds me of what it was like to love reading.' He's murmuring so quietly that I'm not sure if he's talking to me or himself. 'As a child, I'd peer into every wardrobe in the hopes of finding a door to Narnia, and look out for enchanted castles every time I walked through a forest. I remember begging my mum to leave a window open every night so Peter Pan's shadow could find its way in. I looked up at the top of every tall tree in case there was a magical land up there, and thoroughly investigated every rabbit hole in case it was an entrance to Wonderland. I was always the odd one out as a child, but I never felt that way, because of books. And now, so many kids must come in here and feel less alone because of you. This place is beautiful, Marnie. A real sanctuary for readers. Every inch of it *shines* with your love for books. People must step in and never want to leave.'

I get the feeling he's talking about himself, and if he didn't want to leave, that would be fine with me.

'Unfortunately most of them leave without buying anything.' I try to match his cheery tone, but it's a sad fact of life – a vast majority of my customers come in to browse but leave empty-handed.

'Let me guess, they come in to find things they want to order on Amazon?'

'How'd you know?'

'Because the world is not as it used to be. While that's a good thing in some ways, a lot of the joy from when we were children has been replaced, but a place like this stands still in time. You can't make books modern. All right, the words inside them can be different, the language has changed, but children reading in centuries gone by read exactly the same way as we do today. No tablet or phone with all-singing all-dancing updates, just good old-fashioned paper and words. That should be celebrated. I'm sorry I didn't know that before. I didn't realise how special you...' He falters. '...I mean, this place is. I wouldn't have...'

He doesn't continue the sentence and carries on wandering, cradling Mrs Potts in one arm, the other holding her steady and scritching her ears while he takes in every detail of A Tale As Old As Time.

'Pay-it-forward board.' He reads aloud as he stands in front of the honeycomb-shaped board on the wall across from the counter and reads one of the book-shaped tags. 'What's a pay-it-forward board?'

I give him a brief explanation of the idea behind it. 'People pay extra to put money on a tag, and the tags can then be used as payment for anyone who can't afford a book but needs one.'

'Seriously?' He turns to face me, and I can once again imagine a soft look on a face I can't imagine at all.

'Yeah. You see it in coffee shops and places like that, so I thought why not with books too. Not everyone can afford to walk around a bookshop and buy everything they want. If parents are struggling to put food on the table and pay the bills, buying books for their child is the last thing on their mind, and libraries are few and far between now. No one should be deprived of a book to escape into.'

He's quiet. Maybe I've hypnotised him because he's absent-mindedly stroking Mrs Potts, looking in my direction, and I think there'd be an entranced look on his face.

Eventually he shakes his head and I get the feeling he's blinking rapidly behind his visor. 'That's amazingly lovely. I like your faith in people. The idea that anyone is generous enough to help out those less fortunate than themselves. To give something away with no recognition and for nothing in return. Does it get much use?'

I grimace. 'It's gone a bit wrong. No one's used it for ages. There's a sign on either end of the counter pointing it out, but people ignore it. Those two tags are ones I put up. Rick thinks it would only ever be used by greedy scammers who want something for free anyway.'

'Rick's a cynical twit who steals flowers,' he says with a shrug.

I can't help laughing. 'You're not wrong there. I also feel like I'm talking to the most cynical bloke on this side of the River Wye, and yet somehow, *you* like the idea?'

'The world would be a better place if more people did things like this.'

'I was thinking of taking it down. It's become nothing more than a cobweb holder. The tag idea was intended to bring people together, but lately the only thing it's done is destroy what little faith in fellow humans I ever had.'

'Don't say that. You're a shining light in a dark world. If you're giving up on humanity, there is no hope for the rest of us.'

I'm not sure I've heard him correctly. A shining light? Me? I'm the dullest, most boring person in the universe, ever. I've barely existed in the past couple of years and A Tale As Old As Time has suffered because of my grief. The only thing about me that shines is my oily hair if I've got caught up in a book and forgotten to wash it. I want to ask him to clarify that remark, but he comes towards the counter and I'm not brave enough to push it. I most likely misheard, but if I didn't, I want to keep that sentence just for me and hold onto it, always.

He puts Mrs Potts down on the counter. Mrs Potts isn't allowed on the counter and immediately walks across the friendship questionnaire and leaves cat hair all over it. I lift her down onto the floor and shove a packet of Dreamies at Darcy.

I'm not even pretending to work now. I *can't* take my eyes off him and it's pointless to even try. There's something about him that's utterly magnetic, and I watch as he gets down on his knees to feed her a few of the turkey-flavoured treats and there's that familiar groan of discomfort as he stands back up.

'Hi.' He takes a step back in surprise when he realises I'm staring at him.

'Hi.' Just having him here makes me smile. There's something about his presence that's reassuring. I feel less alone than I have in months, like I could turn to Darcy with any problem and he'd have a practical solution and words of comfort or advice.

'I like...' He takes that step back towards the counter, seeming to lose the thread of the sentence.

We're staring at each other. He's so close that I could reach out and touch him and I'm a little bit floored by how much I *want* to touch him. I wish I could bring my hands up and push that hooded visor up millimetre by millimetre, hold him against me, trace my hands over his face and feel every little imperfection he's hiding. I want to tell him he's beautiful because no one who speaks the way he does could ever be anything but.

I want to kiss him. The thought appears suddenly, but once it's there, it's like a flashing neon sign and I'm certain he can hear the electronical buzzing inside my head. My attraction to him has been gradually growing over the weeks but I've always dismissed it. You can't *like* a man you've never even seen, but standing here, face to visor in front of each other, I realise you can *very much* like someone you've never seen.

Somehow he's gone from standing to leaning on his elbows on the counter, and if I reached out, I could tangle my hand in the front of his suit and haul him closer, drag his mouth to mine and smash my lips against his... visor. And the prospect of kissing *that* isn't particularly attractive, but there's something about the man underneath...

He's close enough that I can hear the way his breathing has sped up, and he must be able to see the sweat prickling my forehead. I can sense his eyes on me, and it's a flutter I haven't felt for a long time and didn't think I'd ever feel again. Butterflies are flittering around inside me. He's so near and yet his suit is like a wall between us. Even though it's just material, it seems wider than the hedge that separated us at first, but now, right now, it also feels like it would melt away under my fingertips with just one touch. We're so close. Breaths away. My forehead is millimetres from resting against his. He lets out a happy-sounding sigh. My tongue wets my lips and my fingers reach out for him, to touch his face, stroke away his disguise, prove once and for all that he's not—

'Apples!' He bolts upright and takes such a large step back that he stumbles over Mrs Potts and grabs a display table to stay upright, sending a snowstorm of flyers cascading to the floor. At first I think it's some kind of sanitised swear word, but then he clarifies. 'Do you like apples?'

I feel like I'm wading through cotton wool as I try to process what just happened. 'Apples?'

'You know, the fruit? Round, green, tastes of apple? Best known for growing on trees and keeping the doctor away when consumed on a daily basis?'

'As random questions go...' I say with a bewildered shrug, trying to work out where this shift in conversation is going.

'I've got an influx on my trees at the castle. I'll get you some apples!' He nearly falls over his own boots as he dashes for the front door, clattering headfirst into it because it's locked and fumbling with the key until it lets him out, and I watch it swing shut in his wake.

We nearly kissed. Did we nearly kiss? *Can* you kiss a man whose face you can't see? Can you *want* to kiss someone when you've never seen them? Every time I've had a crush on someone, it's always been about looks. There's a quote by Victor Hugo about the power of a glance. *Few people dare now to say that two beings have fallen in love because they have looked at each other, yet it is in this way that love begins, and in this way only.* It's uncomfortably accurate, no matter how much we claim not to be superficial.

'Apples,' I mutter as I leave the sanctuary of the counter and crouch down to collect up the flyers, and Mrs Potts sits watching the door, waiting for Darcy to come back.

'Cats are so lucky not to have these problems,' I tell Mrs Potts, who *really* doesn't appreciate how uncomplicated her feline life is.

After I've paced the floor for ten minutes, tidying display tables that were already tidy, Darcy reappears with a gentle knock and lets himself in, carrying a bucket in one hand.

He's still wearing the Hazmat suit, but he's recovered his composure better than I have. I'm still breathing hard and I run a hand through my short hair self-consciously because seeing him has made my legs go shaky again, surprised that he came back after that... whatever that was.

'Sorry about...' He waves one hand towards the door like that single gesture encompasses everything neither of us can put into words. 'It's been a long time since I was amongst books. The new-book smell overwhelmed my brain and I forgot myself for a moment there. Won't happen again.'

'At least we can both agree on how deliciously good new books smell.' I paste on a smile. Am I glad or disappointed? He's being a mature, sensible adult. I cannot kiss Darcy. If that had gone any further, would he have taken off his disguise? Or would I have ended up with my lips smushed against the plastic visor? Either way, it's a good thing we didn't get to find out. 'That is a *lot* of apples.'

'The trees have outdone themselves this year.' He hefts the bucket onto the counter. 'They're a quintessentially autumn fruit and I know how much you like all things autumn.'

'I do.' I'm smiling at him again and it should probably be awkward, but it isn't, and I wish I could tell if he was smiling back because it's really disconcerting not to know.

Mrs Potts rubs around his legs, and he bends down to stroke her again, and I *love* how good he is to my cat.

He stands back upright and glances in the direction of the door again. 'Before I go, I wanted to do something while I'm here.'

'What's that?'

I can *hear* the grin in his voice. 'Buy a book.'

'Any specific book?'

'Yes.' With that, he strides off into the shelves, and I listen for the sound of his footsteps as he heads towards what I'm fairly sure is the modern-day fairy-tales section.

It isn't long before he re-emerges with *Once Upon Another Time* and puts it on the counter without a word.

'Seriously?' I raise an eyebrow.

'I thought I'd give it another go. After everything you've said about it, I thought... maybe I'd like to see what *you* see in it.'

His voice is stuttery and he sounds nervous, but I don't think

I've ever smiled so widely that there's a genuine possibility my face would split into two halves before. Every time I try to stop, my smile gets wider. 'U.N.Known wins over everybody in the end. You don't have to buy this. I've tried to give it to you once.' I push the book towards him and he puts a hand on it to stop it moving and whisks a ten-pound note out of his pocket, holding it out to me between two glove-hidden fingers.

It's not a fight I'm going to win, so I take the note and put it in the till. I pack the book in one of our paper bags and pop a free bookmark in with it and hold it out to him, and his fingers brush against mine as he takes it, and even with his gloves between us, there's still a spark that sends the butterflies fluttering around inside me.

'When I leave my Tripadvisor review, you'll be getting five stars for service with a smile.' He takes the bag with what would definitely be a sarcastic grin.

I can't *stop* smiling when he's around, that's the problem. And he'd better be joking about the Tripadvisor thing.

While I'm still lost in thought, he pulls a hand out of his pocket and holds out a wad of notes to me.

'What's this?'

'Ten tags on your pay-it-forward board, please. A tenner each.'

'You can't be serious. That's a hundred quid.'

He moves the hand holding the money closer to me, but I'm totally lost for words. 'Darcy...'

'Take it.' He gives a decisive nod.

'That's incredibly generous.' My fingers touch his hand as I take the notes, ding the till open and put them in, and then crouch down to get ten book-shaped cardboard tags from underneath the counter.

'Once upon a time, I was a book-loving kid who couldn't afford to buy books. The library was my second home. So many libraries are gone now. It's really special that you do this. A lifeline for someone who needs a book to escape into. The people who can't afford it are probably the ones who need the escapism the most. Let me know when those are gone.'

How can he be serious? When customers have put tags on that board before, it's been with a fair bit of pushing on my part, and Darcy comes in and adds ten without a second thought.

He's either a millionaire or he's simply the loveliest man in the world, and I don't think he's a millionaire.

'Only if you write them.'

'Oh, no, no, no, no, no.' He pushes himself up off the counter and steps quickly away, and while I'm usually clumsy and grace-less, tonight I have cat-like reflexes as my hand darts out and catches hold of his. My fingers curl tightly around his palm, holding him in place.

For just a second, the world stops turning. Everything outside of our joined hands fades away, and there is nothing but my fingers curled around his glove. I didn't realise I was going to touch him until my hand was holding his, stopping him from refusing such a simple request.

I intend to persuade him, but my mouth is suddenly dry and the feeling of his hand in mine has made me forget what we were talking about. Nothing seems to matter apart from that touch.

Instead of the usual buzz and hum of working on a busy street, everything is silent and calm, and while it could be put down to the fact it's after closing time and it's dark outside, I think it's more to do with Darcy's hand soothing some restless part of me, and I wish the gloves away so hard that surely a fairy godmother is going to pop up and magic them out of existence at any moment.

His covered head has dipped towards our hands and he swal-lows *hard*. He's so close that I can see the rise and fall of his chest and hear every shallow breath.

Without letting go, I try to regain some composure. 'You have the most beautiful handwriting I've ever seen.' I give his hand a squeeze, and his other hand curls around the counter edge as if it's made his knees buckle. 'Leave some little part of you in the shop. Your handwriting belongs in a fairy tale; it will make each one even more special. Please.'

His fingers squeeze mine and he gives one nod, which seems like it took a lot of effort, and his fingers flex, like he's realised we're cutting off the circulation in each other's hands, and I blink back to awareness to find Mrs Potts has returned to her window seat and is washing her paws in her basket. Darcy and I have clearly been staring at each other long enough for her to give up hope of any more Dreamies, and she's a very tenacious cat.

'I'm sorry, I shouldn't have...' My eyes are on our joined hands and so are his. I go to pull my hand away, and his fingers tighten as though he wants to hold on. I squeeze his hand back and look up at his visor, hoping that somehow I'm looking into his eyes, and that's enough to make him shake himself and yank his hand away sharply.

I take a fortifying breath and paste on a smile. 'So just write that it's worth ten pounds, and you can specify if it's for a certain book or a certain genre or...'

'Anything they choose? I have no right to dictate which books should bring people joy.'

Quite a change from the guy who threw *Once Upon Another Time* back over my hedge a few weeks ago. I can't get rid of my smile. For someone who says he's a non-reader, he's the biggest booklover I've ever met, and the bar for booklovers is set pretty high in a bookshop. 'I agree, but some donators have been quite pernickety about it and only want to put up a tag for a book they approve of.'

His scoff says it all and I push a marker pen towards him.

He looks between me, the tags on the counter, and his own right hand. It's like he's at war with himself. His gloves are thick leather and I doubt he could hold a pen with them on. And it hits me again. If it's this much of a big deal for him to take a glove off, he's never going to take anything more off, is he? Is he ever, *ever* going to trust me enough to look at me without a barrier between us?

Right now, it doesn't seem like it.

Eventually he sighs and removes the glove finger by finger, revealing a right hand that's a mass of scars.

Although he immediately pulls his sleeve down as far as it will go, he's not quick enough for me to miss it. His hand looks gnarled with silvery scars. Raised lines and marks of discolouration that shouldn't be there, the healed remainders of some kind of injury, and when his fingers pick up the pen, they're bent, like they've been broken and healed not-quite-straight.

There's a tremor going through them and I realise how self-conscious he is – because of me. I turn away and busy myself by picking cat hair off the friendship form on the counter, but I'm transfixed by the way his fingers move. His handwriting is truly beautiful, each word is so neatly printed that it could have been done by a machine and each capital letter has swirls and flour-ishes like twirling vines, and it is *just* his handwriting, not some complicated calligraphy with a fancy pen, just him and a Sharpie.

Is it weird to be sexually attracted to someone's handwriting?

The second Darcy has written the last tag, he yanks the glove back on. I'm trying not to watch him, but he's *right there*, in front of me; his aftershave is all around; the feel of his hand is still in mine, as if he's taken over all five of my senses.

I hand him a box of drawing pins and he gathers the tags and takes them to the honeycomb-shaped corkboard and pins them up carefully, painstakingly arranging them in the most eye-catching style.

I don't mention his scarred hand. He knows I noticed it, and if he wanted to explain then he would have, but I can't help thinking about it. What had to have happened to someone to give them that kind of injury? By revealing his hand, has he inadvertently let me in on the 'something' that happened to him?

'Well, that was unexpectedly fun.' He returns the drawing pins and picks up the bag with *Once Upon Another Time* inside it. 'Thank you for having me.'

I can't find the courage to say I can't remember the last time I had such an enjoyable evening, so instead I say, 'Come again sometime. You can keep the suit on.'

He tips an imaginary hat in my direction as he heads towards the door, stopping to say goodbye to Mrs Potts on the way. With his hand on the door handle, he stops and turns back. 'Marnie... thank you for making me feel normal.'

With that, he's gone, but I keep looking at the empty doorway for a long time afterwards. That's the thing, isn't it? *He* makes *me* feel normal, like I'm not alone in the world, like there's someone out there who understands what it's like to feel lonely, and I understand his desire to hide away and escape people's gazes and judgement too.

I can still feel the imprint of his hand in mine, and I can't help but wonder how long it's been since Darcy let someone get close enough to hold his hand, and why it's so special that he let me. He could have pulled away... but he didn't.

And that has to mean something.

11

It turns out that a lot of people want new friends. I never realised my idea would hit such a nerve, or that I wasn't the only adult who found it hard to meet people with the intention of friendship. I posted my idea about friendship dates on Ever After Street's social media, and within a couple of hours, my inbox was inundated with requests to be matched up with potential new friends, and now I'm running around like a headless chicken trying to find its head blindfolded.

After a few conversations with Darcy this week, we decided the best thing to do was to put the friendship form online for locals to fill in and then invite everyone to a friendship evening in the bookshop. Display tables have been cleared of books, covered with pretty tablecloths, and I've ransacked the nearest supermarket for a selection of party food. Ali is manning a tea, coffee, and hot chocolate station, and we're having an evening of no-pressure, easy-going bookish chat to see if anyone hits it off naturally, and I'm going through the forms, trying to see if anyone's favourite book choices suggest they'd have something more in common, and any matches are being sent on a friendship date in Darcy's garden.

Cleo's here, supposedly for her friendship date with me, but I haven't had a chance to breathe yet and she's running around like the decapitated chicken's head trying to find its body, having unwittingly taken on the job of co-organiser and started spotting potential friendship matches right alongside me.

Darcy has taught me how to use a chainsaw so my hedge is neatly cut now, apart from the uneven chunks where I accidentally scalped parts of it, but at least there's a wide walkway so I'm no longer afraid of customers being attacked by delinquent foliage if they dare to set foot outside.

Six sets of tables and chairs are set up next door, our gates are open, and matched couples are being directed out of my garden and into his, where there's tea and a buffet provided by Lilith, and Darcy's nowhere to be seen. I'm hoping he's at least watching from a window or something. I was hoping he'd find a way to get more involved, but so far his only involvement has been setting up the date area in his garden and babysitting Mrs Potts for the evening because she wouldn't be happy with this number of extra people in *her* bookshop.

'Look, those two are hitting it off.' Cleo points to Mickey from The Mermaid's Treasure Trove and Lissa from the Colours of the Wind museum.

'Those two are already best friends, but good spotting. Look, what do you think of these two?' I point out a man and a woman whose forms are in front of me. 'She put Rachel Joyce as her favourite author, and he said *Away with the Penguins* is the favourite book he's read this year. I think there's some crossover between those authors... Maybe those two would have a lot of book recommendations to share.'

'And these two guys both put Adam Kay as their favourite

author.' Cleo points to two men, both standing awkwardly in different places, sipping their respective mugs, and both looking like they're having second thoughts about coming tonight.

'And look, these two both say they like romance novels, which you don't often hear from a guy.' Cleo and I are sliding forms around like *Britain's Got Talent* judges trying to decide on finalists, and she points out the man in question and, on the other side of the shop, a woman who wrote a comment on her form about loving romance novels for the belief in a happy ending. There's something about them that seems like a good match, and I meet Cleo's eyes and know she's thinking exactly the same.

I didn't expect to be doing this with anyone, but it feels nice. I nudge my arm into hers. 'This is fun.'

'We make a good team.'

For the first time, I feel like I'm an integral part of something important. Me, Cleo, and... I glance towards the wall that separates my shop from The Beast's Enchanted Rose Garden. There's just one part missing. None of this would be happening without Darcy and it doesn't feel right that he isn't here.

Cleo goes to collect the two Adam Kay men, and I take the Rachel Joyce woman over to the *Away with the Penguins* man and introduce them. After a quick chat with me as intermediary, I learn that he's Italian and has only just moved here, and she's a single mother and was living in Manchester but recently came back here to raise her daughter close to her parents.

'My bad grasp of the language makes me avoid conversations usually. I am too scared for romantic dates,' the man says, 'but a friendship date is less intimidating.'

'Exactly,' the woman agrees. 'I'm not ready to date again after my divorce, but there's never a bad time to make friends.'

'And bookish friends are the best kind of friends,' I say,

directing them through the children's section to the back door and round to Darcy's.

The man goes first, and as she passes me, the woman fans a hand in front of her face and whispers, 'The bookish gods of gorgeous men are smiling upon me tonight.'

'We should do a singles night next.' Cleo bounces up, nodding towards the two grumpy-looking men who are now deep in conversation and looking much less grumpy than before.

'I was just thinking that.' I watch the retreating backs of the Italian man and Manchester woman. 'If friends can connect over books, why can't people connect romantically over them too?'

She waggles her eyebrows as we send the two guys on their way round to Darcy's garden too, and then goes to introduce the two romance lovers.

The matches just keep coming, to the point where the six tables and chairs aren't enough, it's too late to get any more, and we've got a waiting list of couples to go on a proper platonic date round there. Cleo's not wrong that the bookshop setting is conducive to getting people chatting too, and a lot of people who haven't been matched via forms have started talking to each other over books, and broken off into couples or small groups to have a natter. A Tale As Old As Time is filled with chatter and laughter, and although tonight wasn't about selling books, people keep coming to the counter with books they've found, and I've done better business in this one evening than the rest of the week put together.

There's an ease that we're all in the same boat. A sense of camaraderie. Everyone here tonight has come because they would like to meet new friends and each one of us knows that's not as simple as it sounds.

People are chatting, laughing, leafing through books to share favourite paragraphs or illustrations with other once-were-strangers. People are swapping numbers. Someone's set up a WhatsApp group and is inviting everyone to join. Someone else has suggested that we could start a monthly book club, and I've already been asked twice if this will be a regular thing. People have bought tickets to the upcoming festival and are chattering about it enthusiastically. It's making my cold, jaded heart feel alive again.

I had given up on ever finding people like me. Accepted that I would always be on the edges of society, never really fitting in, but as I stand by the counter, that sense of fitting in fills me again, and I look around, warmed by the number of people who have thanked me for doing this platonic singles night.

This is what we always wanted A Tale As Old As Time to be – a hub that's about so much more than just selling books, a place where people can find real connections, whether with fictional characters or with other people, and for a moment, it feels like my mum is standing here beside me.

I record a video, spinning my phone in a 360-degree turn of the shop so I can send it to Mr Rowbotham and the Herefordshire council as proof that a *Beauty and the Beast*-themed bookshop has something to offer Ever After Street and deserves its place here.

'I never want to forget this night either.' Cleo appears next to me having just returned from seeing off one friendship couple who are going on for a drink elsewhere, and sent another two women on their way to a friendship date with copies of Tilly Tennant books clutched in their hands. 'It's been so much fun.'

'It's kind of evidence.' Apart from Darcy, I haven't told anyone, but I can't hide it any longer as I tell Cleo about Mr Rowbotham's letter and the council's threat.

'Oh my gosh, no. A Tale As Old As Time is my favourite shop in the world. They can't shut it down. It'd be like shutting down a piece of my heart.'

'Mine too.' I hadn't intended to cry tonight, but her kind words make my eyes threaten to fill up.

'We'll save it. You, me, and...' She gives me a hug and glances towards the wall behind me like she can see the flower shop beyond. 'Him. Some weird guy none of us have ever seen.'

'He's just...' I clutch at straws for a word to describe Darcy. It's not weirdness, it's... lack of confidence. Lack of trust in other people and a certainty that he will be judged and disliked based on what he looks like. '...a little unconventional.'

'That's okay, all the best people are.'

The *Alice in Wonderland* quote puts a smile back on my face, and I try not to think about how much I wish Darcy was here to share the joy of this night.

It's 8 p.m. that night when Cleo's downstairs, seeing off the last of our guests with a promise of hosting another friendship evening next month, despite the fact I have no idea if we'll even *be* here by this time in November. After a full day of work, then setting up, then hosting the friendship dates, matching couples, and keeping an eye on everything, I've been on the go since breakfast. My feet are killing me, my back started protesting by lunchtime and hasn't quietened down since, and all I want to do is catch up on the sleep I didn't get last night for worrying about today's event. But tomorrow is a working day, the shop needs to be returned to normal, eleventy billion plates and cups need to be washed up and returned to the castle where Darcy borrowed them from, and Cleo's helped more than enough already, I can't expect her to help with clean-up too. It feels like I'm going to be here until 2 a.m. as I clatter the first lot of tableware into the sink upstairs and turn on the hot water.

There's a knock on the other side of the wall.

'Darcy?' I look up in surprise.

'Successful night, by the looks of it?' His voice is muffled through the brickwork. I've always known I could hear him through the wall, but it's the first time we've tried talking through it.

'I think so. Everyone seemed really happy. I've been added to chat groups, exchanged more phone numbers than I know what to do with, and inadvertently volunteered to start a book club *and* do this again sometime. Thanks for all your help.'

'We've got a problem on this side, Marnie.'

My stomach sinks. I'm too tired to deal with any problems. He hears my groan of despair before I have a chance to formulate a response.

'There's one date left.'

Oh, hell's bells. There's someone still over there? How the heck did we miss that? I thought we'd cleared out any stragglers. I swear out loud at the thought of having to traipse all the way down the stairs and over to Darcy's again. 'I'll be round to clear them out now.'

I don't expect his response to be laughter. 'I don't mean that. I mean there's a table set up for one friendship couple who haven't had their date yet.'

'Oh, come on, don't tell me I've missed someone.' I wrack my brains. The forms were a lot to keep on top of, but I thought I had a better grasp on them than that. There can't still be someone down there waiting, can there?

'You and Cleo, you flipping idiot!'

I've never been called an idiot with such affection before and it makes me laugh. 'I can't, Darcy. I've got to clean—'

'You two come through the back and unlock your front door on the way so Mrs Potts and I can come in and clean up in there.'

'Don't be silly, this is—'

'It's not optional. I didn't want to get involved with the people, but the one thing I can do is clean up, as long as I'm left alone. So get Cleo and make the most of the last date of the night. There's tea that isn't going to stay hot for long if you don't hurry up.'

Tears prickle my eyes and there's a lump in my throat. I've *never* met anyone kinder or more thoughtful than this man. I put my hand on the wall, palm flat against the painted plasterwork, wishing he could feel it. 'Thank you.'

I don't want to leave cleaning up to Darcy, but the thought of sitting down with a hot cup of tea makes me want to cry with longing, and I go downstairs, find Cleo where she's rubbing carpet cleaner into a coffee stain on the bookshop carpet, and drag her through the back door.

Entering Darcy's garden tonight *is* like walking into Wonderland without all that pesky falling through rabbit holes stuff. It's what I imagine the Beast's rose garden must've been like. Inside the gate, he's put up a topiary archway with pink roses woven through it and fairy lights wrapped around it. There's a neat path leading up the garden alongside the hedge, to a set of two wide steps up to a closed back door and a patio area where a gazebo has been set up for the buffet. The rest of the garden has grass that's so neatly cut, it looks like it could've been done with scissors, and the empty chairs and tables are now in tidy stacks, apart from one, which has got a steaming teapot and dainty china cups on it, and a large serving plate piled high with pastries and cakes. He must have raided the buffet before it was ransacked and put aside the best for us.

Also on the table are two hand-cut roses in a vase filled with twinkling fairy lights. The gazebo is strung with fairy lights too, and unlike my haphazard branch-fest, his hedge is cut in a neat box shape and has got warm-white fairy lights threaded throughout it that he's surely only put there for tonight. Around the edge of the grass is a gravel path lined with vintage-looking stone planters filled with orange and rust-coloured autumn roses. No wonder he spends so much time out here. If my garden looked like this, I'd probably be fonder of the outdoors too.

The scent of roses is strong in the air. It's a scent that wafts over the hedge occasionally, not just of one rose, but a blissful concurrence of the scent of each rose, and it's a heady floral mixture that could be bottled and sold as the most elegant perfume.

'How can someone who calls himself a beast be hiding such a beautiful garden?' Cleo pulls out her chair and sits down to pick up the teapot while I set the teacups and saucers out. 'Aren't you ever tempted to try to catch him? See what he's hiding?'

The image of his bent fingers and scarred hand flashes in my head, and I let my fingertips run along one of the beautiful roses in the vase. It's a white rose with red-edged petals, such a contrast that it would make anyone stop and stare. 'No. Because it's about more than what he looks like.'

I'm not even sure it *is* about what he looks like. He keeps cutting off that 'deserves' word, the one I can't stop thinking about, and I keep wondering if this is less about Darcy being accepted and more about Darcy feeling like he doesn't *deserve* to be accepted, for whatever reason. 'He's been an absolute rock since this started. He makes me feel like I've got someone battling alongside me, and *that* is what makes a relationship. Too much emphasis is placed on looks these days. "Handsome" is considered a top-tier compliment. If we like someone, is handsome really the nicest thing we can say about them? Do they not have other personality traits apart from being nice-looking? Aren't they kind? Funny? Do they get us in a way that no one else does? Deep? Intelligent? Caring? Handsome is the least important thing someone can be, but the world makes it seem like the *most*.

Anyone who doesn't fit a traditional mould is left feeling like an outsider.'

'If anyone's going to help Darcy with that, it's you.'

We both take a sip of our steaming hot tea, which goes some way towards negating the chill in the late-October air and I pull apart a croissant while she puts a whole cake pop into her mouth.

'Maybe I could persuade him to come to the book festival,' I say around a mouthful of flaky croissant. 'If he'd wear some kind of costume or something. I could do with a helping hand there, and he's been involved since the beginning.'

'I could help. What do you need?'

'Really? You don't have to. You've done more than enough tonight.'

'I'd love to. I love books and I love this place. Tonight was really fun and I love the company. Bookish people are awesome.' She lifts her teacup to toast against mine, and I grin because I think exactly the same. Bookish people are the best people, and it's been great to spend time with her. We're getting on as well as I always thought we would. 'I'm good at crafts. I love making stuff. If you have any old books, I'd be happy to host some kind of work-shop on reusing them. I could do a demonstration and then show other people how to make something. There are these really easy book page roses...'

'Seriously? That would be wonderful.'

Cleo goes over all the things she knows how to make with book pages, getting excited at the prospect of hosting a bookish craft class, and I can't help thinking about how lucky I am. A few weeks ago I felt totally alone in the world, and now I've made two amazing friends who are both happy to do *anything* to help me and my shop, and everyone from Ever After Street came tonight, even though I've done nothing but push them away in recent months, and their support made me feel like I belong here.

* * *

It's been a couple of days since I last emailed U.N.Known a chatty email about books. He hasn't responded, but there's something about this night that I want to share with him. *Once Upon Another Time* is a lot about friendships and the people who come and go from our lives, and I think he's someone who would appreciate this idea.

When I get home that night, there's one more thing I have to do before I fall into bed.

> Hello again. I know you probably wish I'd leave you 'alown', but I can't give up that easily. *Once Upon Another Time* is such a special book, and I wanted to share a bit about Ever After Street and why it's so special too.

I tell him about this being a place where children can go to believe their favourite fairy tales are real, and then start typing about the friendship dates tonight and attach a few of the pictures I took, wanting to show the pure joy on customers' faces.

> There's so much we can do with this, but my shop is in real danger of being closed down. So much of A Tale As Old As Time has revolved around *Once Upon Another Time*, and in a weird circle-of-life way, you seem like the only person I can turn to. Friendship and books go together like tea and biscuits. Reading is like going on a date in a way. You spend endless nights on dates with books, learning their story and deciding if they're a perfect match for you.

Although my goal is to get him to agree to appear at the book festival, this is just a conversational email to try to make him

understand *why* my little bookshop on Ever After Street means so
much to me and why I keep emailing him when he probably
wishes I'd stop.

He responds almost instantly.

And books always get you into bed on the first date…

That falls flat if you don't read in bed.

Does it come across as sleazy to say, 'At least you're guaran-
teed a happy ending?'

Honestly? Sleazy.

I add a laughing emoji so he knows I'm joking.

A lesser-known member of the seven dwarves, left out of the
Disney movie for obvious reasons.

I laugh out loud, waking up Mrs Potts. This guy is so uninten-
tionally hilarious and there's something about him that puts me at
ease. I stare at my inbox for a few more minutes, but it doesn't
seem like he's going to reply again.

Please give us a chance. I know you're anonymous, but you
wouldn't have to give away your real name. We could put things
in place to make you more comfortable, like a ban on taking
pictures, and a screen or something to shield you from view.
You're not the only one who wants to hide away on Ever After
Street, and everyone's very accommodating of that. I have a
neighbour who stays hidden and he came over in a Hazmat suit
the other day – maybe something like that could work for you

too. A costume, maybe? On the Sunday evening, we're holding a costume ball where everyone is invited to come dressed as their favourite literary characters. You wouldn't look out of place and no one would ever need to know your true identity. A world exclusive Q&A with you would make this festival unbelievably special. It could be the difference between being the first of many opportunities to spread bookish joy or the last days of a bookshop existing on Ever After Street.

I hit send and sit back, not expecting another reply until my email pings again.

I'll give it some thought.

I victory-punch the air. It might not be a glowing agreement, but it's more than I ever expected to wheedle out of him after those first one-line emails, and it lets me settle down to sleep with a smile on my face, and it's all because of one man. Not the unknown one on the end of an email, but the one who gave me the confidence to do this – the unseen one who I imagine every time I close my eyes.

12

_____

It's just after five a few nights later, and I'm upstairs in the kitchen making two cups of tea because Darcy is about to come over and neaten up my badly chainsawed hedge when there's a commotion outside. I hurry over to the window that looks out onto the back garden, and see Rick huffing and puffing his way in the gate, his arms full with a folded-up table, chairs, and a picnic basket.

'This is private property.' I march down the stairs and stand on the doorstep, glaring at the man who's invited himself in and is now struggling up the path under the weight of folding garden furniture. 'What do you think you're doing?'

'Nice to see you too, Marn.' He flashes me a smile so dazzling that it suggests he's recently had his veneers re-whitened. He's found his way to the centre of the garden, put down his picnic basket, thrown the folded-up chairs against the hedge, and is now unfolding the tiny wooden table he's brought with him.

'What are you doing?' I repeat.

'I've heard this little shop had such a thing as friendships dates, but I missed the chance, but better late than never, so I've come for *my* friendship date.' His eyes run up and down my body, making me feel objectified. 'Friendship and maybe more, eh?'

'Friendship dates can only be provided if you've filled in the questionnaire and been matched with a potential bookish friend. As someone who doesn't read, I can't imagine it would suit you very well.'

He clicks the table legs into place and goes to retrieve the chairs. 'I do have one specific friend in mind. Maybe you know her? She likes... um...' He has to stop and think about what I like. 'Books! She likes books. And... dogs?'

'Cats!' I suppose I should be grateful he got the books bit right.

'Yes, yes, it was one of those two, and she's a big fan of...' His face contorts as he tries to think of it. '...Cinderella?'

'My shop is called A Tale As Old As Time and you think Cinderella is what it's named after?'

'Ahh, I knew I'd got it right.'

I roll my eyes and don't bother dignifying his comment with a response.

He unfolds both chairs and sets them opposite each other at the tiny table. 'Your dinner awaits, madame.'

'I'm not hungry and you're not welcome.' My stomach betrays me with a loud growl of hunger. I'm starving but was saving myself for the tea and biscuits I was about to have with Darcy. 'We've broken up, Rick, why are you doing this?'

'Well, you like Cinderella, and she had to go to balls and stuff to meet Prince Charming, didn't she? I thought I'd save you the trouble and Prince Charming could come to Cinderella.' He opens the picnic basket and starts whisking things out of it. He lays the table with two plates, a selection of forks and knives, and two fluted wine glasses, then he gets out a covered salad bowl and places it in the middle of the table, followed by a fancy-looking covered stand. When he removes the cloche with a flourish, I look in horror at the contents, which would've been better off staying hidden.

'For madame, the finest *escargots au vin blanc de, er, aphrodisiac* and for monsieur, *le enjoyment de la aphrodisiac* later.' He says it in what is probably supposed to be a seductive accent.

I fold my arms. 'I'm vegetarian.'

'Oh, well, they're snails. They eat plants, they're practically plants themselves, aren't they?'

'Not quite how it works, Rick.'

He looks decidedly put-out. 'You need to tell people about these whims of yours, Marn. How else am I supposed to know?'

'I've been a vegetarian for over ten years! We dated for one of those years. You cooked for me often. You knew.'

'Ten years?' He claps his hands together. 'Well, you're long overdue a night off then.'

'Again, not quite how it works, Rick.'

He makes a sound of annoyance like it's somehow my fault. 'Well, there's a nice Parisian salad for you to enjoy.'

'Salad? Urgh. Who the heck brings a salad to a romantic meal?' If he knew me at all, he'd know there are a lot more Parisian food groups that I'd have been more impressed with, like croissants or patisserie.

'Never mind, you'll enjoy this.' He bends down to the picnic basket again and returns with a bottle of posh wine, which he shows off like a prize on a gameshow. 'Only the finest for my beloved. Imported from *Par-ee*. Not cheap.'

'I don't want wine, Rick! It's five o'clock at the end of a long day. I want to...' Spend time with Darcy. '...go home and put my feet up with a big mug of tea,' I say instead, because Rick knowing anything about Darcy will only lead to trouble.

'What could be more comforting than salad and wine?' He pulls out the chair and bows. '*Vous êtes...* um... *chaise*, madame.'

Even I know enough French to know he just called me a chair rather than invited me to sit in one. 'No, thank you. I'm not sitting down with you.'

'Your mum would've thought this was really romantic. She loved this garden, didn't she?' He's deliberately baiting me as he sits down, uncorks the wine and fills up both glasses and then piles salad onto his plate.

He's got another thing coming if he thinks bringing up my mum will get him the reaction he wants. 'Rick, this is not okay. You cannot just invite yourself to dinner on someone else's property. Please leave.'

'I didn't invite myself to dinner – I invited you. It's not my fault if you're going to be a stick-in-the-mud. I'm here for my friendship date with my pre-chosen *friend*.' He waggles both eyebrows. 'What's your problem, eh? Do I need to be a customer to participate in your friendship dates or something? Go and get me one of those silly books so I can buy it off you and then we can enjoy ourselves.'

I often wonder how I ever liked this man, but Rick wasn't always like this. He was romantic and charming, once. But then he got into a social media spat with a minor celebrity and internet fame came a-calling. He became known as a 'chef with attitude' who wasn't going to stand for a celeb trying to get something for nothing. Suddenly he had millions of followers and sponsorship deals, and the attitude he purveyed online spilled over into real-life too. He started throwing money around and thought big, flashy grand gestures that he could post photos of on his Instagram account were the way to sweep me off my feet, when what I really would've liked was a quiet evening at home without his phone beeping every two seconds.

'You're trespassing. I want you to leave.'

'Well, tell you what, you call the police, tell them your very handsome and very charming boyfriend has just surprised you with a very fancy dinner and excruciatingly expensive wine, and let's see if they make it the crime of the decade and blue-light it all the way here to escort me from the premises, hmm?' He makes the toddler-esque noise of a police siren. 'Stop being so ridiculously silly, Marnie. Sit down and have a glass of wine to loosen-bloody-up.'

I re-fold my arms and tap my foot in annoyance, staying glued to the doorstep. My heart is beating faster and not in the good way. Rick is just being his typical overbearing self, but I'm alone with someone who won't leave. I have no control over this situation. I can't physically push him away and throw him out the gate, I can't call the police and ask them to remove him because it's not a crime, and he won't listen when I tell him to go.

My mum *would* have thought a romantic Parisian garden picnic was the act of the world's most perfect boyfriend, but I also feel vulnerable and unsafe and like he's trying to manipulate me by bringing her up in the first place, and she would've told me to get far away from anyone who makes me feel like that. Even if it meant poking him in the eye with one of his snails.

Violence aside, I catch sight of the kitchen light I left on upstairs. 'You know what, I was in the middle of something, excuse me a minute.'

I go inside and back up the stairs, glad of the excuse to get away from him. I lean my forehead on the kitchen wall and take a few calming breaths, trying to stop the fight-or-flight rush of adrenaline coursing through me.

'Are you okay?' Darcy's voice comes through the wall. 'I was about to come round and saw there'd been an invasion of something a lot more unwelcome than Japanese knotweed this time.'

He's not wrong there.

'Want me to come and get rid of him?' There's the sound of his hands smacking together. 'I can be quite scary, so I'm told.'

'You? Scary? Never,' I say with a laugh. I'm touched by his offer, but the last thing I want is Rick knowing anything about my relationship... friendship... whatever it is with Darcy, and any confrontation between Darcy and Rick seems like a situation that could quickly get out of control. 'No, thank you. I'm not going back out there; he'll get bored eventually.'

I peer out the window. Rick has got lettuce leaves hanging out of his mouth while he chews through them with two front teeth like a rabbit, and I make an all-too-familiar noise of frustration. 'I had things to do tonight. *We* had things to do tonight. I haven't talked to you all day, I miss—' I stop myself. I can't *miss* him just because I haven't talked to him since last night. The highlight of every day lately has been seeing Darcy in the evenings, and I don't want Rick to take that away.

'Do you want to go for a walk?' he says after a moment of silence.

'A walk?' I say it like I've never heard the word before. 'With... you?'

'Y-yeah.' He sounds unsure, and like he might be recalibrating this as the worst idea he's ever had. 'It's a gorgeous evening and I've been wanting to show you the castle gardens. Do you want to walk up there with me?'

'I'd love to,' I say instantly, because it sounds like he could change his mind at any second. I've never seen Darcy outside of our gardens or my shop. I know he flits back and forth between here and the castle, but he always seems to take hidden shortcuts through the forest, because on the rare occasions that anyone sees him coming and going, it's always the briefest flash as he disappears into the distance.

'Okay. Good. I think.' I can hear the trepidation in his voice.

'Bring Mrs Potts. I'll carry her if she gets tired. Meet you out front in five minutes?'

Aww. One thing they never teach you in Disney movies – you can identify a real gentleman not with fancy bottles of wine and expensive dinners, but if he offers to carry your elderly cat should the need arise.

I bribe Mrs Potts from her window seat with Dreamies and strap her harness and lead on, and have one final glance out the window to where Rick is now poking snails into his mouth and has started downing my glass of wine as well as his own. He won't even notice I've gone.

I lock up behind me and take a breath. It *is* a beautiful autumn day. The early evening sun is low in the sky, and there's a warm breeze that sends yellow leaves falling from the trees on Ever After Street, and I hadn't realised how much I'd come to appreciate the regular hit of fresh air or how much I'd miss our nightly garden routine.

Within moments, Darcy emerges from his shop in his usual disguise. He's wearing black boots that come up to mid-calf with his jeans tucked into them, a dark jacket, and his usual cap, scarf, and sunglasses, and I can't help the spike of disappointment that he still feels like he needs them.

'Hi.' There's a moment of awkwardness where he goes to greet me and I'm not sure if he's going to hug me or not, and for one split second, I think he's going to lean in and kiss my cheek, and I almost headbutt him in the chest when he bends down to stroke Mrs Potts instead.

He holds a hand out, inviting me to start walking, and I jiggle Mrs Potts' lead to get her to walk along too. It might be unusual to see a cat on a lead, but she's used to it from walking to work with me every day. She keeps looking behind her to check Darcy is coming too and only trots on happily when he makes reassuring noises, and I'm once again struck by how much she likes him, and vice versa.

'Don't usually see you out and about on Ever After Street,' I say casually as we wander past Mickey's Mermaid's Treasure Trove shop, full of antiques and curiosities and ocean-themed decorative bits, and then take a shortcut between Mickey's outside wall and the Neverland Sweet Shop and onto the narrow path that cuts through the wooded area behind the shops on this side of the street.

'Don't usually go out and about on Ever After Street.' He sounds like he wants to be more annoyed about it than he actually is, although once we're off the main street and have the privacy of the trees, the tension that was squaring his shoulders visibly disappears. 'Speaking of, why *are* you out walking with me when there's bottle of wine in your garden that looked like it cost more than a monthly electricity bill? I take it you didn't tell Rick you were leaving?'

'Where would be the fun in that? Let him marinate in his snails and eye-wateringly expensive wine. He's like one of those scam callers. You engage them for a little while, then leave the phone on the table and go to make a cup of tea while they carry on talking – at least if they're trying it on with you, they aren't pestering anyone else in that time. They want to waste my time, so I enjoy wasting theirs instead.'

Darcy laughs like he isn't sure whether he should laugh or not. 'You're comparing your ex to a scam caller?'

'He's similarly annoying and similarly dangerous in that you don't know what he's going to do with your personal information. The only difference is that Rick's got enough money of his own that he doesn't want mine, unlike the bloke who phones up claiming your internet is about to be cut off or offering you a free grant for solar panels or loft insulation. So thank you for being a dashing hero and rescuing me tonight.'

His laugh is as sarcastic as his tone. 'Something I'll never be.'

I don't know if he means the 'dashing' part or the 'hero' part, but I glance up at him, trying not to make it obvious how desperate I am to know *everything* about him... Probably as desperate as he is *not* to share.

I reach out because I want to playfully poke him or something, anything for a moment of touch, but I end up just holding my hand out until the backs of my fingers brush against the sleeve of his jacket and hover there for a moment. He looks down and his other hand reaches over, the backs of his fingers touching mine for a moment before he drops his hand, clears his throat, and looks away sharply.

'Have you always been a gardener?' I ask, trying to cover the awkwardness.

'No.'

I wait for him to elaborate, but he doesn't. After we've spent so much time together, I'm still surprised by the one-word answers in the face of a direct question, but I'm not giving up that easily. 'What did you do before?'

'I was an international spy. I'd tell you about it but I'd be breaking the Official Secrets Act.'

'You're hilarious.' I give him a scathing look. 'You could've just said "I don't want to talk about it."'

'Marnie, you don't understand the meaning of "I don't want to talk about it." No matter what I don't want to talk about, you have a way of wheedling it out of me.' His head shifts as he glances down at me and then sighs in resignation. 'I worked in a library.'

'I *knew* you were a booklover in disguise.' I glance up at him and his disguise. 'I mean, not literally. I don't think you're disguising being a booklover, you're disguising...' I decide not to give voice to any of my theories about his reasons for staying so covered. 'In a library here?'

'No. In London. I lived there. I only moved back here after—' He cuts the sentence off abruptly and doesn't start a new one.

After. That word again. Confirmation that something happened to him and there was a before and an after. 'Where did the teaching creative writing come in?'

I keep my eyes focused on Mrs Potts walking in front of me, but I sense the movement as his gaze falls onto me again, like he was hoping I'd forgotten about that.

'That came later,' he says eventually. 'When I was still living in London, I had... good fortune. I fulfilled a lifelong dream and I wanted to give something back. I wanted to inspire kids who had nothing and thought good things only happened to other people. It was... probably the only part of my life that I'm still proud of.'

'I would *love* to host a regular creative writing class at the bookshop. It's something Mum and I talked about years ago but then the diagnosis came, and...' I shake my head. 'If you ever want—'

'*Never.*' The vehemence in his voice makes Mrs Potts look round and he murmurs something about her looking tired and picks her up for a carry, focusing so intently on settling her in his arms and murmuring to her that he doesn't give me a chance to push it any further. 'This way.'

We've slowly climbed up the hill of the forest, leaving the river that runs past our shops far behind. The castle is far above us and off to the right, but Darcy inclines his head, indicating that we should leave the makeshift path we've been meandering along. Unlike the Full Moon Forest on the other side of the street, there aren't any proper paths in this part of the woods, only routes that have been worn down by dogwalkers, but I follow his lead, and off the track, we come to castle walls that blend into the trees where the ivy has covered the ground, trunks, and the old stone of the walls, and masses of brown and yellow autumn leaves are collecting in piles.

He shifts Mrs Potts into one arm and then takes my hand and lifts it until he can place it carefully on her side to hold her steady. The unexpected touch surprises me, his gloved fingers on mine, curling over ever so slightly, lingering long after my hand is in Mrs Potts' soft grey fur. I look up and hold his eyes through his glasses, and I desperately wish I could see his face.

I could reach up right now and pull his scarf down and his glasses off. It would be like ripping a plaster away. It's the only way to *prove* that whatever he looks like makes no difference to his personality.

But it's not *just* about that. I don't want to see what Darcy looks like – I want him to *show* me. I want him to trust me enough to *know* that he could look like the most hideous beast in the world, but he would still be *him*. I want him to realise that he deserves to be loved and accepted, no matter what.

And then I blink again, and as if he can read every thought that just flashed through my head, he drops his gaze and lets go of my hand and I push out a shallow breath.

His free hand goes into his coat pocket and he pulls out a set of keys and lets us in to a fortress-like gate built into the wall with a rusting 'keep out' sign on it, disguised by long tendrils of ivy.

When we're inside, he puts Mrs Potts down, hands her lead back to me and locks up behind us, while I look around in awe.

I saw some of the castle grounds from the window when I came to the ball earlier this year, but nothing prepared me for the scale of it. There's neatly cut dark green grass for as far as the eye can see, interspersed with pristine gravel paths and parterre gardens laid out in geometric patterns with water features, statues, or topiary shapes in the spaces between each ornate clipped hedge. There are leafy trees that look like they've been painted by an autumnal artist, with circular flower beds at the base of each trunk, covered with mulch for now, but I can imagine them bursting with spring colour next year.

As we wander further through the immense grounds, there's a glass gazebo strung with tendrils of a hanging green plant and solar-powered fairy lights that illuminate as dusk starts to fall.

'Do you really do all of this?'

He nods. 'One of the reasons I expect customers to pay for their own flowers – most days, I'd rather be here than at the shop. This is my full-time work. This is what I love.'

I love the passion in his voice, and the calmness that's come over him since he closed that gate. When he's outside, it's like he's constantly aware of running into someone, but this place obviously brings him peace. It's special that he brought me here. Darcy doesn't share much of himself; even now I'd call us friends, he's still cagey and liable to snap if I ask the wrong questions, but this... This is a huge part of himself and he's willingly shared it with me.

'My father installed most of it when he was alive. He was the gardener here for decades. He was friends with the viscount who owned the castle, and he made a promise to keep the gardens as perfect as they always should be. Even years after the viscount disappeared, a fund had been set up to ensure he was always paid. He worked his fingers to the bone in creating these amazing gardens that no one would ever see because the castle was out of bounds, but it was important to him, a way of honouring his much-missed friend. And now it's his legacy too. It's nice to know the gardens are being seen again now Witt and Sadie are living here.'

'No wonder they're going to start hosting weddings. Especially in the spring when the trees will be covered in blossom, the flower beds bursting with colour, the weather warm enough to dance the night away in those open-air gazebos, the scent of roses in the air...'

The one thing I notice are the roses everywhere. They're not ostentatious, but every hedgerow has climbing roses weaving throughout it. Every statue in the centre of the geometric low hedge designs has a potted rose at its base. One of the parterre designs is in the shape of a rose and the gaps between each hedge are filled with beds of roses. Some of the clipped topiary bushes are rose shaped.

It's quite possibly the most beautiful thing I've ever seen. 'People would be so lucky to get married here. These gardens will be in family wedding photos one day soon. Your dad's legacy will live on because of you.'

I don't realise I've affected him until he swallows hard. 'I've never thought of it like that before. It's only ever been somewhere for me to hide away. I never realised anything good could come from it too.'

I look at him, again desperately wishing I could see his face, and even more desperately wishing he wouldn't push me away if I tried to hug him.

'You can just imagine strolling through here, arm in arm with someone you love, watching the sun set over the mountains...' Instead of poking and prodding any further, I nod towards the hills in the distance where the sun is heading downwards.

I'm not sure which one of us is more surprised when Darcy holds his arm out, silently asking me to slip my hand through it, and I do so at super speed in case he changes his mind. I edge closer to him as we walk, letting my fingers curl into the sleeve of his jacket and holding his arm as tight to my body as I dare.

The fresh scent of his aftershave combines with the scent of roses in the air and that sense of peace settles over me too. It's been a while since I felt happy, but in this beautiful place with this beautiful man beside me, it's easy to believe I could be again one day.

'This was my dad's private garden.' When we get to old redbrick walls and a limp wooden gate that looks like it might blow down in the next gust of wind, Darcy extracts his arm from mine to get the keys from his pocket again. 'The viscount gifted him this space to do whatever he wanted with. He'd always wanted a rose garden but had no space at home, so that's what he grew here.'

Inside the gate, there's a long archway built of climbing frames with roses scrambling all over them, and outside of that are rows and rows of rose bushes with paths between them. Most of them are dormant for winter already, some still have leaves but bare stems where he's deadheaded the spent flowers, but plenty are still flowering too.

I carry Mrs Potts as he shows us around. I've tried to imagine where Darcy works, but I'd never imagined it was somewhere this beautiful. There are white roses that look like they've been splashed with pink raindrops and yellow and orange roses that fade to pink as the flowers mature, and bursts of pink and purple flowers all the way through the walled garden.

'This is where I grow all my stock, and this...' He invites me into a long greenhouse. 'This is where I do all my breeding. This is what I wanted to show you.'

The greenhouse has got workbenches running along both sides of it, one side covered with an array of gardening tools and empty pots, and the other covered with rows of seed trays full of tiny rose sprouts and potted larger seedlings.

'This is the rose I'm breeding this year. It's a hybrid of that one and that one.' He points to a tray of young plants and then to a mature yellow rose and a lilac rose further along the workbench. 'It should grow with lilac petals with blotches of yellow, but each one will be unique. I remember you telling me your mum loved roses, and I thought... What was your mum's name?'

'Rosalie. That's why she was so drawn to them – people called her Rosie for short.'

'I thought I might name it the Rosalie rose...' He speaks fast, as though he thinks I'm going to object. 'I print up information cards with each plant so I can add a little bit about her, if you'd like. "Rosalie Platt loved roses and was a much-loved mum and book-seller" or something. You can decide.'

'Rosalie Platt was never too old to believe in fairy tales,' I say instantly. A Tale As Old As Time only exists because of her conviction that it was never too late for a fairy-tale ending.

His voice is thick with emotion. 'I thought you might like her name to live on. I'll be selling them as cut flowers and as plants for people to grow themselves, so anyone who buys them will know her name, and have them for many years in their gardens. And obviously I'll plant some in your garden too, and if you'd like any for family or friends to remember her by, they're yours.'

I don't know when I started crying, but tears are pouring down my face and trying to swipe them away does nothing to stem the flow.

'I don't know what to say.' I sniffle but there's no hiding how touched I am. It's the most thoughtful, kind gesture, and *he* has got the most beautiful heart of gold, and I'm at a loss for how to get across how much this means.

I reach out and deliberately take his right hand. He knows I saw the scars the other day, and he's going to object but I don't let him. I hold his gloved hand between both of mine and squeeze it. 'That's the nicest thing anyone's ever done. She'd love that. *I* love that. Darcy, you are...'

He's closed the greenhouse door behind us, so Mrs Potts is safe and has gone off to watch a spider knitting its web in a corner.

'I want... I *need* to ask you something.' I swallow hard and take a deep breath. 'Take off your glasses. Please. You're the most beautiful person I've ever met, and I've never even looked into your eyes. Let me say thank you face to face.'

'Marnie...' He looks down at where I'm still clutching his hand, looking like he wishes my grip wasn't so strong.

'Whatever you're hiding doesn't make you a beast...'

'Maybe the physical side doesn't.' It's a soft under-the-breath mutter that proves this goes a lot deeper than the scars he keeps hidden, and I squeeze his hand even tighter, keeping my gaze on his face, challenging him with my eyes alone, like a staring contest with an unseen opponent.

Eventually he sighs and gives one curt nod, and I let his hand go so he can turn away and adjust the cap and scarf, as if he's trying to make sure that I don't see a millimetre that he isn't ready to reveal, then he turns back, his dark glasses in his hand, and I'm looking up into Darcy's blue eyes.

And they take my breath away because I didn't think we'd ever get to this point. I didn't think he'd ever trust me enough for something so intimate, and it's not like my tears had stopped anyway, but they spill over again, streaming down my cheeks because I'm bursting with emotion and crying is the only outlet.

'That's most people's reaction to seeing me.' The corners of his eyes crinkle up like he's smiling behind the scarf.

I give his arm a gentle smack. 'Happy tears, you know that.'

'I do.' His eyes look as though they're starting to water too.

There's a bandana under the cap that I hadn't noticed before, pulled right down over his eyebrows, and his eyes are such a beautiful light blue, deep and filled with so many emotions, his pupils wide, and I reach up and cup his face through the scarf, letting my fingers rub over the cable-knit layers of black fabric. He doesn't drop eye contact and this feels like such a fragile intimacy. If one of us dares to even breathe, the spell will be broken.

'How can someone who creates such beauty ever think of themselves as a beast?' I murmur.

He shakes his head without dislodging my hand. He's not disagreeing, he's just letting me know it's something he can't answer, and I'm not going to push him any further.

Instead, I let my thumb rub his hidden cheek, enjoying the moment, especially when his eyes start to slip closed and his head dips towards me, as though he's enjoying it too. The swell of affection for him spills over and before I know what I'm doing, I've pushed myself up on tiptoes and pressed my lips to the scarf against his cheek.

His body goes rigid and without giving him a chance for the fight-or-flight response to kick in, I slip my arms around his neck and pull him down for a hug.

At first he grunts an objection and his hands touch my hips to push me away, but I don't let him. I've wanted to hug this man since the first moment I spoke to him, so many weeks ago now, and he's not getting out of it that easily. I squeeze his shoulders, let one of my palms rub across his shoulder blades, and hold him tight to me. Minutes pass but I don't give up, until finally he lets out a shuddery breath and squeezes me back, giving in to letting himself be hugged and hugging in return.

'Thank you for the rose. And for bringing me here.' With the hug, I'm trying to get across what I can't put into actual words. I doubt Darcy has ever shown this place to anyone, and the thought gives me a little flutter of hope that I might be starting to mean as much to him as he means to me.

His arms tighten around me and through many layers of material, I feel his lips press against my shoulder. His earthy aftershave engulfs me, and his body has melted against mine, and I lose track of time as we stand there holding each other. If I live to be 100 years old, I will never experience a hug that's as extraordinary as this one.

And then Mrs Potts attacks the spider, making a clang as her paw hits the metal greenhouse frame and reverberates, and Darcy lets out a yelp and jumps away from me.

'Oh God.' His eyes turn from relaxed to horror-filled. 'I'm so sorry. I shouldn't have done that.'

'Why not?' I say, surprised at his reaction. 'It was just a hug.'

'Because... you... I...' He growls in frustration and looks skywards, clenching his fists like he's angry at himself. 'I can't ever let someone get close to me again.'

'Why not?' I can't help the sting of disappointment. I didn't expect him to fall into my arms, but I didn't expect the instant rejection either.

He paces, trying to think of an answer, and then his head snaps up and he looks me in the eyes again. 'Because the last time I did, it nearly killed me. Literally.'

'Darcy...' I reach out for his hand but he snatches it out of my reach, and turns away to put his glasses back on.

'I don't deserve to find love again and I don't deserve anyone to love me. Don't convince yourself I'm something that I'm not.'

And that's the problem, isn't it? I think the only thing that's happening here is Darcy convincing *himself* that he is something he's not, and more than anything, I wish I understood why.

13

'You want to *what*?' I say into the phone receiver, surprised by the request of the man on the other end. My tone probably sounds like he's just asked me something unforgivably rude, but I can't get my head around what I've just heard.

'Two tags on the pay-it-forward board, please. Ten pounds each. Such a precious thing to do. Can you give me your PayPal address?'

I reel off the shop's email account that's associated with the online payment platform and thank him, bewilderedly, as he transfers the money while still on the line.

Why is a total stranger phoning up from the other side of the country to put money on the pay-it-forward board? How has he even heard about it? I write his two requested tags out in a daze and thank him profusely as he hangs up.

I'm just about to take them over to the board when the phone rings again. 'Can you put your friendship form online?' A woman's voice comes through from the other end. 'I'd love to be matched with a new bookish friend, but I'm not local enough to attend the friendship nights.'

I take the receiver away from my ear and squint at it. How do people know? Was the friendship date night really so much of a success that people have been sharing their experience of it far and wide?

'We're, er, thinking about it,' I stutter down the line.

Before she hangs up, the woman insists on giving me her name and email address so I can let her know when friendship-finding goes online, and insists on sending a photo of herself, despite the fact I reassure her that a photo isn't necessary.

It's been the most bizarre of all bizarre mornings so far, and it's only five past nine.

I take the tags over to the pay-it-forward board and the phone rings again before I've stuck the second pin in, and I rush back to answer it.

'Hello, could you put a fifteen-pound voucher on your board for me? Who do I make the cheque out to?'

This is madness, I think to myself as I give her our details and write another tag with the hand not holding the phone. Good madness, but madness all the same. How do they know?

I'm just about to go online and see if there's been some big influx of hits on the Ever After Street website or something when Cleo bursts in, thick blonde hair flapping behind her. 'Have you seen this?'

She's waving around a copy of *The Wye Word*, one of those free local community magazines that are distributed in stacks on buses and in shops for anyone to take. 'It's been picked up by the main news aggregator sites and shared online thousands of times.'

'What?'

In the magazine she puts down on the counter is a two-page spread about A Tale As Old As Time.

The headline reads: *Lonely bookseller bringing friendship to Ever After Street.*

'Well, that's insulting,' I mutter. 'Lonely or not, I didn't need the whole world to read it in twenty-two-point Book Antiqua.'

You may think A Tale As Old As Time, the bookshop on cutesy fairy-tale lane Ever After Street is all about whimsy fairy tales, but an unnamed source has been in touch with *The Wye Word* to let us in on a new and unexpected venture the bookshop is undertaking – friendship dates. Yes, you heard that right. Owner Marnie Platt invites you to attend the bookshop's 'friendship nights' to be matched with a potential 'friend' and go on a platonic date to see if you connect with the other person on a 'friendship' level. Just when you thought you'd heard it all, eh? Miss Platt believes that a liking of similar books can lead to a 'special friendship' between bookworms.

'Why are there inverted commas around every mention of friendship? They couldn't be any more disparaging if they tried,' I grumble as I carry on reading, a cold sense of dread settling at the base of my back and slithering up my spine.

We're wondering how many other kinds of 'connections' are being formed in these 'friendship nights'. In fact, we might send an undercover reporter to the next one and find out exactly what this 'friendship' stuff is all about. What do you think, readers? Would you go on a date with a 'friend'? Seems a bit suspect, if you ask us.

'It makes it sound seedy and underhanded, like a metaphor for something more.'

'Maybe they think you're running a brothel.'

'Exactly! And now I've got to worry about an undercover reporter and whether the next group of people will be genuine or wanting to turn it into something sordid for another article. They're trying to cast a bad light on something that was meant to do nothing but good.'

'Marnie, don't worry about it. The only people they're making look bad is themselves. You saw how much fun people had the other night. If you look on Twitter, there's already a comment from Lissa saying she went and it was great fun and she's made a couple of new friends.'

That gives me a shot of hope and I get out my phone and navigate to the tweet in question and the hope quickly turns into horror. 'While it's lovely of Lissa to stick up for us, the only reply she's got is a wide-eye emoji and a threesome gif! This is terrible!'

In the article, there's a photo of the friendship form that looks suspiciously like it was taken on my counter. How has someone got that? Is it one of the people who filled it in for the friendship dates? Or has someone been in here, behind my counter, and pulled a blank one out of the stack and photographed it? Who? And why?

Another highlight of the quirky A Tale As Old As Time bookshop is owner Marnie's benevolent creation of a pay-it-forward board, a chunk of cork on the wall that allows customers to pay any amount of money towards the purchase of a book for someone who needs one. Customers pay their money, pin a tag to the board, and off they go, content in the knowledge that they've given something to a stranger, and unsure of whether that stranger will actually need their money or just grab the opportunity to get something for nothing.

There's also a photo of the pay-it-forward board, and one of me that they've pulled from the Ever After Street website. Next to that is a photo of my flyer about the book festival.

Enterprising booklover Marnie's next venture is organising a book festival on Ever After Street, the imaginatively named Bookishly Ever After, a weekend full of author talks and literary fun, and claiming to have an unmasking of esteemed but secretive author U.N.Known.

'How do they...?' I splutter in indignation. 'That's not confirmed! I haven't told a soul that. They can't print that when it isn't true. U.N.Known hasn't agreed to any such thing and there's no flipping way he will now, is there?'

Cleo pats my hand sympathetically, clearly trying to hide her confusion about how U.N.Known has anything to do with this.

If true, surely the biggest event to rock the publishing industry in years. We'll be waiting with bated breath. Get your tickets now, folks, and see if this Bookish Cupid can indeed unmask the most anonymous author of our time, all while setting you up with a completely platonic new 'friend'. We never expected to use the words 'giant orgy of friendship', but we expect that's what you can expect from a visit to A Tale As Old As Time after the sun goes down... We're not sure we want to know what happens when someone lists their favourite book as *Fifty Shades of Grey*. Anyone brave enough to try it, dear readers?

'This is horrific. How could they do this? Now I have to worry about undercover reporters *and* people making a mockery of it by listing raunchy books as their favourites and thinking they're going to get some kind of bookish one-night stand out of it.'

'All press is good press?' Cleo grimaces even though she's trying to sound upbeat.

'No! Good press is good press, bad press is *bad* press, and this is the *worst* press! It's condescending, defamatory, and downright scornful. What on earth am I going to do?'

She's got halfway through shrugging her shoulders when the phone rings and I pick it up in trepidation. I don't think anything good is going to come from a phone call after *that*.

'Hello. Do you take online orders? I'm looking for the Seasons Edition of *Anne of Green Gables*. Do you have it in stock?'

I still feel like I'm in a daze as I go to mumble a no, then realise which edition she's talking about and overcompensate for my initial disillusionment. 'Yes, I do! It's got the most gorgeous, autumnal, laser-cut cover, perfect gold lettering, and a matching bookmark.' Talking books lets me momentarily forget the bad parts of this morning.

'Let me get my card. How much is postage?'

'I, um, don't really take—'

'Will a fiver cover it?'

I've never done online orders. I've always thought I've got my hands full enough as it is without the extra hassle of having to keep a website updated with stock, and being unable to compete with the mighty internet corporations has made it seem pointless, but that book has been sitting there for an age, it would be stupid to refuse. I enter her card details into the payment system as she speaks and then rifle one-handedly for a padded envelope and address it while she's on the phone.

As I'm doing that, the bell above the door tinkles and a pair of women come in, giggling to themselves. Cleo greets them but they ignore us and disappear between bookshelves.

'Thanks, love,' the woman on the phone says as I pull out tissue paper to wrap her book in. 'Lovely thing you're doing there. I didn't like the tone of that article at all. I'll be in touch next time I need an extra-special book.'

I thank her as I hang up, listening to the giggles of the two women who are taking innocuous books and reading random paragraphs but making them sound like lewd innuendos. '*It is a truth universally acknowledged that a single man in possession of a good fortune must be in want of a...*' one reads aloud while the other one fills in the blank with suggestions far more X-rated than Jane Austen intended.

'Can I help you with anything, ladies?' Cleo gets all protective and goes to stand at the edge of the aisle they're in, and her stern look leaves them with no doubt about how unimpressed we are with their antics, and they put the books they were pulling out back on the shelves and mutter something about us being no fun.

'You gonna invite us to one of your date nights, then? We could show men a thing or two between the pages!' They're still giggling as they flail out the door.

'Honestly, if it wasn't 9 a.m., I'd think they'd just fallen out of a pub.' Cleo leans on the counter from the other side with a huff.

'Is that what we can expect from now on?' I let out a long sigh. 'Mockery, jibes, and people thinking they're going to be set up with some kind of Christian Grey-style sadist if they list their favourite book as *Fifty Shades*?'

'Just ignore them, Mar.' She taps one of the pay-it-forward tags that I haven't had a chance to put up yet. 'At least some people have taken it in the spirit it was meant. You've already got extra tags on the board and had an online order.'

'I don't *do* online orders.'

'Maybe it's a sign that you should start. People all across the country are keen to support independent bookshops. It might bring in extra sales for very little extra effort?'

I let out another sigh, feeling so overwhelmed by it all that I want to cry. Just when things seemed to be going in the right direction, when the garden is looking so much better than it was, when we've had a success of friendship dates and interest in more, and when there's a book festival to put on... When it feels like things will be okay after all, something like this article comes along to strike it down.

'I thought the shop was in trouble...' Cleo says gently.

'It is. And it'll be in even more trouble if my landlord reads this. And someone's already made a complaint about me. What if that person makes another one? What if someone *else* complains too? This might be the final ammunition they need to throw me out.'

The phone rings again and I answer it with all the enthusiasm of a cup of cold tea. This time the person on the other end wants two tickets to the book festival, and I half-expect them to ask if the dress code is latex and if they should bring a whip and some fishnet stockings.

While I'm taking their details, another customer comes in to browse, thankfully alone and thankfully of the non-giggling variety, and Cleo hangs around, waiting by the counter to see if there's anything she can do.

'So do you have any idea who's done this?' she asks when I hang up. 'Who could the "anonymous source" be?'

'No idea. Maybe someone trying to get me in trouble.'

'Any clue who could've taken the pictures?'

I study them again. There's nothi— 'Ahh, look, those are Darcy's tags on the pay-it-forward board. I'd know that handwriting anywhere. So that at least dates it to being taken *after* he put those tags up two weeks ago. There were loads of people in here the other night – it could have been anyone. Maybe that's not the counter in the background of that photo of the form. Maybe it was just one of the people who attended the friendship night who took a photo of their form before they filled it in...' I trail off because I don't believe my own words. That's the wood-grain of the counter. I look at it every day. 'And anyone could've taken a picture of the pay-it-forward board that night. Almost everyone had their phones out at some point. Maybe someone didn't enjoy themselves as much as they said. Maybe someone misinterpreted it and was disgruntled when they *didn't* get set up on a *date*-date.'

I know I'm going to torture myself for a long time to come in trying to figure out who the 'anonymous source' is and probably get no closer to the truth, so maybe it's a good thing when the rest of the morning is unexpectedly busy, but not in a bad way. The phone keeps ringing with stock enquiries, book festival ticket requests, and people asking if the friendship matching thing could go country-wide, and quite a debate has sparked on one of my Facebook booklover groups about whether you *can* find new friends via a love of books or whether this is all a big con to get more money in the till.

And then a wonderful thing happens that reminds me why I do this in the first place. Cleo has refused to leave me by myself to fend off endless calls and the odd jibe from customers, and it's about lunchtime when a little girl comes in, who can only be about six years old.

Cleo is much better with children than I am. 'Are you on your own, sweetheart?'

'My granny's outside.' She points out the window to where there's an elderly lady sitting on one of the benches by the flower beds.

'Does she know you've come in here?'

'She told me to. She needed a rest. She's *ooooold*.'

I laugh, but I know the feeling. I think I've aged sixty years after the unexpectedness of this morning.

'It's Mummy's birthday tomorrow and Granny and me have made her a cake. We came out to buy a present but Granny says everything is too expensive. She saw this and said you could help.'

She's clutching a copy of the magazine in her fist, and I realise she means the pay-it-forward board.

'Does Mummy like to read?'

'Mummy loves to read! She reads to me every night and then I make her stay until I fall asleep and she reads her own book so she doesn't get bored.'

I go over and take one of Darcy's tags off the board and hand it to her. 'This entitles you to choose any book you'd like in the shop. Do you know what kind of books she likes?'

'Kissy laugh-y books! Sometimes she laughs too loudly and wakes me up.'

'Romantic comedies?' Cleo and I raise an eyebrow at each other, and I can't help giggling at her description. The innocence of childhood.

'The ones with pretty covers!' She hands me her scrunched-up copy of *The Wye Word* and takes the book tag, and skips off towards the romance section, and Cleo rushes after her to keep an eye.

I can hear the girl oohing and ahhing, exclaims of 'she's read that one!' and showing Cleo the prettiest covers, and eventually she skips back towards me, clutching two paperbacks. I think the covers being pink and purple were probably the deciding factors in her choices.

'We're doing sums in school, that makes ten.' She pushes them up onto the counter and waves the book tag at me.

It's a little bit over ten, but I don't mind given how happy it makes her. I wrap her choices in gift wrap, and put them into a bag with a couple of bookmarks and a flyer about the book festival, and we watch her skip back across to her grandma on the benches, who raises a hand in our direction with a grateful smile.

It's the uplift I needed this afternoon. 'That's exactly why the pay-it-forward board is there. *This* is the warm and fuzzy feeling I used to get every time someone used it.'

'Why did they stop?'

'Disenchantment?' I shrug. 'I don't know. Maybe most people are cynical, like Rick, and believe it would only ever be used by dishonest people trying to swindle a freebie. Plus, it's hard to get people to part with cash for something intangible, something they'll never see the benefit of, and money is tight for everyone these days. Few people have got extra for themselves, let alone for a stranger.'

'Darcy is not cynical like Rick.' The tag he wrote is still on the counter and she runs her fingers over his curled lettering.

'And that's the paradox that is Darcy. He's cold, hardened, jaded and distrustful, and yet it's like he still *wants* to believe in goodness. He wants to believe people are better than they are. He says he hates people and yet he filled that board without a second thought.'

The little girl didn't take her magazine with her, and Cleo unfurls it and lays it next to the copy we already had. 'Could he have done this? Anonymous source and anonymous neighbour, bit of a coincidence, no?'

'Noooo.' I look up at her in surprise, even though I understand the correlation. 'There's no way. This is the furthest thing from something he'd do. He isn't one for voluntarily talking to people and I can't imagine him seeking out a journalist or saying anything as unkind as this.'

'Did he know about U.N.Known?'

'He knew I was emailing him. I never told him that he'd said he'd think about it. I never told anyone that. I didn't want to get anyone's hopes up, including my own, because I didn't want to be disappointed when he inevitably came back with a no. Darcy was here when I was sorting out the forms the other day, but I'd have noticed if he'd got his phone out and snapped a pic, and he hasn't been alone in the shop to take any photos.'

Judging by the expression on Cleo's face, she realises I'm wrong at the exact same moment as I do.

'Yes, he has, hasn't he? When we had our friendship date and he was in here cleaning up.' I turn it over in my mind. Darcy is the *only* person who's been alone in my shop. He's the only person who would've had a chance to go through the questionnaires and take a photo without anyone noticing. 'This is so unlike him. Maybe he thought he was helping and it got lost in translation. The journalist took nice words and twisted them into something else... Darcy has been nothing but supportive since the moment I met him. There's no way...'

My thoughts are interrupted by the ping of my email account and the email I was dreading pops into my inbox.

It's from the-unknown-author@gmail.com.

I never said yes.

I know that. That article was nothing to do with me. I'm morti-fied. I don't know who told them or how they knew I was talking to you. I honestly haven't mentioned these emails to anyone. I'm so sorry. This is the last thing I wanted printed about me. I'm the one who looks bad.

If this is some way of manipulating me into agreeing, it won't work.

I burst into tears because that's exactly what it looks like, isn't it? It looks like I've released the information to pressure him into agreeing. Cleo chews her lip worriedly as I swipe tears away and type back through blurry eyes.

It's not. I know what you must be thinking, but I don't know how it's got out. I haven't told a soul about our emails, and I've never mentioned your name in relation to the book festival, apart from excitedly telling my neighbour I was going to email you weeks ago. Absolutely no one knew you'd said you'd think about it.

Well, now I certainly won't, will I?

I thunk my head down on the counter. *That* is exactly what I saw coming. His tone is angry, and I decide not to reply again for the moment. Maybe he'll hear me out again when he's cooled off, or maybe I really have blown it for good.

Instead, I fire off an email to *The Wye Word* asking if they're proud of publishing such a demeaning article and asking to know who their anonymous source is, but they ignore the first question and politely inform me that they can't share the names of people who wish to remain anonymous.

I wanted to remain anonymous too. Half the people in my life are anonymous. I wouldn't mind being granted the same courtesy.

14

In recent months, the pay-it-forward board has been mostly cork with a couple of dusty book-shaped tags on it, but by the end of the day, there's barely room to see the board under all the tags. I've had endless phone calls about the book festival and people who want to be matched with bookish friends from all over the country. Cleo stayed for most of the day, refused my offer of paying her, and by five o'clock, I'm exhausted and beyond glad to shut the door for the night and take the phone off the hook.

I go upstairs to feed Mrs Potts and there's a knock from the other side of the kitchen wall. 'You there?'

Just hearing Darcy's voice makes the stress of today melt away. Maybe it shouldn't, because all day I've been fighting that sliver of doubt about him and the article, but I *can't* believe he had anything to do with it.

'You got time to come out? We've got an important job to do tonight.'

We have? I'm not sure what he's talking about, but through every moment of anxiety today, I've clung onto the thought of seeing him tonight. I've looked forward to hearing his calm voice and spending time in his reassuring presence. 'Always.'

No one has mentioned the hug again since the other day, and Darcy hasn't taken his glasses off again since either.

I give Mrs Potts a stroke while she's eating, and she growls at me for fear that I'll steal her kitty biscuits, and I go downstairs and leave the back door open cat-width in case she wants to come out too.

The garden is looking so much better than it was – almost as good as it looked when my mum was here. Surely Mr Rowbotham can't argue with this. The knotweed has been eradicated. The weeds are gone and no hint of the stinging nettles remain. There were flower borders once, now empty, that I've dug over and Darcy's promised to get me some autumn-planting bulbs to fill them with so they'll be full of flowers by the spring. The stone patio that was missing for years has been found again, hiding underneath the tangles of brambles, nettles, and thistles. The cracks between each slab have been meticulously cleared of dandelions, and all that's left to do is jetwash the concrete so it shines. Although the table and chairs were too rusty to save, Darcy has lent me a couple of sets from the castle so it looks like a proper little garden. And although I know we've done it, I can't help feeling like something's missing. It looks as it should, but will it be enough for Mr Rowbotham? I have a horrible feeling that it won't. This isn't *my* garden. My shop belongs to Mr Rowbotham, and I will always be answerable to his every whim. What if he decides he no longer wants to house a bookshop? What if he thinks something else would be more profitable in my place?

I don't know what I'll do without it. Even if I managed to get a job in another bookshop, it won't be here. It won't be *this* shop. It won't have Darcy next door to it. If the worst comes to the worst and I do have to leave A Tale As Old As Time, one of the most devastating things will be the fact that Darcy will no longer be my neighbour.

'Sounds like you've had a hell of a day.' Darcy's voice is right there and I hear the click of his gate unlocking and he appears on the path outside, still wearing his usual disguise. 'Can I come in? I come bearing gifts.'

'You're always welcome, gifts or no gifts,' I say with a grin, although I must admit to being intrigued when he unlatches my gate and lets himself in, carrying a rose in one hand and in the other... an axe.

My fingers brush his as I take the single baby-pink rose with crimped edges and hold it to my nose to inhale the delicate scent. His roses are eternally spectacular, and he deserves more recognition for them than he currently gets.

'Whoever wrote that article deserves dunking into a patch of stinging nettles, naked, with wasps.'

I laugh out loud at the sentiment, although he's a lot kinder than I'm inclined to be towards the writer and their anonymous source. I'm relieved too. More than anything, I didn't want that spiteful article to be his doing, and he wouldn't have said that if it was, would he?

I nod to the axe in his hand. 'And that's your answer? Stinging nettles, wasps, and a spot of axe-murdering?'

He laughs so hard that he throws his head back. 'Not quite. Here, this is for you.'

He whisks the rose out of my grip and replaces it with the axe, taking my hands to position them correctly on the heavy handle.

'It's an axe,' I say, showcasing my talent for observation as he walks up the garden path and lays the rose by the step, ready to go inside.

'To chop the old bench up.' He returns to stand beside me, looking at Mum's bench that's still against the far wall.

'I can't.' The thought sets off an instant panic and I shove the axe back at him, but he refuses to take it.

'Marnie, that bench has three legs and a spindle for the fourth. If anyone dares to sit on it, it will no longer need chopping up and some unlucky soul will be flailing around on the ground impaled by shards of wood.'

'That's fine by me,' I mutter, even though causing grievous bodily harm to my customers isn't *quite* at the top of my to-do list.

He sighs, still refusing to take the axe. 'I know it's difficult. I know what it's like to lose people, but you're trying so hard to save this shop and make use of what will now be a beautiful garden – you can't cling onto something so old and knackered because of the person who once sat there. Come with me.'

I let the axe drop to my side and slip my other hand into his offered glove-covered palm. He tugs me gently, making me follow him onto the path outside my gate, where there's a huge rectangular cardboard box strapped to a wheeled trolley. I crouch down to look at the tiny picture in one corner. It's a brand-new silver ornate bench with three metalwork red roses along the back of it, swirling green scrolls in the arms, and a comfortable looking seat.

'I found it online. I didn't intend to be presumptuous, but it seems only right that a *Beauty and the Beast*-themed bookshop, with a garden the Beast would be proud of, deserved a suitably themed bench to complete it.'

'You're not presumptuous, you're the most thoughtful person in the world.'

'Hah.' His laugh is one of scorn, and I want to take that laugh like a physical thing, screw it up between my hands and throw it at whoever has made him believe that he *isn't*. Even if that person is himself.

'At least let me pa—'

He cuts me off before I can offer to pay for it. 'It's a gift. If you don't want it, I'll put it at the castle. It won't be out of place.'

I'm ridiculously touched by his gesture. I don't know what a bench like this costs, but taking the time to think of it and find it is one thing, but to buy it too... That generosity again. It makes me want to hug him, although I'm not planning on doing that again in a hurry after the other day.

'You don't have to have it.' He jiggles my hand gently. 'I'm not going to use the manipulative "your mum wouldn't want that" line, because I didn't know your mum, but *you* did, so it's your choice. If you want to cordon off that area of the garden and stick an "out of order" sign on the existing bench, that's fine too.'

I think about what he said before, about the castle gardens being his father's legacy. All right, it's not quite on the same scale, but my mum loved our shop's garden. If A Tale As Old As Time is going to stay on Ever After Street, then it should be a tribute to her, not a mausoleum.

'Okay.' I say it so quietly that he has to lean in close and ask me to repeat it, and then he cheers and punches the air with joy, and knowing he's smiling behind the scarf makes me smile too.

I know he's right about the bench and I feel more confident as we go back into the garden and stand in front of it. He demonstrates how to hold the axe.

'It's therapeutic.' He shows me where to aim the first swing. 'I'm sorry about today. You didn't deserve that.'

'It had a good effect too.' I swing the axe, hit the wrong part of the bench and the only thing that crumbles is the leg that was broken anyway. As I try again, I tell him about the extra ticket orders and tags on the pay-it-forward board and then about the little girl who used one of his tags. 'You made her day. She was so happy because of you. And her mum will be overjoyed when she opens her gift tomorrow.'

'Nothing to do with me. That board is there because of you. Maybe this publicity will be good for the book festival too. No matter which way you look at it, a *lot* of people have now heard about Bookishly Ever After who hadn't previously heard about it. And not everyone will be cynical enough to take that article at face value.'

'Yeah, and maybe it will give my complainer something else to complain about.' Thinking about the complainer who started all of this while embedding an axe into wood *is* surprisingly thera-peutic and I hit the bench again, enjoying the thrill when the wood splinters. 'Someone has already taken umbrage with me about the garden, they're going to *adore* the insinuation that I'm running a literary brothel.'

'I'd go to a literary brothel. I'd pay good money to be set up with books I might enjoy.' He can obviously see how much I'm enjoying taking my frustration out on the bench, and points out another area to hit and then stands well clear, and his laugh makes me feel better than I have all day. 'I mean, if actual brothels promise a night you'll never forget, the same could be said of curling up in bed with a good book. I've heard of people who push books on others being called book pimps. *That* would fit right in with a literary brothel.'

It makes me think of that email conversation with U.N.Known the other night about reading in bed. They have alarmingly similar senses of humour. 'I thought you didn't read.'

'I seem to be doing a lot of things I don't normally do lately.' He grunts like he wishes he hadn't said that. 'Seriously, Marnie. No one's going to complain about you. They'll have to get through me first.'

'Thank you.' It makes me feel oddly protected, like Darcy is a good person to have on my side. The warm and fuzzy feelings last for all of 3.5 seconds before the worries of the day come crawling back and I swing the axe into the bench again. 'I've lost U.N.-Known though. He's never going to come to the festival now. I have no idea how the "anonymous source" found that part out. *No one* knew that he'd said he'd come.'

'I thought he said he'd think about it.'

'Yeah, he... Wait, when did I tell you that? I didn't think I'd told anyone that.'

'I dunno.' He shrugs. 'Couple of weeks back?'

Did I? It's easy to talk to Darcy, but do I spill my guts so much that I can't even remember all I've said now?

I'm sure I didn't tell him that though, and it makes the needles of doubt prickle again, but I don't want to believe them. Maybe Darcy did have the opportunity to take those photos in the shop, but there's no way this was his doing. Darcy is honest and blunt to a fault when he wants to be. If he was somehow trying to help and the journalist who wrote the article has taken his words and twisted them, he'd admit that. He wouldn't pretend it wasn't him. And even though I must've told Darcy about U.N.Known over the last few weeks, the published fact that he was definitely coming to the festival is an outright lie. *That* is something I never told a soul because he never said it. It's something that would only have been done with the intention of trying to make my bookshop look bad, and that's not something Darcy would do.

'I tried so hard with him, and someone else has taken that away,' I say with a sigh.

'U.N.Known isn't the only thing that will make Bookishly Ever After a success.' He comes over and repositions the axe in my hands, his fingers lingering over mine on the handle for a delicious few seconds longer than strictly necessary.

I let the comfort of his words and his touch wash over me. 'It wasn't just about that. I think he's lonely. I wanted him to know that people love him. His work is timeless and whatever has happened in his life between then and now, he did an amazing thing that still brings joy to so many people. He deserves to know that. It wasn't about telling the world who he is, I couldn't care less who he is, it was about showing him how important that book is to so many people.'

'You think he's forgotten?'

'I think he's a bit like you. Hiding away from the world, not realising how special he is and how much he matters to people.'

'I'm nothing like that.' After a particularly strong bench hit, shards of wood go flying across the garden and Darcy goes to pick them up before Mrs Potts finds them by getting them embedded in her paws. 'Besides, you have no idea who U.N.Known is. He could live a wild and fulfilling life. He could not want to write any more because his life is so preposterously full and exciting in other ways.'

'I don't think so. He sounds sad and lonely.'

'You can tell that from one-sentence emails?'

'They're not always— How do you know they're often one sentence?'

'You *told* me.' He sounds annoyed by my lack of understanding. 'Ages ago, when you first got in touch with him.'

'Oh, right.' Did I? I didn't think I'd ever said much about U.N.-Known to Darcy, given his dislike for *Once Upon Another Time*. 'His emails sound dull and lifeless. He makes jokes but they sound half-hearted. I thought it might help him to understand how many people still love his book and how A Tale As Old As Time wouldn't exist without it.'

It's a thankfully warm autumnal evening where the air smells of a distant bonfire and brown leaves are floating down from the trees and everything has that crisp feeling of starting over. I'm panting for breath and half the old bench is in pieces on the ground while the other half is leaning on two legs, waiting to be put out of its misery. It's surprisingly cathartic. I swipe my arm across my forehead and find myself smiling for no reason, other than knowing my mum would be laughing at this scene if she could see us now. She'd love the new bench. She'd love how the garden looks. She'd *love* Darcy.

I hold the axe out to him. 'This is fun. You try.'

'I've chopped up my feelings many times. You enjoy.'

'Go on.' I push the axe further towards him. 'If I can say goodbye to this bench, you can say goodbye to... whatever it is that makes you think you need that disguise.'

He looks at me. 'It's not about the disguise. I have scars, you know that. Scars make people ask questions, and I don't want to be asked questions.'

'People wouldn't... No one is that insensitive.'

'Oh, trust me, they are.' The laugh he lets out is bitter and hurting. 'If you look different in any way, people think it gives them a right to comment. Try dying your hair pink or being overweight and you'll see what I mean. If it's not the direct questions, it's the talk they think you can't overhear. The way they turn to their friends and semi-whisper, "What do you think happened to that man?" like something that destroyed my life is for their personal entertainment.'

That's the most he's ever said, the most unguarded he's ever been, and I want to pounce on it and question him, but I also don't want him to feel like he can't open up to me without being interrogated. 'You don't seem like someone who cares what people think of you...'

'It's not about that. It's about what I think of myself. I don't want to be reminded of why I'm like I am. I don't want other people to know. If I'm dressed like this, no one knows that I look different to everyone else. They just think I'm a terrifying weirdo, which is fine by me.'

'So chop up the people who have ever dared to comment.' I hold the axe out again.

He laughs. 'That sounds surprisingly murdery.'

'Metaphorically, you idiot.' I'm laughing too as he takes the axe and holds my gaze behind his glasses, our hands touching on the handle until he dips his head and looks away.

I'm breathing hard in a way that's not entirely from overexertion with the axe, and my breath speeds up when he steps near again and drops an arm around my shoulder, tugging me into his side for the briefest one-armed hug.

'Thank you. First time I've ever laughed about anything to do with my past.'

It doesn't seem like a moment for serious and deep, so I go with the opposite. 'First time I've ever been hugged by a man wielding an axe.'

It makes him laugh again and he drops his arm, but before he's moved away, I nudge his side with my elbow. 'Maybe between us, we can make sure it's not the last.'

'The laughing or the axe-wielding hug?'

It's my turn to laugh. 'Either. Both.'

I watch appreciatively as he stands in front of the bench and tests where the axe is going to hit. He's clearly done this before because he brings it down in one swift move and the rest of the bench crumbles into a pile of wood on the ground and he cheers and turns around to give me a fist bump and I'm sure that he's grinning at me.

He starts collecting up the pieces of bench and taking them to the incinerator drum outside his gate, and I do the same, gathering up armfuls of broken wood and carrying them away to be burnt, and it doesn't feel like as final a goodbye as I expected. It feels like the right thing at the right moment. With the right person.

'Are you helping me build this new bench?' Darcy comes back brushing his hands together and the smell of bonfire fills the air. 'Because I warn you, I'm terrible at flatpack furniture. It'll come out looking like a one-legged giraffe if you leave me unsupervised.'

I laugh. 'Only if you let me make us a cup of tea first.'

'Wouldn't have it any other way.' He goes to wheel the box in from outside.

'Darcy?' I call after him and he turns back. 'Thank you.'

'What for?'

I think about it before answering. 'Being the sunshine after a dark couple of years.'

'I could say the same to you.' He looks at me across the garden, a garden that looks so much different than it did five weeks ago, largely because of him and what he inspired in me.

Things had felt so dark for me that I never thought I'd bring light into anyone's life again, and I don't think he did either, but it feels like two broken people are starting to glue themselves back together again.

Especially when he takes his glasses off to read the instruction booklet and doesn't put them back on, and it fills me with hope that one day it will be more than just the glasses.

* * *

When I get home with Mrs Potts that night, there's an unexpected email in my inbox from the-unknown-author@gmail.com.

Okay.

It's my first time being on the verge of a heart attack, but this is definitely what it feels like.

Okay, what? You'll come?

I'll be there. Feel free to use my name. Publicise it however you want.

I scream and earn myself a kitty-daggers look from Mrs Potts.

What changed your mind?

It takes a long time for him to answer, but it makes me smile when he does.

A reminder of someone I used to be.

15

'So, Bookishly Ever After is next on our agenda.' Ali is the stand-in chairman of this week's Ever After Street meeting because Lilith, the ninety-nine-year-old owner of the tearoom who usually keeps us all in line, has been missing all week due to health issues, and her staff of two are struggling to keep up.

We're gathered in the little clearing in the centre of Ever After Street, surrounded by white wooden fences and flower beds, and everyone has found a spot for themselves on the benches or picnic tables.

'Things going well, Marnie?'

I *loathe* having to speak in front of other people, especially when everyone falls silent to listen to me. The pressure is too great and I end up stumbling over my words and forgetting half of the things I meant to say. Usually I speak as little as possible at these meetings. I watch from the outskirts as the other more confident shopkeepers take centre stage, but the book festival is less than a week away now, and it's become a big deal for Ever After Street.

The article, for all its flaws, has gained some interest, and all the two hundred tickets have now sold out. Witt's assured me the castle can take extra guests if I want to put any more on, and I've been back and forth to the castle all week, starting to get things set up.

I wipe clammy palms on my jeans and take a deep breath. 'Witt and Sadie were thinking of hosting an autumn-themed ball anyway, and they've very kindly let me take over that and turn it into a literary fancy-dress ball. People can come dressed as their favourite literary characters, and there will be prizes for the best costumes. A year's supply of book vouchers and a fresh flower delivery to their door every month, and then two runner ups will get a voucher for a book from me and a plant of their choice from The Beast's Enchanted Rose Garden, and...'

I ignore the murmur that ripples through the gathered residents. It's the first time I've mentioned Darcy's involvement, the first time he's ever been involved with *anything* on Ever After Street, but it doesn't seem right to draw attention to it, so I barrel on. 'On the Saturday, there's going to be bookish crafts and author talks, and a literary-themed afternoon tea, then on the Sunday morning, we've got the author Q&A sessions and a meet and greet so people can get their books signed. I'm going to set up a book swap area at the front of the castle so people can drop off any books they don't want and maybe take home a few that they do, and then to end things on Sunday evening, will be the grand costume ball.'

I get so into it that I forget about my nerves. I hadn't realised how excited I am. There's been so much put into the preparation; Cleo has been helping out at the shop while I've been arranging things at the castle, refusing any payment except taking home a book she'd started reading while the shop was quiet, and it's made me think about hiring an assistant again, although I'm at Mr Rowbotham's mercy and there's no point in hiring someone without the reassurance of a renewed lease. It just so happens that the second day of the festival is also the day that Mr Rowbotham is coming to 'inspect his property' – all the better for him to inspect it while the street is buzzing with booklovers.

'And U.N.Known? That article said...' Imogen from Sleeping Beauty's Once Upon A Dream shop starts. 'He would be a huge draw to this. If you could get him to appear in public for the first time ever... People would be talking about Ever After Street for months. We'd be unforgettable.'

'He's kind of agreed.' I still can't believe that email I got a few days ago and this is the first time I've said it aloud. 'It's just too unreal. How can *I* possibly have influenced this guy who has never done any public appearances before, ever, into coming to ours? Maybe he's playing a joke on me – payback for having the nerve to ask him or something – and he'll be a no-show on the day.'

'Well, that would be his loss,' Lissa from the Colours of the Wind museum says comfortingly. 'Whether he turns up or not, *you* are the person who's going to make this a roaring success, Marnie. You don't need any silly gimmicks.'

It's an unintentional mirror of what Darcy said last week and it makes my heart melt.

'We believe in you,' Mickey adds, and the entire group cheers. For me. It makes me a bit teary-eyed. I can't quite get my head around the fact they're all supporting this, especially after the months of me turning them down whenever they've invited me to do anything.

Trying to control my emotions after their kindness means I'm not concentrating on what I'm saying, and words come out before I've realised it. 'I just hope it's enough.'

'Enough for what?' Lissa asks.

Oh, hell. I didn't want to tell them, and now every eye on Ever After Street is on me, waiting for an explanation, and I don't know how to gloss over it. 'Someone made a complaint about my overgrown garden. The garden's sorted now with Darcy's help, but Mr Rowbotham got his knickers in a bowline knot and reported me to the council, and they're not impressed with the number of customers I bring to Ever After Street, and they're talking about evicting me and using the space for something that would be more popular.'

'They *what*? Oh, those lousy buggers.' Lissa shakes a fist at the sky. 'Corporate greed!'

'Oh, for goodness' sake, Marnie, why didn't you tell us? We could've helped,' Sadie scolds me.

'I didn't want to impose. You've all been lovely to me since my mum died and I've given you nothing in return. You've all got your own businesses to deal with, you didn't need to bother about my woes too.' I decide to be honest. 'And I don't know who made the complaint, I thought it might've been one of you, and it's okay if it was, the garden *was* in a terrible state, it *did* deserve to be complained about. There are no hard feelings.'

A few murmurs go around as they all ask each other if it was them. No one owns up, but they probably wouldn't anyway, not in a group setting.

'Probably just some passing busybody with too much time on their bitter and miserable hands. Someone who gets their jollies off by making life difficult for everyone else,' one of the girls from Christmas Ever After, the year-round festive end of the street, says. 'You know what some people are like. They'll complain about anything if it stays still for two seconds. I bet you get complaints about typos where out of 100,000 perfect words, someone's honed in on the one tiny mistake that's slipped through the net.'

I laugh because it wouldn't be the first time a customer has read the entire book and then demanded a refund because they've found a typo on page 172, and defaced the book to highlight it so I can only resell it as damaged stock.

'You're not going anywhere.' Mickey slings an arm around my shoulders. 'I'll take on the council myself if I have to.'

'A Tale As Old As Time belongs here, Marnie, as do you,' Sadie says kindly. 'When you and your mum arrived, it was a breath of fresh air – the opposite of that fusty old book restorer who used to be there. We'd always said we needed a young and fresh bookshop on this street and your theme fits in perfectly. We're not going to let them close you down over a garden.'

'Why does a bookshop need a garden anyway?' the eyelinered magician from the carousel asks.

'That's what I thought, but I've got to admit that it's become quite important now. It's not the ideal time of year for it, but I could really see it getting some use in the summer months. Like a little outdoor library. I could offer people a selection of books to read and maybe some sort of tea and cake partnership with Lilith...' I glance towards the closed tearoom and it makes me wonder if it will ever open again.

'So it's "growing" on you then?' Ali makes a pun and we all dissolve into giggles, and it's so good to feel like an important part of Ever After Street and part of a real team here.

Feeling accepted makes me think of Darcy, and I look to the upstairs window of The Beast's Enchanted Rose Garden and think about him up there, excluded and alone, when everyone who works alongside him is down here, laughing about a garden that he's solely responsible for.

There are blinds in the upper windows of his shop that are *always* closed, but today... Today, there's a gap between one of the slats, and I'm certain there's a shadow there, looking out.

Come out. I say it in my head, but I know he's unlikely to walk out into a street full of strangers. I let my mouth tip up into a smile instead, hoping I'm looking at where his eyes might be, and for a fraction of a second, one of the slats moves up and down, just once, like Darcy is winking back.

It makes my smile turn into a full-blown grin and I tilt my head and incline it towards the others, silently inviting him to come outside. There's no response from the blind, but I can feel eyes on me, and this time, they're not Darcy's.

Mickey has caught my exchange with the unseen person behind the window. 'We happened to notice you two have been spending time together...'

'He's helped me with the garden. That's all. We talk every day.' I'm playing it down. I don't just *talk* to Darcy every day. I bare my soul to him, but that's not for anyone else to know.

'Oh my goodness, what's he like?' Imogen squeaks, and now every eye on Ever After Street is on me again, and even the birds in nearby trees have quietened down in anticipation of gossip.

'Is he really a beast?' Lissa asks. 'Where did his scars come from? They must be pretty awful to keep them covered the way he does?'

'I've, er... I've never actually seen him.' I was trying not to draw attention to him, but maybe they *should* know. I can't take credit for the change in my garden *or* the boost in my self-confidence. Darcy deserves people to know how special he is.

Almost everyone in the little group is now looking up at his window, and this time when I look up, that gap in the blind has gone. 'He's not a beast. He's... lovely.'

'*Lovely*, eh?' Mickey says with waggling eyebrows.

Usually I'd blush and mumble something incomprehensible, but Darcy deserves better than that. 'Yes. Lovely,' I say with a confident nod. 'He's kind and thoughtful. Protective. Generous. He loves Mrs Potts – my cat, not the teapot – he's the nicest, most non-judgemental person to talk to, but...'

'He makes himself an outsider,' Ali finishes for me. 'He's welcome here anytime. *He's* the one who chooses not to come. None of us care what he looks like or if he wants to wear that hat and scarf.'

I don't want Darcy to be the subject of local gossip, but I *do* want our colleagues – sometimes they feel more like friends lately – to know that he isn't the 'Scary Neighbour' they think he is. 'He doesn't think he'll be accepted because he's chased you all away so often.'

'We're going to have to do something about this,' Ali says. 'He's a part of our little street too. There will always be a place here for him, a safe space where no one is going to judge him. Even if he throws wine bottles at our heads from time to time. *Not* accepting people is *not* what we do on Ever After Street.'

'Is that what we've been doing?' Mickey sounds troubled. 'Excluding him? Gossiping about him?'

'We do, don't we?' Lissa jumps in before anyone can answer. She looks horrified and there's remorse in her voice. 'He's "Scary Neighbour" to all of us. We're all guilty of it, aren't we? We've all sat here and made up theories about what he's hiding. No wonder he never comes out.'

'I didn't realise...' Imogen says. 'I don't give a damn what he looks like, his shop is incredible. Those window displays are the stuff of magic. So many customers talk about them.'

'He's so talented,' I add. 'He grows these incredible one-of-a-kind roses that he's bred himself and no one realises how special they are.'

'But people find it hard to connect to him. His displays *are* beautiful, but customers go into that shop expecting a person to chat to, someone to give them advice about flowers or plants and if he's there at all, then he most definitely doesn't want to be disturbed. People leave empty-handed because they're scared of him,' Sadie says.

'I think he deliberately drives people away so they don't ask questions. He'd rather be seen as a beast than risk not being accepted.'

'That's just heartbreaking,' Lissa says and a chorus of agreement runs through the group, every eye trained on the unseen shadow behind Darcy's window. 'When someone has put up walls that high, they don't need to stay inside them.'

'I'm going to go and buy some flowers today.' Mickey nods decisively.

'Me too,' Ali says.

'My *Beauty and the Beast* display could do with a fresh red rose or two,' Lissa adds.

By the time the meeting ends, having got completely off-track from what we were supposed to be discussing, there are promises from every trader to go and say hello to Darcy today, and I'm unsure if he'll be angry at me for talking about him behind his back, but I've got a sneaking suspicion that Darcy *wants* to be accepted and will secretly be quite touched.

As everyone says goodbye and goes back to their respective shops, Sadie catches me. 'When are you coming for this dress fitting then? It's such short notice, it's a good job we've got another seamstress now and I've got time for this.'

She must have the wrong person. 'What?'

'The dress he's ordered for you?' Her eyes flick towards The Beast's Enchanted Rose Garden.

'What?' I repeat. 'Darcy has ordered me a dress?'

'He hasn't told you?' she says in disbelief.

'No. Not a word.' I glance at his shop too. 'Why on earth would he order me a dress?'

'His email said it was for the costume ball at the book festival – a custom-made yellow Belle gown, no expense spared.'

Everyone deserves to wear a dress like that at least once in their lives. I remember saying it to him weeks ago when I was talking about my love for *Beauty and the Beast*, and I can't believe that he even remembered, never mind thought about getting Sadie to make me a real-life Belle dress. I've always wondered what it would be like to have a dress made for me, but could never dream of spending that amount of money on something I'd wear once, if that.

'You okay?'

I don't realise I've frozen, open-mouthed, and am staring at Darcy's shop until Sadie touches my arm to get my attention.

'Yeah, I just... *Why* would he do that?'

'Maybe he likes you.'

'I know he's let me get closer than anyone else, but *like*? In *that* way? Darcy isn't... he doesn't... I mean, whether he does or doesn't, what kind of relationship could we *really* have? It's okay for a friendship, but I don't know if he'll ever let me get close enough for it to be something more.'

'Is that what you want?'

'I like him, Sadie. Really like him.' I didn't intend to tell her, but everyone watched her and Witt fall in love in the spring, and I know she'll understand. 'I can't wait to see him every day. I miss him when I'm not talking to him. Everywhere I am, I'm thinking about him. I feel this sense of comfort just knowing he's on the other side of the wall. I get butterflies when I'm with him. With Rick, I was always self-conscious and uptight, scared of doing the wrong thing or saying something I shouldn't, but Darcy makes me feel like I *am* good enough just as I am...'

I sigh because it seems hopeless. I know I'm feeling things for Darcy, but how can you love someone who won't *let* himself be loved?

'Never mind, ignore me.' I think about the dress again. I don't know what to do about it. How can I accept such a generous gift?

'He's already paid a deposit.' Sadie can either read minds or my face gives away exactly what I'm thinking. 'It would be unfair to turn down a grand gesture with so much thought behind it.'

'But that fancy-dress night is for everyone else, not for me. I'll be too busy organising everything. It never crossed my mind that I would dress up. I intend to be in the background where no one can see me.'

'In the dress I've got in mind, you'll be centre stage.'

'Sounds like my worst nightmare,' I mutter, even though the thought of wearing one of Sadie's handmade dresses is really a dream.

'Oh come on, you told me ages ago how much you longed to have a *Beauty and the Beast* moment in a yellow ballgown...'

'I know, but...' I struggle to put into words what I'm trying to say.

A grand, expensive gesture is lovely, but what I *really* want from Darcy is something that would cost nothing at all – enough trust to unwind his scarf and let me see him. A hug that doesn't end with him pushing me away. I've always dreamed of a ballroom scene, but not because of the scene itself, because of what it represents – Belle falling in love and the Beast learning to accept that love.

16

After persuading me that a ballgown really is a good idea, Sadie grabbed her kit from The Cinderella Shop and came into the bookshop, where she measured me, drew pattern pieces and pinned them around me, and sketched out what will be the most beautiful dress I've ever seen in my life. Since she left, the rest of the day has been spent confirming times and topics for the author talks and desperately trying to remember if I've forgotten anything and trying to foresee any possible disasters that might strike between now and the weekend, selling a few more tickets, talking books with eager customers, and counting down the hours until Darcy is coming over to fill my empty flower borders with the bags of spring bulbs he's got for me.

I close up at ten to five because Darcy is way more important than any customers who might turn up in the few minutes before closing time. I feed Mrs Potts and make two cups of tea and get some biscuits, and I'm lucky I don't spill anything in my rush to get outside.

'Why did you order me a dress?' I say as soon as I hear his gate unlatch and he appears on the path outside.

'Because you told me ages ago how much you love Belle's dress, and it's a costume ball for literary characters. What better excuse?'

'Darcy, Sadie's incredible and her dresses rightly cost hundr—'

'It has nothing to do with the money.' He lets himself in through my gate. 'I guessed you weren't planning on dressing up, and it wouldn't be right for the organiser *not* to have the most spectacular costume of all. And I thought you might feel more confident in character. I know you're nervous; you doubt yourself and your ability to pull this off, but *I* don't. It might make it easier to push that aside and embody Belle's bookworm spirit. Playing a character is easier sometimes. A kind of disassociation, a detachment, that makes it easier to compartmentalise.'

Is that what he's doing? Playing the role of a beast because it's easier to face life if you're pretending to be someone else? If he calls himself a monster, does it somehow make it easier to cope with his fear that other people might too?

I think I'll probably spend the night of the ball panicking about something going wrong, but I decide not to push it any further. I thank him, but it doesn't adequately express my gratitude. No one has ever *listened* to me the way he does. He seems to understand everything I *don't* say.

I put the tray of tea and biscuits down in the middle of the new rose bench, and he puts the bags full of tulip and daffodil bulbs down beside the newly dug over borders and takes a seat on one side of the bench, and I sit on the other, the tray between us.

After a couple of minutes of silence, sipping tea and dunking Hobnobs, Darcy speaks. 'Do you know how many people I've sold bouquets and plants to today?'

'How would I know something like that?' I try to project innocence, but he saw all those eyes on him at the meeting this morning – he *knows* who we were talking about.

'Well, the funny thing is, the Ever After Street lot have pretty much given up on me lately, but today, they *all* tried to make conversation. I've been invited to lunch, tea, private shopping evenings, been given multiple discount coupons, and Ali brought me a sample platter from 1001 Nights, even after the wine bottle incident. It suggests *someone* has been talking about me...'

I can't really deny it, can I? 'Nothing but the truth. We got onto the topic of my garden and I said you'd helped me. They've always wanted to know you, they just didn't think you wanted to know them.'

'I don't.'

'Don't say that. This is a little community. We support each other. You're part of that whether you like it or not.'

'I'm part of nothing. I can't be part of anything, Marnie. I'm not like other people.'

'No one is like other people.' I can feel my frustration building. What will it take to get through to him? 'Everyone is different. Everyone is unique. Everyone brings different strengths to Ever After Street and everyone is appreciated for who they are. Believe it or not – and I know you don't – but the people here like you.'

'They like some version of me that exists only in *your* head. They don't know me. They haven't seen me. You haven't seen—'

'I don't need to see you to *know* you're the best person who's been in my life for many years.' It feels like there's an impenetrable wall between us and no matter how hard I try, I hit this wall at every turn. His wall. And he's the *only* person who can break it down.

I know that everyone on Ever After Street would accept him, no matter what, but there is nothing I can say to make *him* believe that. I didn't think it mattered at first, but now it's driving me crackers. 'Everyone admires your shop and your work at the castle.

They would *love* to know the real person behind your incredible flower displays.'

'It can never happen. You don't understand.'

'So make me!' The frustration rears its unsightly head again and I snap at him, and then sigh at myself. 'I'm sorry, but you're right, I *don't* understand and I desperately want to. Please, Darcy, *let* me understand.'

I sit back angrily and my shoulders hit the backrest with force and send my tea sploshing everywhere. Darcy doesn't speak, so I eat another Hobnob, and then another with enraged bites, and eventually he sighs and sits back with a groan of pain. That subconscious noise softens my heart towards him. Those noises are something he's never hidden from me, and I'm sure the answer to all of this lies inside them.

He dunks a biscuit and I listen to the forlorn glugging sound when he overestimates the optimal dunking time and loses half of it to the depths of the mug. I turn towards him and lean my head to the side, like it will somehow allow me to get a few millimetres closer to the edge of that metaphorical wall.

His voice is hoarse and so quiet that I don't think I'd be able to hear it if I wasn't sitting right next to him. 'The last time I went out in public, I can still picture the looks on strangers' faces. The fear. The horror. A warning for kids – *that's what you'll end up like if you don't do as you're told.* Someone took a photo like I was some carnival freakshow on display. I always wonder what the guy did with it. Show it round his friends and laugh? Show it to his children as part of a Halloween horror story? Look at it when things get tough and think, "Oh well, no matter how bad life is, at least I don't look like *that*"?' His voice is shaking so much that the bench is juddering with the force of it. 'I was desperate to be discharged from hospital and my physical therapist said they'd never let me go without knowing I was capable of doing normal, basic things, like food shopping, so we went to the supermarket. People acted like he was a zookeeper walking a wild animal. The wide berth. The looks of pity. Confusion about how someone ends up looking like I do. Someone even said to me, "What *is* you?"'

My heart hurts for him, and my mouth has gone dry when I go to speak. 'I wouldn't pay attention to someone who can't even speak in grammatical sentences.'

He lets out a wet-sounding laugh. 'Grammatically correct or not, it hurt more than any of the physical injuries ever had. It proved that I could never live a normal life again.'

'Darcy...' My protective instinct kicks in and I want to wrap him in my arms and growl at anyone who dares to come near, but he's tense, his shoulders hunched and his body taut, and there's no way he'd accept a hug, so I reach over and let my hand slide over his knee, squeezing it gently. 'That's just one person.'

'It was *every* person. Every single one of them looked at me like I'm a monster.'

'No one is a monster. Well, murderers and other criminals, maybe. Are you a serial killer?'

'Not last time I checked.' He tries to laugh, but he sounds so vulnerable, and I realise how much this one incident has affected him. He doesn't *want* to live the isolated life he leads – he pushes people away because he thinks *that* is what will happen if he lets anyone in.

'What happened to you?' I say it quietly, absolutely terrified that this is the question that will make him jump to his feet and bolt back next door, never to speak to me again. I've never tried to pry before, never pushed him for answers, but it's too important to keep dancing around like this.

'You don't know that anything happened to me.' His answer is equally quiet and unforthcoming, and I have to choose whether to continue pushing or not.

I take a deep breath. 'Yes, I do, Darcy. I know you were hurt somehow, injured in some way. Do you have any idea how many noises of pain you make? Every time you get up or sit down, it sounds like your entire body is aching. Please tell me.'

'I can't, Marnie.' He stands up, clearly concealing the noise of pain this time, and the abrupt movement makes my hand drop from his knee and rattle the tray as my wrist falls against it.

One of his kneeling pads is leaning against the hedge and he throws it in front of an empty flower bed by the gate, grabs a trowel, and kneels down to start digging the new bulbs in without another word, conversation clearly closed.

I sigh and do the same. A selection of his kneeling pads have migrated over here, so I pick one up, take a handheld fork and a bag of tulip bulbs, and kneel down at one of the flower borders by the shop wall on the opposite side of the garden.

At first, I just hear the plunge of his trowel into soil and the metal against concrete clink as it hits the edges, but gradually it goes silent and all I can hear is his ragged and unsteady breathing, like I've forced him to think about a past he didn't want to remember.

There's silence for a long time, nothing but the evening chorus of birdsong and the occasional sound of a crisp leaf losing its grip on a branch and being blown to the ground in the forest. I've stopped digging holes for the bulbs because I'm too caught up in listening to his shuddery breaths as he tries to get his emotions back under control, and I fight with myself about whether to go over and hug him or just leave him be.

'I was hit by a train.'

I can't help the intake of breath, partly because I didn't expect him to tell me, and partly because... Bloody *hell*, the impact of that. My mind goes to a million places about what kind of injuries that would result in. No frigging wonder he makes noises of pain every time he moves. I turn around to look at him. 'Oh, Darcy, I'm so sorry. Good lord. I'm *so* sorry.' I don't know what to do with something so unimaginably painful. 'How long ago?'

'Seven years.'

'You were... badly injured?'

'Catastrophically so. That's the word the doctors kept using. I clung onto that, for some reason. Catastrophic injuries. It felt like a good metaphor for what my life had become – catastrophic.' His laugh comes out as more of a scoff. 'Months in hospital. Years more of physical rehabilitation. All the ribs on my right side were shattered. Shards of broken rib pierced my right lung and made it collapse. Broken rib pieces slashed pretty much every internal organ. Fractured skull. Smashed jaw. Smashed eye socket. Smashed cheekbone. Broken pelvis. Broken leg. They barely managed to save my hand. Just about everything you can imagine being broken was broken... Sorry, you don't want to hear my shopping list of injuries. We'd be here all night if I went through them all.'

'Of course I do. I want to know everything, even the hard parts.' I take that as my cue to get up and go over to him. He's got his arms around his knees and is sitting on the kneeling pad now, so I take mine and sit down beside him. 'You're still suffering?'

'No more than I always will. Everything healed eventually. I got mobility back. Broken bones are never the same, and my ribs... well, they had to jigsaw-puzzle them back together with titanium plates, so they ache sometimes, especially when the weather turns cold.'

I reach over and slide my hand over the glove covering his left hand, my wrist brushing against the sleeve of the chunky knit jumper he's wearing, unsure if he's going to shrug me off. 'Your injuries... they changed the way you look?'

'I have scarring. My face was so badly cut up that they had to use skin grafts from my hip to heal it. My nose was broken and healed in a different shape. When a jaw is broken, the masseter muscles overcompensate for the other damaged muscles and they grow and bulge, changing the shape of a face. I'm a mess, Marnie. I need you to understand that.'

'And I need you to understand that it doesn't make any difference. You survived something that sounds unsurvivable. Whatever scars you have, whatever injuries you've recovered from, they're testament to how lucky you are. People would understand. They'd be proud of you for what you've overcome. Your scars are medals of honour for surviving such a horrific accident.'

'That's the thing you're not getting,' he suddenly snaps at me. '*I* survived. Someone else didn't.'

I tilt my head to the side. 'What does that mean?'

'I was on the track because I was trying to get someone else off the track, and... I failed. She died because I wasn't fast enough, good enough, I didn't have the right words, the right actions. I wasn't *enough*. I thought I had more time, in all senses of the word – metaphorically and literally.'

'Someone you knew?'

'My girlfriend. *Ex*-girlfriend. It was complicated. It was a messed-up toxic relationship, we were on-again off-again, but I always thought we just needed to be in the right place and it would be forever. I loved her, and I failed her.'

'That's what you meant about never letting anyone get close to you again,' I say as that sentence he uttered in the castle gardens suddenly makes sense. 'You nearly died in trying to save her. No one could have done more.'

His head is bowed but his scarf moves as he disagrees.

I squeeze his hand. 'What happened?'

'We were on a break. I got a text saying to meet her at the train station early one morning. I thought she had planned some sort of day out for us, hoping to get back together. Got there and there was no sign of her, waited, and then from way up the line, there were shouts from a passing dogwalker, and I just *knew*. I'd never run so fast in my life, and she was just sitting there. I sat beside her. Tried to persuade her to give life another chance – to give us another chance. But nothing I said was enough. I could hear the noise behind me. The tracks vibrate when a train is approaching. So I tried physically lifting her, pulling her out of the way, but she fought me, and then...' He stops, letting me fill in the blank.

He's crying and he pulls his hand out of mine and takes off his glove, muddy from gardening, and pulls his glasses down to swipe at his eyes.

'I'm so sorry,' I repeat, at a loss for anything else to say. Instead of words, I let my hand rub his back and lean over to press a kiss into his shoulder. 'You can't blame yourself.'

'Who else am I supposed to blame?'

It's one of those questions without an answer. 'No one. It's not her fault. No one can help ending up in such a bad place. And it's not your fault – not her ending up there or how you couldn't help her, no matter how hard you tried. Hating yourself and resenting yourself for seven long years doesn't change that.'

I suddenly understand where the 'deserve' thing comes from. Darcy feels like he doesn't deserve to be loved because he blames himself for someone else's death. 'You call yourself a beast not just because of the physical scars but the psychological ones too. You might look different but you *feel* like a monster... which you're not, physically or emotionally. Survivor's guilt... when it sounds like you barely did survive.'

'I'm still here and she is not. By definition, I survived.'

'That doesn't mean you don't deserve to be happy. You deserve to have friends. Colleagues who care about you. A job that brings you joy. You're allowed to share that joy with the world rather than skulking around, growling, and pretending your roses aren't as unique as they are.'

He hasn't put the glove back on his left hand, and even though it's his undamaged one, it still feels special when he reaches out and traces across my palm. His fingers touch mine one by one, and after what seems like a lifetime of holding my breath, they slip gently between mine and his hand closes tight around my hand.

I bite my lip to hold back the sob. I don't know how long it's been since someone held his hand, but this is the first ever moment of skin-on-skin contact with nothing between us. 'You ever talked about this before?'

'No. It was a long time ago. It doesn't matter now.'

'It always matters.'

'To you.'

'To me.' I think for a minute. 'Have we accidentally turned into the Chuckle Brothers?'

He lets out a loud guffaw and every inch of tension dissipates and I can feel the way his body sags. I'm the only person on earth who Darcy has ever been this open with, and it makes me feel exceptionally humble.

'Are you okay now?' I don't realise how hard I've been holding back tears until my voice wobbles on those words, and he hears it too, judging by the way he lifts my hand to his mouth and presses his lips to it through the scarf.

'I died that day, Marnie. My life as it was ended then and there.'

Something niggles at me about his wording, but I squeeze his hand because that's all I can do – hold and listen.

'It was the metaphorical death of the person I was. Until recently I've felt like the good parts of me died and the horrible parts survived. The part that died was the part that still believed in good things – in magic, in fairy tales and happy endings, in there being any good in the world, and what was left in that hospital was a monster who didn't deserve to still be here. I had a job I loved but I wasn't physically able to continue. My so-called friends disappeared like snowflakes in sunlight. The only person who was there for me was my father, and his support got me back on track. Doctors saved my life and then nature saved my soul.'

'Nature... the castle gardens. That's when you got into it?'

'Yeah.' He sounds far away, lost in memories, and for the first time tonight, they don't sound like they're all bad ones. 'When I was discharged, I was still in a horrendous state. I couldn't live alone, so my father let me move here and stay with him. I needed adjustments – handrails, bath aids, wheelchair access because walking was hit and miss back then, and bless his soul, he let people come and put in everything I needed, and he looked after me like I was a child again. He was seventy-three years old, and yet, at thirty-one, I was the one who needed disability aids and daily nurses visiting. A weird kind of ironic role reversal.'

His laugh is tight and so is mine.

'But I refused to go out. By then, my injuries weren't as raw as they were at first, but I still saw the looks from the people in the supermarket every time I closed my eyes, and I didn't want to repeat the experience. The castle gardens were my dad's pride and joy. It was the weirdest, contactless job, and as I got stronger, he made me go with him. I had no interest in the outdoors back then, I'd never grown a thing in my life, but he thought it was the perfect way to ease me back into the land of the living. The path through the forest between his house and the castle was always quiet, and the gardens themselves were completely private. I didn't have to worry about being seen there. I'd struggled with focus and concentration since the accident, but the rules of gardening were the first things I could keep straight in my head. I pruned things, repotted things and found joy in watching them grow and flourish. I found peace with my hands in the earth. The first thing I ever grew by myself was a rose. I'd taken a cutting from one of my dad's rose bushes months before, expected it to die, but it grew, and the day that first rosebud opened into a flower, I sat on the ground in front of it and sobbed my heart out, because this monster had brought about a beautiful change in the world. I had been responsible for so much misery, and for the first time, something was better than it was before, because of me. He died three years ago, and I took over full-time – my way of honouring him and what he'd done for me.'

There are tears rolling down my face and I'm in serious danger of causing him more broken bones if I squeeze his hand any harder. '*Everything* is better because of you. Look at what you've turned that one rosebud into, and how much you've overcome to get this far. Even your handwriting, Darcy. You've got the most gorgeous handwriting I've ever seen, and that can't have been easy after...'

He laughs that sarcastic laugh again. 'That was my stubborn streak. The early days were a haze of pain and strong medication, the injuries all blended into one, but when they took the bandages off my hand, it was... a shock. I'm right-handed and I remember staring at this battered, bloodied, bruised hand and thinking I'd never write again, and writing had been a big part of my life up until then. I did a lot of pen-on-paper work. It wasn't the worst injury, but it felt like the most life-altering one. And as the swelling went down and it started to heal, I taught myself to write again using children's handwriting workbooks, and my obnoxious side pushed me through. It was something I was in control of. It became one thing I *could* do, by myself, just for me.'

All of his handwritten notes suddenly mean so much to me. I've always loved his handwriting, but I never realised how much it represented or how much it meant to *him*. 'Can I just say that I really *love* your stubborn streak?'

He laughs, genuinely this time. 'Been a long time since anyone loved anything about me.'

I squeeze his hand pointedly. 'No, it hasn't.'

He surprises me by dropping his head to rest against my shoulder just long enough for me to turn and kiss the top of his baseball cap. I expect him to object but he doesn't.

'You know it's freezing, right?' he says after a while.

'I do.'

'You know it's, like, 8 p.m., right?'

'I do.'

'You know we should go inside, right?'

'I do.' Instead of letting go, I squeeze his hand tighter. I *am* freezing. That cup of tea is making its presence known in my bladder, but the absolute last thing I want to do is let go of his hand. 'Seriously considering pitching a tent here just so we don't have to say goodnight.'

'That would be okay with me.'

The only part of my body that's warm are the fingers that have been entwined with his, and I clasp his hand between both of mine and lift it to my mouth until I can press a kiss to the back of it and I feel the shiver that runs through him. I can't find the words to express how much it means to me that he opened up, so I touch my lips to the base of his thumb and trail kisses down to his inner wrist and finally press one into his palm, right onto his life line.

'You said you stopped believing there was any good in the world, but you *are* the good in the world, Darcy. They say that if you passed yourself on the street, you wouldn't recognise it as you because in mirrors and photographs, we never see our true reflections, only what we think we look like. It's other people who see who we really are. We hide from our own reflections until someone comes along and holds up a metaphorical mirror, making us see ourselves as they see us. And you *desperately* need to see yourself as other people would see you.'

A full-body shudder goes through him. His glasses are still off so I lean over and press my lips to the skin just under his left eye.

He freezes for a second, and then lets out a sigh and leans into it, so I do it again, mirroring how much I wish I could stroke his face and touch my lips to his. And for the first time, it doesn't feel like such a distant impossibility tonight.

17

The morning of the book festival dawns bright and cold, with birds singing in the trees and crisp brown leaves to kick up as Mrs Potts and I walk through the forest to work. It's been raining for days and the river is gushing below us, crashing through the depths of the forestry, winding and dangerous. The banks are steep, the rocks sharp, and if you fell in, you'd have very little chance of climbing back out, but up here, the tree branches are bare enough to let the sunlight through and it's already started to dry up the muddy paths, and it reflects the positivity of my mood.

I never in a million years thought I could do something like this, and now it's actually here, it feels exciting rather than overwhelming. I've prepped everything, I've got help from Cleo and my Ever After Street colleagues, and the panic I was expecting this morning simply hasn't arrived. Rather than something I'm doing alone, it's become an Ever After Street event and everyone's pitched in and made me feel like part of a team rather than as isolated as I've felt without Mum.

Ever After Street is busy for a Saturday morning. It's almost 9 a.m., there's an hour before the castle opens, and I settle Mrs

Potts in her window seat and open the shop. One of the girls from Christmas Ever After has volunteered to cover A Tale As Old As Time for the day, because I need to be in two places at once and I don't want to close with the extra booklovers who might be passing by.

She's happy to look after Mrs Potts too and I make sure she's got my number and an overflowing tin of Dreamies, and instead of being nervous, I'm excited to get up to the castle before opening time and help with any last-minute preparations.

Mickey and Lissa are setting up the book swap tables in the courtyard, already stacked up with books locals have donated, and I've added in my damaged or otherwise unsellable stock, and inside, Sadie and Witt are arranging the castle's theatre room ready for the author talks early this afternoon, and I thank them for all they're doing and go to find Cleo, who's commandeered one of the ballrooms and has got various tables set up, and stacks of deconstructed books and craft supplies. The first item on the festival agenda is Cleo taking a class on repurposing books that have come to the end of their lifetime, and she'll be teaching a morning of classes on various book-themed crafts.

'Book paper roses here.' Cleo gives me a hug when I come in and shows me around each station, pointing out the first table with a vase displaying a bouquet of roses made out of book pages.

'Darcy would like that one.' The sentence leaves me with a jolt of sadness because this is something I wish I could share with him. He's done so much to help me and to make me believe I can do this, but he hasn't made any mention of actually coming so I assume his initial refusal still stands.

Cleo looks like she can tell what I'm thinking. And there's nothing anyone can do about it, so she opts for distraction instead. 'Wreaths made from book pages here.' She leads me to another table that's stacked with pages she's pre-rolled, and then points out the two other crafting stations in the huge room. 'Book page pinwheels here, and make-your-own greeting cards over there.'

Everything is running like clockwork so far, and as I walk around the castle, saying hello to colleagues that I'd never considered friends until now, I wonder if maybe a book festival is exactly what Ever After Street needed to bring us all together. I've always thought that books have a way of doing that.

As 10 a.m. comes and visitors start streaming in, I join Cleo's class and make a rose for Darcy with the surviving pages of a damaged copy of *Pride and Prejudice*, because I think he'll appreciate it, and I can't help looking around as I fold squares of book paper into triangles to form the petals.

There are so many people here. More than I ever expected. Over fifty people have turned up for the morning of bookish crafts, and everyone seems to be having a good time. Cleo's got quiet Disney music playing in the background and the age of our attendees ranges from young to old and everyone in between, giving a real multi-generational feel, and it makes my heart soar to see so many grandparents helping young grandchildren to glue their paper petals into position, because if they're doing this together, they must be doing other bookish things together and sharing a love of reading through families and across generations.

After a morning of crafting, there are author talks in the theatre room of the grand old castle. Our three local romance authors chat about different aspects of the writing and publishing process, from getting a book deal to creating memorable love interests and building settings. Ali has volunteered as the host and he sits at the side of the stage, asking questions and keeping conversation up with enthusiastic ease. It's fun and easy-going and the theatre seats are filled with readers, listening to each author's every word, some scribbling down notes and questions to be asked at the Q&A session tomorrow.

The afternoon brings with it the time for a literary afternoon tea, where ticket holders are gathered in one of the castle's entertainment rooms. Lots of little tables have been set up, and the three authors are mingling and chatting. There's a buffet of finger food that Cleo's arranged with Lilith's daughter-in-law, who's been hastily brought in to cover the tearooms in Lilith's absence, and our guests are enjoying miniature sandwiches, scones, and bite-sized cakes, along with copious amounts of tea, and as this is a more child-friendly part of the event, Cleo's love of *Alice in Wonderland* has crept in, and children can choose between book-shaped biscuits, 'eat me' cupcakes, and a selection of squashes served in mason jars with 'drink me' tags attached.

By the time 4 p.m. rolls around and people start leaving for the day, I'm left feeling utterly joyful at the success it's been, and with a sense of disbelief that it's all gone without a hitch. I never imagined that I could do something like this, and somehow, I have. *We* have.

Even though Sadie and Witt insist they don't need any help, I stay to tidy up, as do most of my other Ever After Street colleagues and between us we clear up the food and tidy away chairs and tables. Mickey mops the floor, and Lissa goes around with a binbag collecting any debris guests have left behind. Everyone seems happy to help and it makes me feel that sense of community again. The fact that one person can have a slightly barmy idea, and then everyone pitches in to make it come to fruition.

It's what I love most about Ever After Street.

* * *

Sunday morning is a damper affair as the rain pours down again, and I'm glad that today's activities take place inside. A Tale As Old As Time is closed today, so I've brought Mrs Potts with me, and

I've got her tucked under my arm inside my jacket as I hold an umbrella over both of us and hurry through the woods towards the castle.

Judging by the sludgy puddles squelching around my welly boots and the crash of the river rushing through the gorge below us, it's been raining for most of the night, although I was so pleasantly exhausted when I got home that I must've slept through most of it.

This morning is the author Q&A session followed by a book signing, and when I arrive at the castle, I strip my coat off, leave my umbrella in a stand in the foyer, and make sure Mrs Potts is dry and safely on her harness as we go to see where we can help with the setting up.

The book swap tables, greatly diminished after their popularity yesterday, have been hastily dragged out of the rain and into the castle foyer, and Mickey and Lissa are setting them up all over again. There are two ballrooms in the castle – the one on the right of the grand entrance hall is closed off, although no one seems to know why, and the one to the left is where the author Q&A and book signings are taking place, and everyone is in there getting things ready. A small stage where a live band would usually play has now been commandeered for the Q&A session, and there are three tables spread around the perimeter of the huge room where the authors will sign books, and each author is currently setting out their own tables full of paperbacks and promotional materials.

The ballroom is pre-decorated for the literary costume ball later, but it's so dull outside that Witt has put all the fairy lights on early to cheer the room up, which gives it a sparkly, magical feeling, like we really are standing in an enchanted castle.

Festival attendees start arriving, and I keep Mrs Potts in my arms so she's not getting under anyone's feet. I don't know if it was the best idea to bring her, but I don't like leaving her home alone for long days, and she seems to be enjoying all the fuss she gets when being introduced as the bookshop cat.

Ali chairs the Q&A like a pro, and I stand on the edges of the huge ballroom and watch, my tablet in one hand with a list of pre-prepared questions in case there's a lull, but the attendees are so immersed that we easily fill the allotted time with questions and overrun with even more, and eventually the authors head to their tables for the book signings and I wander away, knowing that as soon as they're done, it will be all systems go to clear the ballroom, ready for the costume ball to kick off at 6 p.m.

In the grand entrance hall, Witt has brought in a makeshift stage and a freestanding spotlight, just in case U.N.Known really does turn up. I'm convinced he won't, but it's been such a great weekend that it doesn't seem to matter any more. I thought no one would come without some big draw like finally revealing the mystery of the unknown author, but it turns out that some people just really love books, and judging by the bulging till when I got back to the shop yesterday, they also love independent bookshops and want to support them.

This was such a distant pipe dream at first, but now, instead of impossible, it feels like something I'd like to do again sometime. We could make it an annual thing. Now there's been one Book-ishly Ever After, there will be write-ups and reviews online. Lissa's been taking photos for travel destination websites and the Ever After Street blog and social media. There have already been comments from people saying they wish they lived near enough to attend or they would have made plans to come if they'd known sooner. There's going to be a journalist from a national newspaper here tonight so more people will hear about it. Maybe next year, more people will want to come. Maybe more authors will be inter-ested in being a part of it. Maybe there's a genuine possibility that A Tale As Old As Time could play host to a book festival every year from now on, to share a love of books and a way to meet new bookish friends...

...Unless I'm going to be evicted and no longer have a book-shop *to* support. Mr Rowbotham is supposed to be here today. I sent him an email informing him that the garden was ready for inspection and everyone from Ever After Street would be at the castle if he wanted to discuss anything, but he didn't reply, which is either a good sign or a really, really bad one.

After clearing the ballroom and watching the afternoon pass in a blur, I'm still trying to keep my mind off the worst happening when Sadie puts a hand on my shoulder. 'Time to get changed.'

I glance at the Roman numerals of the clock at the top of the stairway in surprise. It's not even 5 p.m. 'It won't take me two hours to get into a dress. There's ages yet.'

'Not for you, my friend.' Her hand tightens on my shoulder, and two others appear from where they were hiding under the stairs.

Cleo takes Mrs Potts and rustles a packet of Dreamies concealed in her pocket, Lissa wrestles my tablet from my hand, and Sadie herds me towards the stairs before I have a chance to protest.

'We've got it covered down here,' Lissa assures me, flicking my tablet on and ticking off an item on one of my painstakingly prepared to-do lists. 'Mickey's around, Ali and Witt are on hand, and we're all taking over while you have some much-needed me time. Well, *you* time.'

That brings to mind pampering images of cucumber slices covering my eyes and green goo spread across my face, which although a nice idea, it's not exactly ideal timing. 'I can have "me time" tomorrow,' I say, knowing full well that Mondays aren't conducive to free time. 'We're in the middle of the most ambitious thing I've ever done. I don't need to soak in a candlelit bath full of rose petals *right* now. I can be ready in five minutes flat. We had a fitting on Friday – we already know the dress is a perfect fit.'

The three of them share a knowing look with each other, and I have a feeling that this is a well-planned intervention and they all know something I don't, and I have very little choice but to go along with it.

I feel like I've been kidnapped by some fairy-tale mafia as I'm ushered up the grand castle stairway, along a lavish hallway, and into a dressing room, where Sadie's cousin, Scarlett, is wielding a hairbrush at me.

While Sadie adds a few final red rose embellishments to the skirt of the Belle dress, Scarlett sits me down at a dressing table and I look at my reflection in the mirror as she whizzes around me, smoothing my face with foundation which leaves my skin glowing, dusting on just the right amount of blusher which makes me look healthy and glowing, unlike when I try to do my own blusher, which usually makes me look like Ronald McDonald. Once my eyes are outlined in black and surrounded by metallic brown and grey eyeshadow, she starts on my hair. I've always thought it was too short to do much with, but Scarlett whips out curling tongs and manages to curl the straight part at the front into flattering tendrils and tease sections of it back to be held in place by red rose clips that match the roses Sadie's using.

By the time she's finished, and Sadie's helped me into my dress, I look in the mirror and it's like a short-haired Belle is looking back at me, and I'm surprised by the magic Sadie and Scarlett have managed to weave. I look like I belong in a fairy tale, and I have never looked like that before.

'This way, my lady.' Sadie does a mock bow as she opens the door and steps through it, ready to escort me to wherever we're going next.

I slip my arm through hers and she leads me along the narrow corridors and back down the stairway to the main entrance hall, past a few curious glances from visitors as my ginormous yellow satin dress swishes along with me, and she stops at the doorway of the closed ballroom, takes out a key to unlock it and lets us in, but she doesn't follow me.

'Enjoy yourself, and don't worry about a thing out here, we've got it covered.' She backs out of the double doors and they shut with a click that sounds loud in the silence.

The bright lights from the chandeliers make it look even darker outside. The early evening light is fading as it filters through the windows. Grey-black clouds are hanging over the castle, heavy rain is hammering down onto the domed glass ceiling, and I'm alone in the empty ballroom, wondering what on earth is going on.

18

It doesn't take long to find out. Within moments, there's the click of another switch and the bright lights of the chandeliers dim to half-light. In the far corner of the ballroom, there's a narrow staircase that leads to a balcony around the upper level, and someone up there moves, and at the top of the stairs in the corner, the Beast appears. Literally.

Darcy, wearing a blue velvet suit jacket, yellow satin waistcoat, black trousers, and a *ridiculously* realistic-looking Beast costume head, slowly descends the stairs with one hand behind his back, and I watch him while trying to make sure my mouth isn't hanging open in surprise.

At the foot of the stairs, he bows. One arm across his chest, dipping the huge Beast head low, and I bow in return, and I *know* he's smiling as much as I am.

'So *that's* why you ordered this dress for me.' It's not what I want to say, but it's the most eloquent thing I can come up with on the spot. Of all the things I imagined Sadie and the others were up to, something like this never crossed my mind.

'It honestly wasn't,' he says as he walks towards me. 'I didn't know if I was going to...'

'...be able to find the courage?' I finish for him when he struggles for a way to end the sentence. There are a *lot* of people in the castle tonight. Even though he's wearing a mask that fully covers his head, I can't imagine Darcy is comfortable in this kind of crowd.

The huge Beast head nods.

'You look phenomenal.' I take a step towards him and reach out to run my fingers over the yellow-edged lapels on his blue suit jacket. It's a perfect match for what the Beast is wearing in the ballroom scene from the animated movie, and it fits him like such a glove that I'm certain Sadie must've had a hand in making it.

I turn my hand around so my palm rests on his solid chest. 'I thought they were being suspiciously vague about why this ballroom was closed off tonight. This is your doing?' Of course it's his doing. Even the ballroom floor is scattered with red rose petals. No one but Darcy would've thought of something like that.

'Maybe.' I can imagine his blue eyes winking at me. 'You once said that you've always dreamed of a "tale as old as time" moment in a ballroom one day, and we're in a ballroom, in a castle, and you're wearing the most beautiful dress I've ever seen. It seemed like a good time.'

'I didn't know they made masks that were so realistic.' I lift my hand from his chest and stroke the face of the Beast mask, and look up into the blue-coloured glass eyes of the costume head. That's the only possible place to see out, so his real eyes must be behind there somewhere too. I cup the Beast's cheek and let my fingers drift through the brown fur. Two shades of brown velvet surround the eyes, leading to pointed ears and up to forwards-facing plastic horns. There's a big brown flat nose, and the mouth has got two fangs sticking out from the bottom jaw. The entire thing covers his neck and goes down inside the white dress shirt under his yellow vest.

'I wanted to see you kick arse tonight. I wanted to see this whole weekend be the success you deserve it to be and I didn't want to *not* be there for you because of my own limitations. Friends are supposed to support each other.'

'Friends,' I echo. It's not enough, and the butterflies I'm feeling right now are *not* friendship butterflies.

'It's all we can ever...' He trails off, either unable or unwilling to finish the sentence. Which is good because I'm unwilling for him to finish it too. I don't want him to cut this off at friendship. I never thought it was possible to fall for someone you've never fully seen, but I've *fallen* for everything about Darcy, and seeing all of him doesn't seem important any more.

He shakes himself and does a good impression of the Beast's growl. 'Never mind all that. Look at you, Belle.' He lets out a long exhale. 'You look resplendent.'

He holds his hand out for mine, and I slip my fingers over one of the brown fur-covered paw gloves he's wearing. He lifts my arm and encourages me to do a twirl, and I spin around so my skirt flares out.

My dress is a yellow satin off-the-shoulder ballgown, with a boned bodice and a tiered skirt with ruched layers and glittery swirls of gold embroidery. At each ripple of the skirt, Sadie has sewn a sparkly fabric red rose. The heavy satin covers many layers of delicate organza that form the voluminous underskirt and give the dress its classic Belle ballgown shape. It's the furthest thing from something I would wear in real life, but it seems right tonight – like a step out of real life is exactly what I needed, and somehow, Darcy knew that.

Being under his gaze feels like a wave of red heat travelling up my entire body from the tips of my toes to the rose clips in my hair, and I'm blushing as I spin around, holding onto his hand like it's a lifeline.

'Thank you.' The words that come out are hoarse and I have to wet my lips and try again. 'None of this would be happening without you. Not the dress, but not the book festival either. Without your support and encouragement, I'd probably still be crying in a patch of stinging nettles in my overgrown garden.'

'Mrs Potts would never have let you sit there for that long without being fed.'

The laugh cuts through the weird tension between us since he mentioned the word 'friends' when I'm almost positive we're *both* feeling something a lot more than that.

One hand has remained behind his back, and now he holds it out, offering me a single stem red rose.

It's a beautiful, multi-layered flower with petals that are a bright rich red in the centre and almost burgundy on the outer edges, and my fingers brush against his fur-covered ones as I let my hand cup the huge flower and bring it to my nose to inhale the timeless scent.

'This is from the first rose bush my dad ever grew. An old cultivar that he imported from France decades ago. Hypothetically speaking, if there ever was a Beast, growing roses in his castle gardens in eighteenth-century France, this would likely have been one of them.'

To say my knees go weak is an understatement. I'm so touched that he hasn't just brought me a rose, but *this* rose, one that obviously means a lot to him and he knew would mean something to me too. 'You've put so much thought into this.'

'I wanted to give you a fairy-tale moment. You deserve to feel as special as you are, and I don't think many people make you feel like that.'

'I don't think many people make you feel like that either.'

'I don't des—' He abandons the sentence when I frown at him.

Instead, he takes the rose gently from my hand. At first he goes to tuck it behind my ear, but that would disturb the clips Scarlett's put in my hair, then he looks for somewhere on the dress to stash it, but short of shoving it down my cleavage, there's nowhere for it.

He laughs with embarrassment, because when a man looks at your body so intently, it's not usually because he's trying to work out where to put a rose. 'Well, this is awkward.'

It makes me laugh too. A bit of normality in an otherwise unreal night.

'I'll just put it over here.' He inclines his head and walks towards the grand piano at one side of the ballroom. He gets his phone out of an inside pocket in the Beast's blue suit jacket and fiddles with it before putting it down on the lid of the antique piano. 'Unlike in *Beauty and the Beast*, I can't stretch to getting the piano to magically play itself. A playlist will have to do.'

There's a nervous energy that being *so* close to Darcy brings with it, a mixture of excitement and anticipation. He's going to ask me to dance, and it's the strangest mix of joy that he's literally tried to recreate a moment from a fairy tale for me, and maybe... disappointment, because, even though it's a fantastic mask, he's still *wearing* a mask, and if tonight really was a fairy tale, I'd be dancing with Darcy as he really is.

'Would the Belle of the ball give me the honour of sharing a dance with the Beast?' He comes back with one arm outstretched, holding his fur-covered hand open for mine as 'Beauty and the Beast' starts playing from his phone.

It is, without doubt, the most romantic moment of my life. 'I'd be honoured.'

I'm beaming at him and I *know* he's beaming back at me, and I'd give *anything* to see the smile I can sense in his demeanour, the lightness in the steps he takes as he lowers his head in a bow again.

My breath catches as my hand slides into his and his fingers curl around mine. His right hand touches the side of my waist, fitting perfectly into my curves, warm through the lining of my satin bodice. I have to force myself to breathe again as he steps back carefully, slowly, waiting for me to follow his lead as the song that I've always thought was one of the most beautiful songs of all time plays softly. I feel like I'm caught up in a swirling storm of butterflies, fluttering all around me, making me feel like I'm fluttering inside too. My skin is tingling with anticipation of his next move, the promise of our bodies getting closer, and every one of my senses has been taken over by him. Every atom in my entire body is centred on Darcy.

The waltz we dance is something straight out of a movie, and I'm half convinced this is a dream and I'll wake up at any minute, because moments like this don't happen when you're awake.

As we glide across the glittering ballroom floor, Darcy is the perfect gentleman. A real prince in disguise, tall, chivalrous, and strong. He's wearing an autumnal aftershave and I keep turning my head and taking a big inhale of the scent of spicy pumpkins and cloves and cinnamon and everything else that is this time of year personified. The swish of my dress makes me feel like I'm soaring, spinning in his arms, fizzing every time he twirls me around and pulls me back against him, and the respectful distance between our bodies diminishes each time. I get shivers every time we touch, every little brush as we move around each other feels special, and throughout it all, I don't take my eyes off the blue glass eyes of the Beast mask.

Rain patters on the roof above us, and he doesn't say a word as we dance, but I can sense him smiling at me as we spin faster, sending rose petals swirling in our wake. Happiness is glistening in the air all around us. Life might not be perfect, but for right now, it *is*, and there is nowhere I'd rather be than in the arms of this most beautiful man.

As a second version of 'Beauty and the Beast' finishes, and the anticipation of getting close to him tingles again, he spins me around and tugs me back with a delicious little bit more force. I bump into his chest and my hand tightens on the sinewy muscle between his neck and left shoulder, and it feels like he's feeling that same sense of anticipation.

Instead of twirling me again, his hand slips from my waist and round to my lower back and his head tilts questioningly, asking permission to touch me so intimately, and I nod without a second thought.

I can't see him smile, but I *know* he does as those fingers press into my lower back and he pulls my body tighter against his. My hand is still on his shoulder and my fingers curl into the fur-covered folds of the hood where it covers every inch of his neck and disappears under his shirt. The butterflies that were swirling around earlier feel like they've settled all over me, their wings beating a thousand times a minute, like there's magic sparkling all around the room.

Both his arms slide around my back and hold me tight, and my other hand lays on the curve of his chest. I slip my hand under his blue jacket and it comes to rest right over his heart. The Beast head doesn't extend that far down, and there is nothing but the thin layer of his shirt between my fingers and his skin, and my fingertips feel like five glowing spots, burning at every point they make contact.

He lets out an extended breath and my other hand slips up to stroke through the long brown fur held in a ponytail by a blue bow at the back of the mask, and he lets out a sigh and lowers his Beast head to rest against mine.

It feels like I could slide my hands up and peel his mask off centimetre by centimetre and he'd let me. I want to, but he's never been this unguarded before, and he deserves to know that he *can* be without me trying to push him into revealing something he isn't ready to reveal yet.

The playlist Darcy put on his phone has moved into playing a selection of older Disney classics, but to be honest, it could be playing 'Old Macdonald Had a Farm' and I'd still be happy, just so long as I don't have to move more than a millimetre away from him yet.

His arms tighten and his foam-padded chin moves against the top of my head, being careful not to displace any of Scarlett's meticulous styling. 'You okay?' he murmurs through the mask, sounding blissfully far away and like it's taken a Herculean effort to form two simple words.

I feel it too, lost in the joy of moving around the ballroom with him, no longer dancing, just holding each other. 'Best evening of my life.'

His breath catches. 'Mine too.'

'Because you've always wanted to waltz around a ballroom with Belle?'

'Not with Belle, but definitely with *you*. And not always, but in the past six weeks, I've thought of very little else.'

I've never felt so special to anyone before. How is it possible that someone I've never truly *seen* can make me feel so cherished?

'I know you think I was lying when I said *Beauty and the Beast* is my favourite book, but I wasn't. When I was in hospital, there was this kid in there, and part of his recovery was that his nurse used to take him round to read to the other patients. Not usually something I'd put up with, but I was on strong painkillers and I suppose I gave some kind of hazy consent, and every so often, this kid would come and sit by the bed and read a story, completely unfazed by whatever state his listeners were in, and one day he was reading *Beauty and the Beast*, and something more exciting happened down the other end of the ward and he dropped the book and ran off, his nurse chasing after him, and no one ever came back for it. I guess the staff on the next shift assumed it was mine, and it stayed on my bedside table, and one day, when the swelling around my right eye had started to go down and I was getting some vision back, I picked it up and got totally swept away in the story. The old-fashioned language, the sense of a different time, a world away from our own, and the Beast... the idea that one day someone could learn to see past the hideousness and fall in love with him... It spoke to something inside me. It gave me hope, which was something I hadn't felt in months. When I left, I took it with me, and I've still got it on a bookshelf in the flat.'

'So, what you're saying is... you stole a book from a hospital.'

'I told you, I'm a monster.' At least he's laughing as he says it this time. 'And when I realised what I'd done, I sent them a new copy and a voucher for many more new books, because I'm not *that* much of a monster.'

It makes me laugh and I pull back until I can look up into the Beast's glass eyes again.

'Thank you for making me feel that hope again, Marnie. Getting to know you has been like giving water to a dying rose. I thought I was dead inside, that I'd never have the capacity for love again, and then I heard you wailing like an elephant seal in labour...' He holds his arm out for me to smack and I dutifully do, even though I can't stop smiling. '...and everything changed.'

My hand has stayed on his forearm and I give it a squeeze through his suit jacket sleeve.

'From day one, you've treated me like a normal person. You've never tried to catch me out. You've never disrespected my boundaries. You've made me feel like I fit in. You've reminded me of what it's like to be a part of the world and you've made me *want* that again...'

I slip both arms around him, one around his waist, one around his shoulders, until I'm hugging him as tightly as I can.

'For the past seven years, since the moment this happened, I've never met a person who didn't try to change me. Who didn't tell me I was wrong to back out of life the way I have.' His voice is muffled where the chin of the mask is pressed against my shoulder. 'Doctors, nurses, ex-friends, distant family, complete strangers... Not one person has ever accepted my way of coping. Every single person has made me feel wrong. Unacceptable. Like someone who needs "sorting out". But you... you accepted me as I am. Why did you never try to fix me?'

'Because you're not broken.'

I can feel the words hit him. It's like they knock him off his feet. His legs go wobbly and my arms around him are not just hugging him but holding him upright.

'No one's ever said that before.' I can hear the emotion in his voice and that protective instinct kicks in again, the one that makes me want to hold him tight and snarl at anyone who dares to say an unkind word.

While keeping my arms around him, I pull back until I can look up into his eyes again. 'I can't imagine what it's like to lose someone you love in such horrific circumstances, and to be injured so badly and to live with scars and ongoing pain, and none of us have any right to judge anyone on how they handle it. You don't need fixing. You have never needed fixing. If the attitudes of other people need fixing then that's their problem. The one and only thing you need is to let someone love you – to accept you're worthy of love and realise that having scars doesn't make you an un-beautiful person.'

'And what then? You think that will be the moment that the Beast transforms back into a prince? My scars won't be magically healed when the last petal falls from a rose, doom lifts from the castle, and the homeware takes on human form.'

'Good. Because, firstly, that would be quite strange,' I say to lighten the atmosphere. 'And secondly, because the Beast's defining moment isn't when he becomes human again – it's when he's got Gaston by the neck and is holding him out over the edge of the castle, seconds away from letting him drop to his death, and he pulls him back because in that moment, *he* realises that despite appearances, he *isn't* a beast. He never needed to learn to love Belle – he needed to learn to love himself.'

'Do you know how clichéd that is?'

'It's also true. *To love oneself is the beginning of a lifelong romance.*' I quote Oscar Wilde and give him a stern look. 'Because this isn't about how you look. It's about the anger and guilt that you carry with you. You don't hide away because of your scars but because of the feelings that it might bring up if anyone asks about them. It's never too late to forgive yourself.'

'You make me wish it wasn't.' He pulls back and his paw glove reaches out to stroke my face, one plastic claw running down my cheek with the gentlest touch. 'You have no idea how much I want to kiss you.'

The words are so quiet that I don't think he intended to say them, and it makes goosebumps rise across my whole body. I swallow *hard*. 'That would be okay.'

It would be a *lot* more than that. 'Okay' doesn't begin to cover it, but it sounds slightly more civilised than saying, 'I want to wrestle you to the floor, jump on top of you, and kiss you until your mind has melted so much that you can't even *think* the word beast.'

'I can't...' Even as he says it, his hand slides down my arm and he intertwines our fingers. He looks up, looking around the room, the low light, the ever-present rain beating against the roof, the quiet music in the background, and he tugs my hand gently, leading me across to the stairs he came down earlier. He sits on the third stair and pulls his legs up, turning his thighs into a flat surface and inviting me to sit on his lap.

I perch gingerly on his thighs. The huge skirt of this dress doesn't make it easy to squash up against someone. His arm goes across my lower back and curls around my hip on the other side, holding me steady. He's facing front and I'm sitting sideways and facing the empty ballroom in front of me.

His hands are shaking and his breath is coming in sharp pants. 'Will you just... close your eyes and don't turn around?'

I nod and let my eyes slip closed, and cover his hand on my hip with mine, barely daring to breathe as I realise what he's going to do. He pushes out a long, shuddery breath, and his arm rests against my back as, painstakingly slowly, he removes the mask.

Every instinct in my body is screaming at me to turn around and look at him, but he asked me to do one thing, and *that* is more important than sheer nosiness.

Time passes so slowly that it feels like *hours* go by, even though it's only a matter of moments, and then he's there. His nose touches the side of my face. Soft lips press against my cheek.

Just one kiss, one peck that I can't respond to without turning around and going against what he asked me. My fingers are between his where his hand is still on my hip, and I squeeze them with the sides of mine, trying to get across how much it means that he trusts me *this* much.

His nose presses just under my eye and his lips graze against my cheek again, and I want nothing more than to grab him and haul him into a proper kiss, but this isn't easy for Darcy. There are tremors going through him, and his hand tightens on my hip, his forehead resting against my hair, every shallow breath against my skin making goosebumps rise at the back of my neck, and his lightly stubbled chin tingles against my skin every time his mouth moves.

I could happily sit here for the rest of my life, cuddled up in his arms, swathed in semi-darkness, very far away from the real world. It's his right hand that's on my hip, and without opening my eyes or turning around, I lift it up and gradually pull off the glove that's covering it, and bring it carefully to my mouth until I can touch my lips to his scarred skin.

He shivers but he doesn't pull away. Instead, he kisses my cheek again, our faces sort of resting against each other's, and I hold that hand between both of mine, hoping that actions speak louder than words. I can *tell* Darcy that his scars don't matter, but this is the first time I've had a chance to *show* him.

There's silence between us, long and comfortable. His lips touch my cheek every so often, and I keep lifting his hand and kissing the scars covering the back of it, but all this moment is really about is enjoying the closeness, ensconced in our little corner of the castle, surrounded by the peppery, earthy scent of his aftershave, cocooned by the hammering rain, just being together in a way I never dreamed we would.

'Can I ask you something?' It feels like I've just woken up when I finally make myself speak.

'Mmm.' He sounds like he's in a daydream too, distant and tranquil, and definitely not ready for the moment to end.

'What do you think would happen if I opened my eyes right now?' I squeeze his hand again.

'Absolutely nothing. I think you'd look at me, touch my scars, say they aren't that bad and they don't make any difference to how you see me...'

'Then why do you keep pushing me away? Metaphorically,' I add when his arms tighten around me, physically holding me closer. 'There's a whole castle full of people out there who would love to get to know you. A whole street full of friends and customers, and you keep all of them at a distance much further than arm's length because you've convinced yourself that you know what will happen if they ever see you.'

'I do—'

'It's a self-fulfilling prophecy, you idiot,' I say fondly. 'When you refuse to let anyone in, you become lonely. When you withdraw from the world, you become withdrawn. When you tell yourself you're a monster—'

'You become one?' he finishes for me.

'No.' I give his leg a gentle smack. 'You become convinced that other people will see you like that too. Kindness makes you beautiful, Darcy. Your kindness, your thoughtfulness, and your cracking sense of humour make you the most beautiful man I've ever met. There is *nothing* that can change that.'

He nuzzles against my jaw, and it feels like an invitation, because this chaste cheek kissing thing is nowhere near enough. I move my hand back gently, letting my fingers run up his arm as I lift my arm over his head until it rests around his shoulder and my body has turned to face his. Every movement is slow, giving him time to object if he wants to, even though the way his fingers curl into my thigh suggests he *definitely* doesn't want to.

He makes a wanton noise as my fingers reach around blindly until they find his hair, and I run them through thick, straight strands that start curling at the back of his neck where it gets long.

My other hand comes up and touches his jaw, and my fingertips feel the uneven bumpiness of scar tissue, and my thumb rubs across the deep dip of a scar in his stubbled chin. It's barely the whisper of a touch and every single breath sends a fire of anticipation racing through my veins. My heart is hammering and my pulse is thundering in my ears. I didn't realise how desperately I want to kiss him until this moment.

One of his arms is still around me and the other is trailing up and down my back, making me gasp every time he skims the bare skin of my shoulder blades, and my thumb presses into his jaw, turning his head towards me.

It feels like *everything* has been building up to this moment.

My eyes are closed and we're guided by touch alone. I lean my forehead against his and let my nose rub against his and he lifts his head to return the gesture, so close I can *feel* the smile I've only been able to hear before tonight.

His hand gets higher, cradling my head, leaving me with no doubt that he's about to pull my mouth to his and my hands tighten in his smooth hair as a sizzle overtakes my entire body.

It's like the world explodes when our lips finally touch. I've never felt fireworks before, but tonight it's like the fifth of November all over again.

Nothing has ever felt so right or been *so* worth waiting for.

In my head, I'm screaming at myself. *For the love of books, open your eyes. You're kissing a man you've never even looked at*, but something stops me. He's trusted me enough to get *this* close. Maybe one day he'll trust me enough to let me see every scar he's hiding, but until that day, nothing matters more than this gorgeous man trusting me enough to take that final branch out of the metaphorical hedge that protects him.

It turns into a clawing, desperate kiss. His hand in my hair sends rose clips skittering across the floor, and my fingers trace across his ear lobes, my thumb brushing his jaw, tongues tangling with intensity. It's impossible to kiss him *enough* or hold him tight enough, and it feels so *right* that it's overwhelming. It's a kiss that feels so good that it makes me want to cry right into it. Partly because of how good it feels and partly because of how much it means that Darcy has let things come this far.

I can feel how much he's struggling to keep his emotions under control, because I am too. There's never been a kiss that felt this special. I've never felt such a strong surge of love for someone before.

The emotions overwhelm him and he pulls back, panting. He ducks his head against my shoulder, but I stick to my word. I keep my eyes closed. My hand is still in his hair and I move it again, following it until I can press my lips against his forehead, kind of missing and kissing his hairline instead, but it doesn't matter. Touching him somewhere, *anywhere*, is the only important thing.

And then he speaks. Just one word that takes him a *lot* to build up to saying. 'Okay.'

'Really?' I tighten my hands on him.

'I can't do this any more. It's not worth it. I *am* pushing you away, and we've reached the point where I have to choose between losing you and trusting you, and I *can't* lose you. Open your eyes.'

Now *I'm* crying. I rest my forehead against his and press my nose against the side of his face until my lips find his cheek and a shiver goes through him, his hand on my lower back sending one through me too. A tingly, fizzy shiver, and a sense of relief. This is it. Finally. In just one second. One blink.

Suddenly there's a shout from outside and the door bursts open. 'There you are!'

Darcy yelps and scrambles for the Beast mask and I jump to my feet and shield him behind my enormous Belle skirt while he yanks it back on, swearing at shaking fingers, as Rick storms in and hits the light switch, setting the chandeliers ablaze with bright light.

'Sorry, Marnie!' Sadie barrels to a halt after him. 'I tried to stop him but he wouldn't listen.'

'It's okay.' I try to reassure her because she looks distraught. 'If there's one thing we know, it's that Rick is incapable of doing anything he's asked to.'

'Didn't interrupt anything, did I?' he says with a grin in my direction.

Only the most special moment of my life. 'What are you doing here? Why are you at a book festival? You don't even like books.'

'I bought a ticket. I have every right to be here.'

'If I'd have known that, I'd have put a system in place for vetting the guests first,' I mutter, standing on unsteady legs and feeling knocked off-kilter by the interruption.

I glance down at Darcy. He's still sitting on the step, his re-covered head in his hands, and I lean down to touch his shoulder. His re-gloved hand slides over mine, just once, and then he gets to his feet, towering above me.

'Wouldn't mind knowing what you're doing with that *thing*?' Rick demands.

'Who I spend my time with is none of your business.'

Sadie has sidled out the open door, leaving us to it, and Darcy's hand touches my back in silent support, and Rick glares at him. 'I'd like some time alone with my *girlfriend*, if you don't mind, *mate*.'

The word 'mate' has never been spoken in such an un-mate-like way before.

'I don't think she'd like any alone time with you, *friend*.' Darcy's unfriendly tone mimics Rick's, and at full height with the Beast mask over his head, he's an imposing figure, and I can see Rick's blood boiling at being intimidated by someone he thinks is beneath him. This is a situation that needs defusing before it escalates.

Despite the frustration at such an important moment with Darcy descending into *this*, and the exasperation at Rick's truly horrific timing, I reach over and touch Darcy's arm. 'It's okay, let me talk to him. This needs to end and if you stay, he's only going to be interested in getting one up on you and strutting around all over the place. You go.'

'Yeah, mate. You go.' Rick preens.

Darcy hesitates, unsure of leaving me alone with him, but Rick is a peacock, and with Darcy here, his only focus is going to be on parading his pretty tailfeathers in front of him and he's *never* going to listen to anything I have to say. I give his arm a reassuring squeeze and he nods the Beast head in understanding and very, very reluctantly, starts making his way across the ballroom to the door. Darcy bends to retrieve a doorstop and wedges it underneath, deliberately holding it open, and I get the feeling he's not intending to go very far, which is fine by me. I've always felt edgy around Rick, even when we were together, but Darcy's belief in me has given me more confidence than I had a few weeks ago, and I feel like I can speak up for myself now and I have a right to be listened to.

'Marnie?' Darcy turns at the door and the blue Beast's eyes look back at me. 'In case I don't get another chance to say this before the time comes, I'm not going to let you down. And I'm sorry.'

He disappears around the corner and I blink at the empty doorway in confusion at his crypticness.

'What?' I call after him. 'What does that mean?'

'Never mind anything that comes out of that ugly twat's mangled mouth.' Rick approaches me with his arms open, like he's expecting a hug.

'I've just kissed his mangled mouth and it felt very un-mangled to me!' I snap at him, not intending to have let Rick know there's anything going on between me and Darcy.

'You and... *him*?' Rick lets a finger hang in the air, halfway between pointing to the doorway, his mouth hanging open in shock. And then he starts laughing. 'Oh, wait, I get it! You're winding me up! Trying to make me jealous, but it's just too hilarious. This is a publicity stunt for the shop, right? You dressed as that Disney woman in the yellow dress and him as the Beast? Have you joined forces to "win" the costume competition and cheat your way out of having to give any prizes?'

'No, because I'm not a cheater, unlike you.'

'Oh, come on, Marn. *One* mistake. You can forgive me that much, can't you? Come here, let's hug it out.'

He comes towards me with his arms open again, but I whack his hand before he gets within touching distance and step out of his reach. 'Don't touch me.'

'Okay, you're going to make me work for it, fair's fair. Could you give me a timetable for this scheduled sulkathon?' He checks the designer watch on his wrist. 'I mean, are you going to finish punishing me tonight or should I come back next week?'

'Come back *never*, Rick. We're done. We always will be done. I don't want you in my life, and I can't make that any clearer.'

'Oh, now, don't be like that. I come bearing gifts.'

'I don't want any gifts.' I'm trying to be civil to him. In reality, I want to strangle him, but trying to strangle people comes with pesky court proceedings and Rick isn't worth that.

He drops to one knee, producing a ring box from his pocket and flipping it open to reveal a diamond engagement ring that's at least three times the size of the one I once threw out the shop door at him. 'Marry me, Marnie. Again. Let me make it up to you. The one thing your mum wanted was to know she didn't have to worry about you being alone. The size of this diamond proves that I can offer you the world and no one would turn that down based on one minor indiscretion.'

'It also proves that you think money is the only important thing in life.' Instead of feeling angry at him, I suddenly feel incredibly sorry for him. There's a *Beauty and the Beast* quote for any occasion and it brings to mind one about a man Beauty's sister had married. *A gentleman, extremely handsome indeed, but so fond of his own person, that he was full of nothing but his own dear self.* Rick struts around, driving a car that most people couldn't dream of affording, wearing clothes that cost more than anyone would ever reasonably spend on clothing, throwing money at every problem that comes his way. I think of Darcy, the way he not only helped me with the garden, but inspired *me* to do it myself. If Rick had been in my life then, his response to Mr Rowbotham's letter would have been to pay him off, and if that failed, then to pay for some kind of landscaper to come in and make the garden look like it belonged to a country estate. He's a lost soul with such a vapid personality that maybe he feels his money *is* all he's got to offer anyone, and I never realised that before. Maybe what Rick needs is to find someone who loves him, but that person will never be me.

I go over, cover his hand with mine and forcibly close the ring box. 'No, Rick. Not just no, but *never*. I'm sure you'll be the perfect guy for some girl, but we aren't right for each other. I deserve someone who loves me and supports me and champions me. Someone who steps *miles* outside of their comfort zone just to be there for me. Someone who makes me laugh *and* cry in a good way. And you do too. So please hear me once and for all. This has to end. I will never, ever have anything to do with you again. I don't love you – I never did, just like you never loved me. You want the feeling you had back then of being part of a family. Of being a rock when I needed you, but you don't want *me*. Yes, my mum loved you, but she would *hate* the amount of times you've used her memory to try to manipulate me. She would want me to be happy, and if she had lived longer, she'd have realised that would never be with you.'

He splutters, staring up at me open-mouthed. 'Do you know how much this cost? Most girls would be floored by such a gesture!'

'Yes, but I'm not one of them. I like books and drinking tea and eating biscuits. I don't want to zip off to Paris for the weekend at the drop of a hat. I want to curl up on the sofa in front of a crackling fire with someone, cuddling up as we read our respective books. I always, always preferred the Beast to any of the traditionally handsome Disney princes. Most kids had a crush on Aladdin or Prince Eric, but mine was always on the Beast. And that never changed as I grew up and it still hasn't. Please excuse me.'

He's still down on one knee as I walk away, but I don't get very far before he shouts after me. 'You're leaving me for that *abomination*? That *monster*?'

It rubs me up the wrong way and all the goodwill I was trying to channel towards him flies off through the ballroom's windowed ceiling. 'Leaving you? Rick, we broke up a year ago! There is nothing to "leave". Our relationship is well and truly over. Don't ever call Darcy that. He is the furthest thing from a monster. *You*, on the other hand...'

'Darcy? That's *his* name? Hah!' He laughs to himself so much that he overbalances and has to put both knees on the floor to steady himself. 'Well, well, well. Ain't the world a remarkable place?'

'What?' I ask, clearly missing something. There's no way Rick knows Jane Austen well enough to know who Mr Darcy is. I doubt he'd even be able to identify *Pride and Prejudice* as being a book. If Rick knows anything about Jane Austen, he probably thinks she's famous *for* being on a ten-pound note.

'Oh, don't you worry about it, Marn. Who doesn't love a weird and fateful coincidence, eh? Enjoy the rest of your evening.'

I grab the chance to escape the ballroom, although his sudden change in tone leaves me with a sinking feeling – the kind that Belle gets when Gaston sings 'The Mob Song' and starts leading a gang of villagers to storm the enchanted castle with battering rams.

19

Back in the entrance hall, the costume ball is well underway in the opposite ballroom, and out here, it's nearly time for U.N.Known to take the stage. I told him to come and find me dressed as Belle, but I've been hidden away in the ballroom for well over an hour now, so I've got no idea if he's here or not.

Darcy is standing to one side in his Beast costume, and now he's got Mrs Potts in his arms.

'Hi.' I go to stand beside him and reach over to give her a head rub, brushing my hand against his arm as I pull back.

'Hi.' He glances down at me and jiggles his arms gently to indicate my cat, who looks happy and relaxed with him. 'Cleo let me take her for a while. I needed her calmness.'

'Are you okay?'

He makes a non-committal noise. 'You?'

'Yeah. I'm sorry about that, that was the worst timing.' I feel awkward and the atmosphere between us is awkward, like something's shifted in the last five minutes. 'You know there's nothing between me and him, right? It was over long ago, he just refused to listen.'

'I know.'

I touch his arm again, letting my fingers linger on his blue suit sleeve. 'Later, I hope we can continue where we left off.'

The Beast head looks down at my fingers on his arm. 'Well, you might not want to. Marnie, listen, there's something I need to tell you. I'm...' His head lifts towards the door. 'Mr Rowbotham.'

'You're Mr Rowbotham?' I say in confusion.

'No.' He laughs a nervous laugh and inclines his head towards the open doorway. 'He's just arrived. And he looks... wet.'

I follow his gaze towards the castle foyer, the ornate doors wedged open to invite guests in, where Mr Rowbotham has appeared, looking so drenched that someone could've dumped an entire lake on him. He's creating his own puddle where he stands and holding onto a limp umbrella that looks like it gave up the ghost a good few hours ago. 'Which probably means he's been outside to inspect the garden and I'm about to be evicted.'

I try to sound casual, but my heart is in my throat and a stone of dread has settled in my chest cavity. I should go over and speak to him immediately, but maybe it will be a good thing if he mingles a bit and sees people enjoying themselves, and maybe he'll be in a better mood after he's dried off. I see Witt intercept him and offer him a towel, while one of the catering staff hired for the night furtively mops up the puddle.

'Hey.' The brown fur paw reaches out and holds my elbow and waits until I look up and meet the eyes of the Beast mask. 'Not on my watch.'

I casually slide behind Darcy, intending to hide on the sidelines for a while before facing Mr Rowbotham. 'I don't think "your watch" has much to do with his attitude towards non-green-fingered bookshop owners.' I briefly cover his hand with mine. 'But whatever happens, thank you. The past six weeks have been the best time I've ever had, and all of that is because of you.'

'Marnie...'

Mr Rowbotham looks up from rubbing his dark hair dry with Witt's proffered towel and his head swivels in our direction. We stand out because Darcy's costume is two feet higher than everyone else, and my skirt is big enough to need its own post code and I'm not going to be able to hide for long. 'I'll catch you later.'

I slip between someone dressed as Toad of Toad Hall and someone who's come as Paddington Bear and try my best to disappear before Mr Rowbotham notices me. I'm keeping a constant check on my phone to see if there are any emails from U.N.Known, confirming he's actually here, but the inbox stays maddeningly quiet. From a single one-line email, I've arranged a whole evening's activities around this man, and I have absolutely zero idea if he's going to show up.

'Any sign yet?' Cleo is dressed as Alice in Wonderland and she slides through the gathered people towards me. The entrance hall, where the stage for U.N.Known's speech has been set up, is gradually filling with people who have arrived for this moment, and others who have come out of the ballroom to witness the first ever public appearance of such a secretive author.

We're standing by the stairs, lurking behind them in the hopes Mr Rowbotham won't see me, and my eyes flit around the room, but no one who could be U.N.Known stands out.

'He could be *anyone* or he could not be here at all.' I check my phone for the eleventy-billionth time. No new emails. And no one who's looking around the room like they might be hunting for someone dressed as Belle. Apart from Mr Rowbotham. I shift so Cleo is standing in front of me.

'He'll be here. He wouldn't let you down.'

Those words again. My eyes flick to Darcy. He's gone to sit on the opposite side of the room, near the stage, and is stroking Mrs

Potts who's curled up on his lap. That stone in my chest gets inexplicably heavier.

'It was okay to let him look after her, right?' Cleo notices where I'm looking. 'He's brilliant with her and she looked better with the Beast. She can pass for the teapot version of Mrs Potts but no one was buying that she was the Cheshire Cat and it was too late to get her a pink and purple striped jumper.'

I laugh despite the uneasiness I'm feeling. There's an atmosphere in the castle tonight, something in the air that makes it feel like everything is about to change, in one way or another.

'I think she's an emotional support cat tonight. Darcy seemed like he needed her.'

'What happened with you two in the ballroom?' Cleo's oversized black bow headband flops forward.

'Everything.' I sigh. 'And strangely, nothing too. It was... intense. And then it wasn't, and now it feels like a moment we'll never get back.'

'Aww, don't say that. Look at him, Mar. Until a few weeks ago, he was the terrifying shouty guy in the rose shop. And now he's dressed as the Beast in a *very* public place because he wanted to support you. If that's not love, I don't know what is.'

'Maybe.' I try to shrug it off but that sense of uneasiness grows again, and only gets bigger as the lavish clock at the top of the stairway ticks closer to 7 p.m.

The entrance hallway is packed to the brim by the time the clocktower outside starts striking. Seven dongs. On the seventh, Ali gets up and makes his way to the stage. His granddaughters are big fans of *Once Upon Another Time* and would never have spoken to him again if he'd had a chance to chair a discussion with the author and turned it down.

'Well, here we are, ladies and gentlemen.' Ali is dressed as a middle-aged Aladdin and looks out at the gathered crowd, unable to hide the scepticism on his face. 'It's the moment you've all been waiting for.'

There's absolute silence in the crowd. There are costumes everywhere. Mary Poppins is to my left and Where's Wally is on my right. We're all here, united by a love of books and a desire to meet an author who has never been met before. The entire room is holding its breath as one.

'It's time to welcome to the stage, the amazing U.N.Known.' Ali looks around, looking like there's *no* hope of the bloke actually turning up. 'This is a historic moment in the book world, to be granted an audience with such a mysterious writer, so let's all be gentle with our new friend, and give him a warm welcome and show him just how much we love his wonderful book.'

The audience start clapping – a partially expectant clap and a partially muted one, subdued by the clear doubt that U.N.Known is going to be here.

I'm watching, waiting like everyone else in the room, feeling more and more nauseous with every second that passes. I've done all of this on a false promise and the majority of my day tomorrow is going to be spent refunding ticket prices for disappointed customers. My eyes fall on Darcy. Those blue glass eyes have found me across the room, across all the people in between us.

The sudden ding of a new email makes me jump. Seven o'clock on the dot, as though it was scheduled.

I look down to get my phone out, and when I look back up, one person who was sitting is now standing. And he's the only person wearing a Beast costume.

What?

I scrabble to unlock my phone with fingers that have gone clammy. Because Darcy is not just standing. Darcy is making his way towards the stage.

And in that moment, I know exactly what that email is going to say.

Everything that is real was imagined once. I'm sorry I didn't tell you.

I feel like I'm hearing everything through water, and yet, nothing has ever made more sense. Of *course* it's him. Of course it is. *That's* why he replied to my emails when he's never replied to anyone else's – because they were *mine*. That's why Darcy knew what U.N.Known had said in his emails when I *knew* I hadn't told him. That's why he knew they were often one sentence long. The way he said writing was his life once. He used to teach creative writing. *Once Upon Another Time* was published seven years ago, probably not long before the accident. The job he loved that he couldn't continue. No wonder U.N.Known never wrote another word after *Once Upon Another Time*. No wonder his first email told me he was dead – because that's what Darcy felt. The Unknown Author died on the day Darcy *nearly* died. *Everything* he's said makes so much sense now. Even *I* mentioned the similarities between them. Darcy's initial hatred of *Once Upon Another Time* despite claiming to have never read it. That day he bought the book in the shop. It felt important, and it was – he must have blocked out that entire chapter of his life, and buying that book was a small window back into it.

Even tonight. *I'm not going to let you down. Marnie, listen, there's something I need to tell you.*

I hear Ali say '*You?*' in disbelief as he steps up onto the stage.

'Is this for real?' Cleo's practically vibrating beside me. 'Or is he covering for the real one? No one knows who U.N.Known is so he could be, literally, anyone, and if the real one didn't show up, you had a back-up plan of Darcy stepping in? It's not like anyone would know, is it?'

'This had nothing to do with me.' I don't know if I want to laugh or wail. 'He's Darcy. He's always been Darcy.'

'You knew, didn't you?' she says softly.

'No. But yes, in a way. I think I knew without realising I knew. Or without thinking it could be possible. Too many coincidences. Those emails reminded me of Darcy. Talking to Darcy reminded me of reading *Once Upon Another Time* for the first time. I said they were similar without realising *how* similar. I'm surprised, but I'm not surprised. There are so many parallels between them. I noticed them, I just didn't think it was possible that the mysterious unknown author and my mysterious unknown neighbour could be one and the same. And the sole reason he's doing this is because he didn't want to let me down.'

'Awwwww.' Cleo hugs me while bouncing at the same time. 'Now if *that* isn't love then I *really* don't know what is. Someone who has been anonymous for so many years agreed to a public appearance because it would help your business. Now *that* is a man who would do anything for the woman he loves.'

It makes my heart swell in my chest, but I can tell from his body language that he's never been more uncomfortable than he is right now. Mrs Potts is still held carefully in his arms, but he's stiff and awkward with a gait not unlike a wooden plank as he takes his seat on the stage and settles Mrs Potts on his lap, who seems utterly unperturbed by the extra attention.

'So, Mr... um... Darcy.' Ali takes the seat on the opposite side of the stage. He was clearly not expecting this turn of events and doesn't know what to call him, although the comparison to the well-known romantic hero may not be so far off-base if what Cleo's saying is right.

I knew Darcy had pushed himself outside of his comfort zone

to be here tonight, but to sit on a stage in front of a couple of hundred people, to admit who he is and what he used to do... that's so far out of his comfort zone that it's not even in the same stratosphere, and he's doing it *for* me.

'Well, I've got to admit we weren't expecting this, Mr... Darcy.' Ali looks flustered as he shuffles through pre-prepared interview questions on index cards that he probably wasn't expecting to use.

I can see how hard Darcy swallows, his blue Beast eyes not daring to look up from the floor, both gloved hands stroking Mrs Potts like she's giving him a much-needed focal point.

'Well, I suppose we'd best start with a thank you for coming.' Ali puts his index cards on his lap to start a round of applause, and everyone else in the room swiftly follows, and I clap like I'm in a daze. I simultaneously want to stand here and listen to every single word he might say and storm the stage and throw my arms around him.

'I'm sure I'm not the only one who wasn't expecting you to show up, and now I know who you are, I also see why you did, so let's have a round of applause for our favourite bookshop owner, Marnie Platt – our very own Beauty to our very own Beast.' Ali stands to indicate me, and every eye in the room swivels towards me, and my Belle dress feels like it's going to have a *Hunger Games* moment and erupt into flames under *so* many curious gazes.

'There are so many things to ask you that I really don't know where to start. I suppose the obvious one is... why now? Why stay hidden for so many years, but choose now to appear at a book festival?' Ali's eyes fall on me. 'Of course, I have *some* idea myself, but you must've had many requests for public appearances over the years... What is it that makes our little book festival so special?'

Darcy goes to speak, but the words catch. There's a glass of water on the table beside him, and he obviously needs it, but he can't drink without lifting the Beast mask and he's not going to do that on stage. He swallows a few times and tries again.

The moment we've all been waiting for.

'Ever After Street is a very special place, and some of the businesses on this street deserve much more recognition than they get. I have a particular fondness for the Tale As Old As Time bookshop...'

Everyone in the room is completely silent, hanging on his every stilted word.

'Ah, Miss Platt, there you are.'

I groan internally. Speaking of moments we've been waiting for. Mr Rowbotham has finally caught up with me.

Cleo's still standing to my right, enraptured by what Darcy is saying, but he sidles up on my left, still so dripping wet that people nearby step aside to give him space.

'Not a good time,' I say as politely as I can. He clearly has no grasp of how important this moment is.

'A couple of months ago, I made a mistake,' Darcy is saying. 'I did something cruel and vindictive that I shouldn't have done, and my actions caused a problem. I thought my being here tonight might go some way towards fixing that problem.'

What is he talking about?

'You've done an excellent job with the garden, Miss Platt,' Mr Rowbotham says to me.

'You had a look then?' I hiss at the man hovering at my left. Doesn't he realise this is a monumental life moment? It's *not* the time for talking about gardens.

'I did, but only out of curiosity as I happened to be in the area. I must say you've done remarkable work.'

'Curiosity?' What is *he* talking about? Why *are* so many people talking about things that need further explanation today?

'Well, there was no need to bother after the complaint was withdrawn, but I thought I'd pop my head in for a quick look—'

'It was withdrawn?' I turn to him in surprise.

Back on the stage, Ali has gone rogue from the index cards. 'Ah, so you're here in a guilt complex capacity?'

'Not just that,' Darcy replies. 'The people here are my friends and neighbours. They've been kind to me. I didn't want to let any of them down. They deserve better.'

What is he on about? A guilt complex capacity? *What*?

'Yes, I received further communication from the complainant,' Mr Rowbotham says. 'This time saying they'd been mistaken and there was no Japanese knotweed on site, no neglect, no plants of any concern and to disregard their original complaint.'

'But there *was* Japanese knotweed. My friend excavated it. He's a professional gardener and removal expert.' I throw my hand out towards the stage. Maybe if he realises that I'm trying to listen to Darcy, he'll shut up.

'The person was quite adamant they'd been mistaken. They actually wrote at great length about what you bring to Ever After Street and were very keen to suggest I'd be making a huge mistake if I didn't offer you a lease renewal.'

I'm so confused. There's Darcy in one ear and him in the other and I feel like screaming for everyone to shut up and form an orderly queue for life-changing moments. One epiphany at a time, please.

'Does that mean you're going to renew my lease?' I ask, distractedly because I'm trying to listen to Darcy and Ali.

'Mr... Known.' Ali can't decide on which form of address is better and seems to be testing them all out in turn. 'Surely one of the questions you get asked most often is... why all the secrecy? Most authors use their real name or a pen name, they have websites and social media profiles where readers can connect with them, and yet, your identity has always been a closely guarded secret, and my granddaughters tell me there are entire forums on the internet dedicated to finding out who you are. Was it always intended to cause this much furore? A gimmick to get people talking about your book? Or is there something more behind it?'

'I don't know, Miss Platt,' Mr Rowbotham says, but I'm already losing track of *both* conversations.

'Something happened to me,' Darcy says. 'A few months before the book was published. At first I tried to get the publisher to pull the book, but they'd already invested in it and were certain it would be the start of great things. I never intended to be anonymous, but after the accident, I withdrew. I shut myself away from life and the last thing I wanted was anyone knowing my name. I didn't want people googling me. I didn't want anyone digging up any info about what had happened. My agent reached a compromise with the publisher – the book would still be published, but under a pen name. I didn't want to pluck a false name from thin air and pretend to be someone I wasn't, and my editor thought the mystery of the author would add to the ethereal other-worldly feeling of the book.'

Mr Rowbotham is still droning on. 'I'm thinking of selling the building actually, Miss Platt. It's getting a bit much for me. I was relieved to get shot of one when your neighbour bought his property, and now I'd like to spend more time with my wife and son, buy a motorhome and travel together...'

Please shut up. I want to hear about your wife and son and your life problems, just not *now*.

'I'd be happy to give you first right of refusal, if you wanted to put an offer in...'

On the stage, Ali is shuffling through his index cards again. 'We're going to take questions from the audience shortly, Mr Known, but first, I'm sure we're all on tenterhooks to know...

You've been exceptionally quiet in the publishing industry in recent years, but when can we expect another book from your good self?'

Darcy hesitates before he responds. 'I've always thought the answer to that question would be "never", but in the past few weeks, I've been feeling inspired.' He looks directly at me. 'Spending time around books and booklovers has reminded me of how much I used to love writing, and that's something I never thought I'd get back again. I let down people in the industry. I owe an apology to a lot of people. I may well be in legal trouble over the contract I didn't fulfil, but for now, the answer to that question is... maybe *not* never.'

The thought of him writing again – letting himself love something he once loved again – makes my eyes well up with pride and my heart feel like it might burst with joy.

I suddenly realise what Mr Rowbotham is saying. 'Wait, you're asking me if I want to buy my shop?' These are two conversations that should *not* run concurrently.

'If you're interested, Miss Platt. If you can come up with a deposit and then sort yourself out with a business plan and a mortgage, I'd be happy to sell it to you, first and foremost. You only have to look around to see how popular A Tale As Old As Time is – the council agree that it would be a welcome choice to remain in the property.'

'I do!' I say without a second thought. Finally, a chance to be independent, to not have to answer to someone else, but then, as it usually does, reality creeps back in. 'But I can't. I've put *everything* I have into this festival. I've spent everything. The shop's budget for the next year and, if I'm honest, I've gone into my overdraft and my own credit card too. I've got absolutely nothing left to squeeze a deposit from, and I bet you won't wait until I can?'

'Well, now the decision has been made... I really would like to buy that motorhome sooner rather than later, I'm sure you understand. It was actually your boyfriend who persuaded me.'

'Darcy?' Maybe it says something that my mind goes instantly to him. We might've kissed earlier, but 'boyfriend' might be pushing it.

There's a noise from the stage and Mr Rowbotham nods towards it. 'No, that one.'

Instead of a civilised chat between Ali and Darcy, Rick has invaded the stage and is now standing front and centre. His beady eyes search the crowd until they fall on me. 'Marnie, my favourite girl, come up to the front. It's not polite to keep a gentleman waiting.'

Ali looks alarmed and Darcy has sat up straight, his arms protectively around Mrs Potts, who has gone from being calm to looking like she wants to jump off Darcy's lap and make a run for it.

'This isn't a very gentlemanly thing to do,' Ali says to Rick. 'Please step aside, sir, we're in the middle of something.'

I excuse myself to Mr Rowbotham and everyone else I have to squeeze past in my giant dress to make it to the front of the crowd.

'What are you doing?' I seethe at Rick in embarrassment. Not only is he ensuring that every single one of the two hundred pairs of eyes in this room are trained exclusively on me, but he's come clomping right into the middle of Darcy's cathartic moment too. 'These people are here to listen to U.N.Known, not your theatrics. Get down!'

'Oh, please. You're always going on about romance books and *no one* minds bearing witness to a romantic moment.' He drops to one knee and produces the ring box again. 'Do me the honour of marrying me?'

An 'aww' sweeps through the crowd, because they don't know

the history between us or that he's certainly not going to get the answer they're expecting.

I sigh. 'I've said no many times. Why do you think you have the right to not accept the answer you've been given?'

'Because that *Beast* has you under his spell.' He practically spits the word and jabs a finger towards Darcy. 'He's pulled at your heartstrings and forced you to care about him. You're not thinking clearly.'

'The clearest thing I've ever thought is how much I despise you. Stop making a show of yourself, get down, and get out!'

'Not until you say you'll marry me.'

Threats and blackmail. Always a healthy start to a marriage. 'Never. Because I have self-respect. I have standards. I don't want to marry a man who I once caught sullying the romance section by shagging my shop assistant!'

'Self-respect, really?' Rick's face becomes angrier than a lightning fork in a stormy sky. 'Because I don't think it's very self-respectful to be kissing *that*.' His outraged eyes flick to Darcy behind him.

'Rick...' I say warningly. Now there's not just a delusional man on the stage, but a delusional and extremely angry man, and I have no idea how to get him down from there.

'Well, to be fair to the monster, none of us would be here without him.' Rick's menacing eyes lock onto mine. 'You see, Marnie, I'm good friends with Mr Rowbotham. I have a lot of money and sway on my side and it tends to make people open to talking to me. I happened to be passing his office earlier this week, and he let me in on a few, shall we say, trade secrets. He let me see the name of the person who logged a complaint against you – the reason that we're all here. I didn't think much of it at the time. It was a name I didn't recognise...' He does an exaggerated nonchalant shrug. 'Until tonight, when *you* told me who that name belongs to. So, with that in mind, ladies and gentlemen...' He gets to his feet with a bow. 'It's my pleasure to introduce both The Unknown Author, *and*, Marnie, your complainer, Mr Darcy O'Connell.'

I refuse to give him the satisfaction of being shocked. I don't want to believe him. But then I think of what Darcy's just said. *A couple of months ago, I made a mistake. I did something cruel and vindictive.* And then there was what he said earlier. *Not on my watch.* Not on his watch because he'd withdrawn the complaint. Because he told Mr Rowbotham that he was mistaken. And it conveniently doesn't suit Rick's narrative to mention that bit.

I fold my arms and stare him down defiantly. He is *not* getting the reaction he wants from me.

'Aren't you even the slightest bit surprised?' Rick demands.

I watch Darcy. He's protecting a stressed-out Mrs Potts with his arms as he sits forward, looking like he's about to stand up, but I'm probably the only one who knows how much effort it takes Darcy to get up after sitting for any period of time. I start making my way to the side of the stage, intending to at least take my cat out of his arms so he doesn't have to worry about her.

And maybe I can shove Rick off too, with a bit of luck. 'I'm surprised you think *this* is the way to get what you want.'

'Oh, I know exactly what you want. I know what *everyone* here wants.'

I see what he's going to do seconds before he does it. 'Rick, don't you dar—'

It's too late. In one swift move, he darts across the stage, his hand coils into the brown fur of the Beast hood and he rips the mask from Darcy's head.

It's like the world goes into slow motion. No one realises what has happened for a few long moments. Darcy is sitting there, unmasked for all to see.

Under the bright light, his skin looks so pale that it makes the darker pigment of jagged scar lines stand out in contrast. His hair is light brown and chaotic from having the mask pulled off. Blue eyes I know so well blink at the crowd in front of him... and he's the most beautiful person I've ever seen.

And then time turns to super-speed as it catches up again and everything happens all at once.

I see the shock cross his features. The absolute fear and horror as his panicked eyes shoot around the room, taking in the hundreds of people, the gasps of shock, the phones held up, camera flashes and the beep-beep of video being recorded, but it takes a few moments for him to register what's happened.

He stands bolt upright, but in doing so, he releases Mrs Potts, who is now clearly terrified, and she jumps from his lap and races straight for the open door. I try to intercept her but I'm not near enough, and she disappears out into the pouring rain, her lead flapping behind her.

'You monster!' At first I think it's someone shouting at Darcy but I spin back around to see Darcy has turned on Rick. 'How can anyone who is lucky enough to look like you be so rotten on the inside? I will never understand what Marnie saw in you – she deserves so much better!'

'What, like you, Beast? How could anyone ever lov—'

He's cut off by Darcy punching him square in the face.

It sends him sprawling onto his backside with blood pouring from his nose, and the crowd lets out a cheer as though this is free entertainment provided by the book festival.

'You had that coming, *mate*.' Darcy glares down at him, and I can't help feeling a little bit of vindictive glee. I've never had anyone defend my honour before, and to be fair, Rick really has been asking for that for a long while now.

'Darcy...' I step closer and hold a hand out to him, but he

shakes his head. His hands fly up to cover his face, and he jumps from the front of the stage and bolts for the open door too.

The entire room is now staring at the doorway in shock. Witt, who was standing nearby as an unofficial doorman, makes a hand gesture to indicate he's going to follow them, grabs a coat, and also disappears out into the stormy darkness.

Thunder claps overhead, so loudly that it shakes the foundations of the castle. Oh my God, Mrs Potts. She's going to be terrified in that. She hates thunder when she's inside in front of a warm fire. I should never have brought her tonight. What was I thinking?

'What on earth was all that about?' I hear mutterings of the people around me. The visitors, the strangers who don't know Darcy, who don't understand why he hides.

'What a lot of drama,' another one says.

'Was that really necessary?' someone else says.

I don't know if they're talking about Darcy's reaction or Rick's despicable actions, but I round on the man in question, who's getting back to his feet on the stage, clutching his bloodied nose but still managing to look thoroughly pleased with himself.

'How *could* you?' I bark at him. 'Do you know what you've done? You had no right to take away his autonomy like that. That was unforgivable.'

'Unforgiveable? Me? What have *I* done?' Rick gives me the worst innocent look since Boris Johnson claimed to have been ambushed by a birthday cake. 'He punched me! I could have him done for assault!'

'You can't do that to another person, Rick! Darcy wore that mask for deep-seated and personal reasons. It wasn't up to you to decide when to take it off.' I look towards the open doorway, hoping that Witt has caught up with him. 'He's going to be devastated. That was the worst thing you could ever have done to him.'

'Good. He deserves to have his ugliness laid bare for all to see.' Rick does another nonchalant shrug.

Ali has gone out to the foyer and is shrugging on a coat, presumably also going after Darcy as thunder crashes again, reflecting my building anger at the smug git in front of me. 'That gorgeous man deserves the world. He deserves people who love him, understand him, and respect him. *You* don't love, understand, or respect anyone, and it makes you a sad, horrible person.'

'You can't say that to me after everything I've done for you. You owe me for making this weekend a success!'

I was about to go out into the night after Darcy and Mrs Potts, but I spin around, the skirt of my dress hitting someone dressed in the red robes and white bonnet of a handmaid as I turn so sharply. 'What?'

'The article in *The Wye Word*. You know, the one that got you *sooo* much attention and let all these wonderful people know about your little book festival and sold the rest of the tickets you were struggling to shift?'

I'd momentarily forgotten that we've got an audience and him pointing them out makes me self-conscious again. 'I wasn't str—'

'You can thank me for that.' He puts a hand on his chest and bows proudly.

'That was you?' I don't wait for him to respond before answering the question for myself. 'Of course it was you. I can't believe I didn't think of it before. I thought that was Darcy – that he'd tried to do something nice and the journalist had twisted his words, but it wasn't, was it? No one needed to twist your words because they were already twisted. I should have known. That whole article absolutely smacked of your disdainful attitude. When did you manage to take the photos in the shop without me knowing? How did you know about U.N.Known's emails?'

'That night I came by for a picnic and you disappeared. I

wondered where the heck you'd got to and came looking. Your laptop was open on the counter, all I had to do was wiggle the mouse and your inbox was on the screen for anyone to see. I assumed you'd gone home, but now I'm guessing you abandoned me in favour of your "Scary Neighbour" instead.'

'*He* is not scary, but you... you're bloody terrifying. Terrifying *and* deluded.'

'He looked pretty scary to me when that mask came off!'

'Scared, Rick, not scary! He's scared of being rejected because of his scars. Scared of being laughed at. Scared of being publicly humiliated, like he has been before.'

'Oh, boo hoo. Guess what, Marnie? I don't care. I can offer you so much more than he ever can.'

'I don't want *anything* from you! You've done more than enough damage for one lifetime!'

'How about a nice little wedding present?' He drops down onto one knee again. 'A little bookshop. They call it A Tale As Old As Time. I hear it's going up for sale shortly. Say yes and it's yours.'

Is he for real? Is he seriously deluded enough to think that would sway me? 'Never in a million years.'

'You'll never scrounge up a deposit without me. You know you won't. Scraping and scrabbling for change, maybe begging the bank to give you a loan, whereas I can – and will – buy it for you outright, and—'

I've heard more than enough. 'When you've quite finished humiliating me about my financial situation in public... It's just a shop. Bricks and mortar. It doesn't matter. People are what matters. The people I love. And what you've just done to the man I love is unforgivable. This is the end of everything. We're done. Never, ever contact me again.' I hadn't even realised I'd made it directly to the front of the stage, until I turn around and find the crowd of onlookers gathered behind me, and I have to push through them to get to the door.

'He complained about you!' he calls after me.

'I don't care, Rick!' I turn back to face him one last time. 'Everything about him is the best thing that's ever happened to me! Including the complaint. Because you're right, none of us would be here without that, and I'm glad that we are. That complaint shoved me outside of my comfort zone and showed me I can do things that I thought I'd never have the courage to do. Without Darcy, I *wouldn't* ever have had the courage to do them. It doesn't matter that he complained about me. I've come to love the outdoors, to really appreciate the value of nature. I've got an incredible garden that's only going to add to the atmosphere of the bookshop next spring. All of that is because of Darcy.'

I can't waste any more time on Rick. The weather is horrific and both Darcy and Mrs Potts are out there in it somewhere. And I need to find them.

20

Lightning blazes across the sky as I get outside the castle and race down the walled stone walkway towards the Full Moon Forest, and it's followed seconds later by a clap of thunder that's so near, it sounds like the sky is going to fall down, and I try not to think about how scared Mrs Potts must be, or what could have happened to her in this.

The Full Moon Forest splits in two – the nice part, full of fairy sculptures and solar-powered flowers that leads back to Ever After Street, and the other part that blankets the castle from the right side, twisting around the river that rages through it, covering the area behind our shops and leading the way through to the row of cottages on the other side where I live, and although I have no idea which way Darcy could've gone, I think he'd have taken the familiar route, the quiet paths between our shops and the castle, where people rarely venture thanks to the muddy pathways and ferocious drops into the river.

I didn't bother to stop for a coat, and the rain is coming down in vicious sheets, stinging the bare skin of my shoulders like needles. Another flash of lightning turns the sky white, and thunder crashes immediately afterwards.

Poor Mrs Potts! I'm never going to forgive myself if anything happens to her.

Mud covers my once-yellow dress and the rain soaks the fabric, weighing it down as I try to run through the trees but my slip-on flat shoes sink into sludgy puddles with every step. 'Darcy! Mrs Potts!'

It's Witt's voice that lifts through the trees in response. 'I'm down by the shop, Marnie! There's no sign of either of them! I don't think he made it back here!'

The words chill me to the bone and I have a horrible sense of foreboding. Prickling goosebumps break across my back and they have nothing to do with the rain belting down. Something is wrong. Where would Darcy have gone if not to his shop? Where would Mrs Potts go? She'd be terrified, and visibility is almost zero; she wouldn't have known which way to turn.

Home, maybe? Cats can find their way home, can't they?

'Ali's gone towards the main street! Sadie's looking in the castle gardens!' Witt calls. 'We'll find them!'

The rain is coming down so hard that it's like a fog has descended across the woods. I can barely see a couple of feet in front of me, and I keep walking into tree trunks that loom out of the darkness, even though I walk this path between here and home twice a day.

The river is raging below me, and I find the fence that runs alongside the ravine and turn in the direction of home, hoping against hope that Mrs Potts would have found her way back there. Maybe Darcy too. Maybe he followed her and they're both going to be sitting on my doorstep when I get back and wondering what all the fuss is about.

I can hear Witt in the distance, shouting Darcy's name, and I do the same as I push onwards, trying to lift my soaking wet dress and clomp heavy feet through mud that's turned into quicksand and each puddle feels like it's sucking my feet in and not giving them back without a fight.

'Darcy!' I yell for the millionth time and get no response.

The fence between me and the ravine down into the river is flimsy at best, with wobbly wooden posts that are too far apart and wire woven in a square formation between them, but I use it as a guide to follow the path home. At least if I get home and neither of them are there, I can quickly change into something more practical than a ballgown and come back out to re-join the search.

The fence is swaying in the gale-force wind as I run my hand along it, shouting for Darcy and Mrs Potts, and then finally, finally, just as I reach an empty space where a fencepost should be but isn't, I hear a voice.

'Down here!'

It's quiet and coming from way, way below. 'Darcy?'

'We're okay! I've got Mrs Potts, she's okay!'

'Where the hell are…? Oh, bloody hell.' I'm squinting at the river, willing my eyes to adjust to the darkness that's so dark, I don't think they *can* adjust any further. Part of the fence has fallen down, the broken posts and flimsy wire are draped across the steep bank, and as I squint downwards in darkness, I can see the unmistakeable shape of a body on the ground, right down by the crashing river.

I try to fight the rising panic. He's alive, I tell myself. He's just spoken so he must be conscious. Maybe it's not as bad as it looks.

'Don't come down! It's too dange—' he yells up, sounding as if the effort of shouting is painful, but I've already gathered up my gigantic skirt and clambered over the broken fencing, because if he thinks I'm leaving him alone on the edge of a raging river, he's got another thing coming.

I try going down forwards, but it's too steep and I feel like I'm going to overbalance and topple headfirst into the water, so I turn around and lower myself onto my front, and attempt to crawl down backwards on my hands and knees, but the wet mud and sodden leaves are so slippery that I end up sliding, trying to use my hands in the bank for purchase, and in possibly the most ungraceful display anyone has ever performed, I come to a stop on my shredded knees, caked in mud, and liberally decorated with soggy autumn leaves, and instantly crawl across wet grass and sharp stones to get to where Darcy's lying on the steep ground, looking like one wrong move will send him sliding into the water.

And judging by the crash of the water and the angry whooshing, it's not a river either of us wants to end up in tonight.

'Thank God I found you!' I want to throw my arms around him and smother him in kisses, but he's clearly hurt or he wouldn't be at the bottom of a ravine, mere feet from a rampaging river.

'You shouldn't have done that. Now we've both got to get up from here.'

I look back up the bank I've just slid down with trepidation. 'Oh, that? That's no big deal.' It's exactly what he said to me about my garden on the day I met him, and back then, it felt like a similarly unclimbable mountain, but *he* made it doable.

For one moment, it's just me and him, face to face, and then he realises I'm looking at him and jerks his head to the side and brings his left hand up to cover his face.

'She's okay.' The fingers of his other hand wriggle gently on the bundle tucked under his right arm, and Mrs Potts' pink leash is wrapped twice around his wrist. 'I was trying to keep her dry but I don't think even the most waterproof coat could stay dry in rain like this.'

I realise why he's lying here in just a thin white shirt and the torn yellow waistcoat that matches my dress – because he's taken the Beast jacket off and wrapped her in it. 'Mrs Potts!'

I'm so happy to see her, I could cry. Or I'm already crying and I'm just so wet that I can't tell. I part the folds of the blue jacket and reach into the carefully created air hole until I can see familiar eyes gleaming back at me.

Mrs Potts looks most put-out and bedraggled, and the jacket is moving where her furious tail is flicking back and forth. She looks like she's plotting revenge on whoever served her the injustice of being outside in a storm, and there won't be enough Dreamies in the world to appease her wrath, but nothing matters as long as she's okay.

'I don't think she's hurt,' Darcy says quietly, but every word sounds like it's hurting him. 'Upset and wet, but she's okay. She must have got disorientated and gone through where the fence should have been. I was going... I don't know where, anywhere, away from there, and I heard her meowing. Her harness was caught on a branch down here.' One finger lifts from her to point at the looming oak behind us. 'She was fighting to get loose, but if she had, I don't think she'd have had the purchase to keep herself out of the river. I couldn't leave her, but my foot caught in the downed fence, and I, er... It didn't end well. But that doesn't matter. She's safe. She's fine.'

'You're not.' I tuck the jacket back in to keep Mrs Potts as dry as possible, although the three of us are so saturated that it's a tad pointless at this stage.

'I'm fine.'

'You're not fine, Darcy. You don't look good.' I duck my head, trying to see under the hand he's holding above his face.

'That's what I've been saying for years.'

I give him a scolding look, but he won't turn to face me so it was probably a waste of a good admonishment. 'You're as white as a sheet, you look and sound like you're in pain...' I let my eyes run down his body and wince at the sight of his left leg. 'And I'm fairly sure ankles aren't supposed to bend at that angle. Is that broken?'

'Yeah. At least a couple of ribs too.'

I try to examine him for further injuries, but it's too dark to see much, especially with his hand still up in front of his face. There's mud all over him, being washed away by the rain, but the one thing I can see is blood. Even in the darkness, red stands out against his pale skin. 'You have a head injury. Let me see.'

'Low-flying tree branch. Or low-flying me *into* an innocent tree branch.' He sounds like he knows the sentence doesn't make much sense. 'It's just a scratch.'

'Scratches don't bleed like that.' The beating rain is washing the blood into his hair, and all I want to do is take hold of his hand and pull it out of the way.

I'm desperate to touch him but unsure of where won't make him hurt more. He's shivering constantly and the rain has soaked his white shirt, making it see-through around the muddy patches and sticking it to his body, and the darkness of raised and jagged scar lines stand out against the blanched fabric, lines that criss-cross his torso, the right side much worse than the left. I can't stop myself touching him. Just gently, letting my hand rest over one of the scars on his shoulder. 'Can you move?'

'My ribcage was rebuilt with titanium plates. I know something in there is broken, and I don't know how many pieces my ribs are in. Any wrong movement could cause something to shift and puncture a vital organ. I don't want to risk it without paramedics nearby. I've had complications from broken ribs before. The best thing I can do is stay still.'

The panic I was feeling had started to abate because I've *found* both of them, but the idea of broken ribs and punctured vital organs sets my dread level soaring again. 'Have you called for help?'

'My phone's still in the ballroom.'

Of course it is. I scrabble to get mine out of the hidden pocket Sadie always puts in her dresses, but I'm too wet and the screen won't respond to my fingers, and I nearly throw it in frustration because it will *not* unlock, and the rain is still coming down so hard that it's going to drown in my hands if I'm not careful.

'Witt!' I shout into the night, and quickly explain to Darcy that I'm not the only one out looking for him. 'Witt, I've got them but we need help. Call an ambulance!'

'Ask for police and then Mountain Rescue,' Darcy says. 'Normal paramedics won't make it down this terrain.'

'I'm on it!' The distant reply comes from the other side of the river after I repeat those instructions loudly, hoping Witt might be less wet and muddy than I am and be able to make his phone work.

Darcy hasn't complained about my hand on his shoulder, so I give it another careful squeeze, but he's still got his head turned away and he won't look at me.

'I'm so sorry I let her go.' His fingers drum gently on Mrs Potts again. 'You trusted me with her and I put my own... issues... before her safety, and I shouldn't have done that. I'm sorry.'

'You don't have to apologise for that. You were shocked. Hurt. *I'm* sorry, Darcy. If I'd had any clue Rick was going to do something like that...' My voice catches and I have to break off. I can't imagine what Darcy felt on that stage. Even in his worst nightmares, he's probably never imagined being unmasked so publicly.

It feels like looking back on something that happened three lifetimes ago, but in reality, it was less than an hour ago that we were all standing in a grand castle, listening to U.N.Known give his first ever public interview.

'It's my fault. I was unprepared. I let my guard down. You've made me believe that people are better than they are, and...' His voice falters too and he trails off.

'*Most* people are. I'm not sure Rick counts as a person after that. You were only up there for me. Without me, you wouldn—'

'Without you, I wouldn't be a lot of things. Including as happy as you've made me in the past couple of months, and I wouldn't change that for anything, not even to avoid what happened tonight.'

Thunder rumbles in the distance, moving further away, but doing nothing to take the rain with it. The wind screams around our ears, strong enough to whip up my saturated ballgown, and I try to hold it up, to shelter him in some useless way.

The hand he's holding up is shivering constantly, and his whole body is being wracked by tremors from the cold. Even his teeth are chattering, and I don't know what to do to help him. I fiddle with my skirt, wondering if I could somehow rip the under-layers off and use them to cover him, although it's so sopping wet that the extra weight on top of broken ribs probably wouldn't be a good thing.

I'm sitting on my knees next to him, keeping my hand on his shoulder, but scared of getting any closer in case I jolt one of his injuries or make something worse. 'Please put your hand down.'

He makes a noise of refusal and it makes me realise I'm going to have to take matters into my own hands. I've never wanted to push him, but he's injured and we're stuck outside in a horrific storm, it's freezing, and this can't go on any longer. I reach out and slide my hand over the top of the one he's holding up, letting my fingers slot between his and curl in. 'You were going to show me earlier, in the ballroom.'

'That was then. I got swept away in the magic of it. Got lost in a fairy-tale fantasy where someone could actually learn to love a beast.'

'Do you know how harmful that wording is?' I snap at him, overwhelmingly infuriated by this whole situation. 'Love is either there or it isn't. Saying that someone needs to *learn* to love you is like telling yourself that you're not good enough to simply *be* loved. I haven't "learnt" to love you – I've fallen in love with you. With your voice, with the words you say, with *who* you are, with every part of you, and now I need to be allowed to fall in love with the parts you hide too.' I curl my fingers into his hand and tug it gently away from his face.

And finally, finally, he lets me.

He lets me pull his hand away and turns his head slowly towards me, and I most definitely stop breathing. I keep my grip on his fingers, holding on tightly, until my eyes lock onto his beautiful blue ones. I've been desperate for this moment for so many weeks now. To see his face right in front of me, because he *chose* to show me.

The head wound at the edge of his forehead is bleeding profusely, the rain washing blood down his face, highlighting scars in his skin. It's too dark to see much, but I can tell his nose is sort of squashed, flat and wide, but in a way that suits his gorgeous face. One side of his jaw is misshapen and covered by the bumpy scar tissue he let me feel earlier. There are deep crevices and dipped jagged lines of the skin grafts he once told me about, and the brow ridge bone above his right eyebrow is over-prominent and bumpy, like it's been broken apart and healed in a different shape to the other one, but there's nothing that makes him not-gorgeous.

He lets out a shaky breath and his eyes close, as though the weight of my gaze on his face is too much. I'm holding my breath and have to drag in gasping lungfuls of air because I suddenly go light-headed.

I can't stop the tears that spill over, mixing with the rain already cascading down my face. 'You beautiful, beautiful idiot.'

'Don't say that.'

'The idiot bit? It's a term of endearment, honestly. And it's true. You're an idiot and you're bloody beautiful.'

'It's dark.'

'It's not *that* dark.' I give him a stern look and squeeze his hand deliberately tighter. 'No one is going to treat you differently because of this. Yeah, you've got scars, you're going to have another one to add to them by the looks of that tree branch wound, but I promise you, you don't look like any kind of monster. You look like a guy who's been to hell and, most importantly, back. And that "back" is all that matters because you're still here, and I can't imagine a world without you in it.'

He chokes back a sob and then groans when it evidently jars the broken ribs, his eyes squeezed shut, and I rub his shoulder, my other hand still reaching across his chest to keep hold of his left hand.

I wait until he opens his eyes again, and I can't help smiling when our eyes meet. 'Can I touch you?'

His eyes squeeze shut again. 'You've already seen the worst of me. Go ahead.'

'The worst of you is not these scars.' I'm shivering from the cold too, but I reach out and let my shaking fingers trace over the deepest dark lines that weave along the right side of his jaw. 'It's that you think anyone would reject you for having them.'

He lets me trail my fingers across the kink in the bridge of his nose and along the exaggerated curve of his right eyebrow. 'Every one of these scars is a testament to what you've overcome. You survived something unsurvivable and came out the other side as someone who makes the world better just by existing, and from now on, I'm going to make sure you know that every single day.'

I press my knees harder into the mud underneath them to ensure my balance is good enough, disentangle my hand from his to use for stability and brace it against the earth beside his head, and lean over to press a kiss to his cheek.

His skin is like ice and he shivers when my frozen nose touches his face, but I've never needed to kiss someone *this* desperately before. It's just a peck on the cheek, less intimate than the kiss we shared in the ballroom, but it's the circumstances that make it so special. He's hurt and vulnerable, and the easiest thing would be for him to retreat inside himself and push me away, but he's chosen to let me be closer than anyone has been in many years.

'That's the nicest thing I've ever felt.' Despite the truly dire situation, there's a hazy smile on his face when I pull away and his light eyes are dazed-looking when he blinks them open.

'I think you're delirious with hypothermia,' I say breezily, trying to cover the panic that he might actually be suffering from hypothermia, given how long he's been out in this horrendous storm with only a thin shirt on. 'And I hope you know I'd still love you even if you looked like a melted Womble.'

The laugh catches him by surprise and is quickly cut off with a noise of pain that turns into a groan of frustration. 'It's not that simple though, is it? I haven't been honest – you know I haven't. What Rick said about the complaint is tru—'

'I know it is, and it doesn't matter.'

'It does matter. It's not the only thing I've been dishonest about. Marnie... I did it because of the book. Because for the past few years, I've been trying to forget everything about that book. It was a reminder of the before times – times I didn't want to remember, and then you moved into the shop next door to me, and it's in your window *all* the time. I see people coming out of your shop with it in their hands. I wanted to burn every copy ever printed, and there you are, keeping it alive, and I've been this horrible, vicious little cauldron of resentment, bubbling with anger, and I wanted to punch a hole through your shop window and rip that damn book to shreds. Without ever having spoken to you, I hated you because you loved this thing that was such a huge part of the life I wanted to forget, and every way I turned, you had it on display for everyone to see.'

'It's okay,' I say because he's getting choked up and it doesn't sound easy for him to get the words out.

'No, let me finish. The least I owe you is an explanation. When I saw that Japanese knotweed in your garden, I saw it as my revenge, a way to spite you. I didn't think through the consequences. I honestly had no idea that it would lead to the council threatening your place on Ever After Street, I thought you'd just get a slap on the wrist and an order to get it removed, and then I heard you crying...'

'Like an elephant seal in labour,' I interject to lighten the mood.

He smiles despite himself and then turns serious again. 'And I realised it was because of me, because of what I'd done, and I felt like I'd become a real monster. And then I spoke to you and you were so nice. You made me feel so normal. You didn't treat me like an outcast when you were the one person who *should* have, and I felt so damn guilty.'

'Is that why you did all of it? Why you helped? Why you were so generous? Why you came tonight? Just out of guilt? Nothing more?'

'I did it because you've had this weird pull on me. Since that first night, all I've wanted to do is spend time with you. I haven't been able to *resist* spending time with you. And I fell in love with your shop. When I saw inside, it reminded me of everything I used to love, all the good things in the world that I no longer believed in. It's such a little haven for people who believe in fairy tales, and somewhere along the way, *I* started believing in fairy tales again. I started believing in love and goodness and joy. When I bought that copy of *Once Upon Another Time*... I'd blocked it out for years, tried to forget every word that was in it, and you made me feel strong enough to read it again, as a reader, not as myself, and... I enjoyed it. It reminded me of the happiness I found in writing, before everything went wrong. I've hated that book for so many years. If I hadn't been so caught up in book deals and word counts, would I have realised what my ex was about to do? Could I have prevented it? I blamed the book for everything, but I'd forgotten that I loved it once. I came tonight because I knew it would get people talking and you deserved that. You love that shop and you *need* to be able to continue making people believe in magic, and *I* need you too as well, because you've made me fall in love with reading again... and with something else too.' His fingers curl around mine and he tugs my hand to his mouth and presses a kiss to the back of my fingers, and then his eyes flick to mine. 'When did you know it was me? Because I know it wasn't tonight...'

'Somewhere between that book coming sailing back over my hedge and telling the guy in the emails how similar he was to my neighbour. You know that feeling when you come to the end of an amazing book and you wish you could go back and un-read it just so you could experience reading it again for the first time? You were so familiar because I've read your words so many times without realising it. Every time we've talked, I feel the same way I felt when I read *Once Upon Another Time* for the first time – like I've found someone who really *gets* me, a real-life version of my favourite book.'

Rain is sticking his hair to his forehead and I reach out to brush it back, carefully avoiding the still-bleeding wound, and his eyes drift closed. 'You have no idea how desperately I want to kiss you, but I don't want our first kiss to be marred by searing agony.'

'We kissed earlier, and we can have another first kiss later.'

'Not really how "first" wor—'

I cut him off with a kiss. Just a peck, while being careful not to touch anywhere that might be hurting. My face is frozen and his lips are like ice, but it feels like our bodies let out a sizzle when our lips touch, and I could keep kissing him forever, but—

'The ambulance is here!' A sodden-looking silhouette of Witt appears at the top of the bank. 'Ali's directing the rescue team through the woods.'

I hate having to leave Darcy, but the best thing I can do is get out of the way and let them help him.

I extract Mrs Potts from his arm and keep her bundled in the jacket as one of the red-clad rescuers appears at the top of the embankment and makes his way down to us. Another one has rigged up a rope system, and between us, he, Mrs Potts and I haul ourselves to the top of the embankment, while three other men attached to sturdy-looking ropes head downwards with first aid bags and a stretcher.

I hear Darcy talking to them and the one who came down for me wraps one of those foil blankets around me, puts a big hand on my back and walks me towards the clearing beyond the Full Moon Forest where the emergency vehicles had to stop.

Ambulance lights are flashing on Ever After Street. I don't think I've ever been wetter in my life. I shiver inside the foil blanket, and someone brings me a cup of tea while I sit at the back of the waiting ambulance and assure them I'm not the one who needed rescuing. They're even kind enough to give Mrs Potts an arbitrary check-over, and tell me that although I should take her to the vets for peace of mind, it doesn't look like anything a few packets of Dreamies won't fix. A kindly paramedic wraps her in a foil blanket too and no one gets scratched as she passes her back to me.

'Well, life is never dull on Ever After Street, is it?' Cleo plonks herself down beside me and wraps her arm around my shoulders, reaching over to tickle Mrs Potts under her bedraggled chin.

We sit in silence and watch the activity all around us. The rescue crew are everywhere. The police have already arrived with hazard tape to cordon off the broken fence. A policeman is on the phone to presumably someone at the council, who is having their ear chewed off about insufficient fencing. Witt is pacing and Ali is wringing his hands together, and all I can think about is Darcy and what he's been through tonight. Surely his two worst fears – being seen so publicly and being injured again, and he's had to face both of them because of me, and I don't know how to help him get past that.

And then they're there. A team of red-suited men are carrying Darcy on a stretcher between them, and he looks even paler in the flashing blue lights up here, and the blood from the cut on his head looks scarily bright, and I watch helplessly as they strap him into the ambulance, and one of the paramedics holds the door open for me.

'I've got her; you go with him.' Cleo gently takes Mrs Potts out of my arms and murmurs to her. 'She can come home with me and I'll open the shop tomorrow, Sadie's taken over at the festival, Mickey and Lissa are... *everywhere*. Don't worry about a thing here.'

Just when I thought I couldn't cry any more tonight, it sets me off again as I wonder how I got so lucky to find such a good friend and work in such a supportive community.

The paramedics cover Darcy with foil blankets, strap an oxygen mask onto his face and put an oxygen monitor on his finger, and I sit on the bench with my hand on his thigh, just about the only place I can touch him without getting in the way, and desperately try to reassure myself that he's going to be all right.

21

There's a certain kind of humiliation to sitting in a hospital waiting room in a mud-stained yellow satin Belle dress. Everyone recognises both the dress *and* the fact that you must've had a pretty bad night to end up in A&E without a chance to change, and I get sympathetic looks from adults and excited looks that quickly turn to terror from children when they recognise my dress and then their little eyes fall on my leaf-ridden hair and mud-smeared, tear-stained face.

They take Darcy straight through from the ambulance and won't let me accompany him any further. I get sent to a waiting room and a kindly nurse makes me a cup of tea and gives me a packet of wet wipes to clean myself up, but it's *hours* before a doctor finally comes out, and I've paced so much that I've probably worn a hole in the flooring that squeaks under my wet shoes.

He tells me they're admitting Darcy for observation overnight due to the head injury and the effects of mild hypothermia, and that his ankle can't be set until the fracture clinic staff are back in work tomorrow morning. They won't let me see him because visitors aren't allowed at this time of night in case they disturb the other patients on the ward. The last thing I wanted to do was leave him alone, and I make the doctor promise to tell him I'll be back first thing in the morning.

It's nearly 1 a.m. when I get a taxi back to Ever After Street and I have never been so glad to see lights still on in the castle. I don't even have to knock before Cleo comes out and envelops me in a hug.

'Mrs Potts is fine,' she says quickly. 'One of the festival guests happened to be a vet. He was dressed as Captain Hook and gave me his hook to look after while he checked her over. Quite an experience, I can tell you. Witt needed to warm up too so he lit a fire and rubbed her dry in front of it. Ali brought her chicken from 1001 Nights – he's her new best friend now.'

She leads me to one of the cosy castle living rooms and we poke our heads round the door to see Ali dozing on a sofa in front of a fire crackling in the hearth and Mrs Potts purring on his lap, looking like nothing ever happened.

Inside the castle, Witt and Sadie have started clearing away the debris from the book festival, and I intend to help, but a wave of tiredness washes over me as the adrenaline from the evening's events dissipates now I know Mrs Potts is okay, and while Darcy is definitely not okay, he *is* in the best place possible.

I gather the clothes I was wearing earlier and strip out of my ill-fated Belle dress, and Cleo insists on walking home with me and taking the long way round, because *no one* is cutting through the forest again tonight.

She makes us both a cup of tea and toast, and won't go home until I've had a hot shower, changed into my warmest pyjamas, and got Mrs Potts settled. It's the early hours before Cleo leaves, and I fall into bed gratefully, counting down the hours until morning, because seeing Darcy again can't come soon enough.

* * *

It's gone 11 a.m. before they finally bring Darcy back from the fracture clinic and put an end to my endless pace-a-thon in the waiting area, and as a nurse walks me down the ward, the sight of him sitting up in the hospital bed makes my eyes water with tears of relief.

I pull the privacy curtain round and stand at the end of the bed and lift a hand in greeting.

'That' – he inclines his head, meaning my tears – 'is not a good start.'

'They're good tears,' I sniffle. 'Because you're...'

'Don't finish that sentence.'

'Perfect.' I finish the sentence.

'Something I'll never be.' He blushes and just the simple act of *seeing* Darcy blush is enough to start me off yet again, so I busy myself with dumping the bag containing the change of clothes I've brought for him at the side of the bed and pulling the visitor's chair as close as I can get it.

He holds his scarred right hand out and I wrap both of mine around it and cling on, and for the very first time, he lets me look at him without anything between us. They've obviously given him a shower and put him in a papery hospital-issue nightshirt. His head has been stitched up and there are a line of butterfly bandages holding the wound closed, and now it looks angry and swollen with splotches of blue-purple bruising starting to show around it. His left leg is wrapped in bright-white fresh plaster from the toes to the knee, and there's gauze taped to his arm where they must've put an IV line in last night but have now removed it.

There are dark circles under his eyes and he looks like he could sleep for three years and it still wouldn't be enough and he is, without a doubt, the most beautiful person I've ever seen.

I kiss his hand. 'How are you?'

'In immense pain, but somehow seeing you makes it disappear.' He pulls our joined hands to his mouth and presses his lips to my fingers. 'Thank you for last night. All of it – from clambering down that bank to coming here with me. The doctor did mention how upset you were at being sent home. And thank you for coming back this morning.'

'Witt knew where you'd left your keys, so he went into your shop, got you a change of clothes and kept your phone safe.'

'Thank you. And thanks, Witt. I didn't realise how...' The sentence catches and he has to swallow and try again. 'I never realised how kind people are. Half of Ever After Street must've been out there looking for me last night and I never thought they cared.'

'Everyone cares. Cleo's running the shop today and she's already texted me six times to say how many people have been in asking after you.'

'Is Mrs Potts okay?'

'She's fine. Ali's been spoiling her and for breakfast this morning, she went to meow outside the door of 1001 Nights. It will be a miracle if we ever get her back now. Even Dreamies can't compare to Ali's chicken.'

He laughs and his eyes meet mine and we end up just looking at each other.

'You have no idea how glad I am to *see* you.' I squeeze his hand again. 'In all senses of the word.'

He smiles. A small smile at first that gradually gets wider and wider, a cheeky glint growing in his eyes until his whole face shines with the width of that smile, and it looks as familiar as it sounds.

'That's it.' I reach out and trace the edge of his lips. 'That's the smile I've been able to hear in your voice. It's exactly as I pictured it.'

'Will you kiss me?' He swallows hard and I can tell from the wobble in his voice that he's still expecting to be rejected. 'If I could move, I would have leapt on you the second I saw you, but I can't, so—'

I cut him off by carefully smashing my lips into his. Well, as carefully as you *can* smash anything, anyway. We both gasp into the kiss and his hand scrunches in my hair and my fingers caress the back of his neck, making him shiver, and—

The same doctor from last night parts the privacy curtain and I pull back with a yelp.

'People have *got* to stop doing that.' Darcy clonks his head back against the metal headrest.

'Good news, Mr O'Connell.' The doctor's face is red as he pretends not to have seen anything and consults his notes. 'Your body temperature is back to normal and your oxygen levels are normal too. As we explained after the X-ray last night, you've got two broken ribs on the left side, both clean breaks and well away from any of your metalwork, and one nicely broken ankle. We'll send you a follow-up appointment to check on the ankle, and the ribs will heal on their own. And now you've got someone with you, I'm happy to sign the discharge forms.'

The doctor turns to me and hands over a 'dos and don'ts of broken ribs' leaflet. 'He's going to need someone with him. Help, support, there's going to be a *lot* that he can't do, especially for the first couple of weeks. Everything's going to hurt for a while, from every breath to every single movement, no matter how miniscule. The broken ribs will prevent him using crutches, so you'll have to borrow a wheelchair from the hospital to get home, and then hire one for the next few weeks. Breathing exercises are explained in there.' He points at the leaflet and then hands over another one about wheelchair hire, and then glances at Darcy. 'I know you're well-versed in managing injuries, Mr O'Connell, but you *are* going to have to take things easy. Keep active, gentle exercise, *no* work. Don't put the slightest bit of weight on that ankle for at least six weeks, and no pressure on those ribs. No stairs if they can be avoided. Any questions?'

I sit back down in the visitor's chair without letting go of Darcy's hand. It sounds horrific. Darcy suffers enough from his previous injuries without adding more to them. And there's no way he can manage all that by himself. 'Come home with me.'

He goes to raise an eyebrow but winces when it pulls on the stitches in his forehead. 'What? Why would I do that?'

'You can't go back to your shop by yourself. Your shop is nothing *but* stairs. And I happen to live in a bungalow.'

'Your girlfriend makes a very good point.' The doctor nods in agreement.

I meet Darcy's eyes and see the smile reflected back at the term 'girlfriend'. We haven't defined our relationship yet, but I like that idea, and his eyes twinkle in a way that says he does too. 'And, quite frankly, you've got *no* idea how terrified I was of losing you last night, and if you think I'm letting you out of my sight for longer than five seconds, you can think again.' I don't realise how stern I sound until even the doctor laughs.

'I'll leave you alone to discuss it while I go to find a wheelchair because you're going nowhere on crutches with those ribs.' He steps outside the curtain and pulls it back.

'I can't just move in with you.'

'Why not? I have a second bedroom so you can have your own space. I read up about broken ribs this morning and it said sleeping upright in an armchair might be more comfortable, and

I've got a *really* comfortable armchair in the living room, and most importantly, *no* stairs. I cannot, and will not, let you deal with this alone. I know you're kind of damned for the next couple of months. You're going to hurt and there's nothing you can do about it, and I'm sorry for that.'

'It's okay. It's only a couple of months. In recent years, I've had no hope whatsoever. Pain is a part of my life every day. Not usually this acute, mind, but... what I mean is, you give me hope that better times are coming, and it's been a long while since I felt like that. The thought of having a future with you makes me feel like I can face anything.'

'So that's a yes then? You're going to come and stay with me while you let yourself heal and let me look after you? Mrs Potts will never speak to me again if she finds out she could have seen her favourite person every day and I didn't let her.'

He laughs, muted by how much pain he's clearly in. 'Okay, okay. I can't refuse Mrs Potts. But, Marnie, this is an awful idea. You're going to hate me. I'm a *terrible* patient.'

'Well, I'm probably a terrible nurse. We're just going to have to be terrible together.'

'Being *anything* together with you is all I want. But this temporary tenancy had better come with one condition. Until I can move well enough to do it myself, kisses on demand whenever I want them.'

I laugh and lean over to kiss him again. 'As rental clauses go, I quite like that one.'

The doctor comes back with a wheelchair and a set of crutches for when the ribs have healed, and a discharge letter. I hover while Darcy inches himself to the edge of the bed to change clothes, reluctant to let me help him, but impeded enough that he doesn't have a choice.

His body is a mass of scars, and he's obviously self-conscious, and one day he's going to let me kiss every single one of them until he believes me when I say he's gorgeous, but for now, just being okay is enough.

22

'Why do we have to go this way? I don't want to see anyone.'

'Well, firstly because I'm not pushing a wheelchair through that muddy forest. Both of us have seen more than enough of that forest for one twenty-four-hour period, and secondly, because Cleo said it was important that I stop by the shop for a minute and I've already texted her that we're on the way. Plus, we need to get your keys from Witt so I can pick up clothes and whatever else you need from your shop. And someone had better make sure that Mrs Potts hasn't actually moved *in* to 1001 Nights. Ali won't be best pleased to be presented with dead-or-otherwise mice in a restaurant.'

The rain of last night is ancient history and Ever After Street is bathed in sunlight as I push Darcy's wheelchair down the cobblestone street on the way back from the hospital. Witt had put a hat and scarf in the bag, so he's wearing a baseball cap pulled down low over his eyes and an oversized scarf is wrapped around him from chest to the bridge of his nose. He can barely see out, and I wish he didn't still feel the need to hide his scars, but it can't be easy when he's stayed hidden for years. And sure enough, as we round the corner and turn towards the narrow part of the road before Ever After Street splits into a wishbone shape, he lets out a groan. 'I *knew* there'd be people.'

Gathered in front of our shops is... everyone. All of our colleagues. Friends. Sadie, Lissa, and Mickey. Cleo. Imogen from the Sleeping Beauty shop. Scarlett and her boyfriend from Rapunzel's hair salon. A couple of people who are covering the tearoom while Lilith is still on health-related leave. Mrs Potts is in her usual window seat in the bookshop behind them.

And they all start clapping when they see us. My fingers are touching Darcy's shoulder and I can feel how uncomfortable it's making him, but I can't help getting a bit choked up. It's like a welcome home party. Everyone's left their shops on a Monday lunchtime just to see us. It makes it feel like coming home.

There's a mismatched pair of stepladders, one on either side of The Beast's Enchanted Rose Garden. Witt is standing at the top of one and Ali is on the other, and between them, they're holding a big white sheet up so that it covers the front of Darcy's shop and hides it from view.

'Oh, what the hell has happened now?' Darcy mutters to the men on the ladders. 'Has someone put my windows through? Or graffiti? That's all I need.'

'Nothing bad,' Witt reassures him. 'It's actually us who've done something...'

Witt struggles with a stutter and Ali takes over the explanation. 'We hope you won't mind. Please know it was done with a huge amount of love and respect.'

Sadie does a quick drum roll and they drop the sheet.

I was already holding back tears, but now they spill over instantly.

They've repainted Darcy's shop sign. Now it just reads The Enchanted Rose Garden. The 'Beast' part has been erased.

My hand is still on his shoulder and I hear his intake of breath as he realises what they've done and the significance behind it.

Ali climbs down from the stepladder and comes over. 'I speak for all of us when I say we never, ever want to hear the word "beast" uttered on this street again.' He holds his hand out to shake Darcy's. 'It's a pleasure to know you, mate. You'll always be one of us.'

Darcy's breathing is shuddery as he shakes Ali's hand, and his shoulders are shaking as he tries to hold back tears. Everyone's watching, waiting for a response. I give his shoulder a squeeze, because I think he's too touched to put it into words.

'Do you know how painful it is to cry with broken ribs?' he eventually chokes out from underneath the scarf still hiding his face.

Everyone laughs, a relieved sort of laugh, like they weren't sure if he was going to take it graciously or yell at them.

I lean down and rest my head against his, holding his shoulder as his hand goes inside the scarf to scrub at his eyes. I want to hug him more than anything, but hugs with broken ribs and head injuries require more navigation than we've got time for with everyone still watching on.

Witt is next to come over to shake Darcy's hand. 'Love ya, my friend. We're all here if you need anything with your recovery. You too, Marnie.' He holds a hand out to shake mine as well. 'If he needs anything he won't ask for, you ask, all right?'

I give him a nod as everyone comes over, one by one, to shake Darcy's hand and wish him well.

Before long, his head is bowed and, under the scarf, he's wiping away tears again. Being accepted is getting to him in the best way possible.

'Marnie,' he whispers, jerking his head for me to bend down and listen. 'Will you help me stand?'

He shifts carefully to the edge of the chair and I crouch to support him as he uses his good leg to push himself upright and slings an arm around my shoulders, using me for support as he stands. My arm slides around him, holding onto his hip from the other side. Apart from the broken bones, he's bruised everywhere and this is clearly hurting, but he's not giving up.

'That's the nicest thing anyone's ever done for me.' His fingers lift towards the shop. 'No one's ever made me feel so welcome, or so wanted, or so accepted. I never thought I could be a part of anything until Marnie, and then all of you, dragged me kicking and screaming into the Ever After Street community. I don't know what to say or how to ever thank you.' He takes a deep breath and gasps in pain because deep breaths and recently broken ribs aren't the best mix. 'But it's time I introduced myself.'

He leans his head to the side and rests his chin against my hair for a moment, his arm tightening around my shoulders. Not second thoughts, just a moment of reassurance before he does what I know he's going to do next.

This is it. Not the moment the Beast turns back into a prince, but the moment he accepts himself for who he is, and hopefully realises that other people will too.

I squeeze his hip as hard as I dare and turn my head until I can kiss his shoulder, and with a shaking hand, he takes the baseball cap off and hands it to me. He pushes a hand through his thick, light brown hair to smooth it down and starts to unwind the scarf. Around and around, slowly uncovering his shoulders, his neck, and then inch by inch, his face. His scarred cheek, the deep welts along his jaw, his once-broken nose, his misshapen eyebrow bone.

Everything he's so ardently kept hidden for so many years.

Darcy O'Connell is standing in the middle of Ever After Street for all to see.

And no one reacts. No one stares. No one peers. No one makes him feel like a museum exhibit on display. No one acts like he's an outsider.

And it's the absolute best thing they could have done. Absolutely nothing to make him feel out of the ordinary in any way. Nothing to make him feel like the centre of attention. Nothing to suggest his scars somehow set him aside from everyone else.

'Let me know when you feel up to a meal out; there's one on the house for both of you in 1001 Nights.' Ali comes over to give him a gentle pat on the shoulder.

'And don't worry about the castle gardens,' Witt says. 'It's the end of the season and you'll be back to fighting fit long before next spring.'

'I was intending to give the lawns another mow before the year is out,' Darcy jumps in, and that's exactly why Witt said it. Just a normal, everyday conversation to show that Darcy uncovering his scars makes no difference whatsoever.

'Well, I can do that. I might own a castle but I'm not completely inept with garden tools. You just concentrate on taking it easy. The only thing any of us want is for you to heal up fast, so we can get to know you as you are, not as you are while in a great deal of pain and clearly struggling to stay upright.'

It's all the hint Darcy needs to sink back into the wheelchair, panting with the exertion, his grip on my hand painfully tight as the impact of being accepted catches up with him.

'We're not done yet.' Sadie comes forward and pulls an envelope out of her back pocket. 'Something for you too, Marnie.'

She's welling up too. Why is everyone so emotional today?

'What is this?' My mouth is open in shock as I rifle through the envelope full of banknotes she's given me. 'There's *thousands* in here. Why are you giving me this?'

'The deposit for A Tale As Old As Time. We all chipped in. After what Rick said last night, we weren't going to let anyone disrespect one of our own like that. Ever After Street wouldn't be the same without you.'

'You can't have a fairy-tale street without a fairy-tale bookshop,' Mickey says.

'We're only doing it for our own benefit,' Lissa says. 'We're secretly hoping you're going to put on another book festival next year. Preferably without any unwelcome interruptions this time. And I've been on the phone to the council this morning and they've started the paperwork for a community protection warning against Rick. He'll be banned from coming to Ever After Street again.'

'But... But...' I struggle for words. 'You *can't* do this. It's too much. It's—'

'Between all of us, it was nothing. A tiny investment in our future too. All these booklovers have bought me out of house and home,' Imogen says. 'Next year we need to do some sort of co-operation and give discounts to Bookishly Ever After goers or something.'

'One thing I've always said is that Ever After Street is like a family. We stick together. We protect our own. We help each other when we need help. We spend so much time here that we become like a second family. You girls are like weird colleague-sisters to me.' Sadie slings her arms around me, Mickey, and Lissa, and beckons Cleo over. 'You too, Cleo. It's about time we got you working here.'

'Cleo's got a job at the bookshop anytime she wants it.' I squeeze her shoulders. 'Apparently I'm expanding into book festivals now too; I'm going to need some help.'

'I'd love it.' She hugs me back. 'But Lilith's daughter-in-law has just told me that Lilith's unlikely to come back and it's set my mind whirring. I want to spend as much time at the bookshop as I can, as long as you don't mind me keeping my ear to the ground about what's happening with the tearoom. Nowhere better for an *Alice in Wonderland* theme than a place that revolves around tea.'

She and the other three girls chatter excitedly about the possibilities and I take the opportunity to sneak back to Darcy. He's wheeled his chair to the window of his shop and turned around, and I perch on the narrow windowsill beside him. 'Hi.'

'Hi.' He's looking out at Ever After Street with the bright autumn sun shining on his gorgeous face, and he blinks down at me like I've woken him up. 'Thanks for holding me up – both literally and metaphorically. I don't think I've ever been this much of an emotional wreck in my life. I never thought...' He tilts his head back to indicate the shop sign above us.

'I know.' I reach over to squeeze his knee. 'I'm ridiculously proud of you. They love you, Darcy. You just need to *let* them.'

I can tell his emotions are raw and on the surface, and also that he's absolutely exhausted. I don't know how much sleep he got in hospital last night, but it doesn't look like it was much. 'Do you want to go home?'

His hand slides over mine where it's still on his knee. 'Not yet. And I kind of feel like I've just *come* home and it's a nice feeling. I don't want to lose it yet.'

Now it's my turn to smile because it's exactly what I've been feeling too. Like I've found a family I didn't realise I had and they've been right in front of me all along.

'What are we going to do next?'

'About...?' I ask.

'My shop, for a start. It's pretty useless to me for the next couple of months. Everything I own is upstairs. The cut flowers are going to die, so I've just given Witt my keys and told him to take them and distribute them to everyone, but I wondered if you wanted to use the space for anything... Another friendship date night or some author events or something. The garden or the shop itself. I have a feeling that A Tale As Old As Time might need to expand in the coming months...'

'Seriously?' I love his belief in me, even when the pinched look around his eyes suggests he's hurting more than he's letting on. 'Cleo's just given me two notebooks that she filled last night with details of all the people who wanted to put their name down for a friendship match next time. There's enough interest that we could make it a weekly thing for a while and it still wouldn't be enough.'

'I'm ridiculously proud of you too, you know.'

I can't help the grin that breaks across my face. 'I want to do more online, like opening up to internet sales. And I'd like to take the friendship thing online too, so people don't have to be local. Maybe some kind of individual book club – people fill in the friendship questionnaire, I choose a book I think they'd both like, and then they discuss it with each other, via whatever means they prefer – email, Zoom, phone, messaging, carrier pigeon, smoke signals, et cetera. It gives them a jumping-off point. It's less daunting to talk to a stranger if you have something to talk about. I could set some questions so they have discussion points, and... who knows what comes next. Maybe it develops into a real friendship.'

'Or *more*. I know how much you love that romance section.' How he manages to waggle an eyebrow with a head wound and a black eye, I don't know.

It makes me laugh and lean over to rest my head gently on his shoulder and he instantly drops his to lean against mine. 'And people pay for this, yes? Because you're not doing it for free; your time and book knowledge is worth more than that.'

'Something small. A nominal fee. Because I can't give up the time for nothing, and it will cut out timewasters too. People doing it "for a laugh" aren't going to pay anything, but people genuinely looking for a new connection would be happy to, and according to

Cleo's notes from yesterday, a *lot* of people are genuinely interested.'

'Good.' He moves to press a kiss into my hair. 'A Tale As Old As Time is so much more than just a bookshop. Do anything you want with my space for the time being, and then we'll rethink it. I want to do something different. Something that helps people like me. Outsiders. Or people who are in a bad place and don't know where to turn. People who want to talk but don't have anyone to talk to. The number of times I've poured my heart out to a tree... I want to do some sort of "gardening as therapy" thing. A way to bond with nature. Somewhere people can go to escape their normal lives and connect with the world around them.'

'I'm sure Witt would be happy for you to use the castle gardens. If people want to talk, you're there, someone who's been through it, who understands without judgement, and if they don't... there's a satisfaction in gardening, isn't there? You watch it happening right in front of you. Weeding is a healthy way to let out some pent-up frustration. And even if you feel completely ineffectual in all other areas of your life, you can dig over a patch of soil and plant a bulb and watch it grow. It's rewarding, and when you're in a dark place, something as small as the promise of a flower opening can be enough to keep you going.'

He's quiet for a while, and then he kisses the top of my head and murmurs three little words. 'I love you. You're the best thing that's ever happened to me. You say no one needed to *learn* to love the Beast, but *this* beast needed to learn how to let love in again.'

'That had better be the last time you *ever* refer to yourself as a beast. If it's not, broken ribs are going to be the least of your troubles.' I hold up a threatening finger and he laughs and then winces when said broken ribs make their presence known.

I lay my head on his shoulder again and look at our friends, neighbours, and colleagues still milling around, chatting to each other and the few customers who have ventured down. 'The only thing either of us really needed to learn was how to see what's right in front of us.'

'Or right beside us through a hedge,' he murmurs.

'When you've healed up, will you cut a doorway through that hedge?'

'I was thinking more along the lines of taking the whole thing down. I don't want anything to hide behind for once, no matter what.'

'That's the best sentence I've ever heard.'

'You have no idea how much I hate having to ask, and when I can move without blinding pain, I'm going to make up for it, but for now, will you *please* kiss me?'

'And *that* is the next best sentence I've ever heard.' I'm grinning as I slide down onto my knees at the side of his chair to avoid the broken ankle, and lean up until I can take his face gently in my hands and make him tilt his head to avoid the wound.

He surges forward and cuts me off with the most tender kiss, just a touch of his lips to mine, that gets more heated as my hand curls into his thick hair, but I'm holding back because of hurting him, and he can't get the angle right without moving, but somehow it's the perfect ending to the chapter we've just come through and the perfect opening to our next one.

When we pull back, I'm as short of breath as he is, and it has nothing to do with any injuries. I sit back on the windowsill and lean my head on his shoulder again, and we sit there in the early-afternoon autumn sun, watching the hustle and bustle of Ever After Street. The sunlight on my face makes me think of Mum and how happy she'd be if she could see this, and it feels like the moment when the fallen rose petals magically rise back up and the homeware becomes human again.

As if on cue, Mrs Potts comes out and jumps up on Darcy's lap, thankfully still a cat and not suddenly a little old lady. It would be a bit weird if she was, to be honest.

Even though I know the next couple of months won't be easy, I've never been happier, and it feels like this is all I'll ever need. My cat and a few books, and just me and Darcy. No Beauty and no Beast, just a bookworm and a rose grower, proving that every story deserves a happy ending, because falling in love really *is* the tale that's as old as time.

ACKNOWLEDGEMENTS

When Marnie mentions the friends she's found in Facebook booklover groups, I was thinking of the friends *I've* found through Facebook booklover groups! I wish I could thank you all by name, but these acknowledgements would be longer than the book itself. I want to say a massive thank you to everyone who I chat to on Facebook, who I've connected with thanks to these wonderful book groups, and to all of you who show me so much support and kindness on a daily basis.

And I want to say an extra thank you to the admins of these brilliant Facebook groups who work so hard to make these little bookish corners of the internet an absolute pleasure to be part of!

Thank you ~
Sue Baker at Vintage Vibes and Riveting Reads
Sarah Kingsnorth, Hazel Elkin, Marie Harris, Louise Hill, Jessica Redland, and Adrienne Allan at The Friendly Book Community
Fiona Jenkins at The Spirituality Café
Anita Faulkner at Chick Lit and Prosecco
Becky Sumner, and Lyndsay and Lyndsey at Book Swap Central
Donna Bryce, Teresa Nikolic, Trina Dixon, Lisa Bedford, Lee-Ann Holmes, along with Karen, Natalie, and Liana at Fiction Addicts at Socially Distanced Book Club

If you're a booklover looking for somewhere to brighten your day, lift your spirits, and make you feel like you've found a group of people who understand why we always buy more books even though we need scaffolding to hold up our current to-read pile, please find your way to these groups! You will be glad you did – although your to-read pile may not!

Thank you, Mum. Always my first and most important reader! I'm eternally grateful for your constant patience, support, encouragement, and belief in me. Thank you for always being there for me – I don't know what I'd do without you. Love you lots!

Thank you to my best friend and beloved fellow house goblin, Marie Landry, for making every day better just by existing. I love you to bits. I'm privileged to call you my best friend, and I can't wait to cwtch in our Scottish castle one day and frolic *adjacent to* the gorse!

Thank you for your continued love, enthusiasm, and support to my wonderful friends Bev, Jayne Lloyd, Charlotte McFall, and Jodie Homer.

Thank you to my fantastic agent, Amanda Preston, and my brilliant editor Emily Ruston, along with the rest of the wonderful and hardworking Boldwood team and the lovely Boldwood authors! It's a joy to belong to Team Boldwood!

And finally, thank *you* for reading! I hope you enjoyed getting lost inside A Tale As Old As Time and sharing Marnie and Darcy's Beauty-and-the-Beast-inspired love story, and I hope you'll come with me again for the next book to see Cleo join Ever After Street too – there are many more happily ever afters to come!

ABOUT THE AUTHOR

Jaimie Admans is the bestselling author of several romantic comedies. She lives in South Wales.

Sign up to Jaimie Adman's mailing list for news, competitions and updates on future books.

Visit Jaimie's website: https://jaimieadmans.com/

Follow Jaimie on social media:

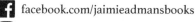 x.com/be_the_spark

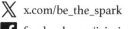 facebook.com/jaimieadmansbooks

 instagram.com/jaimieadmans1

About the Author

ALSO BY JAIMIE ADMANS

The Gingerbread House in Mistletoe Gardens

The Ever After Street Series

A Midnight Kiss on Ever After Street

An Enchanted Moment on Ever After Street

LOVE NOTES

LOVE IN EVERY CHAPTER

WHERE ALL YOUR ROMANCE
DREAMS COME TRUE!

THE HOME OF BESTSELLING
ROMANCE AND WOMEN'S
FICTION

    WARNING:
MAY CONTAIN SPICE

SIGN UP TO OUR
NEWSLETTER

https://bit.ly/Lovenotesnews

Boldw⚭d

Boldwood Books is an award-winning fiction publishing company seeking out the best stories from around the world.

Find out more at www.boldwoodbooks.com

Join our reader community for brilliant books, competitions and offers!

Follow us
@BoldwoodBooks
@TheBoldBookClub

Sign up to our weekly deals newsletter

https://bit.ly/BoldwoodBNewsletter

Made in United States
North Haven, CT
04 January 2024

46985811R00176